SAVAGE HEARTS

FILTHY WICKED PSYCHOS #4

EVA ASHWOOD

———————

Author's Note: This is a dark romance and includes themes that may be triggering for some. Please read at your own discretion.

*For all the readers who've been
begging for a twin sandwich scene.
I heard you.*

RANSOM

Everything fucking hurts.

My lungs burn, and my muscles are screaming from doing this much exercise this early in the morning, but with that Jeep gunning for us, it's not like we can stop. The headlights of the black Jeep flash somewhere behind us, and we duck down another side street, desperate to get away.

At this ungodly hour of the morning, the only sounds on these little roads are our harsh breathing and the beat of our feet against the concrete, but that's not even close to comforting right now. Someone could leap out of the shadows and intercept us, and we have no real idea where we are or what we're heading into.

Nuevo Laredo isn't a massive city, but there are houses sprawled out everywhere, and none of us are familiar enough with this area to make any kind of guesses about what we're heading toward. It flashes in my brain that maybe the Jeep is herding us into some kind of trap, but I shake that off before it can take hold. At this point, it doesn't really matter. We just have to keep moving and deal with whatever happens.

The Jeep's engine roars behind us, and we pick up the pace, taking advantage of the fact that we're more nimble on foot than the Jeep is. But it's still a damned close thing.

"*Fuck* this," I curse with feeling as we stumble out onto the main road again a few minutes later. "Olivia can go fuck herself."

If anyone were to look out their windows right now, they'd see four grown-ass adults running wild through the streets in the predawn hours of the morning, trying to get away from a Jeep.

Part of me hopes Olivia herself is in that Jeep so I can punch her right in her smug face if I get the chance.

Almost as soon as we pause to look around, there's another flash of headlights. I don't know how the hell the Jeep is moving so fast, but it's right there behind us again, downing us in the glare from its brights.

Willow gasps, and before I have time to turn around and see what's up, we're moving again. Vic grabs her arm and yanks her off to the side, and we duck into another alley, sprinting as fast as we can.

"I saw... who was in the... Jeep," Willow pants breathlessly, sounding like she's having a hard time breathing and talking at the same time. "It was... Troy."

My head whips around as I stare at her.

"What the fuck?" Malice growls. He turns to look at her, not slowing his pace. "Are you sure?"

Willow looks like she's going to be sick, but she nods. "I saw him. He's not dead. He must have... must have survived."

Vic grunts breathlessly. "That means Olivia had help. Fuck, I didn't know. I wasn't counting on that."

None of us were, but we don't have time to dwell on that right now. If that asshole Troy has been hunting us the same way Olivia has, then we have to keep moving. I'm sure that bastard has a grudge against us too, considering we almost killed him and ran off with the woman he was supposed to marry.

"Come on!" I tell them, picking up my pace a little bit more, even though it feels like my heart is about to explode. "We can figure it out once we get out of here."

Even though I'm the one who said we'll figure it out later, letting go of it is still one of those 'easier said than done' kind of things. Even as my arms pump and my feet slap against the pavement, my mind starts conjuring up memories of all the shit Troy has done. All the ways he's threatened Willow. The way he was planning to marry her, even though he sure as hell knew she didn't want it.

I think about their engagement party, when he had that proprietary look in his eyes, acting like he had the right to decide who Willow was allowed to speak to, barely standing down because he didn't want to cause a scene.

Olivia might be in this for the money, and she's clearly willing to use her only living heir as a bargaining chip, but Troy is one of those assholes who's just vindictive and petty. He's not chasing us because of money, since he doesn't need us for that the same way Olivia does.

He's chasing us because he can't stand to lose.

Anger wells up in me, hot and intense. I think I might hate that fucker even more than Olivia.

The idea of running from him turns my stomach, and I'm half tempted to stop and try to take the cocksucker out, but it would be a bad idea. We're at a disadvantage, and a pretty big one at that. The thing that matters the most here is keeping Willow safe. Anything and everything else can come later.

So we keep running, sprinting along and ducking through more small spaces. We climb over garden beds and duck under someone's clothes line, trying to put as much distance as we can between us and the Jeep. The more we run, the quieter it gets, and after several agonizing minutes, it seems like maybe we've managed to get away.

There's no more roar of the engine behind us, and the streets are only lit by a few streetlights instead of the glow of those headlights. But we're still running blindly through this unfamiliar town in Mexico, not sure where we're going. It's not like Vic had time to plot a route for us. Those bastards caught us completely off guard.

Wherever we manage to hole up next, we're going to have to be a lot more careful.

And that opens the question of where we can even go. Unless Troy and Olivia somehow guessed we were going to Mexico days ago, they probably haven't been here for longer than we have, but they have more resources than we do. Hell, they might even have people on their payroll living here, eager to help them. It'll be hard to know which places are safe to go to. We need more distance between us, and we need to throw them off of our trail so we can regroup and come up with another piece of this plan.

We were supposed to have more time for that, but here we fucking are.

My mind churns, trying to figure something out as we finally slow our steps. Vic glances around like he's trying to find some sort of landmark to help him orient himself as we step out onto another street.

But before he can say anything, a loud roar cuts through the air.

Fuck. The Jeep.

There are no headlights this time, but there's no mistaking the sound of the engine. The driver cut the lights to blend in with the darkness around us, and the Jeep is gunning toward us, barreling down on us fast.

"Shit!" I shout, and I feel both Malice and Vic move beside me. Vic throws himself in front of Willow protectively, and in that exact second, a gunshot rings out.

Then Vic crumples the ground, going down hard.

Willow screams, the sound high pitched and terrified, and the Jeep's engine roars again.

It doesn't stop or even so much as slow down. It veers slightly off course, whipping past us. The sides are open, and a hand shoots out, grabbing Willow up as it goes by, pulling her on board the speeding vehicle.

She screams again, fighting the hold of whoever the hell grabbed her, but it's not enough.

"*Fuck,* no!" Malice shouts.

"No you fucking don't!" I bellow, right there with him.

I put on a burst of speed, trying to chase down the Jeep, but it tears away into the night, moving so fast I don't have a hope of catching it on foot.

Come on, I urge myself, gritting my teeth. Willing my body to move faster, to at least keep following the Jeep so it can't disappear on me. *Come the fuck on.*

But it's no good. It gets farther and farther away, and eventually, I have to stop running, my lungs burning. With the headlights still off, I can't even see the damned thing once it gets far enough away.

Shit. Fucking goddamned *shit.*

The Jeep is gone, and Willow with it.

For a long moment, it feels like time stops entirely as my mind grapples with that fact, refusing to believe it. Every breath is like inhaling shards of glass, and I fight for air, trying to keep the anger and desperation from clouding my brain.

The only thing that finally cuts through the haze of panic and fury in my brain is a noise from behind me. I turn to look back at Malice, who's returned to the spot where Willow was snatched from us.

He's on his knees on the ground, hovering over Vic's body, and a sickening feeling lurches in my stomach.

Fuck, no. *No, no, no.*

We can't have lost Vic and Willow in the same night. That would just be...

No.

They're several blocks behind me, almost indistinguishable from the darkness around them, and despite the way my muscles and lungs protest, I turn and start to run again, making my way back over to them. My chest is tight, and it's not just from the exertion. I don't know what I'm going to see when I reach the two of them, and if Vic is dead—

I swallow hard against that thought.

As I get closer, I see Malice keeping pressure on a wound in

Vic's side. Vic groans, and even though it's a pained sound, it loosens the knot in my stomach a little. He's still alive.

Thank fuck for that.

Malice looks up when I approach them, an obvious question in his eyes, and I shake my head.

"They got away," I say, voice hoarse. "Willow is gone."

"*Fuck!*" my older brother curses. "Fucking—*fuck.*" His dark eyes flash with emotion, his jaw going tight.

On the ground, Vic doesn't look much better off. His shirt is soaked with blood, but it doesn't seem like he even notices or cares. He closes his eyes and lets out a shuddering breath, and I can see his hands clenching into fists, squeezing rhythmically as he counts under his breath. He has to be in pain from getting shot, but it's losing Willow that's wrecking him now.

Wrecking all of us.

For a moment, we all just stand in silence, staring after the place where Willow disappeared. It's so fucking hard to process everything that's happened. Last night, we were dancing, happy and free for the first time in a long time. We thought things were going to be okay. We thought we could stop running for a bit. Everything felt perfect.

We all fucked Willow, and it was like the final piece of a puzzle clicking into place. Like everything was the way it was supposed to be. And now she's gone. Snatched into a Jeep by her asshole of a 'fiancé,' and we have no idea where she's being taken.

It makes me feel sick just thinking about it.

"Malice," Vic rasps, sounding exhausted but determined. "Help me up."

"Vic—"

Victor cuts him off, shaking his head. "It's not that bad. He just tagged me in the side. And we can't stay here. The longer we stay, the farther away she gets. We need to get moving."

"Where are we even going?" I ask, moving in to help Malice as we get Vic to his feet.

"We know Troy took her," Vic grits out. "So that's somewhere to start. We just need to figure out where the fuck he's going to take her. Come on. Let's go. We need to find a car to hot-wire. You can stitch me up once we're on the move."

That's how I can tell how serious he is about this. He's willing to let someone stitch him up in the back of a moving car. There's no way that'll give him the nice, precise stitches he prefers when it comes to shit like this, and he usually likes to handle this kind of thing himself. But right now, finding Willow is more important. Important enough to cut through the mental hang-ups Vic gets sometimes.

Malice drags in a deep breath and lets it out. "Okay. Right." He glances at me. "You're the best at hot-wiring, so you take point. There's got to be something decent around here we can steal."

I nod.

There's still an empty, gaping wound in my heart, but I try to push that aside for now. We have a goal, and I need to focus on that instead of letting the agony in my chest overwhelm me.

I need to focus all of my energy on one unalterable fact.

My brothers and I will do whatever it takes to get Willow back.

2

WILLOW

Consciousness comes back to me slowly, in fits and starts.

I'm aware of my body before anything else, aware of the ache in my muscles and the way my chest hurts. My head feels fuzzy, and I struggle to open my eyes, but the lids feel too heavy. When I try to think back to what happened, my stomach drops and my head aches, so I take a deep breath against it.

There are...hands on me?

I feel like I'm moving, like someone is carrying me, and thick fingers brush over my body, but they don't feel familiar.

"Hey!" someone snaps. "Keep your fucking hands to yourself. I didn't bring you here so you could feel her up, you jackass."

Wait. I know that voice.

It all comes rushing back to me in a dizzying swirl of emotions and images and feelings. I remember running from the Jeep, Vic going down in a heap in front of me, and someone snatching me away from the guys before they could even react. My eyes snap open just as I'm being set down, and Troy's deceptively handsome face swims into view above me.

There's no expression on his face, but something burns in his eyes. It's not quite triumph, but something darker, something that probably doesn't bode well for me.

"Morning, *honey*," he says, the endearment sounding like poison as it falls from his tongue.

My tongue feels thick in my mouth, and it's a struggle to get the words out. "You're su...pposed to be d...ead."

He snorts, disdain practically dripping from the sound. "You should have told your pet criminal to aim better if you wanted me dead, sweetheart. He didn't hit anything vital. The blood loss almost got me, but hey." He smirks, shrugging with one shoulder. "I have the best doctors money can buy."

"You—"

"That's enough chit chat." Troy cuts me off. "You should go back to sleep for now. It's gonna be a long trip."

I open my mouth to tell him to go fuck himself, but then someone jabs a needle into the side of my neck. There's a pinch of pain, and everything goes hazy until darkness falls over me again.

Whatever they gave me must be strong, because all I'm aware of for a long time after that is small snatches of things. I wake up every once in a while, looking blearily around me, but there's nothing of note to linger on, and I can't seem to stay awake. As soon as I wake up sometimes, the darkness comes for me again, dragging me back under. I don't know if they're drugging me every time, or if it's some kind of delayed release of what they injected me with the first time, but I have no idea how much time has passed or where we even are.

I can tell we're moving though. Sometimes it feels bumpy, like being in the back of a car, and other times it's smooth, but there's still that feeling of motion around me.

Someone holds my head up a couple of times, tipping water into my mouth that I have to work to swallow. I feel raw inside, and the water is a cold shock to my system. Sometimes there's food, pieces of fruit and stale bread, and even though my brain screams through the haze that I don't want anything from these people, I'm too out of it to resist.

When someone helps me to the bathroom, I go with them, letting them lead me there and back, almost like a puppet.

9

It's like being trapped in my own head, knowing this is bad and wrong and terrible, but not having the energy or freedom to do anything about it. As soon as I think I should be fighting back or at least demanding to know where they're taking me, I'm slipping back into the darkness again, completely out of it.

A whimper falls from my lips, and I feel tears sliding down my cheeks, even though I wasn't aware of crying.

I'm lost inside my mind.

I'm lost from the men I love.

I'm just... lost.

———

SOMETIME LATER, I wake up again.

This time, I feel more alert than I have in a while. My head hurts, and it takes me a little while to process everything. I still feel groggy at first, my thoughts swimming around my mind like fog. Trying to latch on to anything specific is like trying to get a solid grip on something slippery and ephemeral.

But then my pulse speeds up as I'm hit by the memory of overwhelming fear.

Everything comes rushing back to me all over again, and I gasp softly, my eyes flying wide open and darting around. I'm in a nondescript room, but at least I'm alone. I'm lying on my side on a bed, and when I try to move to get up, I realize that my wrists and ankles are bound tightly, making it awkward to maneuver.

Something twists around my legs, making me feel stifled and claustrophobic, and when I look down at myself, I realize that I'm no longer wearing the sweaty, dirty clothes that I ran through the streets of Mexico in.

Instead, I'm wearing a long white dress, the thick fabric of the skirt tangled around my legs.

Oh my god. It's a wedding dress.

My heart lurches in my chest, beating sluggishly and then picking up its pace to a wild gallop as I struggle to sit up.

The door opens, and my beleaguered heart jumps again, adrenaline shooting through me like a flood of ice water in my veins. Troy steps into the room, a few men dressed in dark suits following him. As they file into the room, I get a glimpse beyond the door for a second—enough to tell that we're in a house of some kind, but not one that I recognize.

Troy strides toward me, flanked by the men who must be his bodyguards or hired muscle. He comes to a stop by the edge of the bed and looks down at me, smirking as his gaze roams over my bound body. This close, and with a clearer head, I can see that he's favoring his left arm, holding it like it's causing him pain. That must be because of the bullet Victor managed to lodge in his chest.

A vague memory filters into my mind, something I'm almost positive Troy said to me while I was drugged.

Should've told your pet criminal to aim better if you wanted me dead.

Goddammit. We didn't have time to check Troy for a pulse back at the church, and the guys were so focused on getting me out that Vic didn't even bother to shoot him again. But although the single bullet clearly did some damage, it wasn't enough to kill him.

As if he can tell I'm staring, Troy relaxes his left arm a bit, like he doesn't want to admit that Vic managed to hurt him at all. He cocks his head, his lascivious gaze running up and down my body again before settling on my face.

"I'm glad you're finally awake," he drawls. "I was worried you were going to sleep through our big day, and we wouldn't want that. I want you to be awake for every single moment of this. After all, you only get married once."

"Fuck you," I spit, working again to try to sit up as the ropes chafe my wrists and ankles. "You son of a bitch! I will *never* marry you. I'd rather—"

He cuts me off by backhanding me across the face. Hard. My head whips to one side, my entire body jerking on the bed since I can't steady myself with my hands. Pain explodes in my cheek, darkness swallowing my vision for a second before stars dance before my eyes.

The blow was so hard that it nearly knocked the wind out of my lungs, and my mouth falls open as I struggle to draw in a breath.

At least it took something out of him too. He winces when the force of the hit jars his bad arm, and he tucks it a little closer to his body.

"I made a mistake when we tried this the first time," he says, his voice sharper now, tinged with an edge of vicious anger. "I was too easy on you. Your grandmother promised me you could be controlled, and I took her at her word. I thought you were going to see reason, so I didn't break you properly. I'm not going to repeat that error, and I'm not going to tolerate any bullshit. Do you understand me?"

My chest goes tight at the way he sounds. There's true malice in his eyes, something that makes me think of little boys who pull the wings off of butterflies just because they can. He sounds angry —he clearly *is* angry—but a part of him also seems almost gleeful, as if he's looking forward to breaking me like he just promised.

Our gazes lock for a moment, and he drags his tongue over his bottom lip, curling and uncurling his fingers as if he's debating whether to hit me again. Or maybe whether to hit me with an open or closed fist.

But finally, he pulls his attention away from me and glances over his shoulder at one of his men.

"Cut the ropes," he snaps.

A hulking man comes forward brandishing a knife, and I flinch back as he slices through the ropes binding my wrists and ankles. Before I can so much as move on my own, the same guy grabs my arm, hauling me to my feet.

Troy and his guards lead me out of the room and to a different part of the house. While we walk, I try to get my bearings, but I have no idea where we are. It's not Olivia's house, and I've never seen Troy's before, so I wouldn't know what it looks like.

It's on the tip of my tongue to demand to know if he sent more men after the Voronin brothers. The image of Vic crumpling to the ground is etched in my mind, and every time I think of it, I feel bile rise in my throat. I don't know if that gunshot killed him, or if Malice or Ransom got hit too. I don't think the Jeep went back for them after I was yanked into it, but I have no idea what happened after I was knocked out.

But I bite the words back, keeping them locked behind my lips. The last thing I need to be doing is reminding Troy of his grudge against the brothers, and as terrified as I am right now, the only upside of the fact that he captured me is that maybe he'll stop going after them now that they no longer have what he wants.

Beside me, Troy speaks again, and just the sound of his voice is enough to fill me with dread.

"After our first fuckup of a wedding, I decided that this one doesn't need to be as lavish. Who really cares if everyone who's anyone is here to witness it, right? And it's not like you know anyone worth inviting. So we just have one other guest this time."

He opens a door and we walk into what appears to be a small office. There's a desk in one corner, and a small leather couch along another wall. Olivia is sitting on the couch with a cup of tea clasped daintily in her hand.

I haven't seen her since the first wedding, and laying eyes on her now fills me with fear and fury in equal measure.

After everything, my grandmother is still willing to endorse this. She's still willing to sell me off like a piece of livestock, just so she can get what she wants.

"Hello, Willow," Olivia says, her voice cool and detached. "I would say you're looking well, but..."

She sweeps her gaze over me from head to toe and lets the sentence remain unfinished.

My stomach churns just from looking at her. It's hard to remember a time when her petite stature and perfectly styled gray hair fooled me into thinking she was a kind older woman. She's probably been wearing that high society mask her entire life, and even though she still wears it impeccably, I know her well enough by now to see past it.

All the way to the monster underneath.

I take a deep breath, forcing air into my lungs. I know that appealing to any sense of humanity she has is probably useless, but I can't stop myself from trying anyway. The wedding dress is tight around my torso, wrapping around me and only adding to the panicky feeling in my chest.

"Olivia, please," I say, my voice shaking. "You don't have to do this. You and Troy can make whatever deals you need to make on your own. You don't need me for this. Just let me go. I'm begging you."

Troy snorts, and Olivia's passive expression doesn't waver as she shakes her head.

"After all that's happened, you still don't understand," she says.

"That's not how things work in this world, sweetheart," Troy adds, his lips curling into a sneer. "You don't get something for nothing. Sure, I could bail Olivia out and help her crumbling empire, but what would I get out of the deal?"

I ignore Troy, because he's a lost cause. Appealing to his better nature won't work because he doesn't have one. Instead, I focus on Olivia. My grandmother. Someone who's supposed to love me.

"Please," I murmur, tears stinging my eyes. "Don't do this. You know what he's going to be like. You know what he's going to do to me. *Help* me. Please. We're supposed to be family."

Olivia sniffs, taking a sip of her tea. "The time to do each other favors as family has long since passed, I'm afraid. If you had gone into the marriage I arranged for you willingly, it might have been a different story. I would've tried to help you learn how to survive and thrive in your role as the wife of a powerful man. But you ran. You made a mockery of everything I tried to do. And so this is what we are left with."

I swallow hard at the note of finality in her voice. Even though I knew it was an impossible, last ditch hope, something in my heart breaks all over again at her callous words. It's a brutal reminder that although we share DNA, this woman isn't my family in any way that counts.

Looking away from me, Olivia fixes her attention on Troy. "Our deal is still in place."

"*With* the adjustments," Troy points out, sounding a little petulant. "You said it was going to be a simple marriage, and it definitely wasn't."

Olivia waves a hand, a hint of irritation passing over her face. "Yes, yes, with the adjustment. I've accepted the forty-five percent."

"And I've accepted the extra work I'm going to have to do to break your willful granddaughter into a wife I can use. We all have our crosses to bear."

She doesn't even bat an eye at his casual talk of abusing me, and my stomach clenches into a knot as my imagination runs wild, dozens of horrible scenarios running through my mind.

As I work to keep myself from vomiting, the two of them go back and forth in a last bit of negotiation, solidifying the deal they've worked out together. Apparently, my disappearing act has made Olivia have to give up some ground in their bargain, but I can't even take pleasure in knowing that. Because Troy is clearly going to take his anger out on me one way or another, and Olivia isn't going to do a thing to stop him.

In the end, they both seem to be... if not satisfied, then at least in agreement. Olivia rises from the couch, coming to stand behind me.

One of Troy's guards moves to the front of the room, and Troy smirks at my look of confusion.

"What? Were you expecting a priest? I told you this wedding wouldn't be elaborate, and anyone can get ordained on the internet these days. All we need is a witness, and this marriage will be legally binding."

He gestures for his guy to begin with a sharp jerk of his chin.

"We're here today to witness the marriage of Troy Copeland and Willow Hayes," the man intones in his deep voice.

The words twist around me like invisible ropes, and the room goes in and out of focus around me. The drugs Troy gave me have mostly worn off, but they're still in my system, making me feel weak-limbed and disoriented. I shoot a quick glance around the room, looking for any way out—but I can't see one.

Troy's guards have stationed themselves around the space, and between them, my grandmother, and Troy, there are half a dozen people who will try to stop me if I make a run for it. There's no way I'd get out of here in one piece.

It's so surreal, standing rooted to the spot as the words of a basic, perfunctory wedding ceremony are read out in the quiet room.

It was different the first time, when I agreed to walk down the aisle with Troy because I thought it would keep the guys safe. When it was a choice I made, however much I hated it. Now I have no idea where the guys are, or even if...

I have to swallow hard a few times past the lump in my throat.

Vic was shot.

He was on the ground when I last saw him. But I can't think about that right now. If I do, I'll fall apart completely, and I can't let that happen.

Troy's goon drones on for another minute, but I barely process the words he's saying. When he turns to Troy, asking him if he promises to stay with me in sickness and health, it's a struggle not to laugh hysterically.

Troy grabs my hand roughly, slipping a ring on my finger. Then he squeezes my hand so tightly that the metal of the ring digs into the adjoining fingers, a triumphant, ugly smile spreading across his face.

"I do," he says, and it may as well be a death sentence.

"And do you, Willow Hayes, take Troy Copeland to be your lawfully wedded husband..."

I don't even listen to the rest. None of it matters. None of it means anything. Part of me wants to refuse, to tell Troy and Olivia that I'd rather die.

And maybe that's true. Maybe I would rather die than face what comes next... but I can't.

Because if there's a chance the Voronin brothers are still alive, then I have to stay alive too.

When Troy's man stops speaking and looks at me expectantly, something twists in my gut. A gaping hole opens up in my chest, ragged and raw, as I swallow hard and whisper, "I do."

Troy's lips curve into a self-satisfied smile.

"Then by the power vested in me by the state of Michigan, I now pronounce you husband and wife. You may kiss the bride."

The smile on Troy's face shifts to something much less pleasant, and he leans in, gripping my chin hard. I don't jerk away, but every atom in my body crawls at his touch, and when he kisses me hard, I feel sick to my stomach.

Olivia nods when Troy finally releases me, allowing me to jerk my head back. She eyes me with that cool expression, her eyes so emotionless that I think she truly must be a sociopath.

"It's done. Finally," she says. "I know you probably think this is the worst thing that's ever happened to you right now, Willow. But one day, you will appreciate what I did for you."

Without another word, she turns to go. Troy's bodyguards step out of her way as she leaves, letting the door swing shut behind her.

I stare at the door, almost shocked that she still thinks that. As if this could ever be anything other than a cruelty. As if this could ever help me. Nothing Troy could offer is anything I want, and nothing their world of money and lies could provide will do anything to help me out of the hell she's consigned me to.

But now she has what she wants, so I guess none of that matters to her anymore.

A hand touches my arm, and I yank away instinctively. Troy doesn't let me put any space between us though, stepping closer as he grins down at me with lust written across his face. He touches my arm again, deliberately running his hand down from my shoulder in a slow, teasing slide.

"No harm in getting the honeymoon started early, is there?" he murmurs, licking his lips. "It's finally time for me to see if you're worth all the trouble you've caused. You've got more fire in you than I expected, I'll give you that. But I don't mind." His smile widens as he leers down at me. "Breaking you is going to be so much fun, wife."

3

VICTOR

I GRIT my teeth in the back of the car, grateful at least that Ransom is driving.

He's the one who hot-wired the first car we found as we were walking, and he smiled his way past the border patrol as we crossed back onto US soil.

Getting back across the border was easier, since we already had our fake IDs, and the authorities aren't watching for us to be coming *from* Mexico.

Thank fuck.

I shift in place, and my side aches at the movement, throbbing for a solid minute before it settles down. We raided a vet's office for medical supplies after Ransom got us a car. The stitches are the best Malice could do, especially considering the urgency of the situation and the fact that the car was moving at the time, and they're fine.

It still grates on me, knowing that they're uneven. It bothers me more than the pain, honestly, but I'm able to push that aside to focus on the matter at hand.

Ransom and Malice are both in the front of the new car we stole when we ditched the first one somewhere around the Texas state line. I can hear them talking in low voices. Malice sounds agitated, another reason why he's not allowed to drive right now. The last thing we need is to get pulled over because he's driving with his temper.

Ransom is feeling just as frustrated and fucked up as the rest of us about Willow being gone, but at least he can obey the traffic laws while doing it.

While they talk, I use my laptop, doing what I do best. I'm supposed to be healing as best I can, but I've never been good at being idle, even where there's no crisis. Plus, the longer we go without knowing where Troy took Willow, the harder it'll be to find her.

So I search.

We've been able to track him to a degree, using small sightings on security cameras. We have enough to know that he brought Willow back to Detroit, but finding out where the fuck he took her to from there has been the hard part.

I've searched the cameras around his house and his condo in the heart of the city, but there hasn't been any movement at either of those locations at all. Which means he's got her somewhere else. It's smart, all things considered. Bringing her back to one of his known properties would be fairly conspicuous. But him being smart just makes our job harder.

Something feral scratches at the inside of my ribs when I think about how long Troy has had Willow. It's been just over thirty hours now, but a lot can happen in that time. Especially with someone like Troy fucking Copeland.

My chest aches, and I find myself tapping my fingers on the edge of my computer, reverting back to my old coping mechanisms. I can feel myself spiraling a little, and I hate it. If I let myself, I could imagine all the horrible fucking things Troy might be doing to Willow.

He probably won't have killed her, because that would defeat the purpose of all of this, but there are things that can make a person wish they were dead. I know that fact better than most people, and I don't have any delusions that he's going to treat her softly just because he wants to marry her.

But letting those dark thoughts overtake my mind isn't going to help me find Willow, so I take a deep breath, forcing myself to refocus on what I'm doing.

We have a trail of breadcrumbs leading from Mexico back to Detroit, and I go over them again, trying to pick up some hint of where Troy took Willow.

There are a few sightings of him moving through the city, but other than that, I'm drawing a blank. It's like he took her totally off the grid or something, and the thought of that makes my skin prickle with irritation and fear.

If we can't find her...

No.

No, I can't afford to think like that. Troy isn't a criminal mastermind. He's a rich, spoiled idiot who didn't like being told no. There's *something* out there that's going to help me figure out where he took Willow. I just have to find it. For now, she's hidden away wherever that is, and she needs me to keep digging until I find her.

I narrow my focus even more, scrolling back through all the sightings I could piece together. I open a notepad on the side of my screen and start jotting down all the points that connect these places together, anything that could form a trail that might lead to Willow.

The muttered conversation between my brothers in the front seat fades into background noise, no more than static in the back of my head as I work. This has always been my role among the three of us. It's what I do best, and the stakes of my success have never been higher than they are now.

I don't look up again until I hear Ransom curse bitterly from the front seat, the sound loud enough to jar me from my thoughts.

"What—"

But the question dies on my lips as I glance around and see where we are.

I hadn't even noticed that we'd made it back to the city, back to our old turf. It feels like it's been months since we left it, even though it hasn't been anywhere close to that long, and the sight of our warehouse—our home for years—as a burnt out ruin makes my breath stall.

Malice and Ransom have finally switched who's driving, and my twin's fingers grip the steering wheel tighter. Beside him, Ransom's jaw is tight as we slowly drive by the building that was once ours.

The original structure is gone, burnt down to the foundation. Chunks of blackened wood and stone have been piled up to one side, as if someone started trying to clear away the mess but gave up halfway through.

More likely, someone in the area called the city to complain about it being an eyesore, but it was low on the list of priorities.

Either way, the home we made for ourselves—the place where we operated our business, the place where Willow came into our lives—is gone. When Olivia first sent us the video of it, none of us cared all that much. It was more important that we were all together and alive, and we'd made our peace with leaving our old life behind.

Now the sight of it hits me like a wrecking ball. It's just another reminder of everything that was taken from us.

Because of Troy.

Because of Olivia.

Malice clears his throat and speeds up a bit, putting some distance between us and the wreck of the warehouse.

"It doesn't matter," he says, voice gruff and firm. "We said goodbye to it already, and it doesn't change anything now. We'll get a hotel or something and keep a low profile. We just need a place to make a home base until we find Willow."

"Right," Ransom agrees, although he sounds less sure about it.

"Right," I murmur.

We head for a hotel off the beaten path on the outskirts of Detroit, someplace fairly shitty. Those are always the kind of places we hole up in when we need to stay off the radar. If it has beds and internet, that's good enough for our purposes.

This place has a sign outside advertising both free wi-fi and free continental breakfast in the morning, which I know from experience will likely just be those tiny boxes of cereal and some room temperature milk. Maybe a few pieces of fruit that are questionable at best.

"I'll get us checked in," Ransom says, sliding out of the car before heading inside to talk to the man behind the front desk. Malice and I follow a few minutes later, my twin hefting the backpack containing my laptop higher on his shoulder.

"Three room keys then?" the man is asking, glancing between the three of us. He looks half wary, half like he doesn't give a shit, and Malice and I stay quiet so as not to upset the balance of that.

"That would be great, thanks," Ransom says, putting on his bright 'people moving' smile, although it definitely doesn't reach his eyes.

"Okay. You're in two-oh-seven," the front desk guy tells us, speaking mostly to Ransom. "Stairs are just down the hall there. Breakfast is from seven to whenever we run out or remember to start putting stuff away."

Ransom gives him a little nod and thanks him for his help, and the three of us move off down the hall toward the stairs.

"You two get settled," Ransom tells us in a low voice. "I'm going to go find us some food. And some clothes. We haven't eaten in too long."

I'm sure he's right, but I barely register being hungry or thirsty or tired. Aside from my wound twinging, a low burn of pain when I walk or twist a certain way, I'm not really aware of any of those more human needs. My mind is just focused on the tasks ahead.

"Be careful," Malice replies. He grips Ransom's shoulder for a second, sharing a look with him before the two of us head up the stairs to the second floor.

Our room is serviceable, with two full size beds in the center, a TV, and a little desk and chair in the corner. I set myself up there, pulling out my laptop and plugging it in with all of the other things I need for this. Malice stalks to the window and draws the curtains closed, then walks the perimeter of the room to check it out.

Before I can lower myself onto the desk chair, he stops me.

"You should take a shower or something," he says, his dark gray eyes meeting mine.

"If this is your way of telling me I stink, I'll go ahead and let you know that you and Ransom aren't much better. We've been in a car for over twenty-four hours," I mutter.

Malice huffs a breath, not budging. "You've still got dried blood on you. You didn't even take time to clean up after being shot."

I realize with a jolt that he's right. It didn't even occur to me to care about that, and it's one of the first things I would have done if the situation was normal.

When I pull my jacket away from my shirt, it's still soaked through with blood, stiff and crackling from where it's dried. I lift my shirt, examining my wound for the first time since Malice patched me up. My side is mostly clean, but blood is crusted in the stitches, and it probably needs to be disinfected.

I grimace, reacting viscerally to the sight.

It's as if now that we've stopped moving for more than the time it takes to piss and gas up the car, all the little aches and pains are making themselves known. My head throbs, probably protesting the lack of food and water and the blood loss on top of everything else.

I've pushed my body and my mind to the breaking point over the last day or so, and it's not like we were all that well rested before we got to Mexico.

"Yeah," I mutter finally. "You might have a point."

Malice jabs a finger in the direction of the bathroom, and I go without argument, closing the door behind me and standing under the glow of the harsh florescent lighting.

The bathroom is small but relatively clean, and I undress quickly, leaving my dirty, sweat and bloodstained clothes in a heap on the floor. No point in folding them now.

The water hisses from the shower, icy cold at first, but then gradually heating up as it runs. I can hear the pipes clanging a bit as steam starts to fill the little room.

I hiss when the hot water hits my hastily stitched up wound, and I look down at it, examining it more closely. The stitches are uneven but good enough. It's definitely going to scar, but that was unavoidable, really.

All I can think about as I run my fingers over the bumps of the stitches is how that night went. How I tried to step in front of Willow, to protect her. How it was my instinct to keep her from being in the line of fire. I would have taken more bullets than this one to keep her safe, but in the end, it didn't even matter.

I got shot, and she still got taken.

I can see it, almost like it's playing out in slow motion every time I close my eyes. The angle is twisted and wrong from me being on the ground, my head swimming, my vision a little blurry. But I could still see clearly enough in that moment to see Willow being snatched.

I can remember every second of it.

The look on her face of shock and absolute terror.

The way her scream split the night air and echoed even after she was taken.

My eyes snap open, and I realize I'm breathing hard. My heart is racing in my chest, pounding with force against my ribs. I force myself to take a deep breath and then another, trying to focus on what I can control here and now.

I grab a wash cloth from the rack next to the shower and lather it up with the hotel soap, starting from the top and moving down as I clean myself. The water runs murky as grime and blood start to come away, and my eyes zero in on the sight of it.

It doesn't help.

Nothing helps.

I just keep picturing Willow's face.

I keep hearing her scream.

I keep seeing her being driven farther and farther out of reach, until I can't see her anymore.

The emotions are like a tidal wave, and once they reach their peak, I don't have a hope of outrunning them. It all crashes over me, threatening to drown me under the weight, and I gasp for breath.

Willow has always been intense for me. Her emotions mixed with mine, the way I feel about her. It's not like anything I've experienced before, so I have no defenses against it. No defense against the anger and the bone-chilling fear I'm feeling, wondering if she's okay.

I clench my jaw hard, trying to focus on breathing in through my nose and then out through my mouth. I count each breath in, four seconds. Then hold for another four and exhale for the same. But it's not really helping.

I add tapping my fingers to the mix, against my thigh, against the tiled wall, managing to do enough that I can finish showering off and then step out of the shower.

It's all just so much. It's all too much.

Nothing I'm trying is working the way it usually does, and there's none of that familiar settling as things start to calm down. If anything, it just whips my emotions into more of a frenzy, like a hurricane in my head and my chest, everything moving too fast and too chaotically for me to be able to grab ahold and shove it all back down.

The bathroom is suddenly too small. The dingy white walls are closing in, and I whirl around and punch one hard. The pain sends a jolt down my arm, and that cuts through the static in my head a bit, so I do it again.

I start counting, lining up my breathing with each punch. In, out—one. In, out—two. In, out—three.

The world narrows to the pain in my hand and the feeling of the paint from the wall under my skin, sticky with humidity from the shower. The count climbs higher, and I start leaving bloody streaks on the wall from where the skin of my knuckles splits, but I don't stop.

Not until the door swings open and Malice crowds into the small space, pulling me away from the wall.

"Fuck. Come on." His voice isn't gentle, but it is soft.

"Mal—"

"I know," he says, cutting me off. "I sent you in here to clean up, not get all bloody again. And put some fucking pants on."

I pull my hand up to look at it. He's right. The knuckles are a bloody mess. At least patching that up will give me something to do with my hands.

I wash the blood away under the water from the sink and then pull on my old pair of pants, grimacing at the knowledge that they've already been worn for too long without a wash. I forgo a shirt for now, unwilling to put that crusty, bloodstained thing back on my body, and I can feel Malice's gaze on me as I move around the small room.

"You know," he murmurs after a long moment. "Usually, I'm the one punching shit. You're supposed to be the level-headed, put together one."

I snort at that, but he's not wrong. "I feel like... I don't know. I feel like I'm splintering apart. Everything's wrong. It wasn't supposed to be like this."

"Yeah. I keep thinking about the night before all this shit popped off, and how we were so..."

"Happy?" I fill in.

Malice shrugs. "Yeah, I guess. We thought we'd bought ourselves some time, at least. That it would be easier from there on out."

"We got complacent."

"We thought that fucker was dead."

"Olivia wanted us to think that. She hid the truth from us on purpose," I tell him. It's something I've spent a lot of time contemplating over the past twenty-four hours. "Probably so she could use him exactly the way she did. They were both hunting for us, and he managed to get the drop on us because we were entirely focused on her."

Malice mutters a curse under his breath, raking his fingers through his dark hair. "We'll fix it. We're gonna find her."

I swallow hard. I can feel the looming edge of that spiral from minutes ago, right there, ready to consume me again. But I let out a breath and then drag in another one, focusing on Malice instead of the panic.

"We have to find her," I say, and my voice sounds raw even to my own ears. "We have to. I just. I—"

My voice chokes off. I don't even know what words I'm trying to find. I don't know what to say to make it clear how important this is. How badly we need to make sure she's alright.

"You love her." Malice's voice is quiet, but the words feel oddly loud in this small, empty space. It's not an accusation, just him telling me how I feel.

I drag in another breath and then nod. It's strange to think about it, strange to acknowledge that it's true. I certainly never thought I'd feel this way about anyone. After our mother died, I was so certain that the only people I would ever love were my brothers.

And now...

I nod, agreeing with Malice's words.

That starts up a whole new storm of feelings roiling inside me. Because I do love her. That's what this is. That's why I feel so strongly for her. Why I'm so desperate to get her back. Why having her gone feels like I'm missing a piece of myself, and why imagining her being hurt by Troy makes me want to tear down the entire world with my bare fucking hands.

"I never told her," I rasp, my eyes flicking up to meet my brother's. "I never even... I couldn't even touch her for so long, no matter how much I wanted to. Fuck. I wish shit didn't hold me back so much. With you and Ransom, it's not like she ever had to doubt how you felt."

Malice snorts, shooting me a look. "Bullshit. Ransom maybe,

28

but me? Threatening her every other day and getting in her face about shit?"

I shake my head, agitation crawling beneath my skin. "But she still stayed. She still..."

"Yeah, and she stayed for you too. I saw how you two were together, and how she pushed to get that close to you. You think she would've done all that if she had doubts?"

My retort dies on my lips, and I shrug, too many emotions choking my throat.

"She knew," Malice continues, his voice firm. "She knows. And I can tell you that she feels the same way. She never saw you as damaged or fucked up. Not any more than the rest of us, at least. She cares about you just the way you are."

"How do you know that?" I ask, almost desperate for the answer.

"Just do." He pauses, then adds, "It was obvious, Vic. I could see it every time she looked at you. Just like she could see it in the way you looked at her."

I let out another ragged breath and when I breathe in again, my lungs don't protest quite as much.

"Okay," I murmur. "We have to find her, Malice."

"We will," he says, his expression hardening. "I don't give a fuck if we have to turn this whole damned state upside down, or this whole damn country. We're gonna find her."

He reaches out a hand, and the sight of it plunges me into a memory of a different time, years ago.

Malice was younger then, but no less determined. His eyes blazed almost exactly the way they are now as he told me and Ransom that we were gonna make sure our dad could never hurt our mom again. He held his hand out then too, and Ransom and I clasped it in turn, sealing the deal with a handshake that meant so much.

The stakes are just as high now, with the fate of the only person we love as much as each other hanging in the balance.

So I reach out, clasping Malice's hand the same way I did back then. He squeezes, and I squeeze back. For a moment, I'm wrapped up in the knowledge that whatever comes, at least we're all in this together. At least we're not grappling with any of this shit alone.

We hold that for a second, and then we let go, the moment broken. But the impact is still there.

I feel more steady as we leave the bathroom, and I apply some ointment to my wound before sitting down at the desk. My hands don't shake as I pull up my programs, ready to resume the search.

A few minutes later, there's a muffled curse from outside the door, and then Ransom comes in, balancing a drink carrier and several massive bags, as well as the room key.

"Thanks for getting the door," he grumbles, tossing the plastic key onto one of the beds.

"You didn't knock," Malice says, shrugging.

Ransom rolls his eyes and tosses the bags of clothes down on the bed before he starts distributing the food.

It's just fast food, greasy burgers and fries that have already started to cool, and I barely taste it as I eat and sip at the soda Ransom brought for me.

Malice and Ransom give each other shit, but once again, it starts to fade to background noise as I narrow my focus. I tap my fingers on the desk—one, two, three, four, five. I inhale deeply, the scent of grease and salt rushing through my nose.

Re-centered, I get back to work for real.

Once they're done eating and have showered as well, I'll get Malice and Ransom to help me, maybe by turning my digital map into something physical that we can see on the wall. We'll keep working as long as we have to, until Willow is back and safe.

Because I can't live without her. I spent so long fighting it, trying to deny my feelings. But it's not a question. Not anymore.

I need her more than I need air.

And I'll destroy anyone who hurts her or tries to keep me away.

4

WILLOW

GOOSEBUMPS PRICKLE MY SKIN, and I do my best to pull in a deep breath, but all I can seem to manage is a short, sharp inhale.

I'm back in the room I was in when I first woke up in this hell-hole, but nothing about it feels comforting or familiar.

I avoid the bed, sitting on the floor instead, my arms wrapped around my knees, as if I can keep myself together that way. The dress I was forced to get married in hangs off of me in tatters, strips of white satin and lace that don't do enough to cover me up anymore. I still keep pulling the scraps around me even more, and my hands shake as I arrange the pieces.

There's very little light in the room, but I can still catch sight of the red streaks under my fingernails. I curl my hand into a fist, but it doesn't really help.

My body shakes, adrenaline and fear finally starting to leak out of me, leaving me in a state of something like shock. My face is wet with tears, and every so often, another one tracks down my cheeks, spilling over. I don't bother to wipe them away.

I take a breath and then another, trying to keep myself as steady as possible. It feels like if I fall apart now, I'll never be able to put the pieces back together.

Everything hurts, and there's a headache throbbing behind my eye, so I take a note from Vic's book, trying to count each breath, letting it center me a little. But it also makes me think about Vic and the others, and that hurts like an invisible knife being driven into my chest.

More than anything, I wish they were here.

The door opens, and I flinch back, trying to scoot deeper into the shadows. I'm expecting to see Troy or hear his mocking voice, but when I glance up, it's just one of his bodyguards.

That's a relief, but only a small one.

"Come with me," he grunts, and I don't even bother to argue.

I get to my feet, my cheeks burning with shame as the tatters of my dress fall a bit, showing off more scarred skin than I'm comfortable with. I keep my arms wrapped around my torso, trying to keep myself covered as best I can.

The guard looks me over, but there's nothing in his eyes. No desire, but no sympathy either. I might as well be another piece of furniture in the room instead of a living, breathing human being. He doesn't seem to give a shit that his boss kidnapped me, or that I've clearly been assaulted.

Of course not. He works for Troy, and Troy wouldn't keep someone who'd care about something like that on the payroll.

"Let's go."

He turns to lead the way out of the room, and I follow him, flinching at every sound and trying to keep my footsteps steady. My gaze keeps darting around the hall as if I'm expecting Troy to come bursting out of one of the rooms or around a corner, but we make it to a bathroom without seeing him.

"Get cleaned up," the guard grunts. "Your husband is expecting you to join him for dinner. There are clothes in there for you. Put them on or I'll do it for you."

He stares at me expectantly with that same impassive expression on his face, and I pray he doesn't have orders to follow me inside or anything. When I step into the large bathroom, he lets me shut the door behind myself, and I finally exhale.

At least I'm being allowed this moment of privacy.

I don't even want to look at my reflection in the mirror at first. Or even at my body at all. My hands are still shaking as I try to remove what's left of the wedding gown, and it takes a few tries for me to get the zipper undone.

The tatters of satin and lace slide down my body, and I step out of the pool of it as soon as I can. It's chilly in the bathroom, and I feel that air rushing over the scrapes and scratches on my body. The places where Troy got rough.

I swallow hard, a lump rising in my throat.

There's a bruise on my side where he hit me, and when I touch it, it throbs tenderly.

I whip my hand away from it.

When I finally turn to face the mirror, I hate what I see. My hair is a mess, tangled and matted from Troy grabbing it, My eyes are bloodshot and my face is splotchy from crying. More tears fall, and I jerk my eyes down, not wanting to look at myself anymore.

Instead, I focus on the tattoo above my left breast. Right over my heart. The stylized number 24 that Malice put on me what feels like forever ago, and the initials of the brothers.

I turn so I can see the newer addition, which is healed now and no longer has that shine of fresh ink. The flowers stand out beautifully on my skin, wrapped around the harsher lines of the weapon Malice tattooed on me.

If I close my eyes, I can focus on the memory of the hum of the machine, and the way Malice explained why he chose this design for me. How he told me that he sees me as both beautiful and delicate, but also strong and unbending.

I let that ground me, keeping me from breaking down entirely.

Swallowing hard, I turn on the shower and wait for the water to heat up before I get in. I hiss as the spray hits my back, then groan softly. I'm so sore all over, but the hot water starts to wash away the blood and sweat and everything else, and it feels good to clean away the remnants of Troy on my body.

I let the water beat down on me, easing my tense muscles, the sound of the shower drowning out my thoughts.

I wash my hair thoroughly, taking a minute to tame the tangles before moving on to washing myself up, drawing it out for as long as I can.

I'd stay in here forever if I could, but I don't want to run the risk of Troy or his guard coming in to get me, so eventually, I shut the water off and step out of the shower.

Finally, I look a little more human. I don't know if someone cleaned me up when I was brought here from Mexico, and I don't really want to think about it either way. But it feels nice to be clean now.

Thankfully, the clothes Troy left for me are normal, nothing like the wedding dress that I woke up in. Just an expensive looking blouse, undergarments, and some pants that I step into once I've dried off.

The shirt covers my tattoos, but I still know they're there, and I put my hand over the ones on my chest, taking another deep breath.

I think about the Voronin brothers, remembering the last time I saw them. Malice and Ransom, furious and out of breath, trying to keep us all moving. Vic standing in front of me and then abruptly crumpling to the ground, shot. I don't even know where he was hit. I don't even know if...

He has to be alive. He has to be fine.

Neither of his brothers would let him go without fighting like hell to bring him back from the brink, and I know they would have taken care of him. So he must be alive. He's probably out there somewhere being very particular about stitches and wound cleaning.

All three of them are probably looking for me. By this point, I believe that with my whole heart. They've proven time and time again that as long as there's breath left in their bodies, they won't stop trying to find me or protect me.

So I have to survive.

I have to still be alive when they get here.

I have to.

Clinging to those words like a mantra, I finally pull open the bathroom door.

The guard is still there, his arms crossed over his chest. He doesn't say anything, just motions for me to follow him and leads me down another hall and into a dining room. It's not as lavish as Olivia's, but it still manages to be ostentatious. Troy is already there, sitting at the head of the table, lounging like some kind of king on his throne.

He looks up when I walk in on the heels of his guard, and I feel a burst of savage satisfaction at the scratch marks that run down his face.

He might have gotten what he wanted in the end, but I didn't go down without a fight. He took something from me, but at least I took something from him too.

Even if it wasn't enough.

"Sit down, wifey," he says, sounding smug and bored all at the same time.

I do as he says, taking a seat gingerly at the table.

A door at the other end of the room opens, and food is brought out on trays. A big roasted slab of meat, vegetables, and bread. It smells good, but I don't move to serve myself, even as Troy starts loading up his plate.

It takes him a moment to notice, and he swallows around a mouthful of bread as he arches a brow at me.

"It's not poisoned," he assures me, smirking. "Why would I do that? You're my wife. It's my job to take care of you, right? So I need to keep you fed."

Every time he reminds me that I'm his wife, I hate it more, and I grit my teeth. "You don't seem to have any qualms about hurting me, so don't act like that means anything."

Troy's smirk just widens.

"Hurting you and poisoning you are two different things." He reaches for his wine glass and takes a swallow, smacking his lips. "I knew you were going to be a wildcat. That's why I was drawn to you. I wanted someone with a spark in her. With some fire. All the

35

other women my parents were interested in marrying me off to would've been too easy to break. Just lying there like limp little rag dolls, taking it. But you? You make me work for it, and I like that."

My stomach turns, and I feel like I might throw up right here at the table. If he notices, Troy doesn't give a shit, because he just keeps going.

"Of course, I'll have to teach you how to behave," he adds with a chuckle. "I need a wife I can take out in proper society, which means I'll have to break you. Stamp out some of that fire. Just enough, you know? That's why we'll be taking an extended honey-moon here. I told my family that I'd be gone for a little while, so that I could have some time with my new bride. Just the two of us. It'll give me a chance to train you."

My skin prickles as revulsion fills me, sour and strong.

"You're such a fucking pig," I spit. "A monster who gets off on pain and power. You think you're some kind of prince or king or playboy? You think you're better than everyone else, but you're nothing but a piece of shit. Just another spoiled brat who never learned to take no for an answer."

Even as the words are spewing out of my mouth, I know I should hold my tongue. I shouldn't be saying any this, because it's just going to come back and bite me in the ass, but I can't help it.

"You're disgusting," I snap. "You talk about all these other women who would just lie there and take it, but you know what I think? I think no other woman would let you touch her with a ten-foot pole. Not for all the money in the world. Because you're a creep and a troll, and they know it. So you have to resort to shit like this, because no one wants you! And why would they? Why would anyone want a disgusting monster like you?"

Troy just listens, sitting there with his wine glass in his hand, letting me go off. He looks unbothered for all of thirty seconds before he stands up and jerks his chin at the two guards standing by in the room.

Instantly, they move, grabbing my shoulders and jerking me up from my seat. I stumble as they shove me forward and then force me down to my knees in front of the table. My heart jackrabbits in my chest, cold fear rushing through me in a wave.

Calm as anything, Troy gets up and walks over. He fists a hand in my hair, grabbing it so hard it makes my eyes water.

"I should choke you with my dick for saying shit like that," he says, his voice even. "But I know you're such a wild little thing, you'd probably try to bite it off. I promise you though, we'll get there. One day, you'll know better than to fight back at all."

I bite my tongue, resisting the urge to spit in his face.

I don't want to make whatever he's about to do to me even worse.

Troy's fingers tighten in my hair, and for a second, his cool façade cracks. I can see the pitiful, petty anger in his eyes, and I know my words affected him more than he's letting on.

"But let me give you just a little taste of what happens when you displease your husband," he whispers, his voice harsh.

He yanks me up by my hair, and I bite my tongue to keep from crying out in pain. The two guards still have a hold on me, and together, they drag me out of the kitchen and down the hall to another room of the house.

It's mostly empty, but there's a trapdoor hatch set into the floor.

One of the guards hauls it open, and I peer down into a coffin sized space under the floor.

Oh god. Oh fuck. No.

My breaths turn shallow as panic overtakes me. I try to back away, but the other guard keeps a tight hold on my arm, not letting me move.

At Troy's nod, the two burly men shove me down into the little space, and before I can get my bearings, the hatch is slammed closed. Over the sound of my frantic heartbeat, I can make out the sound of a lock clicking into place.

I'm locked in. Trapped.

Footsteps echo overhead and then... nothing.

I'm locked in, and I'm alone.

It's dark, and I can barely see my hands in front of my face.

There's nothing down here, no room for anything else other than my body, and I curl into myself as much as I can in the cramped confines, trying to remember how to breathe. There are tiny gaps in the floorboards, so I don't think I'll suffocate down here, but the air feels thin as it rushes into my lungs. I get lightheaded, which makes my heart beat even faster.

My head starts to swim, and I feel like I might pass out, panting through my mouth, every fiber of my being raging against this enclosed space. My hands scrabble at the trap door, trying to find a latch or a handle or something, even though I know it's useless. They locked me in. I heard it.

Swallowing hard, I force myself to breathe in through my nose and hold it for a bit, counting under my breath the way Vic does when he's overwhelmed. *One. Two. Three. Four.* I let it out slowly and then do the whole thing over again.

I tap my fingers against my thighs, and the feeling of the fabric of my pants under my hands is grounding.

I'm still here. I'm still alive.

Each little ritual helps me cling to sanity, keeping me from spiraling out of control entirely. Tears leak from my eyes as I hold on to a single mantra.

Survive. Survive. Survive.

5

MALICE

I HURL a chair across the room, watching with dissatisfaction as it doesn't splinter into a thousand pieces the way I really fucking want it to. The way I feel like *I'm* splintering, coming apart at the seams the longer this shit goes on.

"God fucking dammit!" I snarl at nothing in particular, curling my hands into fists hard enough that my nails bite into my skin. I drag in a deep breath and then shake out some of the tension in my body, dragging a hand over the scruff on my face.

I haven't had time to shave in a while, but none of that shit matters now.

We just lost another thread. Another lead that didn't pan out. It's been several days since we got back from Mexico, and it feels like we're not any closer to finding out where Willow is. Every fucking day that passes with no news and no resolution just makes it worse.

Ransom's jaw is tight, a muscle in the side of his face jumping until he lets out a breath himself.

"We'll just... keep looking," he says, his voice strained.

Victor doesn't even say anything. His eyes are glued to his computer, and his fingers are flying across the keyboard as he searches for something new. All he does these days is search, sifting through information to try to find a lead buried under all the fucking nothing we keep coming up with.

He hasn't torn himself away from his computer for more than a couple hours here and there to sleep, and that's usually only when Ransom or I make him. His face is gaunt, his blue eyes bloodshot, but he still keeps going.

And even with all of that, we haven't found her.

If I feel like I'm about to lose the last shred of my sanity, I know my brothers feel the same. Whatever shit I said to Vic when we first got to the hotel, whatever reassurances I gave him, I've lost sight of them now. I feel like I've got a monster inside me, tearing me apart from the inside out.

All I can think about is how we're failing her. Willow was depending on us to keep her safe, to keep this shit from happening, and we fucking *failed*. And now we can't even fucking find her.

She could be going through all kinds of horrible shit, and we're sitting here in this goddamned hotel room, helpless to do anything about it.

I slam my fist into the wall hard enough to send a jolt up my arm, and then I drop my forehead to rest against the shitty wallpaper, breathing hard.

"How the fuck can that asshole go underground like this? How can we just... lose to him? To *him*?"

"Money and resources go a long way," Vic mutters tiredly. "He can pay to cover his tracks."

"Are we sure he actually brought Willow back here?" Ransom asks. "Maybe he just passed through Detroit and went somewhere else. Maybe we're looking in the wrong places."

I can see Vic's hackles go up, his shoulders stiffening.

"Yes, I'm sure," he snaps, sounding tense and frustrated. "He's here somewhere. I just—I can't make the last connections I need to. I can't track him the rest of the way. He's covered his shit too well."

"Fuck it." I shake my head sharply. "We should go interrogate Olivia. *Beat* it out of her if we have to. She has to know where

Willow is. It's not like she'd let Troy take Willow somewhere without her knowledge."

"We don't know that for sure. And she'll have us arrested if we go anywhere near her," Ransom points out. "Remember, she's got warrants out for all of us now, not just you. Lying low in an ask-no-questions hotel while we search for Willow is one thing, but going after Olivia flat-out would be too risky."

Irritation simmers under my skin. On our drive back to Detroit, Vic alerted us that there are now outstanding warrants for all three of us, proving that Olivia followed through on the threat she made all those weeks ago. She probably knew it would make it harder for us to go after Willow, and it makes me fucking furious that she can throw roadblocks like this in our way from her goddamned ivory tower.

"Well, what the fuck else can we *do*?" I growl. "Just sit here?"

Ransom grimaces, shoving a hand through his messy brown hair. "I don't like it any more than you do, Mal. I'd love to give Olivia a piece of my mind—with my fucking fists. But if we get thrown in jail, we can't help Willow at all."

"*Fuck!*"

I punch the wall again, because I know he's right. But I hate it.

"Let's just... start at the beginning again," Ransom suggests, even though he sounds as exhausted as the rest of us. We've gone over it so many times, and we're no closer to knowing anything. But it's not like we can just give up. "What do we know?"

"We know Troy came to Detroit," Vic responds automatically. "I've tracked him to the city, but no farther than that. The only contact he had with his family was telling them he'd be away for a while. He hasn't been to the offices of their corporation either. He's basically vanished."

"And taken Willow with him," I mutter. "There are only so many places he could be fucking hiding."

Vic spares me a glance. "It's a big city, Malice. And like I keep saying, he has the money to stay completely under the radar. I'm sure he has the resources to cover his tracks and hire a team of bodyguards who'd help him hide a captive."

He says the last word like it tastes sour in his mouth, and it makes my stomach turn just hearing it. My Solnyshka is too damned strong to just be some fucker's captive, but right now that's basically what she is.

I pace the room, feeling pent up and caged in. I'm ready to leave this fucking hotel and tear this whole goddamned city apart if I have to, destroying it from the ground up to find Willow.

Every second that passes is like a knife in my heart, twisting deeper and deeper. The more I think about what she might be going through, how she might be suffering, the sharper that knife becomes and the more viciously it cuts.

I open my mouth to say something, but then Vic suddenly sits up straighter. There's something sharp about his posture, an edge of alertness that wasn't there a moment ago.

"Wait," he says.

Ransom is at Vic's side in a heartbeat, and I'm right there on his heels, energy and adrenaline churning inside me. We peer over Vic's shoulder, not quite sure what he's found yet. His fingers move across the keys, typing even more furiously, and then he sits back.

"Here," he says, his voice shaking slightly. "I found something. It's a property I think Troy bought a while ago. Fuck, he hid his tracks well. He went through a shell company to purchase it, and there's almost no connection between him and this house. But it's his. I'm sure of it."

"What does this mean?" I ask, getting right to the point.

"It means it's a place he has that we didn't know about before. I'm almost certain it belongs to him."

We all tense at that, spinning out on the implications.

"Can you get footage surrounding the area?" I ask Vic, gripping the back of his chair. "We've gotta know if it's his. If he's there."

Vic is already working on it as I speak, his eyes narrowed.

"It's remote, outside of the city," he says, speaking slowly as he follows the trail of information he's digging up in real-time. "Looks like some kind of cabin in the woods. Maybe he bought it as a sort of safe house in case he ever needed to lie low. Or as someplace where he could do shady shit without being seen. Let me see what I can piece together."

It's another tense few minutes as we watch my twin work. Rushing him isn't going to help anything, I know that. But at the same time, I feel like I'm champing at the bit, wanting him to hurry up, desperate for this to be *something*.

Finally, Vic pulls up some blurry footage.

"This is from about a week ago," he says. A couple of cars with tinted windows are driving up a twisting road, which I assume leads to the cabin he found.

"There's not a lot of traffic in this area," Vic explains. "Almost no cars use this road. And the timing works out right. So—"

"So that's probably her," Ransom finishes.

"It's as solid of a lead as we've got," Vic agrees.

My muscles tense, ready for action. I can't fucking wait any longer.

"It's good enough to act on," I tell them, clapping my hands on the back of Vic's chair and stepping back. "Let's go."

Ransom gives me a look, although he's already moving toward the cabinet where we've stashed the weapons we bought over the past few days. "You know this isn't going to be easy, right? Troy's going to have security with him. And considering how well-trained the crew who came after us in Mexico was, he's probably not taking any chances."

I shoot him a dark smile, cracking my knuckles. "Good. I'm in the mood to kill more than one motherfucker tonight."

6

WILLOW

L IGHT SUDDENLY FLOODS the small space I'm trapped in, and I have to blink back tears as it burns my eyes.

When I glance up, Troy is standing there, the smug smile I've come to loathe playing over his lips as he looks down at me.

"Are you ready to be a good girl this time?" he asks, all mocking condescension, as if he's talking to a child or a pet. "Are you starting to learn your lesson, little wife?"

I swallow hard and nod.

I've been locked down here in this little crawl space several times now. Enough that I've started to lose count, lose the tether of time as the days bled together. I don't even know how long I've been here anymore.

He's let me out to eat sometimes, and he's forced himself on me again too.

Through it all, I've somehow managed to keep some small thread of my sanity intact, not letting this break me. I keep the sound of Malice's voice in my head, telling me I'm strong, and that's helped in my darkest moments. In my time alone, I've been putting together a plan for how I might get free of this, building it in my mind while I try to numb myself to what's been happening to my body.

I've been giving Troy what he wants ever since my outburst that first night, since disengaging makes it seem like he's breaking me the way he wants to. Not fighting back makes him smirk that awful smirk, but I'm hoping it's also making him more complacent.

It's a risky plan, especially since Troy has proven himself to be more cunning and vicious than I first thought. But it's the only possible escape route I can see, so I have to try. No matter how dangerous and soul-crushing it is.

The worst part is that sometimes I can't tell if it's an act anymore. The lines between the lie and the truth are just as blurred as the amount of time I've been here, leaving me feeling disoriented and numb, like a stranger in my own body.

Fuck. Maybe he really is *breaking me.*

Troy reaches down to take my arm and help me out of the cramped space, and I want to flinch back away from him, but I force myself not to.

He notices the way I keep myself pliant and loose in his arms, and he smiles approvingly.

"There you go," he croons, and the fake kindness in his tone makes nausea roil my stomach. "You're learning so well. You'll be fit to appear on my arm in public in no time. I'll get you cleaned up, dress you in something other than the shit you used to wear, and no one will ever guess that you're the daughter of a whore, will they? They'll never know that you're just polished up trash. My pretty little *wife.*"

As if he can't help himself, he drops his head and bites my neck, and I press my lips together, my toes curling against the hardwood as I struggle to keep myself from reacting to the pain. When he drags his tongue over the bite mark, I squeeze my eyes shut, making sure not to let a single tear fall.

He won't win.

I won't let him win.

Troy draws back, studying my face for a second before nodding in satisfaction.

45

"Come with me," he says, his tone returning to that falsely gentle lilt that I despise. "I'll help you get cleaned up."

He says it so magnanimously, as if it's not his fault I'm streaked with grime and dust and dirt in the first place.

Jerking his chin and gripping my arm, he leads me down the hall up a set of stairs to the second floor. When we get to the bathroom attached to his bedroom, he starts taking my clothes off. I just stand there, lifting my arms when he urges me to and stepping out of my pants. His hands grope at my body, and I fight the urge to shudder with revulsion as my skin crawls from his touch.

I bite the tip of my tongue, focusing on the self-inflicted pain over every other sensation in my body.

"In you go," Troy says, helping me into the shower and turning it on.

You can do this, I remind myself. *You have to be strong. If you let him break you, then you're never getting out of here. You just have to endure it. You just have to get through it.*

Luckily, Troy doesn't climb into the shower with me, and I'm allowed at least a few minutes of privacy behind the glass shower door. I clean up quickly, scrubbing the dirt away, knowing that the phantom feeling of Troy's touch is just going to be replaced as soon as I get out of the shower.

I don't have any delusions that he pulled me out of that hole just to chat.

I also don't dare take too long, so as soon as I'm clean, I turn off the water and step out. Troy is waiting for me, holding a towel. But instead of offering it to me, he holds it in his hands, just out of my reach. His gaze burn as he looks me over, those cruel eyes following the path of drops of water as they slide down my skin.

I can feel it when his gaze lingers on my scars, and something in his face twists a bit.

"You really are lucky." He snorts a laugh. "I married you even though you're deformed like this. No one else would have. But unlike some, I can see past that. I can see the potential underneath the mess. I always knew an ugly girl would be a better fuck, and I was right. One day you'll thank me for choosing you."

His words remind me suddenly of what Olivia said to me the last time I saw her. That someday I would be grateful for this. It just makes me hate Troy—hate *both* of them—even more.

They both buy into this delusion that somehow they're doing me a favor. That me being a poor nobody forever wouldn't have been so much better than this hell.

Dropping the towel, Troy reaches out and skims his palm up my side, dancing it over the curve of my hip. Unlike when the Voronin brothers—especially Vic—used to touch me, he avoids my scars, as if he can't stand to touch them.

His hand moves up my arm and into my wet hair, and when he threads his fingers through the damp strands, I brace myself to be yanked toward him.

For once, he's more gentle than I expect, and he pulls me closer and kisses me.

Instead of jerking away or going stiff the way I want to, I force myself to kiss him back. I have to close my eyes, screwing them shut tight so that I can't see his face, and even then, his scent invades my senses, his tongue slipping into my mouth like a probing slug. My stomach twists, and I wonder if he can taste the bile that's rising up in my throat.

But I guess he can't, because he makes a hungry noise in his throat. And that little bit of participation on my part is enough to make him pull back after a moment, looking pleased.

"You're learning," he says with a nod. "Aren't you?"

I nod back stiffly, my arms limp at my sides.

"That's good." His all-American good looks are at odds with the salacious hunger in his eyes. "You're being very good for me, little wife. Maybe I'll give you extra dinner tonight if you keep behaving."

My stomach cramps in response, but I'm glad it doesn't growl out loud. Troy has been restricting my food, only giving me scraps when he feels like it, after he's finished eating, and hunger is right there with exhaustion at the forefront of my brain.

I nod again, doing my best not to let the hope show on my face.

"Good girl." Troy gives my cheek a little pat, and then a sharp slap. "Now go lie down on the bed and get ready for me."

My cheek stings, but I do what he says, my feet shuffling into the bedroom.

I hate the sight of this bed by now, but I make myself lie down anyway, still naked and damp from the shower.

I know what comes next, and my body is already tensing in anticipation.

Troy comes into the room a moment later, and his eyes are all over me.

"You know," he muses, palming his cock through his pants. "I do sometimes miss the way you used to fight back with everything you had. That was hot. But I'm pleased with your progress. You'll be a good little wife in no time."

Revulsion creeps through me, but I push it down, watching as he comes closer.

"Spread your legs," he tells me, and I do it.

My heart rate picks up as my adrenaline kicks in, but I try to hide it, keeping my breathing even the way I've been practicing during the many long hours in the hatch.

And then Troy is right there, crawling up over me. He touches me as he moves up, grabbing my breasts roughly, tweaking the nipples. His eyes are dark as he looms above me, and he drops his head, ready to steal another kiss.

That's when I move.

There's an ugly lamp on the nightstand next to the bed, one I've been forced to stare at before, while Troy has been forcing himself on me. I grope for it now, grabbing it around the middle. It's heavier than I expected, but I manage to swing it and smash it right into the side of Troy's head.

He jerks sideways and then reels back with a startled grunt. "What the fuck?"

"Get the fuck off me," I rasp, swinging for him again.

"You little bitch." He throws his hands up, partially blocking the blow this time, his face blotchy with rage. "You must really like it down in that hole. If that's the case, I'll leave you down there until you can't remember what light is."

He lunges for my throat, his hands out, but I'm ready for him. I bring my legs up between us, using them to keep him from getting too close, and he grunts when my knee hits him in the stomach. I drop the lamp and try to roll out from under him, crawling away down the bed.

A hand closes around my ankle, tight as a vise, and I kick hard, but it won't let go.

"No you don't," Troy spits. He starts trying to drag me back, hauling me in, and everything in me screams in protest.

No. No!

I have to get away now. This is my one chance. If I don't escape on this attempt, he'll never let his guard down again. He'll keep me bound day and night, and he'll make sure I pay for what I've done.

If he manages to get the upper hand, I'm done for.

My other foot is still free, and I lash out with it, catching Troy right between the legs. He grunts in pain, and I kick him again, hitting his bad arm this time.

That's enough to get him to let me go, and I gasp for air, throwing myself off the bed and taking off running. I'm still completely naked, but I don't have time to throw anything on. Every precious second counts, and I'll need each one of them to try to find a way out of this house. I've only been in a few rooms, almost always accompanied by guards, so despite my best efforts to piece together the layout of the large space, I only have a vague idea of where the exits might be.

There are also at least four guards here somewhere, but Troy didn't bring them with him when he came for me today. Still, I'm sure he's already alerting them to my escape attempt. I need to get out before he can send them after me.

My heart is pounding in my chest, and I take the stairs so fast that I almost go tumbling down them, barely catching myself on the banister. I know the downstairs part of the house a little better than the upstairs, since this is where the dining room and the room with the hatch are.

When I reach the hallway at the bottom, I debate for a half second, torn between turning left or right. My hands shake with the overflow of adrenaline as I force myself to make a snap decision and turn left, racing down the corridor toward what I hope like hell is the front of the house—or even the back, as long as there's a door that will let me out.

I turn at the end of the hallway, and a desperate sob tears from my lips as I see what looks like the front door.

Please, please, please.

The door looms ahead, and I put on a burst of speed, my entire body aching as I reach for the knob. It's locked, and I scrabble at the deadbolt—

But before I can turn it, a furious roar sounds from behind me.

Troy.

He tackles me sideways, knocking me away from the door and bringing me down to the floor in a heap.

"Going somewhere?" he pants, his artfully styled hair disheveled from our struggle. "You fucking wish. You're mine now. I fucking *own* you, and I'll keep you here for as long as I have to. There's no way out, you little bitch."

He's clearly furious, his brown eyes snapping, his nails digging into my skin. He spits on my face and then punches me, making pain flare in my cheekbone. My vision goes blurry around the edges as he rises to his feet, looming over me. He grabs my legs and starts dragging me away from the door, my bare skin sliding painfully over the hardwood floor.

I can see my window for freedom closing, and it makes me frantic.

No. Dammit, not like this.

I'm not going to be thrown back into that hole. I'm not going to be dragged back into his bed. I won't let it happen. I'd truly rather die than let Troy keep me here.

That thought lights something inside me, and I let out a feral scream, twisting and kicking with everything I have. I manage to yank one of my ankles out of Troy's grasp and kick the back of his knee, and he goes down with a grunt, catching himself with one hand. I try again to scrabble away, but he lunges for me, wrapping his arms around my waist and sending us both crashing to the floor again.

We roll and scrabble, elbows and knees and fists flying. He's bigger than me, and surprisingly strong for someone raised in the lap of luxury, and manages to shove my arms over my head, using his weight advantage to keep me pinned down. He's breathing hard, and I can see a sheen of sweat on his forehead, gleaming above the bruise and the trail of blood from where I hit him with the lamp.

But still, despite his obvious pain and the fury burning in his eyes... he's hard.

"Gonna teach you a real lesson," he grunts, wrapping one hand around my throat. "Gonna make sure you don't forget it this time."

He starts to squeeze, and I buck my hips beneath him, trying to throw him off me. I can hear the sound of shouts, and I know his guards are coming. Once they get here, I'll be too outnumbered. All that will be left is for them to watch as Troy fucks me. Possibly even *kills* me.

"Fuck... you," I choke out, because if I really am about to die, I want those to be the last words he ever hears me say.

He bares his teeth, something halfway between a snarl and a sneer. "You won't be so mouthy when I'm—"

Bang!

The sound of a gunshot in the distance cuts him off. Both of us jerk in surprise, and my heart stutters as several more shots ring out, followed by loud voices yelling indistinguishable words. The noises get louder, coming from the back of the house, and alarm flares in Troy's brown eyes as he stares down at me.

Then footsteps thunder down the hall toward us, and his head snaps up.

My gaze follows his just in time to see Malice, Ransom, and Vic burst into the entryway from the back of the house.

7

WILLOW

My heart stops when I see them.

Malice is flanked by his brothers, as always, and all three of them are heavily armed.

For a split second, I think I must be losing my mind. Maybe I really am broken. Maybe I'm still in that crawl space, hallucinating all of this.

But then Malice lets out a wordless sound of fury, and it breaks the spell. Troy moves like he's going to get up and do something, but before he even has a chance, Malice is on him.

He snatches Troy away from me, the muscles in his arms bulging as he drags him off of me. Troy swings at him, landing a punch on the side of Malice's face, but it's like Malice can't even feel it. He shoves Troy backward, bearing down on him like a train as he slams him against the wall.

The force of it looks hard enough to crack some ribs, and Troy grunts—but Malice doesn't pause for even a second. Shoving his gun in the waistband of his pants, he grabs a wicked-looking hunting knife from a sheath at his hip and drives it through Troy's hand, impaling it against the wall.

Troy screams in pain, and as the sound echoes in the foyer, Vic strides forward, a savage look in his eyes. He grabs Troy's left hand

and shoves it against the wall just above shoulder height, making Troy scream again as his bad arm is torqued into a painful position. Then Vic stabs him through the palm just like Malice did, pinning Troy up like some kind of butterfly on a corkboard.

I sit up, barely aware of the cool hardwood under my bare ass as I stare at the scene before me in shock.

Malice is all towering fury, burning hot and fast the way he does, while Vic exudes more of a silent anger, a simmering rage that lashes out fast and deadly. Ransom steps forward too, looking more like his brothers than he ever has in this moment, his handsome features as hard as stone.

The three of them move in tandem, attacking Troy. Vic goes for the wound in Troy's shoulder, jabbing his fist against it.

Malice aims for the face, punching him in the nose, the eye, the cheek, leaving him a bloody mess.

Ransom takes body shots, driving his fist into Troy's gut in a way that makes him groan.

"You bastards," Troy grunts, struggling to free himself. "You won't... get away with this. I'll have you killed for this, you—"

He cuts off with a scream as Vic jostles the knife piercing one of his hands, and he slumps, breathing hard and fast.

I just keep staring.

Part of me can barely believe this is real. That they're here. Victor is here, *alive*, and I saw him get shot. The whole time I've been away from them, I wasn't even sure that he had made it through the night I was taken. I have a split second of being unsure, worried that he's a ghost. That me thinking I see him is proof that this is a dream or a hallucination. That my mind has finally broken from all the torment I've been through since Mexico.

Maybe this is just my brain blocking out the truth by making up this scenario. By giving me the thing I want the most, the brothers here with me, when in reality I'm just getting assaulted by Troy with no end in sight and no help coming.

Troy howls in pain again, and I shake myself.

No. It has to be real. It has to be.

Everything catches up to me in a rush as my mind struggles to process it all. Being locked in that crawl space, barely eating, Troy forcing himself on me again and again. My emotions spike, and I sway as I clamber to my feet. My legs are shaking like they can barely support my weight, adrenaline rushing through me and making my skin go cold and clammy.

A tiny noise escapes my lips, barely audible over the other sounds filling the entryway, but Ransom turns toward me immediately.

"Willow," he says, his voice hoarse with relief as he rushes over to me.

That seems to spark Malice and Vic out of their rage, and they leave Troy where they've pinned him to the wall and come over to me too.

For a moment, all I can do is stare at them as they gather around me. I'm overwhelmed, shaking and lost, and when I open my mouth, nothing comes out.

"Hey," Ransom murmurs. "You're okay now. Angel?"

"She's in shock," Vic says.

"No surprise after what that fucker has probably been putting her through," Malice growls.

"Willow, nod if you can hear me." Ransom's voice is low, worry shining in his blue-green eyes.

I look at him and feel myself nod, even though I'm not really aware of having given my body that command.

He grins, bright and perfect. "Good girl. There you are. We've got you. We're going to get you out of here. Fuck, what did that monster do to you?"

He takes in the sight I must be, my hair wild and matted, bruises on my skin from fighting with Troy, my face gaunt and my eyes hollow.

Malice makes a noise low in his throat, almost like a wounded animal. He takes his jacket off and passes it over to Ransom, who helps me wrap up in it.

"There you go," Ransom murmurs. "It's okay, pretty girl. We've got you. I'm so fucking sorry we didn't get here earlier. But we're here now."

And they are.

All three of them are here, gathered around me until I can't even see Troy anymore. They're here, solid and real, not just figments of my battered, tormented mind.

"I—" My voice gives out, and I swallow and try again. "I can't believe you came. You found me."

"We'll always find you," Malice says. "Always." But the strength of his words isn't mirrored in his face. There's a tortured expression there, something haunted in his eyes. "We tried to come sooner. As soon as they took you. We tried to get to you."

I nod because I know. I know they would have been here the very same day I got here if they could have. I can picture them frantically searching, tearing the city apart to find me. There's no doubt in my mind about that.

Ransom reaches out and touches my face, drawing my attention back to him. He pushes my hair back, tucking it behind my ears as Troy lets out a low moan behind the brothers.

"What happened?" Ransom asks. "What did he do?"

In truth, even though I lived it, I don't want to think about it. I don't want to bring it all back up. But the three of them are all looking at me intently, so I try to get my mouth to form at least some words.

I lick my lips, and it takes me a few tries to start speaking.

"He... he got me back here, somehow. I was out of it for that, so I don't know how. When the drugs started to wear off and I woke up, I was... I was in a wedding dress. He and Olivia forced me to marry him, to go through with the deal."

Malice's jaw clenches, rage swimming back to the surface of his stormy dark eyes. Vic's face is set in hard lines, his entire body almost unnaturally still, as if there's so much chaos inside him that one tiny movement will unleash it all.

"Then he..." I swallow. "He said we had to consummate the marriage, and he—"

I wrap my arms around myself, and I notice distantly that my breathing is turning sharp and shallow again. My teeth chatter, and I can't force any more words out.

"It's okay," Vic tells me, his voice soft even though his expression is anything but. "You don't have to say it."

They can put the pieces together, clearly. They did burst in on Troy on top of me, and he's made enough threats that they can understand what went on here. At least most of it.

I lower my eyes, suddenly feeling... I don't know. Still overwhelmed and angry and hurt more than anything else.

"I'm sorry," I whisper.

Fingers slide under my chin, and when I look up, it's Malice tipping my face up. His nostrils flare with each breath, and there's so much rage in his eyes, but I know it's not directed at me. He's angry *for* me instead.

"You don't have a fucking thing to be sorry for," he says, his voice a low rasp. Then he steps closer and wraps his arms around me, enveloping me in a tight embrace as he presses his lips to my tangled hair.

I melt against him, because it's what I've wanted to do the whole time I was apart from these men. I wanted to sink into them, to let them make me feel safe. To have them remind me what it feels like to be loved.

We stay like that for a long moment, and Malice doesn't let go until I do, as if he would've held me like that until the end of time if I needed it. But as we separate, his whole expression shifts. Whatever tenderness was there for me is blotted out by the anger and hatred that fills his face as he turns back to Troy.

My onetime captor is sagging against the wall, his head lolling to one side. I didn't notice before that he'd passed out, but with both of his hands stabbed through, his injured shoulder torqued, and the beating that the three brothers gave him, it's no wonder.

Malice strides over to him and grabs a fistful of his hair, yanking his head up. Troy moans something incoherent, and Malice smacks him hard across the face.

"Wake the fuck up," he snarls. "I want you conscious for this."

Troy blinks a few times as he comes back to himself, pain and fear filling his expression. He finally gets his bleary eyes to focus on Malice, and there's no trace of that smug superiority from before. Now he just looks terrified, every bit the shitty little coward he's always been deep down.

"You hurt someone I love," Malice says, getting in his face. "And now you're gonna find out what happens to people who do that. It doesn't end well."

He pulls his gun from his waistband and shoves it between Troy's lips. Troy tries to fight against it, gagging and choking and trying to spit the metal barrel out, but it's no use. His struggle only makes his hands pull harder against the knives stabbed through them, and with each yank, he blubbers with pain.

His eyes are wild with fear, one of them nearly swollen shut, and there are tears at the corners of them, threatening to fall.

Malice's finger tightens on the trigger, and my pulse skyrockets. Before I can think about what I'm doing, I throw myself forward, stepping between Ransom and Vic.

"Wait!" I stammer out.

Malice hesitates, but I can still see his finger curling around the trigger. I swallow hard, forcing the panicky, shaky feeling aside for a moment. I need my head clear for this.

"Wait," I say again, my voice stronger this time. "You can't kill him."

8

MALICE

Distantly, I know Willow is saying something, but her words barely even register through the haze of red that fills my mind. I'm like a beast in this moment, a demon made of pure fury. A fucking grim reaper with only one purpose on this earth.

To end the man in front of me.

After what he did to Willow, he deserves it. He deserves to die in the most painful way I can fucking think of, to feel every ounce of pain he probably caused her.

My finger wants to keep curling against the trigger. To pull it and splatter this fucker's brains all over the wall of the prison he kept Willow in.

But I hear her say I can't kill him, and when she repeats it, her voice taking on a more urgent tone, I jerk my head to the side to look at her, breathing hard. The gun doesn't move from Troy's mouth.

I shake my head, practically vibrating with fury. When I speak, my voice is a strained rasp, and the words come out more growled than spoken.

"You can't stop me from killing him," I tell her. "You can't ask me to do that."

What he did to Willow... that shit hits close to home. I know how it feels to be powerless, to be used. I know how it fucks with your head and tries to break your spirit.

"Malice—"

"No," I growl. "He touched you. He hurt you. I'm gonna kill him for it."

Willow shakes her head. "I know. Malice, I know. But just... wait. Please."

I drag in a deep breath and then another. The monster in me is saying *fuck it*. Telling me to pull the trigger. To end this man's miserable life now and give him what he deserves.

But Willow looks at me with those luminous brown eyes, and she says 'please,' and I have to listen.

Every part of me resists it though. It's a slow, torturous thing as I drag the gun from Troy's mouth, my muscles hardly wanting to cooperate.

Willow swallows hard and moves forward on wobbly legs. Vic and Ransom are right there, supporting her, helping her come closer and making sure she doesn't fall.

She takes a few steps toward me and Troy, her eyes hard.

Troy starts to struggle more as she nears him, but it's weak. It's the struggle of someone who has no fight left, like a wounded animal that knows it's going to be killed as soon as the trap closes around its leg. He doesn't have the strength to break free, and he's clearly realized by now that we took care of his bodyguards on the way in.

It was messier than I would've liked, with too many close calls where either my brothers or I almost got shot. But we didn't have time to make it a cleaner operation. Vic did as much recon as he could, but we made the choice to go in partially blind—and it's a good fucking thing we did. If we'd gotten here any later, I'm not sure I would've ever forgiven myself.

Willow comes to a stop just a few feet away from Troy.

Even though she has to still be in shock, she looks so strong now. Although my brothers are still flanking her, she's standing on her own now, the shaking in her legs subsiding a little, her head held high.

Pride flares inside me.

No matter what this fucker did to her, he didn't break her. He didn't destroy her strength or her spirt. She's facing down her tormentor, her nightmare, standing up to him without flinching, and I love her more intensely in this moment than I ever have before.

She draws in a deep breath, her shoulders rising and falling as she gathers herself. When she speaks, her voice is low but audible.

"Do you remember what I said to you when you brought me to that room to marry you?" she asks him.

Troy blinks at her, not saying anything.

I shake him a little, narrowing my eyes. "She asked you a fucking question."

He rasps something unintelligible, but it doesn't matter, because Willow answers for him.

"I asked that you and Olivia just make the deal without me," she whispers. "That you leave me out of it. I begged you both to just not make me do this. But you said no. You said you can't get something for nothing, and you insisted on making me your wife. You wanted to be married to me. So now... I'm going to take what's owed to me as your wife."

Her voice twists on that last word, and it's almost enough to make me shove the gun back in his mouth and empty the entire clip. But I don't, because I'm starting to understand what Willow is getting at. Admiration floods me all over again for this beautiful, indomitable woman—so soft and delicate, but with a core of steel that runs all the way through her.

"Do you understand what I'm saying?" Willow presses, taking a step closer to him. "You forced a ring onto my finger. You bound my life to yours. You said it was your job to take care of me. So now you're going to make sure that your precious little 'wifey' is taken care of. You're going to sign everything you own—your fancy houses, your shares of your family's company, all of it—over to me."

Troy scoffs, some of his smug asshole nature coming back to the surface now. I'd be impressed that he can manage such a holier-than-thou look while impaled to a wall if I didn't want to blow his head off.

"No," he bites out. "Why the fuck would I do that?"

I grin at him, and I can tell from the fear that floods back into his face that the look on mine is just as feral and vicious as it feels.

"I'm so fucking happy you said that," I murmur quietly, moving in closer to him.

Troy's face goes white. "W-why?"

"Because now I get to make you say yes."

To give him a little taste of what I mean, I grab one of the knives from Troy's hand, yanking it roughly out of the wall and out of his palm in one vicious tug. He screams in pain, and the sound is music to my fucking ears—but it's still not good enough. It might *never* be enough.

Vic slides into place once Troy's hand is free and grabs his wrist, keeping him pinned to the wall.

I glance over my shoulder to where Ransom is still standing with Willow. "Ger her out of here."

"No." Willow lifts her chin, shaking her head. "I want to stay."

I blink in surprise, clenching my jaw as I meet her gaze. "It's gonna be bad, Solnyshka," I warn. "You don't have to watch this."

But she just straightens her shoulders, her brown eyes flashing. "I want to."

We stare at each other for a long moment, and I consider arguing with her. After all the shit she's been through, this isn't what she should be seeing. The last fucking thing she needs is more violence. But I take in the set of her mouth, the way she's holding herself, and all I see is her strength. She might look fragile, but she's not, and I can't deny her a chance to see what happens to the man who hurt her so badly.

So I nod.

When I turn back to Troy, all I know is purpose. Somehow, Willow being here to watch just makes it even more intense. I want her to see what happens, what I'll do to anyone who tries to hurt her, as if somehow that might make her feel safer after all of this.

I flip the knife in my hand, catching it by the handle over and over again. Troy's hazy eyes follow the movement, and I smirk at him, rage and vengeance overtaking everything else.

"You're gonna wish you'd taken her offer the first time," I tell him honestly.

And then I move.

With a quick flick of my wrist, I use the knife to cut through the waistbands of his pants and boxers, leaving them with no support so that they fall down around his ankles.

He gasps in shock and anger, and I bring the knife right up to his dick, letting him feel the sharp edge on his most sensitive bits.

That makes whatever indignant shit he was going to say die right in his throat, and he whimpers.

"Yeah," I tell him, my throat so tight with anger that the words are hardly more than a rasp. "I know what you've been doing with this, you piece of shit. You've been sticking it where it doesn't fucking belong, haven't you? And maybe if you don't know how to use it right, you shouldn't have it."

Troy chokes out a wordless noise of fear, but I ignore it. I wrap my fist around his dick, squeezing hard enough to hurt, and then slash the knife downward, severing it with one clean cut.

He screams in pain, his eyes rolling back and his entire body bucking against the wall, as if he's trying to somehow escape the confines of his own skin. Too bad for him, that's not possible. The noise he's making is too fucking loud though. I feel confident that we've taken care of all of his bodyguards, and this place is so remote that there's almost no chance anyone will hear us.

But still, his increasingly high-pitched scream grates on my nerves, so I shut him up by shoving his bloody severed dick into his mouth. He almost chokes on it as I stuff it between his lips, shaking his head and groaning, but I don't stop until it's finally muffled some of his sounds.

It's quiet enough now that I can hear Willow's small intake of breath behind me, but even though I'm acutely aware of her, I keep my focus on Troy.

Beside me, Vic's eyes are glittering with their own kind of anger and determination. He has another knife in his hand, and he stares at Troy with that cool, calculating look he gets sometimes.

"I think I owe you a little something," he says. "You wanted to leave me for dead, didn't you?"

Troy starts to shake his head, but before he can try to say anything around the dick gag, Vic stabs the knife into his side, mimicking the wound my twin is still favoring from getting shot.

From there, we take turns, each of us getting our pound of flesh for all the pain and torment this asshole has put Willow through. Vic stabs him in different places, twisting the knife in deep, and blood stains Troy's clothes, dripping down to the floor.

I need something more visceral than that. More up close and personal. So I hit him, hard, over and over again. My fist collides with his side, and I don't let up until I hear the crunching of his ribs. I hit him in the face, breaking his nose, leaving his mouth and chin a bloody mess.

Troy doesn't take it well.

There's no more of that smug bullshit, that pompous attitude where he thinks he's calling the shots. Within a few minutes, he's reduced to a sniveling mess, crying and screaming and shaking where he's held against the wall.

Behind us, Willow just watches it happen. Ransom has a hand on her shoulder, but neither of them move as Vic and I keep torturing Troy.

It doesn't take long before he breaks.

Finally, the fucker manages to spit out his own dick, letting the bloody, limp thing flop to the floor with a wet sound. His voice is wrecked, halfway between a sob and a scream as he cries out, "Okay! I'll do it! I'll do whatever you want, just please... fucking stop!"

A savage, dark part of me wants to keep going. Wants to take him all the way to his limit and then past it. I want to get in his face and tell him he probably didn't stop when Willow begged him to, that he probably just got off on it even harder.

But there was a purpose to this beyond just making him hurt, so I nod and force myself to step back.

I yank the other knife out of his hand, and Vic and I haul him away from the wall. He can barely stand, his legs shaking from how much pain he's in and his pants still bunched up around his ankles. He leaves a trail of blood as we drag him between us, following Willow down the hall to a small office.

"This is where I got married," she says, her voice a little hoarse. "Seems right that this is where I should get my due."

"Fuck yeah, it does," Ransom tells her, still staying close by her side.

I have no fucking clue what needs to happen next, but luckily, Vic does. He steps smoothly into control of the situation.

"Sit him at the desk," he tells me, and the two of us drag him over that way. Troy basically collapses onto the chair as soon as we set him on it, his head lolling forward. The stump of his dick has stopped bleeding so much, but his thighs are coated with red. I don't think he's in any danger of bleeding out, but we need to get this done quickly anyway.

"Stay awake, asshole," I grunt, gripping his hair and forcing him to lift his head. "Vic, what does he need to do?"

"He'll need to sign papers transferring ownership of all of his assets to Willow. Give me a sec."

Vic opens Troy's laptop and presses Troy's finger to the small fingerprint reader on one side of the laptop's keyboard, unlocking it. He spins the laptop on the desk and leans over it, clicking and typing away. A few more times, he demands a password or a piece of information from Troy, who seems to be so broken down by this point that he offers up no resistance, spitting out whatever Vic wants to know.

Once he's done handling the actual transfer of money and assets, Vic prints out a document and slaps it down on the desk in front of Troy, who's struggling to keep his eyes open.

"We'll need to get it in writing," Vic says coolly. "Confirming that you want Willow to have everything."

Troy rouses a little at that, glaring up at Vic balefully. I spin the office chair a little and rest my foot on his crotch, pressing the toe of my boot against his balls right below the bloody stump of his dick.

"Sign it," I bite out. "Or I'll cut these off too."

He whimpers, squirming in his seat, but when Vic hands him a pen, he does it, scrawling a shaky signature at the bottom of the page.

"There. I did what you said," he rasps, dropping the pen to the desk with a clatter. "Now you have to let me go."

I chuckle, the beast inside me rising up once again.

"There's just one problem with that," I tell him. "You took something that didn't belong to you. And the moment you touched Willow, you signed your own fucking death warrant. We were never going to let you live after that."

And Troy, the stupid fucker, actually looks shocked. There's a look on his face like this is the last thing he expected to happen, and I would laugh if I wasn't so deadly serious about this shit.

"You—you can't," he splutters. He surges up from the chair but then immediately stumbles as his body reminds him that we just beat the shit out of him half an hour ago. "You *can't*."

Ransom snorts, his arms folded. His eyebrow ring glints in the light as he tilts his head. "Come on, Troy. You had to know how this was going to end for you. And after all, how often has someone telling you 'you can't' stopped you from doing something?"

His eyes are hard, and Troy glances away from him, trying to appeal to Vic next.

"Listen," he says quickly. "You want money? I've got money. I can give you as much money as you want. Whatever it takes to make this go away."

Vic lifts an eyebrow. "But all of your money is Willow's now. So what do we need you for?"

That seems to hit Troy like a slap in the face, and his expression twists from wide-eyed and pleading to something ugly.

"You don't know who you're dealing with," he snarls. "You don't know who the fuck I am. I am *Troy Copeland*! My family is one of the most prestigious and powerful in this whole damned city. You're a bunch of lowlife fucking criminals. You can't order me around."

"We already did," Ransom says. "We ordered you around, killed all your guards, and beat the shit out of you. Give it up. You've got nothing."

"No!" he screams. "*No!* It's not over! I won't—you can't—"

I ignore his outburst, looking to Willow instead. Waiting for her command. She's the only one who could stop this, and honestly, I'm not even sure she could get me to walk away now if she asked. The monster inside me is crying out for blood, and it won't be satisfied until Troy is dead on the floor.

Willow meets my eyes, and I can tell she understands. That she's ready.

She gives me a small nod.

I look back to Troy, crossing the distance between us. He's backed himself into a corner in his rage and fear, and I close in on him, my gaze intent on his bloody, bruised face.

His chest heaves, and I can tell each breath is causing him pain. Good.

I get right in his face and lower my voice, even though I know he can still hear me.

"*Ty obidel zhenshhinu, kotoruju ja ljublju. Esli by ja mog ubit' tebja sto raz, ja by ubil,*" I tell him in a low voice.

His eyes flash, and it doesn't matter if he understands the words or not. The intent is clear.

I grab the knife out of its sheath at my side, already stained with his blood. With a quick jab, I shove it upward between Troy's ribs, and he gurgles out a cry of pain.

His body jerks as the knife pierces his heart, and then he crumples to the floor, his eyes wide and unseeing.

9

WILLOW

I STAND FROZEN, watching as Troy dies.

Unlike when Vic and Malice tortured him earlier, it's not big or loud. Just a stab and a gurgle and the flash of a bloody knife as Malice withdraws it.

Troy falls to the floor, and I wait to feel something like relief that he's gone, that he can't hurt me anymore. But I don't. There's nothing but that strangely numb feeling that I've had since the brothers showed up.

I was so relieved to see them at first, and for one bright moment, everything felt okay. But now I feel removed from the moment. Like everything that's happening around me is happening to someone else.

Stepping forward tentatively, I stare down at Troy's body.

He looks so small and nonthreatening now. Nothing more than a pile of flesh and bones, his pants still twisted around his ankles and blood smeared over his skin, not able to hurt me or anyone else ever again. All the same, my flesh crawls at the memory of his smirk and the coldness of his eyes.

"We need to get the fuck out of here," Ransom says, breaking the spell I'm under. "Let's take care of this place and make ourselves scarce. I don't want to be here for another second. And you shouldn't be here any longer either."

He addresses the last bit to me, giving me a concerned look.

Of course he's looking out for me. All of them are.

Ransom's words are enough to make them all spring into action. They move like a well-oiled machine, and it reminds me strangely of the time they all showed up to my old apartment to handle the aftermath of Vic killing Carl.

The three of them fall into their roles so easily, doing their particular jobs to cover up the murder.

Victor grabs Troy's laptop so he can go through it later. "There might be stuff on here that we can use against Troy's family or Olivia," he says.

Then he sets to work making sure that there's no security footage that can tie them to this place. Nothing to lead back to the brothers.

Ransom and Malice are on the more destructive duty of burning the place to the ground. Malice starts making sure all the bodies of the guards are ready to go up in flames, and Ransom comes back from their car with the accelerant to speed up the process.

I just stand there, wrapped in Malice's jacket. It barely covers my ass, leaving me feeling a bit chilly and exposed, but it's better than being naked. And at least it smells like him, the musky, spicy scent calming my nerves a little. I stare around the house, still feeling disconnected from it all, like there's a sheet of glass between me and the rest of the world, and I can only watch what's happening.

This place was my prison for... I don't even know how long. Days? A week? Two? Long enough that I built it up in my head like it was some kind of fortress I might never leave. But standing here now, it seems just like a regular house. Just a place where someone might live.

Not a place that was a living nightmare for me.

"Is that all the guards?" Ransom asks as he passes Malice.

"Yeah. I counted 'em."

Ransom nods, spreading the acrid smelling liquid around. "Vic, we close?"

"Just about," Vic replies, focused on the computer in front of him. "Making sure there aren't any cameras I missed. Are we going back to the hotel from here?"

Malice shrugs. "Not like there's anywhere else to go, really. And it's getting late."

They start talking about where they want to go next, what happens from here, and I remember, sort of distantly, that their warehouse was burned down. They're homeless now. And I guess I am too. It's not like I can go back to the apartment Olivia was paying for.

The brothers talk and plan lightly as they work, but I don't have anything to add to the conversation. I didn't have any plans beyond escaping from Troy, and it still hasn't really sunk in that I've done that. That I'm free.

A hand on my shoulder startles me out of my thoughts, and I jump, turning to see Ransom standing there. He still has that concerned look on his face, and his voice is soft.

"Sorry. Are you—" He cuts himself off, like he thinks better of asking. "We're ready to get out of here. We've gotta go so we can torch the place."

"Right," I mumble. "Okay."

I let them lead me out, following Ransom and Malice as they head out of the house and through a wooded area toward where the car has been stashed.

Vic is the last one out, and judging from the smoke already starting to billow through the windows, he's started little fires already to help the place go up easier.

We stop before we reach the car, pausing to make sure the flames catch like they're supposed to. It's late in the evening, and I stand shivering in the night air. Heat starts to pour off the house as it burns, but that doesn't help warm me up.

I feel a familiar panicky, fight-or-flight response start to crawl

70

up in me from the flames, and I remember with a shudder all the times I've come up against fire in a bad way. With the Voronin brothers, I'm starting to associate it more with them coming to my rescue, but that trauma is still there, making me want to turn away. But I force myself to stand still and watch it, not wanting to leave until the whole house is burning, fully blazing in a fire that would be impossible to put out.

It doesn't take long, and I stare at the inferno until my eyes are burning from the smoke.

Finally, the guys usher me away from the burning cabin, leading me to their car. I get buckled into the back, and it could almost be like any other time I've ridden with them, if weren't for... everything else.

Malice starts the car and we drive away, leaving the burning house behind.

It's dark, and there aren't any streetlights to illuminate the path as we weave through a densely forested area. I close my eyes, leaning my head back against the seat, trying to steady my breathing and slow the beat of my heart.

When I feel a little more calm, I open my eyes and swallow hard. "How... how did you find me?" I ask.

"It wasn't fucking easy," Malice says. "That slimy fucker covered his tracks better than we thought he would."

"We searched everywhere we thought he might have taken you, but he wasn't popping up anywhere on the cameras I could check," Vic explains. "Not near where his parents live, not near his own properties, not near his offices. Then I found out about this place that he recently purchased, and that connected the dots."

I remember what Troy said to me about how he told his family that he would be unavailable for a while. That he was taking an extended 'honeymoon,' so he could 'train' his wife. So he could take the time to break me. I'm not sure how much he told them about what he actually planned to do to me, but I'm sure they had no illusions that I would be treated well. And I'm also sure that none of them voiced any objections. They raised him, after all. They

71

brought him into this world of wealth and power and violence, so I wouldn't be surprised if they're as awful as he is.

I shiver, wrapping my arms around myself, trying to push Troy's voice out of my mind. I have to remind myself that he's dead now. His corpse is probably becoming a pile of ashes at this moment, and he can never hurt me again.

We're still driving down a single lane road, surrounded on either side by trees. I don't recognize the area, but it hits me how far outside of Detroit we must be. I can't even see a glow of lights on the horizon from the city itself. Troy had me out in the middle of nowhere, in an area so remote that no one would come looking if they didn't have a reason to.

Even if I *had* managed to get away from him, it would have been ages before I made it to anyone who could help me. He had me isolated, truly trapped with him.

The thought makes me want to throw up.

It takes the better part of an hour to get back to the city, and we pull up to a hotel that looks like it's seen all kinds of sketchy shit go down. This must be where they've been staying since they got back from Mexico.

It's another harsh reminder that their own home is gone, and I swallow hard, hating my grandmother more than ever for everything she's done.

Once we get out of the car, the three of them basically form a human barricade around me to keep anyone from seeing me the way I look now, hustling me inside the lobby and then up the stairs.

As soon as we get to the room and the door locks behind us, the three of them immediately start tripping over themselves to do what they can to make me comfortable.

Ransom rummages in his suitcase and comes up with clothes for me to change into.

"When's the last time you ate?" Malice asks, his voice full of gruff concern. "You should probably eat something. I can run out, or we can order in. Whatever you want."

"I'll go down the hall to the ice machine and get some water,"

Vic offers. "Are you thirsty? Do you want a soda or something else?"

"Maybe a shower first," Ransom throws in. "And a change of clothes. You'll probably be more comfortable."

"Anything you want, Solnyshka." Malice's gray eyes burn with intensity. "Just let us know."

I smile a little, touched by their concern. They all look so anxious in their need to make sure I'm alright, and I know it's because of how much they care for me.

"A shower would be good," I murmur. "I want to feel clean. And then maybe some food."

In truth, I'm not hungry at all, but I know I should eat. Even though I'm too numb to really register it now, my body is under-nourished from the time spent in captivity.

"There's soap and shampoo and shit in the bathroom," Malice tells me. "I'll grab some food and be back by the time you're done."

I just nod, flashing them all a weary, grateful smile before making my way into the bathroom.

It's small and cramped, nothing special at all, but at least I know it's safe. I strip out of Malice's jacket, letting it fall to the floor while the water heats up in the shower.

Once it's just above tepid, I step in and start washing up, wanting to cleanse my skin everywhere that Troy touched me. I close my eyes, trying to relax, trying to breathe, but I still feel weird. *Wrong.*

The door opens after another minute, and I peek around the shower curtain to see Ransom stepping inside, closing the bath-room door behind him.

"Just me," he says with a smile, holding his hands up. "I just didn't want you to be alone. Is it okay if I stay?"

I nod, and he smiles wider. He strips down, tugging his shirt over his head to reveal his cut torso and the tattoos snaking over his skin. Then he reaches for his pants, watching me for any signal that he should stop. I nod again, swallowing, and he shoves them down, baring his pierced cock and muscled thighs. He kicks his shoes off along with his pants and then steps into the shower to join me, pulling the curtain back in to place and moving in behind me.

At first, he doesn't touch me, just watching as the water runs down my skin. I gaze at him too, drinking in the sight of his handsome face, his eyebrow piercing, and the brown hair with highlights of copper strands that darken as the water soaks into them.

"Fuck," he murmurs finally. "You have no idea how good it is to see you. Not even like this—I don't mean just because you're naked. I just... missed you, angel."

"I missed you too," I whisper back. "All of you."

"We were all going a little insane without you," he admits with a crooked grin. It doesn't reach his eyes, which turn a little haunted as he speaks. "Malice was... well, you know, *Malice*. And Vic barely left his computer to take a shit and sleep. None of us could function beyond what we needed to do to get you back. Because we need you. You keep us together."

I can picture it easily, the way Malice would have been on the edge of losing his shit, angry and intense, and Vic's single-minded focus.

"But you were together before you even met me," I point out, tilting my head to let the water from the shower hit me at a different angle.

Ransom shrugs. "We were, but it's hard to imagine it now. I don't think any of us could ever go back to the way things were before we met you, even if we would've said things were good back then. That's just because we didn't know how perfect they could be. You've changed us a lot. And we wouldn't have it any other way."

Warmth blooms in my chest. I smile a little, happy to hear that. I hate that they were so worried about me, but it feels good to know that while I was holding on to memories of them to keep me from losing myself to my fear and pain in Troy's hold, they were holding on to me as well.

I want to tell him that. That I thought about them every day. That I pictured their pep talks, their strength, their resilience, and that it kept me sane in a way that nothing else would have. But the words won't come. I don't want to talk about the pain I endured in that house with Troy, and even thinking about it makes my head throb.

Ransom seems to sense that there's some war going on inside me, or else it's showing on my face pretty clearly, because he just smiles and moves closer.

"We're together now," he murmurs. "All of us. And everything will get better, I promise. One step at a time, you know?"

I nod because he's right. "Okay."

"Let me take care of you, okay? Let me help."

I nod again, and Ransom reaches for the little bottle of shampoo on the shelf in the shower. He lathers up his hands, filling the shower with the scent of generic shampoo, and then starts washing my hair gently. The dyed brown locks are a mess of tangles and knots from it being damp when I fought with Troy, but Ransom's fingers are soothing as he works the knots free and lathers my hair up.

He talks softly about nothing really, just filling the silence as he muses about what Malice might get for dinner, running down a list of the restaurants nearby, and how they've tried takeout from most of them. He talks about how Vic supposedly hates onions, but how he definitely ate some on a cowboy burger while he was deep in concentration trying to track me down.

It feels domestic and soft and safe, and I try to let myself sink into it, focusing on the good things here and blocking out the bad. The roar of the shower, the feeling of Ransom's sure fingers in my hair, the trickle of suds and water down my back as he tips my head back to rinse my hair clean.

He keeps water and shampoo from getting in my eyes, and then smiles when he straightens me back up. Without making me ask him to keep going, he grabs the body wash and lathers up a wash cloth, then starts to clean me up. He lifts my arms, carefully scrubbing at every inch of my skin, and when he moves over my torso, I gasp softly as the cloth brushes across my chest.

Ransom grins, stepping a bit closer to me in the confines of the old bathtub. He fits a hand behind my head and tilts my head up a bit, then drops his own head. His mouth is just an inch away from mine, leaving me to close the distance if I want to.

And I do.

I missed him. Missed *this*. Missed being taken care of and looked out for.

He makes a low noise into our kiss, his mouth moving against mine, and I clutch at his shoulders, needing something to hold on to as my head starts to spin. The kiss heats up, his hands roaming over me, slipping over my curves and the scars on my torso, slick with water and the remnants of body wash.

I wait for the familiar heat to pool in my belly, for the fire that usually comes with kissing any of these three brothers... but it's not there. Instead, there's a rising tide of bile, and rushing feeling of panic.

Something in me rebels against this, and that hazy veil that I couldn't shake before is back, making it hard to think or feel. I start shaking, and I pull back a little, feeling like I might throw up.

Ransom notices immediately. His shoulders stiffen, and he pulls away completely, looking down at me with a worried expression.

"Are you okay?" he asks, a droplet of water clinging to the piercing in his eyebrow as his brows furrow.

I swallow hard, trying to breathe through the roiling in my stomach. "Yeah. I—I don't know what's wrong with me. I'm sorry."

I frown, glaring down at the shower floor, because what *is* wrong with me? This is what I wanted. Ransom, Malice, and Vic. I wanted them even when I shouldn't have, when they pissed me off or scared me more than anything, so why is it that now I suddenly can't do this? Now, when all I wanted was to be back with them? Now, when I'm finally safe?

"Hey." Ransom's voice is soft. He reaches out like he's going to touch me, but then seems to think better of it. "It's okay. Let's get you dried off and dressed, alright?"

I nod, but I still feel... wrong. Off balance and out of sorts, like I'm living in a body that isn't mine. And angry that the feelings I *want* to be experiencing have been replaced by awful ones instead. Instead of feeling hungry for his touch, I feel almost claustrophobic, making me want to crawl out of my own skin.

Since I'm as clean as I'm going to get for now, I let him help me out of the shower. He grabs a towel and hands it to me, and I grit my teeth as I take it and dry myself off. I know he'd rather do it for me, another way to take care of me and be close to me—but he clearly doesn't want to upset me again, and I hate that.

"You've been through a lot, angel," he murmurs, as if he can read my thoughts. "More than we even know, probably. You don't have to be alright on your first night back. Or even the second. It's gonna be okay."

He says it like he means it, and I know he must. None of the brothers would ever hold my pain or trauma against me, not when they're so familiar with trauma themselves. But I still feel crushed.

"What if... what if I never get better?" I mutter, the words spilling out of me before I can stop them. "What if I'm just... *broken* now?"

"You're not," he says firmly. "Listen to me, pretty girl. You've been through something horrible. Something no person should ever have to experience. And you made it through that, which is a testament to how fucking strong you are. How powerful and unbreakable. But no one could blame you for needing time to heal from that. And just because you're strong, that doesn't mean you have to be completely alright. Not right now, and not ever. It's okay to not be okay."

I nod mutely, putting on the dry clothes he offers me.

He grabbed me a pair of boxers, some oversized sweats, and a t-shirt, and they all smell like him. Just like with Malice's jacket, it's a comforting reminder that I've got my men back. That they're all here with me.

When we step back into the main room, Malice, true to his

word, is back from his food run. He and Vic both turn to look at me, and I can see the concern in their eyes.

"I grabbed some sandwiches," Malice says. "Can you eat?"

"I'm just really tired," I tell him, wrapping my arms around myself even though I'm no longer chilled. "I'll have something in the morning."

He looks like he wants to argue, but instead, he just nods.

I go to the bed farthest from the door and curl up on it, putting my back to the guys. I can hear Ransom murmuring to them in a low voice, probably telling them what happened in the bathroom.

Tears leak from my eyes, spilling down my cheeks and soaking into the scratchy material of the pillowcase. No matter what Ransom says, I feel like there's something wrong with me. Like even though I survived my time with Troy, he took something from me that I might never get back.

My gut churns with worry and disquiet.

I wish I could fall asleep sandwiched between all of my men like I did the night before I was taken. I hate that even though they saved me and we're back together again, they somehow still feel too far away.

Maybe Ransom is wrong. Maybe I really am broken.

My thoughts keep tumbling over and over, but after a while, I finally fall asleep, my body and mind too exhausted to cling to consciousness any longer.

WILLOW

I'm in the middle of a nightmare when someone wakes me up. I don't even know what I was dreaming about, but I feel my heart racing and there's that spike of adrenaline pumping through me. Distantly, I can tell someone is saying my name, and I realize there are hands on me. I'm half awake, half still in the dream, and the hands feel threatening. They're holding me down, trying to keep me pinned, and my heart rate jacks up even more with the fear of it.

I thrash on the bed, pushing those hands and whoever they belong to away, a strangled, "No!" bursting out of me.

The sound of my own voice somehow wakes me up the rest of the way, and I blink, seeing Malice sitting on the bed with me. He's not touching me anymore, his hands held up so I can see he's not a threat.

My chest heaves as I fight for breath, putting one hand over my heart to try to calm myself down. I force myself to breathe in and out, purposeful, counting the way Vic does. Malice reaches out like he's going to touch me, but he stops before he gets too close, something flashing in his stormy gray eyes.

Ransom must definitely have told them what happened. How

hard it is for me to be touched right now. And now Malice has seen it for himself.

"Are you okay?" he asks, his dark brows drawing together.

I swallow hard and nod. "Yeah. I'm fine. I'm okay."

I'm definitely putting on a brave face, but I don't want to seem weak right now. I don't want to *feel* weak.

Malice just looks at me, and I can tell he sees right through me, the way he always does.

"Solnyshka, I know," he says, giving me a look. "I know how badly it can fuck you up."

At first, I just blink at him, but then it hits me in a rush that he *does* know. After what happened to him in prison, he definitely understands what I'm going through right now. Honestly, he's probably the only one I know who would get it. Vic has plenty of trauma from what their father did to them, so I'm sure he can understand a lot of what I'm feeling right now too. But Malice was assaulted in prison, so even more than his twin, he can probably relate to the way I feel like I barely belong in my own body right now.

I pull my knees up to my chest, wrapping my arms around them as I look at him, taking in the strong lines of his face and the scruff of a dark beard on his jaw.

"Did it help?" I whisper softly. "When you killed the guy who... did that to you in prison?"

His eyes harden, but he has a thoughtful look on his face as he nods. "Yeah, it did. But... not as much as I'd hoped it would."

I swallow, my stomach twisting. He really does understand, then.

"I thought seeing Troy die, seeing him crumpled up and unable to hurt me again, would help," I whisper. "And it did, a bit. But the part of me that he broke still feels broken."

I hate saying it out loud like this. It makes everything I'm feeling seem more real, as if giving words to it means it's never going to be fixed. But Malice doesn't look disgusted or angry—at least, not at me. He's not even looking at me with pity in his eyes.

His jaw is set tight, and he curls and uncurls his fingers in a way that makes me think he's either wishing he could reach for me and pull me into his arms, or that he's wishing he could resurrect Troy so he could torture and murder him all over again.

"I remember how it was that first night after I killed the gang member who assaulted me," he offers. "I was running on a high from doing it, from taking back what he took from me. I knew that it was going to change shit for the better, and I wanted it to feel... I dunno. Different. I wanted there to be this shift—not just externally, but internally. I wanted to erase what had happened, but after I killed him, I realized how impossible that was. Nothing could erase it or undo it. Not even killing him."

I nod along with him because that's exactly it. I thought there would be some shift between Troy being alive and Troy dying, and all I felt was just numb. Even though there's a feeling of relief that he can't hurt me again, all the ways he *did* hurt me are still lingering at the edges of my mind, ready to break into my thoughts at any moment.

"How long did it take?" I ask, trying to keep the plaintive note out of my voice. "For you to start feeling better? To start feeling more like yourself?"

He shrugs, lifting one muscled shoulder. "I don't think I can really put a number on it. It wasn't like I woke up one morning and had completely forgotten about it. But it stopped weighing on me. I found my purpose and my strength again. It was gradual though. One step at a time."

"That's what Ransom said last night," I tell him.

Malice snorts. "Yeah, well, he gets things right sometimes. But it's true. It won't always be like this. You're fresh out of that shit, so it's still deep, and it still cuts you up when you think about it. But you won't always feel like this."

He says it with such complete conviction, and he's the only person right now who could say it like that and make me believe it. Because he lived it. He lived it, and he's here, strong and confident and not shattered into a million pieces. A part of my brain whispers that Malice is just stronger than I am—but then, he thinks I'm strong too. He believes in me.

Now I just have to believe in myself.

Malice's gaze drops from my eyes to the spot on my shoulder where he gave me my last tattoo. Almost under his breath, as if he's talking to himself just as much as to me, he murmurs, "*Mjagkaja i krasivaja, no so stal'nym pozvonochnikom.*"

I don't know what the words mean, but the warmth and pride in his voice as he speaks makes my stomach flutter, a welcome distraction from the agitation prickling beneath my skin from the remnants of the nightmare.

"Thank you," I whisper. "For talking to me about this. I know it's probably not easy, but it helps to know I'm not alone."

His eyes burn as he leans a little closer to me. "Of course. I figured you'd know by now that there aren't a whole lot of limits on the shit I'd do for you, Solnyshka."

That makes me smile, just a little. "Thank you for coming to get me too. I don't know if I said that last night. But you and your brothers saved my life."

Several strong emotions pass across his face in quick succession, too fast for me to identify, but raw and real all the same. He nods, holding my gaze as if he wants to make sure I believe his next words.

"If there's one thing you can count on in this whole goddamned world, it's that me and my brothers will *always* come for you," his voice dropping low as if he's making a vow. "No matter what it takes. No matter what the risks. Nothing can keep us from coming to your side. I love you, Solnyshka, with my whole fucking heart. And I can't live without my heart. Just like I can't live without you."

I nod, tears burning in my eyes. He's said those words to me before, but they hit me almost harder in this moment than they did then—partly because they almost seem unnecessary by now. Every single thing Malice does is a declaration of how much he loves me.

"I love you too," I murmur back. "With my whole fucking

82

heart. I didn't want to live without you or your brothers either. There were times... when I almost wished I was dead. But I knew I had to keep living so that I could get back to you."

Malice makes a noise low in his throat, a rough, pained sound. I almost regret telling him that truth—admitting that I almost wished for death—but at the same time, I've never been able to hide anything from these men. They've seen my best and my worst, and incredibly, they seem to care about me because of *all* of it, not just the good stuff.

We stare at each other for a long moment in silence, something unspoken passing between us. His dark gray eyes are just as intense and piercing as always, and all I can do is look back at him, feeling something grow in the air around us. It's tender and raw, but in a good way, like we're seeing the deepest parts of each other and it's only strengthening the bond we have.

I can see the desire in his face. Desire for me, desire to help me —all of it. And I feel a faint stirring of that inside myself too.

Fuck, I want to kiss him so badly.

I want to feel his arms around me, to feel him claim me.

But another part of me still rebels at the thought.

I know Malice isn't Troy. He's a better man than Troy could ever be, and despite the roughness and darkness in him, he's always taken care of me. So it's not like I'm afraid to have Malice touch me. But it's almost like my body can't distinguish between a touch I crave and one I fear right now. It twists me up inside that I can't take comfort in him the way I want to. The way I know he wants to.

The moment lingers, and I know that if this was another time, I'd already be on my back on the bed with Malice buried inside me, his large body looming over mine as he filled me up so completely that I couldn't think about anything else.

But neither of us moves.

Me, because I can't, and Malice because he's following my lead. It turns awkward, at least in my mind, and I look away from him to the rest of the room, which is surprisingly empty.

"Where did Ransom and Vic go?" I ask as the little bubble of tension between us dissipates. For now, at least.

"They went to get food," Malice says, sitting back on his heels on the bed. "We ate the sandwiches last night, and we saved one for you, but it probably won't have kept very well in the mini-fridge. So they went to get something else."

Almost as if on cue, the door opens a second later, and his two brothers come striding in. They're mid argument as they come through the door, Ransom gesturing with his hand even though it's weighed down by a bag of food.

"For fuck's sake," he says. "It's not that big a deal, Vic. It's not like I'm saying we should start living on cheese fries and apple pie. It's one fucking day."

"That's beside the point," Vic replies. His face is impassive, but there's annoyance in his blue eyes. He's also carrying a bag of food, one even bigger than Ransom's. "As I've said already."

Ransom rolls his eyes. "Listen, you got your way, didn't you? Do you have to be right about every single thing?"

"I don't *have* to be. I just am."

"What the fuck are you two bickering about?" Malice interjects. He eyes the bags in their hands, and I blink when I realize just how loaded down the two of them are. "And are we feeding a fucking army?"

"Your brother, in his infinite wisdom—" Ransom begins.

"Oh, now I'm just *his* brother," Vic mutters. "Charming. Lovely."

"As I was saying." Ransom talks louder. "Vic decided we needed to get a bunch of health food shit, and started driving clear to the other side of town to go to some place with stir fry and wheatgrass and whatever other hippie shit because—"

"Because Willow needs to regain her strength," Vic interrupts. "She needs to recover. We don't know what that fucker was feeding her while he had her, and it's up to us—"

"To pamper her a little," Ransom continues, cutting him off smoothly. "Which is why I said we needed to stick to some comfort foods. Burgers. Milkshakes. Things that spark joy. Not rabbit food."

Malice just gives them both a look like they're ridiculous. "So you couldn't compromise."

"Getting both *was* the compromise," Ransom mutters.

Vic shakes his head, putting the bags down on the desk in one corner. "Look, if I had my way, I would have been able to cook for Willow myself. That's what I *should* be doing. But since I can't, this is the next best thing." He folds his arms, a stubborn look crossing his usually impassive face. "I'm not going to apologize for that."

Memories of all the times Vic has cooked for me or shared his food with me flood my mind, and something tugs at my heart as I realize how much it's a part of his love language. Long before he could admit he wanted me or even liked me, he was doing sweet little things like cooking soup for me when I was sick or letting me use his peanut butter when he wouldn't let his own brothers touch it with a ten-foot pole.

"You don't have to apologize," I tell him softly. "I really appreciate that you guys cared so much about what I would want, and about what would be good for me. I wish you could cook for me too, Vic. But you're right, this *is* the next best thing, and it means a lot. I want to try everything you guys bought."

I smile at him, and although the lines of stress don't leave his face, his expression softens a little as he offers me a small smile back. Ransom takes a breath and blows it out, his shoulders relaxing as some of the tension drains from his posture. I know they're all worried and stressed, more protective of me than ever, and they're trying to take care of me with food the way they do in every other way.

Malice digs out some paper plates from a tub full of random stuff in the corner, and between the four of us, we split up the food. It really is an interesting mix of burgers and chicken nuggets and fries alongside salads and stir fry and a fruit platter. I take a little of everything, noting happily that I actually do feel better enough since last night to actually want to eat.

I sit on the bed cross-legged, and Malice and Ransom take the other bed, leaving Vic in the chair at the desk. There's a certain stiffness to the way Vic moves as he takes food for himself, like he's favoring his side and twisting to avoid hurting it, and I remember with a jolt the night he was shot.

"Are you okay?" I ask him in a rush. He must be, since he didn't seem to be in much pain when he was hurting Troy last night, but I have to ask. I have to know. "You got shot."

Vic smiles, sipping from a bottle of water. "I'm alright," he assures me. "They hit my side, but Malice dug the bullet out and patched me up. I'm not thrilled about the messy stitches, but it's healing just fine."

I breathe out a sigh of relief while Ransom mutters under his breath about how he wasn't the one who suggested doing stitches in the back of a moving car.

The brothers bicker and banter amongst each other the way they do, and it's soothing as we all tuck into the food. But eventually, Vic brings us back to business.

"We need a plan going forward," he says. "I know you probably need more time to rest, butterfly, but—"

"No, I understand." I nod emphatically, trying to ignore the way my stomach tightens around the food I just ate. "There are still loose ends. We're not safe yet."

He nods. "Troy is gone, so he's no longer a threat, but Olivia still could be. As far as she knows right now, she's won. She thinks you're still holed up with Troy, and to the best of our knowledge, no one knows he's dead yet. He went far off the grid in order to remain alone and undisturbed with you, so his family hasn't heard from him in days and won't expect to for a while longer. But that won't last forever. Eventually, the burned out cabin will be discovered, and news of his death will spread. Once that happens, Olivia will realize her plan didn't work out how she intended. We need to deal with her, to make sure she can't come after Willow anymore."

"Should we leave again?" Ransom tosses out as he picks up a french fry. "I mean, at this point, there's nothing keeping us here, right? So maybe the best thing would be to just get out of Detroit altogether."

"We could. But there's no guarantee Olivia wouldn't try to chase us down again." Malice grunts. "I can't imagine she's going to take us killing Troy and making Willow a widow lightly."

Vic nods, staring down at his plate thoughtfully as he uses his fork to make sure the food he piled onto it doesn't touch at all.

"You're right," he murmurs. "The longer this goes on, the more personal it gets. She was willing to sacrifice Willow to achieve her own ends, but at some point, it became about more than that. It's about punishing Willow for defying her. It's about power, control, and revenge. So even if pursuing us wouldn't be the logical choice, I wouldn't put it past her to do it anyway."

"So we're right back where we started," Ransom says, frustration creeping into his voice.

"Not necessarily." Vic shoots me a look, pride shining in his eyes. "Willow has resources now, thanks to her quick thinking. She would've inherited a portion of Troy's estate no matter what, as his legal wife. But since he transferred everything to her before he died, she has both money and his shares of his family's company. That means she can meet her grandmother on even ground. Level the playing field between them."

My heart clenches with worry, and I put down the rest of my burger.

"I don't want to run," I announce firmly, shaking my head. "I want to stay and stand up to Olivia. Like Vic said, the playing field is more even now. She has resources, but so do I. Except... I'm worried about you guys. What if she tries to blackmail you again? I don't want you to get arrested."

For the first time since I was reunited with the men, Ransom grins the way he used to—a sexy as fuck curve of his lips that's both charming and wicked. His blue-green eyes gleam as he tells me, "Oh, don't worry, pretty girl. We have a plan for that."

"What?" I ask, glancing between the three of them.

"So, while we were searching for you, we spent a bit of time talking about this problem," he explains. "Olivia holding shit over our heads, always being able to blackmail us. We found out on the way back to Detroit that she must've turned in the evidence she had against us to the authorities, because we *all* have warrants out for us now, not just Mal. But we've decided to beat her at her own game."

"What do you mean?"

Vic smiles, and although it doesn't have that same charming tilt to it that Ransom's smile has, it's just as beautiful to see.

"A while ago, she had us steal something from a judge," he tells me. "It was one of the assignments she gave us before we knew that she was X. And when I was doing recon on him, I found out he was cheating on his wife."

I grimace. I think I remember them telling me about that job, and having three men whom I know would never leave me or even look at another woman, I feel sorry for this judge's wife. But then my nose wrinkles as I ask, "What does that have to do with getting Olivia off your backs?"

Malice smirks, grim and vicious.

"Well, it just so happens that he's the judge who signed the warrants for each of us. So, we're going to get evidence of his cheating and blackmail him into recalling those warrants."

11

VICTOR

Willow's eyebrows jerk upward as she processes that bit of information, and she chews on her bottom lip anxiously.

"Are you sure that's going to work?" she asks. "It seems risky."

"Oh, it'll work," Malice tells her. "This judge has... questionable sexual appetites at best."

"Malice is right," I tell her. "The ironic thing is, I don't think Olivia knew about that part of his secret life at all. I'm fairly certain that the flash drive she had us steal from his house was just related to some iffy financial dealings. So if she was hoping to use that against him, her threat definitely won't be as strong as ours."

"Hell no, it won't." Ransom grins. "This fucker will probably do just about anything to keep his wife, or the general public, from finding out about the fucked up shit he gets into when he tells her he's working late. These kinds of assholes will do whatever it takes to keep their reputations intact, and we're not even asking for that much. Just the recall of three little warrants. We'll make sure Olivia can't hold the threat of prison time over our heads anymore."

Willow nods slowly, still looking worried. "I guess that's the best plan we have."

Malice and Ransom crumple up their trash from the meal and

start to get up, clearly getting ready to head out. Her head snaps up to look at them as they move, and there's something wild in her eyes.

"Where are you going?" she asks, looking tense.

"It's okay," Ransom assures her. "We're just going to get moving on this plan. The faster we get shit settled, the sooner we won't have to look over our shoulders anymore, right? We're gonna go stake out the judge and gather some evidence."

I watch Willow take that in. She glances at the clock on the bedside table and seems surprised that it's already late in the afternoon. She slept late, but I'm glad she did. We all did our best not to disturb her, since she needed the rest, clearly.

"We'll be back before you know it," Ransom promises. He winks. "We've just got someone's life to threaten to ruin."

Willow nods again, although I can tell she's not quite comfortable with the idea of them leaving.

But they have to, and she keeps her gaze locked on them as they pull on their jackets. Ransom comes over and snags a fry from the pile in front of Willow, popping it into his mouth before leaning a little closer so that their foreheads are almost touching.

"You just focus on relaxing, okay? Take a nap, watch some cable. Whatever you need to do. We've got this."

"Okay," she murmurs. "Come back soon."

He chuckles, his voice warm. "As if we could stay away."

Malice doesn't come over or say anything, but he gives her a look that's heavy with significance, and Willow smiles a little shakily. So clearly she gets the message.

Malice and Ransom leave, and as the door closes behind them, she lets out a breath. She seems to deflate a little, staring down at the food on her lap like she doesn't want to eat any more of it. With just the two of us, things have lapsed back into quiet, and I have a feeling that all of her fears and worries are rushing in to fill the silence.

After what she just went through, it makes sense that she

would be nervous to be separated from us, getting caught up in all the awful memories she has now.

But I don't want her to get dragged back down into that. I don't want her to lose herself to that dark place.

I'm not Ransom, good at talking these things out and putting people at ease. He has a way of bridging gaps between people that I've never fully understood. And I'm not even Malice, with his forceful personality that allows him to just barrel on through things and manage to help somehow.

What I *do* have is the memories of my brothers helping me when I've needed it. How they've always managed to tether me to them when I start slipping away into myself, pulled down by my demons and the trauma branded into me by my father.

What they always do is remind me that there are people who care. That there is life outside my own head. That they're there for me.

So that's what I can try to do for Willow.

I roll the desk chair over to her bed and pull the plate of food from her lap. She looks up at me, surprised, and I stab the fork through some of the veggies on the plate, offering them up to her.

"You don't have to feed me," she murmurs, her pink tongue darting out to lick her lips. "I'm okay. I can..."

"I want to," I tell her. "Please? Let me help you."

She opens her mouth and then closes it, and when she meets my gaze, I can see she's affected by the offer. Touched by it.

"Okay," she whispers and lets me feed her several bites.

She eats in silence, chewing and swallowing, accepting each new bite of food I feed her. It's intimate and caring, and for the first time since she was taken from us in Mexico, a warmth spreads through me, banishing the cold, empty feeling in my chest. I like being able to take care of her like this.

"You're sure you're okay?" Willow asks after a bit. "From the bullet wound, I mean. You went down so hard, and I thought—"

She shakes her head, obviously not wanting to finish that sentence.

"I'm fine. It missed anything important, so it was just some pain and some blood. I've had worse."

"You guys always say that," she mutters.

I shrug a shoulder. "It's true. Grim as it is. But the truth is, I'm fine. I promise. The worst part of it was getting stitches in a moving vehicle."

She makes a face, exhaling a puff of air that's almost a laugh. "I can't believe you did that."

"I had more important things on my mind. We had to get moving so we could get to you."

I don't want her to feel guilty when I say that, or to blame herself, but it's true. The most important thing in that moment was getting to Willow, and I didn't care about how uneven the stitches would be or how unsanitary the back of that car was. It bothers me a bit, now that we have her back and I can actually focus on anything besides the search for her, but it's manageable. It's the kind of thing that the old version of me probably couldn't have ever gotten past, but the new version of me has different priorities.

It was painful and terrifying becoming this version of myself, letting the beautiful woman in front of me get under my skin and change me. But I like who I am now so much more.

"Can I... can I see it?" Willow looks almost nervous to be asking, like she expects me to say no, but I could never deny her anything. So I take my shirt off, letting her see the bandaged wound on my side.

Anguish crosses her face, and she brushes her fingertips near it.

Goosebumps erupt in the wake of her touch, and I tense, my body reacting to her the way it always does—full-force, an instant response.

It's almost overwhelming, having her touch me again after what feels like so long without it. I've gotten used to her touch, more comfortable with it than I ever was before, but there's still an element of sensory overload to it.

I don't know if it's because of how much I feel for her or if it's just because I'm still getting used to casual touches, but it's like every nerve in my body is attuned to her touch.

To distract myself, I focus on her. I look her over, noticing the shadows under her eyes, the way she seems worn down and thinner than she was the last time I saw her. Just a bit of her blonde roots are starting to show beneath the dark color she dyed her hair, barely noticeable, but present. She has bruises on her skin, and there's also a graze on her shoulder where the collar of the shirt she's wearing slips down. It looks fresh and painful, probably something she got in the last day or two—maybe even last night.

"You're hurt," I murmur, nodding at it.

She looks and grimaces, swallowing hard. I don't ask her how she got it. I can picture it pretty well.

"It's fine," she says. "Ransom got a chance to look me over in the shower last night. I don't have any injuries that are too bad. Nothing as bad as what you have, by a long shot. It's raw, and it hurts a bit, but it should heal up okay."

She's right. It should heal up okay, but *okay* isn't good enough when it comes to my butterfly. I hate that she's hurting at all, and I want to do everything I can to help her heal up faster, and to heal well.

Without another word, I get up and go to the first aid kit we assembled out of stolen products from the vet's office in Mexico. I grab some antibiotic ointment before striding back over to her. It's second nature to dab some of the medicinal smelling ointment onto my fingers and reach out to her, but I pause before I touch her, waiting.

"May I?"

Willow bites her lip and then nods.

I dip my chin in acknowledgment and then start smoothing the ointment over her skin. She tenses up, just like I did when she touched me a moment ago. My fingers go still on her shoulder, and I can feel her practically vibrating beneath them.

"Are you alright?"

"Yes." She exhales a shaky breath, and some of the tension bleeds out of her, but not enough.

I hesitate for another moment, not moving at all until she relaxes a bit more. Then I finish putting the ointment on her and replace the cap on the little tube.

"I hate this." Willow sighs, drawing my attention back up to her immediately. "I hate how I don't feel like myself anymore."

Her words strike a chord with me. I know exactly how she feels, even though I wish I didn't. I can vividly remember having that thought almost verbatim after one of my father's worst 'training' sessions. My fingers tap against my thigh as I work to shove down my own demons, determined to battle them back so that I can help the sweet, perfect woman before me conquer her own.

"You're still you," I assure her, my voice low. "It might be a new version of you, and things might never be quite the same as they were before, but you're still Willow. Still beautiful, still so strong. Still my butterfly. Still the most amazing woman I know."

Her chest rises as she drags in a long, shaky breath, her eyes shimmering at the corners with unshed tears. It's clear she can't quite believe everything I'm saying, and I can relate to that too. Reassurances and kind words can't always penetrate the clamor of other, worse voices in our heads. But I mean everything I just said, and I'll tell it to her every day if that's what it takes, until she can see all of those things in herself again.

Emotions build inside me as I gaze at her. I've always felt a bit closed off from my feelings, locked inside myself by my old trauma. But I can feel new words bubbling up, straining to escape my mouth as if they have a mind of their own and demand to be said.

"You're the best person I know, butterfly," I murmur. "And I lo—"

Willow's eyes widen as she registers what I'm about to say.

"Don't," she blurts quickly, cutting me off.

I close my mouth, my heart hammering. There are more tears swimming in her eyes, threatening to fall as she shakes her head.

"Please don't," she whispers. "Not like this. Don't say it now, not when I'm broken like this. When I can't even stand to be touched. Can't hug you or kiss you the way I want to."

I stiffen, my jaw clenching as I take in her sad expression. I hate seeing her like this. Hate knowing she's in so much pain. That she thinks she's broken.

So even though this woman could tell me to walk into a burning building and I'd do it, this is the one time I *can't* do what she's asking of me.

"I love you," I tell her, letting each word fall from my lips with clarity. Letting her hear the truth behind each syllable.

She blinks, sending tears spilling over her eyelids and down her cheeks. I want to wipe them away, but instead, I open my mouth and speak again.

"I love you," I repeat, the words pouring out of me. "Right now, in this moment. Not later. Not after you've had more time to recover. I love who you are, *always*. Every part of you, in every way. And you will *never* be broken in my eyes."

My chest tightens, my entire body overwhelmed by the rush of emotions flooding through me. The day I saw that trucker put his hands on Willow and ended up stabbing a knife through his hand, it was like the door I was trying to keep closed on my feelings was blasted open. But this? This is like the entire wall has been demolished, every bit of armor I've ever erected around myself falling away in my need to make Willow understand how deeply I care for her.

"You never treated me like I was broken for not being able to handle being touched," I continue, my voice hoarse with feeling. "You never stopped caring, even when I tried to push you away. So I'll never treat you like you're broken, butterfly. Because you aren't. And no matter what happens, I'll always love you. I couldn't stop even if I tried."

12

WILLOW

Something cracks open in my chest as Victor's words wash over me.

It makes my chest ache, deep and throbbing, the raw honesty of his confession hitting me hard. But at the same time, it also soothes some of the pain I've been carrying in my heart. Like a balm against the darkness that's been threatening to drown me ever since I woke up in Troy's hold.

I missed all of the Voronin brothers so much, and as much as I tried to reassure myself that I was going to see them again and that they would come for me, I had no way of knowing if that was true or not. It's like it's hitting me all over again that they *did* come.

They spent days locked in this room, searching for any sign of where I was.

They fought their way through Troy's guards and took him out.

And they saved me.

Tears run down my cheeks, spilling over and sliding down my face, but I don't reach up to brush them away. Instead, I reach out for Vic, taking his hand. Our fingers lace together like they were made to interlace just like this, and I lean forward, needing to be closer to him.

Vic leans in as well, and we meet in the middle, our foreheads resting together. I wish I could do more in this moment. I wish I could kiss him or hold him or crawl onto his lap and ride him slow and deep—anything to show how deeply his words are affecting me right now.

But Vic doesn't seem upset that this is all I can offer right now. He doesn't seem like he feels the lack. His bright blue eyes are shining, and there's a small, breathtaking smile on his face as he keeps talking, his voice low and insistent.

"I mean it, butterfly," he murmurs. "You saved me. Did you know that? You changed me. And at first, I was so angry about it. Change was never a good thing, and I liked my well-worn routines and the way I had my life ordered. In my mind, everything that was different was your fault at first, and it made me so uncomfortable. But then you became so important to me. With every conversation, every time you let me in, every time you made me feel like I could matter to you... you showed me that things could be different. There was a part of myself that I never believed existed, and you showed me that it did."

I let out a shuddery breath, wrapped up in his words. "It was always there," I tell him. "At least, I hoped it was."

Vic laughs quietly. Then his expression turns more serious, and I feel his soft sigh ghost against my lips.

"I always knew I was going to be the odd person out," he murmurs. "Malice was going to fuck and fight his way through life the way he wanted to, and Ransom was going to find someone to settle down with eventually, because he's like that. And I was just going to... be there. Behind a screen, keeping the world at arm's length."

It makes me sad to hear him talk about himself like that, but I do have to admit that when I first met him, it seemed like that was what he wanted. To be alone with his computer, handling things behind the scenes and not letting anyone but his brothers get close.

"Would you have been happy like that?" I ask him, my voice low.

He's quiet for a moment, breathing in slowly while he gathers his thoughts.

"I thought I could be," he admits after a while. "I thought that was what I wanted. Or at least, I thought I would be content like that. No one ever made me want anything different. Until you. You made me feel things that I'd never felt before for anyone."

"I still say I'm not that special," I mumble.

"You are though." He squeezes my hand. "No one else has ever gotten close, butterfly. No one else has ever made me *want* before. I saw how easy things were between you and my brothers, and I was so sure that it was never going to be like that for us. That I would want you—need you—and never be able to cross the gap. Never be able to even touch you the way I wanted to, without it being a horrible thing that made you realize how broken I am."

"You're not—"

He smiles, cutting me off as his thumb rubs gently over my knuckles. "I know that now. Thanks to you. Because you *saw* me, and you never once shied away. You kept trying, even when I didn't give you a reason to."

"The thought of being close to you was reason enough," I whisper. "I just wanted that so badly. You made me feel like I wasn't alone, even in the times I felt most lost and afraid." More tears well in my eyes, and I blink a few times, letting them fall. "Every time we talked, even in the early days when it was just by text, I felt better. You filled up a part of my heart that had always been empty, and the more full it got, the more I felt the bad shit being chipped away. I just wanted more and more of that."

He swallows, closing his eyes for a moment. When he opens them again, his blue eyes find mine as if he never wants to look anywhere else.

"I wanted to be that for you," he says softly. "I wanted to help, even though I never felt like I knew how."

"You did. You helped so much."

I pause, holding on to this moment as a bubble seems to surround us on the bed. Part of me wants to pull back so that I can look him in the eyes more easily, but another, bigger part of me can't stand the idea of losing this connection with him right now. So I stay right where I am, letting the warmth of his palm and the light pressure of his forehead against mine ground me.

"I love you, Vic," I say, blinking again because I don't want my freely flowing tears to obscure my view of his beautiful eyes. "I love you so much. I love that you let me in and let me see you—even the parts of you that you thought would scare me away. I love that you trust me to push you a little. I love that you work so hard to make sure we're all safe, and that you never stop trying. I love your organizational systems, and that we both feel the same way about peanut butter."

That last bit makes him chuckle, and he closes his eyes again, like he's savoring my words.

"I should have known right then that there was no way I could keep myself from falling for you," he says, something warm and fond in his voice. "I've never bonded over peanut butter with anyone else before."

"Of course not. Because your brothers are both crunchy peanut butter loving heathens," I murmur back, and he laughs again.

It's funny that we're barely touching, only our foreheads and our linked fingers, but this moment feels even deeper than the first time we had sex. It's so intimate, like we're baring our souls to each other and they're reaching out to touch as well.

"You saved me too," I whisper to him after a beat of silence. "When I was... when Troy had me, I just kept thinking of all of you. Thinking about how Malice said I was strong and how Ransom told me I could do anything and how you made me feel grounded. It kept me sane in there, when everything was so bad."

Vic's fingers spasm a little around mine, and there's something deep and unreadable in his eyes.

"What did you think about?" he asks.

"I had such clear images of you counting and measuring your breathing. When I was trying not to panic or go insane in there, I

99

would do that. It made me feel closer to you, and it kept my head clear."

I don't go into more detail than that. The last thing I want right now is to start thinking about being locked in that little crawl space under the floor in Troy's house. My heart rate speeds up just thinking about it, and as if he knows, Vic squeezes my hand again. His thumb resumes its slow and steady movement over the backs of my knuckles, and the touch is soothing, grounding me in this moment.

I let out a breath I didn't realize I was holding and breathe in Vic's familiar scent, reminding myself all over again that I'm safe now. He has me.

"I hate that you needed to use any of the coping tools I use."

Vic's voice is heavy, and for a second, I can so clearly pick up on the fact that he and Malice are twins. Malice keeps his rage closer to the surface, but Vic has it in him too—and they'll both gladly unleash it on anyone who hurts someone they love.

"I'm glad we could be there for you," he adds. "Even when we weren't there physically. We're always going to be there for you. I hope you know that. No matter what it takes."

"I know."

The certainty of it is soothing. Almost everyone I've ever had in my life has let me down in the end, abandoning me or betraying me to serve their own ends. But the Voronin brothers will never do that. The bond we share is deeper than that, and it feels good to have one thing in my life that I can trust implicitly.

We stay like that for a moment longer, just breathing each other in, soaking up the closeness. It feels like we're breathing in tandem, our hearts on the same rhythm. Like we're so in sync that nothing in the world could break us apart.

Even when we finally move away from each other, straightening up and letting go of each other's hands, that connection remains, tethering us like an invisible cord.

"Are you done eating?" Vic asks, glancing down at the food.

"Yeah." I smile. "I'm good."

He nods, gathering up the trash from the meal and making a face at the pile that his brothers left on their bed.

"You should get some more rest," he tells me. "You're still recovering."

The minute he says it, I can feel how tired I still am. My body aches, and there's a headache forming behind my eyes—the kind I get when I'm too worn out. My whole body feels like overcooked pasta, floppy and barely able to support itself. But I think about how I woke up after that nightmare, feeling like I didn't know where I was, so on edge and afraid. That probably wore me out more than anything else, and I don't want to go back to that.

"I don't really feel like sleeping," I mutter, not quite meeting Vic's gaze.

He doesn't press me for more information, and there's something in his expression that tells me he understands how I feel without me having to go into detail about it.

He's always so good at that. I swear he can read me like he's got an open line directly into my brain sometimes.

"Okay," he murmurs. "Then how about we turn on the TV and relax that way? Watching cable is the best thing about hotels. Or at least that's what Ransom always says."

I nod my agreement, and Vic shuffles things around. He steals the pillows from the other bed and props them up on mine, fluffing them and arranging the sheets.

I scoot up and make myself comfortable, hugging one of the pillows close. Vic climbs up beside me, keeping some distance between us as he settles in.

Just like before, when Vic was anxious about being touched, there's tension between us—although now the roles are reversed. But I can feel it, crackling and electric in the space between our bodies on the bed. There's so much want there, so much desire, and it's coming from both of us. I want more than anything to just roll over there and tuck myself under his arm. To rest my head on his chest and feel that closeness. And more than that, I want to act on those feelings that rose up before, in the wake of our confessions.

But I know I can't. I'm still not ready for it, and Vic doesn't push for anything. He *understands*, which helps more than he'll ever know.

Picking up the remote, he scrolls through the TV guide channel for a bit before turning to one of the home improvement shows I like so much.

"Oh, this one," he comments. "This isn't one of the better ones."

I glance over at him. "How do you know? I didn't think you really watched TV."

He shrugs lightly. "I don't, normally. But I did some research."

"On home improvement shows?" I furrow my brow, confused. Of all the things for Vic to put his considerable talent at hunting down information toward, this one seems very strange.

"Yes. And the concept of home improvement itself, I guess. At first, I just wanted to see how accurate these shows are when it comes to showing the process of remodeling a home. I assumed a good amount of it was just dramatized for the show, and I was right about that. Some of them get it closer than others, and some are just full of drama. This is one of the dramatic ones."

He nods to where the woman in overalls is talking to the home owners. And he's not wrong. This is one of the ones where a family calls in an expert to renovate their house, and usually they either don't have enough money or the house turns out to be in worse shape than they thought, and it all gets very emotional.

As if on cue, the wife in the couple starts crying on camera, talking about how their baby is only five months old and has barely been able to sleep at night because of a heating issue with the house.

"We're all just so exhausted," she says, weeping to the designer. "When she's not sleeping, we're not sleeping, and we're at the point where we're considering just paying for a hotel for a while, because we can't go on like this."

The shot shows her holding the baby, rocking her in her arms, and then zooms in on her exhausted face.

Yup. Definitely dramatic.

"But why?" I ask Vic, turning back to him.

"Because drama sells," he explains with a shrug. "Probably more than discussing crown molding or outdated HVAC systems."

"No, I mean... why did you do all that research?"

"Because you like these shows," he answers, as if it should be obvious. "At first, I wanted to know why. They didn't seem all that entertaining, and you were so fascinated with them. I wanted to see if there was something I was missing. And then I just wanted to feel... closer to you, I guess. I wanted to understand you better, so I started with something you enjoyed. It helped me keep my shit together when you had to stay away from us. I imagined you in your apartment watching a show like this, and it made me feel like we were there together."

"Oh." For a second, I just stare at him, surprised and touched. "You really do love me, don't you?"

His brows pull together, a confused look crossing his face. "Of course I do. Did you not believe me earlier?"

It's such a classic Vic response that I can't help but laugh a little. "Of course I did. Don't worry."

We go back to watching the show, and the designer lady faces the camera, explaining the problem to the audience as if we didn't just see it happen on the screen.

"The Hampton family thought they were saving money by having a friend from Joshua's job come in and do their HVAC work for the last few years. But our team uncovered more problems than they were bargaining for once they went in."

The shot cuts to a close up of mold, thick and dark, as well as termites in the wall.

"Gross," I mutter. "They're definitely not coming in under budget."

Vic snorts. "They'll be lucky if they're not bankrupted by the end of this. They're going to need a completely new HVAC system run through there because of the friend cutting corners, and the termite damage looks extensive."

"Maybe they should have called you in instead."

"Absolutely not." Vic snorts under his breath. "Unlike Joshua's friend, I know what my skills are. Home renovation is not one of them."

In the end, he's right. There's a whole section of the episode where the Hamptons have to borrow more money from the wife's family in order to complete the work. They lean heavily on the fact that they have a new baby, and of course in the end, the house is beautiful.

"Notice how they didn't show them fixing any of the termite damage," Vic comments. "Which opens up the question of if they even did or if they just slapped a new coat of paint on the walls and called it good enough."

I laugh as the next show comes on, one where a husband and wife team come through and each try to convince the homeowners to go with their vision for renovating the house.

"This is one of the ones you like better, isn't it?" Vic says, lifting an eyebrow as if wanting to confirm his guess.

"Yeah." I grin. "I like when they change the house completely. It always starts as a regular old house at best and a total disaster at worst, and then it turns out so beautiful and bright in the end. And the couple always has such interesting ideas."

We watch the show together, getting caught up in it as the homeowners, two men who are preparing to adopt their first child, give the hosts a tour of their house. It's a beautiful ranch style place that seems to go on forever, and I sigh dreamily at the walk-in closets and the big, bright kitchen.

Vic laughs under his breath, and I shoot him a look. "What?"

"Nothing. It's just nice to see you enjoying yourself. And that *is* a very nice kitchen. Well organized."

"Of course that's what you'd notice," I tease back, shaking my head. "There's not even anything on the counters, so how do you know it's organized?"

He nods at the screen. "The fact that there's nothing on the counters. That means it's all put away somewhere. Probably with a system that makes sense for pulling things out and keeping them in order. I bet they don't have to worry about someone coming through and leaving chip bags all over the place."

"Not until their new kid arrives, at least," I add.

"Then it'll be like living with Malice and Ransom," Vic mutters, and I laugh.

"I'd really like a skylight in here somewhere," one of the men on screen says, gesturing around their bedroom. "Natural light is incredibly healthy."

Vic rolls his eyes. "Oh, yes. Just grab a sledge hammer and put a skylight in the bedroom. What a wonderful idea."

"What's wrong with a skylight?" I ask him.

"Nothing. But the attic is definitely above the bedroom."

That makes me burst out laughing. It's not surprising that Vic has memorized the layout of the house already, just from watching one quick tour of the place.

When they go into the kitchen, the other husband starts listing his plans for new appliances, and the two designers nod along and take notes.

"That's the ugliest backsplash I have ever seen," Vic says later, when one of the designers shows his mockup for the house. "It doesn't match anything in that kitchen."

"It kind of hurts my eyes to look at it," I agree. "What would you do?"

"Something neutral," he replies immediately. "That way if I wanted to repaint or get new appliances, it wouldn't all have to be ripped out."

"Sensible." I smile, nestling deeper into the pillows.

The combination of the shows I like and Vic's running commentary lightens the pain in my chest even more, and after a while, I start to nod off. I can still mostly hear the TV, and I'm not sleeping deeply enough to dream, thank goodness. But lying next to Vic feels restorative in its own way, and I drift in and out, comfortable and relaxed.

I lose track of time, and when the door opens, I blink awake to see Malice and Ransom coming back in.

I rub my eyes as Ransom makes his way over to the bed, sitting down on the other side of it.

"Hi," I mumble through a yawn.

"Hey, sleeping beauty," he replies, grinning.

Malice comes to sit at the foot of the bed, leaving me with a brother on all sides of me. They're surrounding me, and it makes me feel so safe. There's nothing here that wants to hurt me, but if there was, they wouldn't let it get through.

"Did you get what you need?" I ask, shaking off the last of my doze.

Ransom makes a face, puffing out his cheeks like he's holding in vomit. "Yeah, and then some. I saw shit I never wanted to see."

I wince at that, not eager to know the details of whatever weird sex stuff the judge is into. It's got to be bad, if it will work for blackmail.

"So it was good enough? You guys are going to be safe?"

That's the most important part of all of this. If whatever this judge gets up to while he's sneaking around on his wife isn't enough to keep him in line, then finding out about his weird kinks or whatever will have been for nothing.

"Yeah. Definitely," Ransom confirms. "I can't imagine this guy won't go along with our plan with what we've got. I wouldn't want it getting out if I was into that kind of shit, married or not."

I sigh with relief, a little bubble of hope rising in my chest. If the men are safe from being arrested, that will help me sleep better at night. I can't bear the thought of any of the brothers being arrested—especially not Malice, after what he went through the first time he was locked up.

"We'll go ahead and mark that off the list, then," Vic says, breaking into my thoughts. "And move on to the next part of the plan."

"Which is?" I ask, glancing his way.

"Preparing to face Olivia."

Just hearing her name makes me feel sick to my stomach, but he's right. Facing off with her is the next big thing we have to do. As awful as Troy was, as disgusting and cruel as he could be, Olivia is the one who set everything into motion. She's the one we have to set our sights on next. We need to get her off our backs permanently somehow, or we'll live the rest of our lives looking over our shoulders.

"Do we have anything to work off of?" Malice asks.

Vic nods. "I've been digging through Troy's laptop, and I've got some information about his family that we can use. Like most rich assholes, they're clean on the surface, but it just took a little digging to find what I wanted."

"Do you think they know that their precious little Troy is no longer with us?" Ransom asks.

"As far as I can tell, no one knows anything. Troy was off the grid up in that house, out of touch with everyone. I feel like if there was news of his death already, it would be everywhere."

We all nod in agreement at that.

"Even if they wanted to keep it quiet, it wouldn't be that easy when it's someone like Troy Copeland," I say, and the name tastes bitter in my mouth.

He's dead, I remind myself. *You saw him die. Painfully.*

That last thought is a bit vicious, but I don't try to push it aside. I'm learning to embrace my vicious side, which is probably thanks to Malice's influence. I'm not mad about it though.

"We have a limited window," Vic is saying as I tune back into the conversation. "I think it's best if we make our first move before everyone finds out what happened to Troy. Him going off the grid the way he did could actually work in our favor here. We don't want to waste the opportunity."

Malice smiles, and there's a sharp, deadly edge to it.

"I agree. We should pay a little visit to Olivia soon," he says. "Someone should let her know that things have changed."

13

WILLOW

A DAY LATER, after the brothers have paid a little visit to Judge Bailey and put the fear of god into him—or rather, the fear of having his disgusting private life broadcast to the entire world—I leave the hotel with Ransom.

It feels weird to not have to be hiding anymore, after spending so long looking over my shoulder, terrified of being caught. We're still trying to stay under the radar until we're ready to face Olivia, but with her still thinking I'm holed up with Troy, that's not a huge concern at the moment.

Malice and Vic weren't too keen on staying behind at the hotel though—especially Malice. The three brothers have been so much more protective in the couple of days since they rescued me, almost to the point of smothering me with attention. I can't blame them for that, considering I was snatched away from them and dragged off in a Jeep while they watched in horror.

Ransom has always been affectionate and possessive with me, but it's all been turned up a notch. He keeps an eye out on our surroundings as we step outside the hotel, making sure nothing and no one can get close. A man leaving right behind us gives me a second look, and Ransom glares at him with such intensity that the guy immediately averts his eyes and hurries to his own car.

"Ransom." I purse my lips, shaking my head.

"What?"

"Are you going to give the stink eye to anyone who even looks at me funny?"

He shrugs, tucking his hands into his pockets as we cross the parking lot. "Why the hell not? You can never be too careful. And they shouldn't be looking at you anyway."

I shake my head, equal parts amused and touched by the complete sincerity in his voice.

When we get to the car—which they told me is one they stole on the way back from Mexico, swapping out the car Ransom hot-wired shortly after I was abducted—he opens the door for me before I can even reach for the handle. I'm sure if he wasn't trying to give me a little space, he'd probably buckle my seatbelt for me too, but instead, he waits for me to get settled before closing the door and going to the driver's side.

He starts the car, and we peel out of the parking lot, heading to a shopping center outside the heart of the city.

"I almost didn't think Malice was going to let us leave without him," I comment as we drive.

Ransom snorts. "He's in mother hen mode—although he'd kill me if he knew I called it that. And I can't really blame him for not wanting to let you out of his sight. The only reason I didn't freak out is because I get to stay with you the whole time. Watch, if we're not back in a couple of hours, he's going to be calling every two minutes to make sure we're alright."

"You're *all* in mother hen mode," I correct him. "But I get it."

He snorts in amusement, but he doesn't disagree with my assessment.

"Anyway," he continues, "Mal and Vic have their own jobs to do, so they'll have plenty to keep them busy while we're gone. We've gotta make sure everything is in place before we approach Olivia. Like Vic said, this is our best opportunity, and we don't want to fuck that up."

We already have a date in mind for when we'll make that move, but everything has to be ready first.

Honestly, all of it makes me anxious. I don't want to see Olivia or talk to her, but I know I don't really have a choice if I want to ever be free of her. Eventually, she's going to realize that Troy is dead. Killing him only bought us a temporary reprieve.

Having the brothers on my side does make me feel better about it though. I have a real family for the first time in my life—ride or die people who would do anything for me.

No matter what Olivia throws at us, we can handle it.

"It's going to be okay," Ransom says, as if he can sense the way my thoughts are going. "Vic's going to plan this whole thing to within an inch of its life, and Malice is great at adjusting in the moment if need be to make sure it will go off without a hitch. It's going to be fine."

"What are *you* going to do?" I ask him.

He grins. "Keep them from going to their extremes and making shit crazier than it has to be. That's my specialty."

We both laugh at that, and it feels good to be able to find some humor in all of this.

Ransom drives us to a shopping center I've never been to before, and we get out, stepping into a dress shop. It's not as fancy as the places Olivia took me to, but it's definitely more upscale than the places I used to shop. But that's not really hard to do.

A sales woman greets us brightly as we walk in, glancing past me to Ransom, her eyes sparkling. "Please let me know if there's anything I can do to help you and your... friend," she says, beaming at him.

"I think we'll be okay," Ransom replies. "But thanks."

He steers me past her, not quite touching me. We move past row after row of colorful clothes until we get to the section full of fancier gowns. There are so many of them it makes my eyes blur. All kinds of fabrics and colors and lengths, patterns and designs jumping out at me.

The truth is, before Olivia, I never really knew how to shop for myself. I bought the things I could afford, which was never anything luxurious or all that nice. Now that I have a chance to buy things that are pretty and purposeful, I feel like a fish out of water.

I wander the racks, looking at dresses, pulling a couple off the rack and then wavering. I have no idea what I'm looking for when it comes to cut or color or anything.

"This... fits," I say, holding up a powder blue dress for Ransom to see. "I think it does, anyway."

He looks it over and frowns. "That sure is a color, though. Do you like that one?"

I shrug. "I don't know. Blue is nice. I guess."

"Blue *is* nice. That looks like an Easter egg gone wrong. And it's not your color."

"How do you know what my color is?" I ask.

"Angel, I've been checking you out for months now. Trust me, I know your colors."

My cheeks flush as he makes a show of checking me out now, and to my relief, it doesn't set off that awful sick, shaky feeling in my chest. Instead, I just laugh and put the Easter disaster dress back on the rack.

"I have no idea what I'm looking for," I finally admit.

He smiles, coming over to the rack I'm going through. "Luckily for you, I'm here. I know this is usually Vic's job, but I wanted to have my turn," he says, teasing. "I can dress you just as well as he can."

"You know he's going to make some comment about the dress not being symmetrical enough if we don't pick the right one," I tease back.

"We don't want to risk his wrath. Symmetry it is then."

Weirdly, that task is a bit harder than it should be. There are so many dresses that are cut higher in the front than the back, or on one side than the other. Ransom holds up a bizarre black number that has one sleeve and is shorter in the back than the front, and we both shudder before he puts it back.

It's interesting, watching his process for picking things out. He does seem to have an eye for color, and he stays away from the pastels, instead pulling out dresses in reds and greens and rich, dark blues. He finds one in a shimmering gold, pulling it out and holding it up to me.

It's off the shoulder a bit, and it will definitely show off more of my scars than I'm used to, but Ransom has that look in his eyes.

"Are you sure about that one?" I ask, shifting a little nervously.

"If you don't want to try it on, you definitely don't have to," he replies. "But I think gold would look amazing on you. It'll add to how bright you already shine."

I look at the dress and the look on Ransom's face and then nod. "Okay, add it to the pile."

He beams at me, and seeing that look definitely helps. I want to shine. I want to try to rise above the darkness and pain that I feel stuck in lately.

We go through a few more racks, and Ransom makes a case for more dresses. The growing pile in his arms is getting a little out of hand, but it seems like he's excited for me to try them all on. There was probably a time when I would have been excited to do it too. Now it just feels like a means to an end.

But getting back to the things I enjoy is part of healing, probably, so I take a deep breath and brush off the misgivings, trying to feel some pleasure here.

"We'll go from least likely to most," Ransom says, handing me three dresses. "That way we can eliminate them quickly."

"You're starting to sound like Vic," I tell him, smiling.

He rolls his eyes. "Don't tell him that. I'll never hear the end of it."

I just laugh and take the dresses into the dressing room. I get undressed quickly, not wanting to spend more time than I have to out of my clothes in this place I'm not comfortable in yet.

The first dress is blue, and I can already tell I'm not really going to like it. The material is scratchy, and instead of showing off my assets well, it just makes me look boxy.

I also can't reach the zipper.

"Everything okay in there?" Ransom calls.

"I need a little help," I call back. "I can't get the zipper up."

There's a soft chuckle from outside, and then he comes in, closing the little door behind him.

I can feel his eyes on me as soon as he steps in, and he swallows as he looks me over. There's no question what he's looking at. I'm half in the dress, the zipper undone down my back, hair spilling over my shoulder where I flipped it forward to try to get it out of the way of the zipper.

It's not what I would have called alluring, but Ransom's eyes are burning into me, the heat palpable.

All of a sudden, the small room is full of tension, and it's climbing by the minute.

If this were weeks ago, I would have teased him a little. I would have looked forward to the touch of his fingers as he zipped me up, trying to tempt him into touching me more.

Ransom knows that, and I can see it on his face as he meets my eyes in the mirror. There's a flare of heat there, turning the blue-green depths just a bit darker.

For a second, neither of us moves, locked in this moment, and my heart beat speeds up a bit, not with anticipation, but with something like dread.

But then Ransom clears his throat and visibly holds himself back. He swallows hard and then smiles, moving in closer to do up the zipper.

His touch is careful, not straying more than it needs to in order to get the zipper up, but it still makes goosebumps spread over my skin. Just the proximity of him in the dressing room, the small space filled suddenly with the scent of him, makes me wish things were different.

"There you go," Ransom says, stepping back, putting distance between us. "I like the color on you, but I'm not sure about the cut of it. You're gorgeous in anything, but this dress is kind of shapeless. What do you think?"

He pushes his hands into his pockets, and he doesn't seem upset, just waiting for my opinion on the dress.

The way he is with me now, the patience he and his brothers have for me, it makes my heart swell. I watch him in the mirror, and the words bubble up before I can even think about them, almost as natural as breathing.

I meet his gaze in the mirror. "I love you."

I can see the second the words hit him, and Ransom reacts immediately. His eyes flare with pleasure, and a huge grin breaks out over his handsome face. He's shining with pure joy, so intense and happy it's like basking in the sun to see it.

His hands come up to my shoulders, and I don't flinch as he turns me around to face him.

"Say it again," he says.

So I do. "I love you, Ransom."

He takes in a deep breath, and his eyes are shining. He looks like the words have hit him right in the chest, and he even puts a hand up over where his heart is, like he's trying to keep all his feelings from pouring out all over the place.

I watch his face, captivated by how open and full of emotion he looks right now.

Finally, he just grins, his eyes searching my face for a second. "I love you too," he says. "This is going to sound crazy, but go with me, okay?"

"Okay," I reply, laughing a little.

"I think a part of me loved you since the first moment I saw you. That moment we met on the street and you had been crying, remember?"

I nod, breathless with the knowledge that he remembers all that. It feels like it was so long ago. Like it happened to someone else. So much is different now, and I couldn't have imagined back then that I would have ended up with the very handsome man who stopped to talk to me that night. Or that I'd want to. Everything about him had screamed predator, and now I know that he—and his brothers—can be dangerous when they want to be, but that there's so much more to them than that.

Ransom grins even brighter. "I threatened to beat someone up for making you cry, and I meant it, even then. Even then I had the urge to protect you."

"Why?" I ask him.

"Well, back then I thought you looked sweet. I thought that anyone who would make you cry deserved to get their fucking ass kicked because you didn't deserve it. Now... now my brothers and I would do anything to protect you, Willow. Whatever it took."

"I know," I murmur softly. "I know you would." They've more than proved that. They somehow found me when Troy had me locked away. They managed to kill him and pull me out of that hell, and I'm forever grateful to them for that and all the other rescues they've pulled off for me.

"I appreciate it more than I can say," I tell him.

Ransom shakes his head. "You don't have to say it. We know. Malice, Vic, and I are all different people. We're brothers, but we're not really that similar."

I grin. "You're telling me."

"And somehow, you're still our perfect match. You fit with us so well. All of us. No other woman could say the same. You're just so perfect, Willow."

"Even... even though I'm like this now?" I ask him, somehow needing to make sure. It's silly, since he's saying all this now, even after what happened to me, but I just need to hear it. "Even though I'm all broken, and you can't even touch me?"

"Willow," Ransom says firmly. "Nothing would make you less than perfect to us. I can speak for my brothers when I say that. It's not about being able to touch you, and you've been through something fucking awful. No one's holding that against you. It doesn't change you. Who you are inside."

I look up at him, confused. "But I feel like a completely different person."

"Maybe some things about you are different," he allows.

115

"Maybe it's going to take some time for you to get back to who you think you're supposed to be. Maybe you have to heal some before you can like the things you used to like. But the parts of you that we fell for? The parts that make you Willow Hayes, badass bitch and sweetheart? All of that is still there. It might feel further away right now, but it's not gone. Nothing could kill that in you."

He sounds so sure of himself, so determined to get me to hear what he's saying and believe it, and that, combined with everything else he's said, makes my heart swell. It's everything I needed to hear right now, and I lean up, putting my arms around his neck so I can kiss him.

Ransom kisses me back, responding immediately. As if I needed it, his almost instinctual response is just more proof that he always craves me. That even what Troy did to me and all the horrible abuse he put me through will never stop Ransom from wanting to be with me.

But as soon as his mouth comes alive over mine, I tense up.

Ransom presses in closer, deepening the kiss, and my stomach coils with fear and nausea. For a split second, I'm back in that house, and it's not Ransom holding me close, kissing me because he loves me, but Troy, holding me down and kissing me because he can.

I squeeze my eyes shut tighter and drag a ragged breath in through my nose. I try to fill my lungs with Ransom's unique scent, letting it chase away the bad memories so I can push through this.

I want this. I want to be able to kiss and touch my men the way I used to. I want to go back to being the uninhibited sexual creature I discovered inside myself thanks to them. I fought so hard for that, to be comfortable and not shame myself for my desires.

Being held captive by the trauma Troy inflicted on me feels like taking a giant step back.

I must make some noise or go stiff or something. Some way that Ransom can tell. Even though I try to keep going, clinging on and kissing him harder, as if I can brute force my way past my trauma and find some pleasure on the other side... Ransom knows better.

He gently pulls back and unwinds my arms from around his neck. He kisses my knuckles softly before releasing my hands, so tender and understanding.

And then takes a step back, putting more distance between us.

"I'm sorry," I blurt, the words spilling out of me. "I'm trying—I don't want it to be like this."

"Willow." His voice is soft. "It's okay. One day, I'll fuck you like you want. My brothers and I will erase every memory of Troy left on your body. We'll remind you who you are and why we love you, and it'll be fucking amazing. We'll overwrite every bad thing that's happened by worshiping you like the goddess you are. But not yet. When you're ready, and not before."

"What if... what if it takes too long?" I ask, unable to hold back. "What if—"

"Then we'll wait," Ransom replies, like it's the easiest thing in the world. "We'd wait forever for you, pretty girl."

It's just as sincere as the words he used to tell me he loves me, and all I can do is nod, tears burning in my eyes.

His expression hardens a bit, and he lets out a shaky breath.

"That fucker got off too easy," he says darkly. "I wish I could go back and make him hurt the way you're hurting. Vic and Mal both got their chances to make him bleed, and I wish I could've taken a turn too. He deserved to suffer way more for what he did to you."

"You're starting to sound like Malice now," I say, smiling a little. "That's both your brothers in one day."

Ransom huffs a laugh, the harsh edge of anger bleeding out of his face. "Don't say that. I have to be the rational one of the three of us, or we'll never get anything done."

"I think you guys take turns being the rational one." I pause, considering. "Or at least, you and Vic do."

He laughs again, and the tension in the little dressing room starts to ease. The moment breaks, and he tucks my hair behind my ears as we smile at each other.

"I don't think this is the dress," I say, finally answering his earlier question.

"Agreed." He moves in to help me with the zipper without being asked. "On to the next one, then."

It's easier than it probably should be, to go back to dress shopping after that. The weight of our conversation is still there, the meaningfulness of the words we spoke lingering in the air between us, but we focus on other things for the moment. Ransom stays in the dressing room with me while I try on more dresses, helping me get into them and take them off.

In the end, the gold dress wins out, and he looks very pleased with himself as I survey my reflection.

"I told you," he says. "You shine. Nothing could dim your light when you look this good."

"I do like it..." I chew my lip, gazing at our reflections in the mirror.

"Then we're getting it."

His decisive tone makes me grin. I love how all he cares about is whether I like something, whether it makes me happy. And as long as it does, then he wants it for me too. I don't even bother to look at the price tag, since I know it'll probably make my heart stop —and the truth is, I can afford it now. Besides, I'm basically buying myself armor to wear to my first meeting with Olivia since the wedding. So it's worth splurging on whatever makes me feel the most confident and powerful.

I slip out of the dress, and Ransom hangs it back on a hanger as I pull on my street clothes. Then we step out of the dressing room and head to the register to purchase the dress.

On the way out of the shop, Ransom wraps an arm around me, and the small touch doesn't make me flinch or tense up the way I'm expecting it to. I can even lean into his side a little as we head back to the car with the garment bag in tow.

It feels like progress.

Not quite as much as I'd like to have made, but progress all the same.

14

WILLOW

A FEW DAYS LATER, I stand looking at my reflection in the mirror. I'm wearing the gold dress Ransom picked out, and I let his words replay in my mind as I smooth down the skirt of it, trying to feel more confident.

At least the cuts and bruises from everything that happened to me while I was Troy's captive are slowly fading. Still visible, but not as dark and grim as they were at first.

Just a few months ago, I would have been trying to cover them up the same way I used to always try to cover up the scars. The old urge to hide everything is still there, but I push it back, not letting it take over. Honestly, the dress I'm wearing tonight doesn't leave room for hiding. It's off the shoulder and has short sleeves, showing the bruises and my scars, and I won't try to put coverup on them.

No long sleeves, no makeup.

The truth is, I've fought my way through a lot to get here. I've been dodging death since before I even really knew it. All the way back to when Olivia killed my birth mother and tried to kill me, setting fire to our house to make it seem like an accident. Somehow, I managed to come through that in one piece.

I've been through a hell of a lot, and every mark on my body is proof that I'm a survivor.

That despite what happened to me, I'm not done fighting yet.

There was definitely a time when I felt like I was weak, or when I doubted my own strength to push through. But even then, I was fighting. Dealing with Misty, putting myself through college as best I could, trying to make a better life for myself with the little I had.

It makes me feel strong as I stand before the mirror, and I drag in a deep breath, nodding to my reflection. With the dress and my face lightly made up, I look good. My dyed brown hair spills over one shoulder in soft curls, pinned on one side, and although I still prefer my natural blonde color, the darker color seems to fit the occasion. I look like I can walk into a fancy party and hold my own.

And that's what I intend to do.

I step out of the bathroom and into the main room of the hotel room we're all still sharing.

The guys are already ready, Ransom and Malice sitting on the beds while Vic checks last-minute things on his computer. When I step out of the bathroom, all three of them look up.

They're a bit dressed up too, in dark slacks and well-tailored blazers, their shirts underneath the only pops of color in their ensembles.

I can feel all three of them looking at me, their gazes starting at my head and moving down, taking in my outfit.

It's the first time Malice and Vic are seeing the dress, and as Ransom tears his focus from me for a second to take in their expressions, he looks smug and pleased, as if he's even more sure that he made the right call in picking out this particular dress.

"Do you like it?" I ask them, smoothing my hands down the front of it again.

"You're stunning," Vic replies, not taking his gaze off me.

"Looks like you're not the only one who can pick out a dress, Vic," Ransom says to his brother, grinning.

Vic just rolls his eyes, and Malice doesn't let his eyes leave me for a second. There's a look in the dark depths of his irises that lets me know exactly what he's thinking about, and a flicker of heat flares in my belly.

If things were different, I'd be hoping for one of them—all of them, really—to touch me. To slide their fingers down my arm or dip them under the neckline of the dress. But now the thought of it makes my stomach twist with nerves, that hint of nausea still there, proof that I'm not over what happened to me yet.

None of the guys have rushed me or pushed for anything, all content to let me move at my own pace, but I still hate it. I want to feel normal again.

"Fuck, Solnyshka." Malice's hoarse voice draws my attention back to him and his brothers, breaking me out of my thoughts. "You look..."

He trails off like he doesn't have the words for it. There's more than heat in his eyes, and when I glance at Vic and Ransom, I can see it's the same for them. There's pride there too, shining at me from three directions, and something that looks kind of like awe.

That knowledge makes my stomach clench in a different way. A much better way.

It makes me feel powerful, having these three men feel this way about me. It reminds me that I'm strong the same way the scars and cuts and bruises do. That I can get through this, because I've come through everything else that's been thrown at me.

I can do this.

"We should get going," Vic says, running a hand over his hair even though there isn't a single dark strand out of place. "The invitation I found said the party starts at eight."

"Yeah, but it's more normal to be fashionably late to these things," Ransom replies. "You know how these rich fucks love to make an entrance. Everyone's already there, and they get to show off their outfits or their jewels they just bought from exploiting children in other countries."

Malice snorts and Vic shakes his head, but Ransom does have a point.

"Are you ready?" Vic asks me, looking into my eyes.

I take another deep breath, shaking out my hands to dispel a little nervous energy.

"I don't know," I tell him honestly. "I don't know what's going to happen tonight."

"We've covered all the bases we can," Malice says, glancing to his twin for confirmation.

Vic nods. "We're covered. All that's left to do is go talk to Olivia. If you're ready, butterfly."

I lick my lips, glancing at all three of them in turn. If I had to go do this by myself, it would be much harder to agree, but knowing they'll have my back and will make sure nothing bad happens tonight—as much as they can, at least—helps so much.

So I nod. "I'm ready."

Malice claps his hands once. "Then let's go do this shit."

He leads the way to the door, and we follow him out, getting into the car. For once, Vic lets Ransom ride shotgun, sliding into the back with me.

Once we pull out of the small parking lot and get onto the highway, my heart starts pounding, thoughts of how tonight could go wrong racing through my head. What if the judge they blackmailed went back on the deal? What if Olivia tries to grab me right there at the party? What if it's all a trap?

Before I know it, I'm breathing harder, swallowing and trying to get a handle on myself, but it's hard. Olivia's already proven how dangerous she is, and that she's willing to do whatever it takes to get what she wants.

Killing Troy was one thing, and at least as his widow, I have more power in this world now. But Olivia is going to be even trickier to deal with. What if she—

My rambling train of thought is cut off by a hand sliding into mine.

I glance down to see Vic's fingers lacing through my own. His large hand envelops mine, and he squeezes lightly, offering comfort.

"It's going to be fine," he murmurs. "Breathe for me."

I force myself to take a deep breath and then another, clinging on to his hand as tightly as I can.

Breathe, Willow. Just keep breathing.

The party is being held at a high-rise building in the heart of Detroit, and it only takes us about thirty minutes to reach it. There's a valet out front, but Malice parks the car himself, and we all get out, heading for the door together.

There's a doorman checking people's names off a list, and I square my shoulders, trying to channel calm and give the impression that I'm supposed to be here.

The doorman looks us all over and raises an eyebrow.

"Name?" he asks, sounding half bored, half like he's pretty sure he's not going to find my name on the list.

"Willow," I tell him. "Willow... Copeland."

It tastes bad in my mouth to say it, but I know it's our ticket in. The guys tense behind me, and I swear I can feel a shift in their emotions like a physical thing. They hate that name as much as I do, or maybe even more, if that's possible. But it's part of the plan. They know I have to do it.

The doorman nods, marking my name off. "Welcome, Mrs. Copeland," he says. Then he glances at the guys, looking a bit skeptical.

"They're with me," I explain.

For a second, it seems like he's going to protest, but then he nods, ushering us inside. I'm sure it's not the first time someone has arrived at one of these kinds of parties with their bodyguards in tow, and it's not like the doorman knows of any reason not to let them in.

"The elevator is down the hall to the right," he says. "Head up to the roof."

"Thank you," I reply, and we walk down the hall, our shoes echoing on the marbled tile as we make our way to the elevator.

Malice jabs the button for the roof, and the three of them move in to surround me protectively. The odds of us being attacked in the elevator are almost zero, but it does make me feel better to have them so close.

The ride up takes less time than I wish it would, and as we near the top of building, I lift my chin, putting my game face on before the elevator doors slide open.

The rooftop is lavishly decorated with twinkling lights, gold accents and ornate ice sculptures. Waiters weave skillfully between guests, offering little canapés and flutes of champagne.

The guests are the usual set for this kind of thing, the same sort of people who showed up to the engagement party Olivia threw for me and Troy. Most of them were probably at the first disaster of a wedding too, although I wasn't paying enough attention that day to recognize any of them. They sparkle in their finery, glittering with jewels, expensive watches, and designer clothes.

The occasion is an anniversary party for Troy's parents—a big, fancy rooftop party for all their friends and people they want to impress or do business with.

Troy told me about the party when I was still in captivity at his house in the middle of nowhere. It was supposed to be our first outing together as a married couple. The first public appearance he was going to make with me as his wife. He took great pleasure in telling me that I would be expected to attend and make a good showing, and I can only be glad that it worked in my favor now.

Because it got me in the door.

My men and I walk across the rooftop, cutting our way through little clusters of mingling guests. I can feel people watching us, their gazes sliding from me to the three brothers. Whispers start up around us as we move, and I can pick up a few of them as we go.

Not everyone recognizes me, especially with my hair a different color, but the guys stand out, even dressed up. They just don't have the look of people who belong with this crowd, and it shows.

But we came here with a purpose, so we ignore them for the most part.

Olivia is easy to spot, wearing a silver dress and standing near the bar. She's talking to an older man, a glass in her hand, but once the man drifts away to speak to someone else, she glances to one side—and her eyes lock with mine.

Her head jerks slightly. Several emotions pass over her face, and I can tell she's surprised to see me. Then her eyes flick toward the guys, and her carefully crafted mask cracks for just a moment.

Disdain and hatred cross her features, showing how truly ugly she is. But then she gets herself together, smoothing her face back into that expression of neutral politeness that seems to disarm people and win them over. She pulls out her phone from a tiny clutch in her hands and raises it to her ear, keeping her locked on us the same way someone might watch a pack of wild dogs.

"Let's go," Malice murmurs, and I nod.

We make a beeline toward her, and Olivia returns the phone to her clutch after a moment as her gaze runs over me. If she has an opinion about my outfit, she doesn't say anything as we reach her. Instead, she glances past the men as if she expects someone else to be there.

"Where is Troy?" she asks. "And what are you doing here?"

"I was invited," I reply coolly, ignoring the question about Troy for now. We'll get to that, eventually.

"I know that. But your little band of criminals weren't." Olivia's tone turns icy as she adds, "You're making a mistake, Willow. You're a fool to keep dragging them into this. I thought you claimed to care about them."

"I *do*," I shoot back.

"Then you should let them go. Bringing them here, constantly hanging around them? It could so easily destroy their lives."

It's so clearly a threat, and Malice reacts to it, stepping forward a little. Fury radiates from him, and even though he doesn't make a move to hit Olivia or even get close enough to hurt her, it's obvious that he wants to.

"Willow didn't drag us into anything," he snaps. "We'd stand by her side no matter fucking what."

Olivia looks at him with a cool expression, her gray hair

glinting in the light as she tips her head slightly to one side, her eyes narrowing.

"You should have learned your lesson," she says. "You were meant to be a lap dog, and dogs who don't obey get put down." She never raises her voice, but there's something in her tone that makes a shiver run down my spine. "I thought someone would've taught you that lesson while you were in prison, but clearly it didn't stick. When you get sent back, I'll make sure you become someone's bitch."

It's a shockingly crude thing to say, and seems at odds with her refined outfit and the way she's holding herself. The words lash out like a whip, and protective fury fills me in a rush.

I step forward, putting myself between her and Malice, poisonous words gathering at the tip of my tongue. But before I can say anything, there's a commotion behind us.

I turn my head in time to see several cops making their way in, pushing their way past the guests and coming toward us. My pulse jumps, even though we were expecting this too.

Olivia must've called them. That's who she was on the phone with.

The other guests have all abandoned their conversations and are watching as the police make their way across the rooftop. We have an audience now, and I can feel my pulse in my throat as my entire body prickles with nerves.

Olivia looks smug, lifting a hand to gesture them over to us as if they weren't already headed our way.

"Did you call us out, Mrs. Stanton?" one of the officers asks.

She nods. "Yes, officer, I did. I believe there are warrants out for the arrests of all three of these men." She gestures to them, her eyes glittering. "I just wanted to do my civic duty and inform you that they were here. And I didn't know what they were planning to do, showing up at a party like this where they clearly don't belong."

The cops exchange looks and then glance at the three brothers.

"Names?" one of them asks the men, and all three of them give their names.

I watch in silence, doing my best to keep from grabbing them and making a mad dash for the elevator. We've been on the run for so long, and this is bringing up vivid memories of that night at the bar we went to, when Malice was nearly arrested and we only escaped because a fight broke out and gave us cover. The impulse to create some sort of diversion so that we can flee again is almost impossible to push down, but I do my best to school my features, not letting my fear show on my face.

"I'll have to call it in, ma'am," the cop who seems to be taking the lead says, glancing at Olivia.

"Whatever you have to do," she replies with a fluttering wave of her hand.

At least they're planning to check on the truth of her claim before they put cuffs on the guys. That's something.

It's a tense few minutes as one cop makes the call. A low buzz of murmured conversation springs up around us again, although I can still feel people cutting glances our way, curious about what's going on.

Then, finally, the cop comes back over, reaffixing his radio to the belt at his waist.

"I'm sorry, ma'am. It seems there's been some confusion," he says, jerking his chin toward the brothers. "There *was* a warrant out for their arrest. But it's been recalled."

There's no change at all in Olivia's expression for two or three heartbeats as she processes that information. Then shock registers on her face, her jaw falling open.

I let out a breath, my lungs burning from holding it for too long. *That's right, you fucking bitch. You don't win this round.*

15

RANSOM

Beside me, Willow lets out a short, barely audible breath. My shoulders relax a little at the confirmation that our plan worked. Judge Bailey came through on his promise and recalled the warrants Olivia set up for the three of us—and our blackmail material was definitely better than hers, or he probably would've tried to go to her to see if he could get her to sweeten whatever deal she offered him to sign off on the warrants in the first place.

"Was there anything else, ma'am?" one of the cops asks.

Now that it's clear they were called out here for nothing, they only seem to be giving Olivia basic respect, based on who she is. She's still gaping, her mouth hanging open just a little wider than is probably fitting for polite society, and I fucking love to see it.

A kind of savage satisfaction fills me as I watch her expression change. She no longer has the upper hand over us, and she's finally realizing it. All that smug satisfaction she was exuding just a second ago is bleeding away, as if she's finally realizing that Willow is a true force to be reckoned with.

Too bad for her she's so slow on the uptake. My brothers and I have known that truth for a long fucking time, and we're prepared to have Willow's back for whatever comes next.

"Ma'am?" another cop prompts Olivia. "Was there any other

reason we were called out? Do you have any charges to make against these men?"

He glances at us, and even though we've just been cleared, I can feel Malice stiffen beside me. It's old habit for all of us, a natural distrust of cops and an instinct to be ready to fight at a moment's notice if need be.

But right now, it's not needed.

Olivia snaps her jaw shut, then shakes her head. "No. I suppose not. I'm very sorry to have wasted your time."

"Not a problem."

The cops leave, and most of the party goers seem to lose interest as they realize they won't be getting a big show of anyone being dragged away in handcuffs. But I can still feel glances being cast our way, Olivia's peers probably trying to evaluate what's going on with her, and why the four of us are talking to her.

Ignoring the stares from those nearby, Olivia takes a step closer to Willow, fury overtaking her face.

"What did you do?" she hisses.

Willow just smiles at her, as calm as can be. You'd never know that she was worried at all before we got here, and my chest swells with pride for how she's playing this so well. I swear I'm falling in love with her even more, watching her handle this.

"We just took a page out of your playbook," Willow tells her grandmother, speaking in a low voice. "It turns out blackmail can be shockingly effective as a tool for getting things done. Or undone."

Understanding flares in Olivia's eyes, and she splutters with anger. "You—how *dare* you—"

Before she can finish that sentence, two new people emerge from the crowd, stepping forward to join us. I recognize them from both the wedding we interrupted and photos that came up during our search for Troy's hiding place.

They're his parents.

They look as snobbish and inbred as everyone else here, dressed to the nines for this party. They come to stand beside

Olivia, their gazes sliding over Malice, Vic, and me like we're trash not fit to grace their presence.

I roll my eyes. *Fuck these assholes. We have the upper hand here.*

"What is going on, Olivia?" Troy's mother bites out. Stella Copeland might be beautiful, with her dyed blonde hair and elegant outfit, but she has this look on her face like someone near her stepped in dog shit and is tracking it all over her fancy party. "The police, here? I asked them why they came, and they said they were called out by you."

Troy's father, Alexander, looks at Willow, and the contempt on his face is so easy to see. It makes me bristle, wanting to put myself between him and her, to protect her from his shitty judgment.

But I know I don't have to. My girl can hold her own with these people. She's strong enough for that and then some.

"We knew you made a deal with Troy for her hand in marriage," Alexander says, sniffing as he turns his attention back to Olivia. "But you assured us that she wouldn't be a problem. That *they* wouldn't be a problem."

He jerks his head at the three of us.

"Yes," Stella agrees, her lips set tight. I'm sure there would be a frown line between her eyebrows if she hadn't been Botoxed to within an inch of her life. "And this very much looks like a problem. You know how important this party is to us. We invited potential business partners to this event. It was supposed to go off without a hitch."

They're both looking to Olivia for answers, and it's really fucking satisfying to see that she doesn't have any for them.

"I know." Olivia's voice is curt, and her back is still ramrod straight, but there's something in her eyes that looks unsettled.

Good. How does it feel to not have the upper hand for once, bitch? I think viciously.

Since Olivia's words didn't actually explain any of what's going on, and she doesn't seem to have anything else to say, the Copelands wheel on Willow.

Stella takes a step closer, getting into Willow's face.

"I warned Troy against this," she spits, her upper lip curling. "I told him that you would be a problem. That you were going to be a black mark on this family and our good name. But he promised me he could keep you in line. We even let him step away from his duties at the company to take the time to make sure you were ready to be presented to polite society. Clearly, he overestimated himself."

She started off speaking quietly, but by the end, her voice has risen a bit, and Alexander puts a hand on his wife's shoulder and pulls her away from Willow.

"Not here, Stella," he says, his voice sharp and low. "This isn't the time or the place. Troy will have to deal with her, that's all. We will remind him that he has a duty to this family, and that it includes keeping his little... *projects* at home until they can be controlled properly."

It's a fucking disgusting way to talk to and about a human being, and the fact that they're discussing Willow like she's some kind of stray Troy took in and hasn't housebroken yet gets my hackles up.

I can't hold back any longer, so I step forward, catching the Copelands' attention.

"That's gonna be pretty hard for him to do," I tell them with a savage grin. "Seeing as he's not alive anymore."

There's a split second of silence while they absorb that, and then Stella gasps. "*What?*"

Malice steps up beside me, crossing his arms over his chest as he stares them down.

"You didn't wonder why he wasn't here yet?" he asks, his voice hard. "It's because he's indisposed. Permanently. Which you might have found out about already if you hadn't supported him going off the fucking grid with Willow. I know you rich fuckers are fucked in the head, but you let him hold Willow captive while he tried to break her. You all knew about it. Don't even try to tell me you didn't. And you accepted it."

"How dare you—"

"Shut. The fuck. *Up*," Malice snaps, cutting Troy's father off. He's taller than Alexander by a good few inches, and even with the man trying to draw himself up to look intimidating, he's got nothing compared to the raw violence Malice exudes. "You knew he'd be unreachable, and you knew why. You gave him the space to use and abuse Willow, and that's why you neglected to find out that his cabin burned down. With him inside."

There's a small intake of breath from Olivia, and I swing my gaze over to her, watching her digest that new piece of information. I can tell she recognizes the symmetry of it, and she should, considering she burned down a house herself once. She killed Willow's mom in a fire, forever altering the course of Willow's life. And now we've done the same to her, in a way, snatching away her deal and killing the monster Willow was forced to marry.

"Alexander," Stella says, her voice a harsh whisper. She puts her hand on her husband's arm, clutching it through his suit jacket. "It can't be true, can it? Troy can't be—"

Her other hand comes up to her mouth, trembling just a bit.

Alexander takes a bit longer to snap out of his shock. He blinks at us for a long moment and then looks to his wife. "I... I don't know."

"It's true," I tell them with a shrug. "We're not gonna waste time trying to convince you. You'll find out for yourself soon enough once you go check out his little hideout in the woods. You should've kept that little monster on a shorter leash. Maybe told him 'no' a time or two, so he'd know the meaning of the word."

"He was our only son," Alexander snaps back, his face purpling. "And now he's—"

Vic cuts him off with a scoff. "I highly doubt you care all that much about him. It's the *legacy* you're mourning, isn't it? The fact that he was your only heir. You didn't care about him as a person. None of you know what it means to care about someone as a person."

Something passes over the older man's face, making it twist

into an ugly shape. It's easy to tell that Vic is right, although I'm sure Alexander would never admit it. Troy was their only son, and I'm sure they're horrified to hear of his death—but not for the reasons that any good parent would be.

As if he's just had the same thought I did, Malice snorts.

Alexander hears the noise and whips his head toward Mal, nostrils flaring as he glares at him. "You wouldn't know a legacy if it slapped you in your face," he spits. "Don't presume to judge me."

Malice's smile is more a baring of teeth, like an animal about to bite. "I was judging you long before this moment, don't worry about that."

Stella still looks stunned, shaking her head as she clutches her husband's arm. She hasn't shed a single tear though, and it just proves even more strongly that these rich families are mercenary and heartless. They try to talk down to us, acting like we're not even worthy of breathing the same air as them. But at least we take care of our own, for reasons that have nothing to do with money.

And they're about to find that out.

Alexander doesn't seem to want to take his chances with Malice, understandably, so he turns on Willow instead. He takes a step forward, eyes narrowed at her.

"You will regret this," he hisses. "I knew you were going to be a poison as soon as my son brought you up. I thought that perhaps the part of you that had Stanton blood would be enough, but I see the trash won out. I will make your life a living hell for what you've done to my family. I'll ruin you. I'll *destroy* you."

Willow doesn't so much as flinch back away from him, but I can sense the way she tenses under the onslaught of his vitriol. I wonder if it reminds her of Troy, and it takes everything in me not to lay Alexander flat on his back with a single punch.

Vic steps up this time, his face neutral but his eyes burning. "You should be careful what you say next, Mr. Copeland," he murmurs.

"Excuse me?" Alexander's voice rises, and he tamps it down to a strained whisper as he grits out, "Don't think you can threaten me."

"It's not a threat. Not really. More of a warning. You should watch what you say and do."

"And why is that?"

Vic shrugs. "Because thanks to our connection with his widow, I have access to several of Troy's protected files. Files that show things I very much doubt the Copeland family would want brought to light."

Stella narrows her eyes at him, shaking off some of her shock. "Just what are you implying?"

"That your family isn't as clean as you'd like to pretend you are. And if you come after Willow or me and my brothers, we'll reveal that fact to the world," Vic says. "I can destroy your reputation in this city with the push of a button. And you're not going to stop Willow from taking what's owed to her either."

"What do you mean?" Alexander demands, his gaze flying from Vic to Willow. "Nothing is owed to her! Not from us."

Willow lifts her chin as she faces down her raging in-laws. She looks like a fucking boss-ass bitch in her gold dress, standing strong and tall like a queen, and I can't tear my gaze away from her.

"Before Troy died, he signed everything over to me," she tells them. "I was already legally owed a portion of his estate as his widow, but I guess he wanted to make sure I would be truly taken care of." Her voice twists a little on those last few words, and I can hear the weight of her trauma behind them. Then she clears her throat and adds, "So he left everything to me. Including his money and his place on the board of your company."

There's near pin-drop silence in our little circle as she lets them take that in, and then Troy's parents explode.

"Absolutely not!" Stella hisses, practically vibrating with rage. "You must be out of your mind if you think we are going to allow this. You're nothing! You're no one, and you have no right to—"

"You will regret this," Alexander cuts in, a sheen of sweat

covering his brow. "You little *bitch*. I know you're responsible for this. You and your... men must have killed Troy."

Malice shakes his head. "We're just the messengers. We don't know how it happened. Lots of weird shit goes on in the backwoods. We were never seen around there."

A grin tugs at my lips, although I don't let it take over. Malice's words are a subtle nod to all the work Vic did making sure that there's absolutely no evidence connecting us to Troy's death. The house was decimated, leaving no fingerprints and nothing more than a pile of ash and bones, and there's no footage that could possibly tie us to that location. All the reasons that Troy was so hard to find played into our favor when it came time to end him. There was no one around to witness his violations of Willow, but that also means there was no one to witness us murdering him.

The Copelands will never be able to link us to Troy's death, and Malice is making sure they know that.

Alexander is fuming, his hands clenched into fists at his sides. His face is red, and the sheen of sweat on his forehead has turned to beads that are trickling down his temples. He's probably never been in a physical fight in his fucking life, but right now he looks like he wants to punch someone in the face.

Stella stares off at the cityscape in the distance, which is clearly visible from our rooftop vantage point. Her face crumples a little, like it's finally hitting her that her son is dead and not coming back. A few wrinkles manage to form despite all the Botox I'm sure she's been pumped full of, and it makes her look older, probably closer to her actual age.

"Troy..." She makes a little noise, covering her mouth with her hand again. "I can't believe it. My boy."

"Oh, don't give me that shit," I snap. I move closer to her, suddenly even more pissed off by the first real hint of sadness I've seen from her all night. "Don't act like he was some innocent little boy who got caught up in the wrong shit. You raised a fucking monster. Whether you knew who he was on the inside or just turned a blind eye to it, your son was a piece of shit."

135

She looks taken aback, her eyes wide, but I'm not fucking done. All the helpless rage I felt when I watched Willow be snatched away in that Jeep, or when we burst into Troy's cabin and found her naked on the floor, is surging out of me, finally given a release.

"She's worth more than all of you," I growl. "And it's about fucking time you realize she's not someone you can step on. She's not your pawn. Now she's playing on the same level you are, with the same kinds of resources you all like to throw around. The only difference is, she has the three of us to back her up."

Olivia and the Copelands are all staring at us, stunned looks on their faces. I know they'll rally soon enough and start trying to find some way out of this corner we've boxed them into, but like Alexander said, this isn't the time or the place. Hell, they probably won't even publicly acknowledge that their son is dead tonight, since it would ruin the optics of their party.

So for tonight, there's nothing they can do except glare at us like they're trying to burn us alive with just their eyes.

Willow reaches down, giving my hand a squeeze. I can feel the slight tremor in her hand from all the adrenaline that must be coursing through her, but her voice is steady as she speaks again.

"You did this, you know," she says quietly, addressing her grandmother. "I never wanted to be part of your world, not once I realized what it was truly like. I asked you—*begged* you—to let me go, and if you had, I'd be long gone with my men by now. You never would've seen me again. Never would've had to deal with me. But you insisted I become part of your world." She takes a breath, and the gold of her dress gleams as it shifts a little. "So now I am. I have everything Troy once had, and I intend to use it. I'll see you at the next board meeting."

With that, she releases my hand and turns on her heel to leave.

Malice, Vic, and I follow right behind her, more than ready to be done with this place. But before we can get far, Olivia jerks herself out of her frozen state and rushes toward us. She grabs Willow's arm, yanking her granddaughter around to face her.

"You've impressed me," she says, although it's definitely not pride glinting in her hazel eyes. "I didn't know you had it in you to be so devious. So gutsy. But you'll never survive in this world."

I move in, putting myself between Olivia and Willow, making her let go of Willow's arm or risk me doing it for her.

"I wouldn't be so sure about that," I snap. "I've never known anyone like Willow. She's a goddamned warrior. And if you'd paid enough attention, you would've known that too."

Malice growls under his breath in agreement, and Vic nods. The three of us close ranks around Willow, blocking her from view of her grandmother as we make our way toward the elevator, and I can tell from the whispered voices around us that despite Olivia's and the Copelands' best efforts to keep their masks of polite civility in place, everyone here knows that some shit just went down.

Good. Because we're just getting started.

16

WILLOW

We pile back into the elevator, and I can feel the attention of everyone at the party on us, watching as we step inside. It makes my pulse race, being this on display, but I try not to let it rattle me —at least, not outwardly.

I keep my head high, my shoulders back, and Malice punches the button for the floor we want, letting the elevator doors slide closed.

Once we're out of view of everyone, I let out a small breath of relief, but for the most part, we all stay quiet. We did what we came to do, but until we're out of the building, it won't feel safe to relax.

The guys stick close to me, keeping me surrounded as if the three of them are some kind of human shield.

We walk out of the building, passing by the valet station and heading toward the car. I can feel the tension building in the air between us as we reach it, all the unspoken words we've been holding inside since we left Olivia and the Copelands behind bubbling up.

Vic opens one of the back doors for me, and I duck inside the car, sliding across the seat to let him climb in beside me. Ransom and Malice are up front, Malice behind the wheel like he usually prefers to be, and as soon as all the doors slam closed, Ransom tips his head back and lets out a wordless sound of victory.

"Fuck yes!" He clenches one hand into a fist, his eyes blazing with accomplishment and pride. He's practically bouncing on his seat with adrenaline. "Did you see their faces? You were so fucking incredible, angel."

"Of course she was," Malice chimes in, shoving the key into the ignition. "She's a fucking queen, and now they're all going to know it."

Ransom chuckles, shaking his head like he's enjoying reliving every moment of our confrontation. "Fucking Olivia with her smug face when she called the cops. Like she just knew she was going to get to see us dragged away. Too bad for her she's not the only one who knows how to blackmail."

"That was a particular high point," Vic agrees, smiling a little.

"And you were right. This was the perfect place to confront her." Ransom cranes his neck a little to look back at us. "Two birds with one stone. We got to deliver the news to the Copelands that Troy the fucking rapist is dead, and make sure they know that we've got dirt on them we'll use if they try to stop Willow from claiming what's rightfully hers. Fucking brilliant."

Malice, in true Malice fashion, cuts in to refocus everyone before the celebrations can go on too long.

"Yeah, yeah, it was great," he says as he pulls out onto the street. "But we need to stay on our guard. We just pissed them the fuck off, and I doubt they're going to let that shit go easily. We don't know what move they're going to make next."

"He's right," Vic replies, nodding. "We can't get overconfident now."

"I know, I know. I just want to savor the victory for a bit," Ransom says, but he gets more serious.

I listen to them past the rushing in my ears, my entire body buzzing like a live wire. There's so much leftover adrenaline coursing through me from everything that just happened that I feel like I could jump out of the car, sprint back to the hotel, and still manage to beat the guys there. Seeing Olivia was terrifying, but it was freeing in a way too.

I'm committed now.

Olivia knows Troy is dead and that I have access to his money and his shares of his family's business. The chance to try to slip away and run from my grandmother has passed, and I'm glad, in a way. Running was never going to be a permanent solution. Even if we managed to evade her, which would've been difficult, I would've spent my whole life looking over my shoulder. I couldn't live like that.

So I'm in this now, until the very end.

As Malice drives, the four of us talk, hashing out what comes next in our plan to get my life back.

"The only downside of leveraging Troy's assets is that now you'll have to get involved with his family's company." Ransom makes a face. "I hate the idea of you being around those fuckheads any more than you have to."

"It's necessary," Vic says, reaching across the seat to take my hand. It's a simple gesture, but from him, even the smallest touches always means so much. "I know it won't be pleasant, but you made Troy sign all of that over to you for a reason."

He looks over at me as he finishes speaking, and I nod. "I did. I have no idea how to navigate all of that stuff, but I know I have to do it."

"Don't worry. I'll help you prepare for it. I have all the information we're going to need. And if I don't, I can find it."

I smile at Vic, always grateful for his help and his diligence.

"Do you think Olivia will try to make a move before the next board meeting?" Ransom asks.

"What can she do?" Vic replies. "We've bought ourselves some time while she tries to untangle how badly she fucked up here, so I think we should be okay for the moment."

We're in as good a position as we can be, but Malice is right. We can't let our guards down. Still, it is nice to have finally won something against Olivia. After months of her having the upper hand, calling all the shots, leaving us to scramble and try to figure out what the next step is, we've finally hit her where it hurts.

Hopefully we can keep it up.

We get back to the hotel and pile out of the car, then head inside. The front desk guy looks at us curiously, taking in our outfits and the way the guys all cluster around me, but he doesn't say anything as we head toward the stairs.

On the second floor, Vic lets us in. As I step through the door, something odd catches my attention. It's a nondescript cardboard box, big enough to hold a good amount of stuff, and it's pushed up against the side of one of the beds.

It looks innocent enough, but my heart rate jacks up at the sight of it. Is this something from Olivia or the Copelands? Some move they're making already? And if so, how the hell did they get it here while we were out? Even *they* can't move that fast, can they? My head swims with possibilities, each more horrifying than the last, and Malice glances at me with concern.

"Solnyshka? What's wrong?"

Taking a step forward, I point to the box. "What is that? Is it from Olivia or Troy's parents? Could they have—"

I break off as a strange look passes over Malice's face. He almost looks a little abashed, but that can't be right. I've never seen that expression on his face before.

He clears his throat, looking from the box back to me. "Oh, that. It's not from them."

"How do you know?"

"Because it's from me. I ran out earlier while you were getting ready."

He walks over and nudges the box closer to me with his foot, and when I stare at it in confusion, he rubs the back of his neck and lets out a sigh.

"It's for you. I... just open it."

He hefts the box, which looks fairly heavy, setting it down on the bed. Still having no clue what's going on here, I sit down beside it and pull open the flaps at the top. My eyebrows shoot up as I examine the contents inside.

Books.

Lots of books.

I pick one up and turn it over so I can see the cover, then glance up at Malice. "Romance novels?"

He nods. "Yeah. They're for you to read, if you want."

"But... why?"

Now he really does look bashful, and it's so interesting to see this expression on his usually so harsh and determined face.

"Our mom used to really like them," he explains, running a hand over his jaw. He shaved for tonight, so his scruff is gone. "And when we asked her why, she said it was because they always had a happy ending. No matter what shit the main characters went through, they always ended up together and happy in the end. So she could read them with no stress, I guess. It helped her because in her job, she saw a lot of death and pain. And our dad was a piece of shit, so maybe she used it as an escape from that too."

His voice turns a little rough as he talks about his mom, and without even meaning to, I drop my gaze to his arm. The tattoo of her name—Diana—curves over his upper arm, hidden by his shirt at the moment, but I know it's there.

"Anyway," he continues, "I thought maybe you'd like them for the same reasons she did. Not to escape us, but as something with a guaranteed happily ever after at the end. After what happened to you, I just wanted you to remember that... good things exist."

"Oh." A lump fills my throat as his words wash over me, and that's all I can get out at first. I turn the book over in my hands, touched more than I know how to say. "Thank you."

He shrugs again, his dark gray eyes locked on me. "I know you've been going through a lot, so I just wanted to help. I'm not as good with the talking about shit."

"You're better than you think," I tell him, remembering our conversation a few days ago after I woke up from that nightmare.

One corner of his mouth twitches upward in a smile, and we

gaze at each other in silence for a moment. Then Ransom chuckles, breaking the moment.

"Vic, remember when Mom got that new book, and it went missing before she could finish it?" he asks.

"I remember."

"We all thought Dad took it just to be an asshole, but now I'm wondering if maybe..." He trails off with a significant look at Malice.

Vic smiles, amusement sparking in his sharp blue eyes. "Anything's possible, I suppose. And Malice does seem to know an awful lot about the structure of a romance novel."

Malice's face shifts from warm and possessive to annoyed in less than a second. "Because I asked Mom," he grunts. "Fuck off."

"We're just saying," Ransom comments, decidedly not fucking off. "There's no shame in it if you wanted to read a good story back then. If you wanted to dream about being some dashing hero."

"It's really very sweet," Vic agrees. There was a time when he might not have joined in the teasing, but now he banters right along with Ransom, arching a brow at his twin. "You could go for the high drama of one of the old school books. Shirt ripped open, hair blowing in the wind."

"I hate both of you. I hope you know that."

Malice flips them off, but there's not much heat in his voice. I've seen the three of them give each other more shit than this, but there's always an underlying layer of love to it. They poke at each other, but it's only because they're so familiar with each other, and it always makes me smile.

Ransom slaps a hand to his chest as if he's been mortally wounded. "Ouch. Hating your own brothers isn't very romance novel hero of you, Mal. I guess you only show your soft side for Willow, is that it? Everyone else gets 'I'll fucking kill you,' but Willow gets 'I got you these books about loooove'."

He stretches that last word out and makes a starry-eyed face, batting his eyelashes like mad.

Vic chuckles, and Malice snatches up a pillow from the bed and whacks it into Ransom's face, making him grunt.

I laugh along with Vic, amused by their banter, but I clutch the book to my chest, already looking forward to starting it. It's a bit silly, but I do really like the gift. And the intent behind it.

Malice got me these books because he wants to help me heal, and he thought it might help.

I still hate that a part of me feels broken, like I've lost some part of myself that I was finally starting to embrace, but I'm starting to realize that as intense as sex with the guys has always been, they love me for so much more than that. I'm finally coming to accept that I can count on them to be there for me no matter what, and that nothing could make them abandon me.

This gesture from Malice is so out of character for him, and I wonder if he chose the books at random or picked out ones he remembered his mother reading. Either way, it shows another side of him that I haven't seen yet, and I like that too.

"Malice," I murmur, getting his attention again. He stops beating up on Ransom with a pillow immediately and comes over to me.

"Yeah, Solnyshka?"

"Thank you. Really." I lean up and give him a little kiss at the corner of his mouth.

It's light enough that it doesn't make me feel jittery inside, but judging from the way Malice smiles, it's enough. He catches my hand with his, stroking his thumb over my knuckles. I can feel the callous on the pad of his thumb, just a little rough, and it helps settle me even more.

"You're welcome," he murmurs. "I just... wanted to do something."

"You did. Even before this, I mean. You saved me."

"I know, but—"

He breaks off, frustration clouding his features. I can see in his eyes all the things he wants to say. That I should never have been taken in the first place. That all of this should never have happened.

I squeeze his hand, and he sighs, drawing me closer so I can rest my forehead on his chest. We stay like that for a few minutes, just taking comfort in each other.

"*Ty zasluzhivaesh' schastlivogo konca, Solnyshka,*" he murmurs in Russian. "*Ya dam tebe ego ili umru, pytajas'.*"

I let the unfamiliar words wash over me, the sound of my nickname mixed in with them. I'm tempted to ask him what he just said, but I don't really need to. I can feel the emotions through the words, and there's something comforting about hearing him speak Russian to me.

We pull back after another moment, and Malice gives me a little smile. Just a quirk of his lips. But it's good enough.

"We should get some sleep," Vic says, glancing from his brothers to me. "It's been a long day, and we have a lot to do to get ready for the next stage of our plan."

Ransom yawns, tossing the pillow Malice was hitting him with back on the bed. "Yeah, good call. I'm wiped."

Now that he mentions it, I'm also pretty tired. I smother a yawn and then move away from Malice to change out of the dress. At first, I start to head toward the bathroom to do it, but then I hesitate. Biting my lip, I plant my feet, remaining right where I am.

I pull the zipper down and shimmy out of the dress, making the gold material shimmer under the overhead light. I can feel the men all watching me, their eyes lingering on my tattooed, scar-marked skin as I bare it. I don't even have a bra on, just a pair of panties, and being this bare in front of them makes heat dance down my spine.

For the first time in a long time, there's no rush of nausea after it.

Part of it is because I know I can trust them to not touch me when I don't want them to, and part is something I can't quite define. Maybe it was confronting my grandmother tonight and telling her and the Copelands that Troy is dead. Maybe that made

145

it feel more real to me—the fact that he's truly gone. Or maybe it's because I reclaimed a little bit of my power tonight.

Either way, I'll take the progress.

I pull an oversized shirt over my head and go get comfortable in one of the beds while the guys change and use the bathroom and do their nightly routines.

Ransom slides into bed with me, wiggling around to make himself comfortable. I pick up the book from the nightstand and crack it open, ready to dive into it.

I'm a few pages in when I feel the mattress dip a bit. I look up to see Ransom peering over my shoulder, trying to get a peek.

"Skip ahead to the good bits," he murmurs, waggling his eyebrows.

"The good bits?"

"You know, when the hero rips his shirt open or something. That's what they always do, right?"

I give him a deadpan look, and he laughs, reaching over to try to take the book and find the 'good parts' himself.

"Nuh-uh, this isn't for you," I say teasingly, hiding the book from him behind my back.

Ransom pouts, sliding his tongue piercing between his teeth. "Oh, I see how it is. Only Malice gets to read the romance novels. I'm crushed, angel."

"You should have stolen Mom's like he did," Vic says, emerging from the bathroom. "It's not Willow's fault you missed the opportunity."

"If you two don't shut the fuck up..." Their brother grumbles under his breath, getting into the other bed. He punches the pillow down and makes himself comfortable.

"That's not very dashing romance hero of you, Malice," I point out, giggling a little as he shoots me a dark, hungry look.

Vic and Ransom laugh, and Malice just reaches out to turn off the light, apparently deciding to ignore us all.

I nestle down, pulling the covers up to my chin and settling even deeper into my pillow. Ransom is still chuckling beside me, his body warm and solid behind mine, not quite touching but close enough that I can feel the heat coming off him. Malice mutters something to which Vic replies quietly, and the sounds of them all around me soothe something deep inside my soul.

I feel more whole with them, like this, than I have in what feels like a very long time.

17

WILLOW

THE NEXT MORNING, I wake up in a cold sweat.

My heart is pounding, and my jaw is clenched hard from the effort of trying not to scream. The details of the nightmare are already starting to trickle away, but there's a sick feeling of dread in my stomach that tells me what it was about anyway.

I lie on my back, glaring up at the ceiling, letting frustration wash away the helpless feeling. It's not much better, but I'm just so tired of these fucking dreams about Troy. I'm tired of having to relive what happened to me when he held me captive, and even if I can't remember everything about the nightmares, the real life memories are still vivid enough to fill in the blanks.

Even after standing up to Olivia and making the choices to take my life back, I'm still weighed down by this shit, and it's exhausting.

"Hey."

I jump a little, turning my head to see Ransom staring at me in the dim light of the hotel room. His face is soft with sleep, and it's clear he knows I was having a nightmare.

"Sorry," I mumble. "I didn't mean to wake you up."

He shakes his head, reaching out to tuck a piece of sweat dampened hair behind my ear. "I'd rather be awake so I can make

148

sure you're okay than sleep while you're suffering. I was about to wake you up if you didn't come out of it yourself."

I swallow hard, trying not to feel guilty about my shit keeping Ransom awake. I know he means what he says, that he'd rather be there for me, but part of me wishes it didn't have to be like that.

"Fucked up from nightmares and covered in sweat this early in the morning," I mutter ruefully. "This isn't very queen-like, is it?"

Ransom grins, shaking his head again. "Only to people who don't know what a real queen looks like. You're more regal than ever, angel."

I don't know how he can say that, but he seems sincere, so I just roll with it. I know I'm not going to get back to sleep now, not after being woken up like that, but before I can roll over to see what time it is, Vic's alarm goes off on the other side of the room.

"Fuckin'—shut it off," Malice grumbles, his face buried in his pillow. "Goddammit."

Vic silences the alarm, sitting up and stretching. "It goes off at the same time every fucking morning, Malice. Stop whining."

"*You* stop..." Whatever else Malice was going to say is lost to the depths of the pillow as he trails off.

Vic is the first one out of bed, like he usually is in the mornings. I know he's been trying to stick to his normal routine as best he can, up early and getting right to work after making coffee in the little machine provided by the hotel.

It's harder when he's sharing a room with his brothers, since they tend to grumble about being woken up.

There's a heavy thud, and then Vic curses. "Dammit! Ransom, for the hundredth damned time, stop leaving your shoes in the middle of the floor. There's a place for shoes, and it's not right in front of the bed. You're not even sleeping in this bed."

He mutters more words under his breath as he aligns the shoes neatly under the fall of the bed skirt.

"It's not that big a deal, Vic," Malice says, finally sitting up and scrubbing a hand through his dark hair.

"That's what you said about the towel on the bathroom floor," Vic mutters darkly.

"I left it there for one second," Malice argues back.

"And that's one second too long."

Ransom chuckles. "He's got you there, Mal. See, Vic? I bet my shoe thing doesn't seem so bad compared to a wet towel."

Malice grunts unintelligibly, and Vic just rolls his eyes and strides toward the bathroom the way he does every morning. He always likes to get in there before his brothers can mess up all of his organizational systems.

"You won't have to deal with our shit for that much longer," Ransom says, stretching as he swings himself out of bed. "You can have your own room soon and micromanage it to your heart's content."

Vic stops in the bathroom doorway, making a face at that. "As much as I want to be rid of your mess, I don't want to miss sleeping with Willow."

His words are straightforward and honest, and I grin, touched by how he says it.

We've come such a long way from him not even wanting me around. Back then, I never would've thought he'd be willing to put up with Ransom's shoes and Malice's towels and the mess of four people sharing a small room, just to get the chance to sleep next to me.

But here we are, and it doesn't feel strange to see Vic want that anymore. Knowing how far he's come—how far we've come together—gives me hope that maybe I can get to a better place too. No matter how hard it is.

Vic had years of trauma holding him back, and he's managed to change and grow, so surely I can too.

A natural order has sprung up in the time since I've been here with the brothers. Vic always goes to the bathroom first, and Malice puts the coffee on, filling the little room with the scent of the dark roast blend all three of them can agree on. Once Vic is done, I go in, brushing my teeth and hair, washing my face, getting dressed. Then Ransom, then Malice.

Vic arranges things for housekeeping, and we sip coffee and get ready for whatever will be happening that day.

Today is a bit different though, because instead of making a plan to go out or do recon or whatever, we start packing up all our stuff.

As part of our plan to stand up to Olivia, I'm essentially taking over Troy's life. All the things we forced him to sign over to me are mine now, and I'm claiming them.

Thanks to Vic's help, I have access to his family's company, access to his money and assets, and even access to his properties. So now it's time to start taking advantage of that. Instead of the four of us living out of this dingy hotel, we'll be moving into Troy's penthouse in the city.

My penthouse now, I guess.

With his access to Troy's laptop, Vic has gotten all the info about the penthouse, and he filled us in on it. It wasn't Troy's main house, just somewhere he stayed when he happened to need a place to crash in the heart of the city. The house where he spent most of his time is in a wealthy, residential neighborhood, but even though it's bigger than the penthouse, there's no way I could live there. It would feel too much like *Troy*. Too much like the place he kept me captive in out there in the woods.

It doesn't take us long to pack, since none of us have much. We've had to abandon everything and run more than once, and I can't help the twinge of pain in my heart as I realize that pretty much all of our worldly belongings are in this small hotel room.

When we finally pile into the car with everything packed tightly in the trunk, Vic gives us the rundown once more.

"It should be fully furnished," he says, looking back from his usual spot in the front passenger seat. "As far as I can tell, Troy bought it furnished, so unless he threw everything out, we should have what we need."

"Hopefully that means it won't be too hard to settle in."

Ransom grimaces, leaning back in the seat beside me. "I don't want to even think about how Troy would decorate a place on his own."

"Probably all pretentious shit. Ugly ass art pieces and shitty furniture," Malice grunts. "Fuckers like him have no taste."

The building itself is industrial and cold looking. It stretches up several stories, barely looking any different than the office buildings that loom on the skyline in the heart of the city.

There's a doorman who watches us with curious eyes as we walk into the building and head for the elevator, but when we put in the code to be let in and then up, he doesn't say anything.

We go all the way up to the fifteenth floor, stepping out of the mirrored elevator onto a completely quiet hall. Troy actually owned the top two stories of the building, so the floor below ours is currently unoccupied. The penthouse is the only residence on the top floor, and the plush carpet muffles our footsteps as we make our way to the door.

"Here you go, angel." Ransom hands me the key they took before they burned Troy's cabin down. "You want to do the honors?"

I take the key from him and twist it in the lock, and the door swings open, granting us entrance to the penthouse.

The inside matches the outside, for the most part.

The appliances are all shiny and silver, gleaming almost like new in the overhead lights. There's a marble island separating the living room from the kitchen, with leather covered barstools pushed up to it.

"Big kitchen, at least. I bet Vic is already planning all the meals he's gonna make in here," Ransom teases.

"And deciding which cabinets I'm going to claim before the two of you can destroy them," Vic mutters back, making me grin.

In the living room, a long leather couch takes up most of the space. There's a thick white rug under the glass-topped coffee table, and the couch is pointed toward a massive flat screen TV built into the wall.

We walk the whole place together, checking it out and

poking our heads into each room. There are two bathrooms, both fully decked out with elaborate showers and double sinks. One has a huge tub as well, sitting right under the window that runs the length of the wall. There are four bedrooms—three normal sized, and one massive one, which one of the bathrooms is attached to.

Once we've done a sweep of the whole place, the guys split up, each of them taking a section.

There aren't a lot of Troy's personal belongings here, making it clear that he truly didn't spend a lot of time living here. It's a relief knowing this isn't a place where we're going to have to deal with lingering traces of him, and the guys take it one step further, even.

They go around with big garbage bags, filling them up with everything that was Troy's personally. His clothes from the closet and dresser, his toiletries, anything that could remind me of him.

"It's your place now," Malice says as he passes by with another full bag. "His shit can go in the fucking dumpster."

I smile softly, grateful to them for this. I don't want reminders of Troy here. Not when I have enough of those in my head already. At least this isn't a place Troy ever held me captive, so there are no horrible memories like that.

"We're trashing the bed," Ransom says when the guys are done taking stuff down to the dumpster behind the building, not trusting the trash chute. "You should get the big bedroom, angel. Since it's your place now."

"Where are you guys going to sleep?" I ask, glancing at them.

"There are enough other rooms for us. And you shouldn't have to sleep in a bed that fucker ever touched."

I chew on my lip, not sure how to pose what I want to say. But luckily, Vic speaks up before I have to figure it out.

"I already said I don't want to have to sleep apart from Willow," he says, shaking his head. "We've played the game of picking and choosing who gets to sleep with her on a given night long enough."

"What are you suggesting then?" Ransom asks.

"One big bed," Malice answers, speaking for his brother. "Big enough for all of us." He glances at me. "If that's okay with you."

I nod, a broad smile blooming on my face. "Yeah. I love that. I like the idea of having you all close. Can you guys handle having to sleep in the bed together?"

Vic shrugs, his blue eyes meeting mine. "Malice snores, and Ransom is a clinger, but it won't be the worst thing in the world."

"I don't fucking snore," Malice shoots back.

"Yes, you do," Ransom and Vic say in unison.

"And sometimes you even talk in your sleep," Ransom adds. "Usually, it's threats."

"I'm gonna threaten you in a minute," Malice mutters under his breath. "We have shit to do."

Ransom's still laughing as we head out of the penthouse and back down to the car. Now that we're going to live here, the place needs to be stocked with stuff. The guys lost most of their shit between their warehouse burning down and fleeing to Mexico, and pretty much all of my stuff is gone too. So it's a good excuse to go shopping.

With a pang, I remember going shopping with Olivia, back when I thought she was going to be something good in my life. I remember her encouraging me to get the finer things, talking me out of cheap sheets and bad furniture.

But I push that away. This is different.

For one, the guys make it a lot more fun. They bicker between themselves as we walk around store after store, picking things out. Vic buys all new kitchen stuff, delighted with the idea of arranging things to his liking and starting fresh in a kitchen he can make his own.

We get a new bed and frame, a massive California King that will have to be delivered. Picking out sheets for it is another journey, with Vic lecturing us about how thread counts don't really mean anything.

"Feel that," he says, holding out a package of sheets to me. I rub my fingers over the ones on top and make a face at how rough they are.

"I hate those," I tell him.

"Those are supposedly high thread count, Egyptian cotton sheets. They cost more than a cheap mattress."

"Okay, but what about these?" Ransom asks, holding up some satin sheets in a bright red color.

Vic just gives him a look and Ransom laughs, putting the sheets back.

In the end, we settle on some that are a nice crisp gray color, and soft enough that I want to wrap myself up in them. We get new pillows, new comforters, new everything.

We pick out end tables, and once it's clear that we're using Troy's money to pay for all of this, Ransom throws in a new gaming system too.

"May as well use that big-ass TV for something," he says with a shrug.

It's a long afternoon of shopping, and we head back to the penthouse in high spirits. The prospect of getting it all up to the top floor is a little daunting, but even that can't quite snuff out the spark of excitement I feel at having all this new stuff. It's stuff I picked out myself, stuff Troy has never touched before. That means a lot right now.

We take turns heading up to the apartment with loads of our new purchases, Malice doing most of the heavy lifting, with Vic supervising and Ransom bringing up the rear.

I grab a few of the lighter bags of stuff, and then turn around to see someone familiar heading toward me on the sidewalk. The guys are upstairs, and for a second, my breath catches.

Joshua.

I haven't even really thought of him since that date we didn't go on, and it feels like so long ago now.

"Willow?" he asks, smiling uncertainly. "Hey, I thought that was you."

"Oh, hi," I reply, feeling awkward and unsure how to navigate this conversation.

Unlike Troy, Joshua always seemed like a perfectly nice guy. He was nice enough in our few interactions, just... not my type. I never felt anything while I was around him, and when he asked me on a date, I mostly agreed just because I was still trying to pretend there was nothing between me and the Voronin brothers. I still wanted to fit into my grandmother's world, and I thought dating a nice, ordinary guy would be the way to do that.

Then Malice put an end to any thought of me going out with him, and it never really got resolved. I never actually told Joshua that I didn't want to go out with him, but I guess me getting engaged to Troy sent the message.

"I'm surprised to see you here," he says, shoving his hands into his pockets. "You know, after everything."

For a split second, I think he knows about how Troy kidnapped me and held me captive, and my heart rate kicks up a notch.

"W-what do you mean?" I ask him.

"Your wedding," he explains. "Pretty much everyone heard about your big wedding to Troy being interrupted and you being snatched right from the altar."

"Oh." I breathe a little easier. That probably *was* big news among the circles people like Joshua travel in. "Yeah, that was... something."

He nods. "But I guess you two got married anyway, right? And now Troy's dead?"

"Yeah, there was a fire at his place up in the woods," I say, which is the truth. "It was a tragedy." Which is a massive, massive lie.

"I'm sorry for your loss. I can't even imagine what..."

Joshua's voice trails off, his gaze flicking over my shoulder.

I can feel the Voronin brothers approaching before I even see them, the three of them moving as a unit to crowd in behind me. They're radiating protective vibes, sizing Joshua up and making it clear that his presence is not wanted.

Joshua's eyes dart from me to the three of them, and when Malice drops an arm around my shoulders, his eyes widen. Something flashes through them, and I can't tell if it's fear or suspicion or what, but he definitely seems even more unnerved.

I get it, in a way. He was just about to offer me condolences on my dead husband, and now three tattooed, dangerous looking men are surrounding me possessively, clearly staking their claim on me. I'm not exactly painting the picture of a grieving widow.

But I don't want to.

It's one thing to not admit to being involved in his death, but it would be another thing entirely to have to pretend to grieve his loss. I've had to lie at various points in my life, and I can do it when the need arises, but I'm not that good of an actor.

"Anyway…" Joshua clears his throat, backing away. "I uh, need to get going. I'll see you around, Willow."

He takes one last look at the guys and then makes his way down the street again, walking faster than he was before.

Malice's eyes follow him until he disappears around the corner, and then the three of them help me with the last of the stuff.

"I don't know who the fuck he thinks he is," Malice grumbles.

"It was fine," I tell him. "We were just talking."

"Yeah sure. Talking. I remember that fucker."

I roll my eyes, going up onto my tiptoes to press a light, placating kiss to his lips. "He's not cut from the same cloth as Troy, at least. When I told him I couldn't go out with him that night, he didn't even do anything. He just accepted it."

"I meant what I said that night. And I'll still do it if I have to."

"Oh, that's the guy you almost went out with." Ransom glances down the street to where Joshua disappeared as he put the pieces together. "I didn't know you went for that type, angel."

His tone is joking, but there's a flare of possessive fire in his eyes.

"I don't," I tell him, stepping closer and resting a hand on his chest. "You know what my type is?"

"What?"

"You." I glance from him to Vic and Malice. "All of you."

"Good answer, Solnyshka." Malice's hand comes to rest on my hip, giving a little squeeze as all three men surround me for a moment. Although Malice and Vic have more similar facial features than Ransom, all three of them look so alike in this moment, wearing nearly identical expressions of possessive heat.

I bite my lip, my heart thumping against my ribs as I let myself relish it for a moment. I can't help but be affected by how deeply they've claimed me. It's intense, but I like it. I like how much they want me.

We break apart after a moment, although I notice that the guys make a point to never leave me outside on my own for even a second after that. It doesn't take long to finish unpacking all of our new purchases, and once the bed gets delivered a little while later, we start putting everything together. Malice and Ransom tackle the task of assembling the bedframe as the huge mattress leans against the wall next to a comfy easy chair we've put in the corner.

I start putting groceries away in the kitchen, pleased that Vic seems to trust me with this task, even if he'll probably rearrange it all later anyway.

My phone buzzes in my pocket a few minutes later, and I pull it out, smiling when I see who the text is from.

Speak of the devil.

Vic's name flashes at the top of the screen. He's somewhere in the apartment, probably setting up his computer in the room he's chosen for his stuff when he's not sleeping with the rest of us.

Even now that we've gotten better at communicating with each other in words, I still like the text conversations we have. It's a reminder that this was the first way we totally let our walls down with each other, somehow managing to bridge the gap that existed between us before.

VIC: Save me a cabinet?

ME: I saved you two. Just for your stuff.

VIC: Perfect. I knew I could depend on you, butterfly.

VIC: And you can always have what's mine.

VIC: But just you. Not my brothers.

I laugh at that, but I feel special too.

ME: I'm almost done in here.

VIC: Good. I'm ready to go over stuff with you.

That last text makes me swallow hard. There will be a board meeting for the Copeland Corporation soon, and I'll have to go to it. I can't claim my place if I don't. It's going to be something completely out of my depth, and Vic promised to help me prepare for it beforehand.

Before I can head down the hall to poke my head into his computer room, Vic comes out with his laptop and settles in the living room on the couch.

I go to join him, sitting next to him.

As if he can sense my nervousness, he puts a hand on my knee and meets my eyes. "You can do this," he tells me. "I've got everything you need."

"I know. I'm just a little anxious. But let's get started."

"Okay."

He gives my knee a small, reassuring squeeze. Then he pulls up a chart on his laptop and begins to speak, laying it all out for me.

18

WILLOW

A few days later, I stand in a parking lot, staring up at one of the many large office buildings that stretch toward the sky in the middle of Detroit.

I've never even been this near to an office building like this before, but I have to go inside. The board meeting is being held up at the top, and my stomach is in knots.

I was barely able to consume anything more than coffee and toast this morning, and now I'm regretting even that as sourness tries to climb up my throat.

But I shove it down, swallowing hard and dragging in a deep breath.

Of course, the guys are with me. They can't go up into the meeting with me, no matter how much I wish they could, but having them here right now is comforting. It's better than nothing, that's for sure.

Malice takes my hand in his, squeezing it lightly. "Remember you deserve to be there," he tells me. "You walked through fucking hell to earn that right. Don't let them intimidate you."

"Right." I nod, squaring my shoulders. "I'm not afraid of them."

"Good." He grins, and it's sharp and savage. "Fuck, I wish I could be up there to watch you take down Olivia. I wanna see the look on that smug bitch's face when you beat her at her own game."

"I'll be sure to describe it to you in detail when I get back," I promise, finally smiling a little.

Malice kisses my cheek, his stubble scraping lightly over my skin, and then Vic moves in.

"Deep breaths," he tells me, and I do the breathing technique I picked up from him. "Good. Remember everything we talked about. You know all you need to know to win this. You've got it."

I nod, smiling when he reaches out to brush his fingers over my wrist. From Vic, in public, that's practically a bear hug, and it goes a long way toward making me feel better.

Ransom dips in next and kisses the corner of my mouth, careful not to smudge my makeup.

"Give 'em hell," he murmurs. "Show those rich fuckers that you're worth a million of them."

"I'll do my best," I whisper back.

All three of them are so confident, so *sure* that I can do this, and I soak it all up, letting it chase away the dread that's been building up in my chest since I woke up this morning. Even if I have to go up there by myself, I won't truly be alone.

So I step away from them, stiffening my spine and moving toward the building's entrance with quick strides.

Even as the distance between us grows, I can feel their support, their love. It's something I'm carrying with me, something nothing can shake.

I've been reading some of the romance novels Malice got for me in my downtime and before bed, and I smile to myself as I step into the cool interior of the lobby of the building. My three men are definitely better than any of the guys in the books I've read so far. More dangerous, but much better.

"Can I help you, ma'am?" the woman behind the front desk asks, looking up from her computer at me.

There was a time when just walking into a place like this would have gotten me thrown out. When it would have been so

161

clear that I didn't belong, in my scruffy clothes, shrinking down to try to hide myself.

Now I keep my expression cool and my head held high. I'm dressed up in the kind of business clothes people wear to these kinds of places, a nice blazer in a dark blue color with a pencil skirt and matching pumps.

I definitely look like someone who goes to important meetings all the time, and the outfit was chosen specifically for that. If I'm going to do this, then I'm going to do it all the way.

I've learned a lot more about this world that my grandmother inhabits since I was first brought into it, and while it won't ever be where I want to belong, I feel less like a fish out of water than before. I'm learning how to function in the upper-class world of wealth, backstabbing, and deceit.

So I walk up to the desk, my heels tapping on the shiny marble floor.

"Yes, hi," I say, smiling at the receptionist. "I'm here for a board meeting with the Copeland Corporation."

"Yes, of course. I'll just need to see your ID."

I pull it out and present it to her, and she nods. "Thank you. Sign in here. It's on the eighth floor. Just take the elevator on the left right up."

"Great."

I sign the sheet she presents me with and then walk to the bank of elevators. Even though I'm alone on the ride up, I maintain my façade of confidence and strength, and when I step off, I keep my gaze fixed straight ahead as I make my way down the hall to the conference room where the meeting is being held.

Of course, as soon as I walk in, all eyes are on me.

Olivia is here, and so are Stella and Alexander, Troy's parents. I don't have to look at them to feel them glaring at me, their fury clear. I'm sure they've been to the burned out wreckage of Troy's cabin by now and confirmed that he truly is dead. But thanks to the dirt Victor dug up on them, they haven't dared to make any moves to stop me from claiming his assets.

162

Although I don't meet their gazes, I let myself look at Olivia briefly, giving her a version of her own polite, empty smile. I'm turning her own tactics back on her, acting calm and sweet on the outside, acting as if everything is fine—and I have to admit, it's satisfying as hell to see the way her lips pinch at the corners in response.

Sweeping past her, I slip into the only empty seat remaining at the table.

Most of the other members of the board look over at me as I settle into the chair, clearly confused about who I am.

"We seem to be missing someone," an older man says. "And we've gained someone new?"

He glances at Troy's parents.

Alexander clears his throat. "This is Willow," he says. "Willow..."

"Copeland," I supply for him, my tone neutral. "Troy's widow."

His nostrils flare, his jaw clenching as low murmurs spring up around the room. Judging by the response from the other board members, I assume that the Copelands must not have announced his death publicly yet. They were probably still trying to decide how best to spin it.

Well, too fucking bad.

"Yes. Troy's widow. My son was... he died recently. In a tragic accident." Alexander's tone is stiff, as if each word is being forced out of him and he hates it. "Willow will be taking over his role in the company and on the board. It's... what Troy wanted."

He swallows hard, and beside him, his wife puts a hand over his on the table. To anyone else, it probably looks like a gesture of support, since they both just lost their son. But I can tell that Alexander's lips are trembling with anger, and his wife doesn't look much happier.

Too bad neither of them have a choice in the matter. I can only imagine that in the days since they were given the news of Troy's death, they've been scrambling to find a way to undo what I did

163

and how I ended up taking over his entire estate. But unluckily for them, our marriage was fully legal. I'm owed a certain portion of his estate anyway due to my status as his wife—and thanks to the papers I made him sign, I got even more than that.

It's all square in the eyes of the law, much like our sham of a 'marriage' was. They could probably take me to court to fight it, but that could end up risking their *entire* estate.

So they're trapped.

Just like I was.

I barely even look at the two of them, meeting the gazes of the strangers around the table instead. Vic did some research on all of them, so I know some basic facts about each one of them. But none of them are my targets here today. That honor belongs to Olivia.

The other board members look surprised, and there are a few murmurs between them as they lean over and whisper to each other, but I don't flinch. I face them down, not wavering, because just like Malice said, I have every right to be here.

I've paid for that right in blood.

"Well, then." The older man—Dexter Carville—clears his throat. "Welcome, Mrs. Copeland. Alexander, Stella, I am so sorry for your loss."

They both nod, and Alexander's voice is tight as he says, "Now that everyone is here, we can begin."

It feels gross being called *Mrs. Copeland*, my skin crawling at the words, but I try not to let it show. That's the role I'm playing today, the part I have to play for this part of the game.

The meeting begins, and as they dive into a discussion of the business, all of it is dry and dull. I don't care about the financials of the corporation or the investment potentials. I only know what Vic and I went over, but I pay attention anyway, listening to all of it since he'll want a full report when the meeting is done.

Multiple people speak, the others nodding along. I hold my tongue and sit patiently, waiting for them to move on to the relevant part.

Finally, Dexter Carville speaks again. "The next order of business is the matter of the construction of the new building this year."

I sit up straighter. *This is it.* This is what I've been waiting for.

"As you all know, we're looking to expand, and we need a new central location to be able to do that smoothly. The building is already designed, and we have the land purchased and ready. There's just the matter of who will be awarded the contract for the work. Mrs. Stanton has suggested Oberon for the construction." He nods to Olivia.

"Yes," she says, folding her hands on the table in front of her. "I do have a stake in this company, but I can assure you that I personally vouch for their work. I've toured their sites, and they've managed to combine efficiency and innovation to a marvelous effect."

"Oberon? I've heard they have a habit of cutting corners to get the work finished on time," one of the women says, glancing at Olivia. "Are we sure we want to entrust such a large contract to them?"

"Their work speaks for itself, Giselle," Olivia replies coolly. "And as part of an... arrangement between Troy Copeland and myself, it has already been agreed upon that the new building contract will go to Oberon."

A rush of hot anger sweeps through me. I already know that the *arrangement* she's talking about is the deal she made with Troy for handing me off to marry him, and I hate that she traded me away like currency just to enrich one of the companies she owns.

But that stops now.

"Actually," I say, speaking up for the first time since the meeting began. "That won't be happening anymore. You made that deal with *Troy*, but I'm here in Troy's place, and I don't agree to award the contract to Oberon."

My grandmother's head whips toward me, her eyes opening wide. If the stakes weren't so high here, I might be amused by the almost comically shocked expression on her face. She shakes her head, her jaw opening and closing a few times before she gets any words out.

"I—you can't—" She presses her lips together, her eyes blazing. "We had a *deal*."

"I know." I smile calmly. "But I'm sure you're very familiar with the fact that deals can sometimes change."

Color rises in her cheeks, and she looks toward Alexander and Stella as if silently urging them to fix this. My stomach twists a little, nerves rising up in me as their gazes meet hers. This is the risky part of our plan. If they side with her, they could ruin my plan.

But my men and I know too much about them for them to risk it. And besides the blackmail we hold over them, there's one added element that I hope will play into my favor: by now, I think they hate Olivia almost as much as they hate me.

She played off of Troy's obsession with me to get the marriage arrangement set up, and even though she had to make concessions as well, she negotiated a pretty sweet deal for herself, nabbing herself a spot on the Copeland Corporation's board and arranging for a lucrative construction project to be awarded to her business, Oberon.

As much as they despise me, Alexander and Stella have some small reason to support me in blocking Oberon being awarded the contract... and no real reason to support Olivia.

So they don't.

Neither of them say a word, refusing to back her up, and silence fills the boardroom for a long, painfully drawn out minute before Olivia makes a choked noise in the back of her throat.

She sits back in her chair, her jaw snapping shut as she stares fixedly across the table, and I have to fight down a triumphant smile.

It's my second win against Olivia, and it feels even better than the first.

"Alright, then." Dexter breaks the silence, nodding once. "We'll go with a different contractor. That can be decided at our next meeting."

They move on to other subjects of discussion, and when the meeting finally wraps up, I drag in a deep breath as I rise from my chair.

Members of the board cast curious looks at me as they gather their things, and I wonder if they're adjusting their initial assessments of me now that I've made my first power play. Maybe they think I picked the wrong battle today, but it doesn't really matter. They don't have any idea of the true war I'm fighting.

As I step out into the hall, fingers dig into my wrist, stopping me short. I turn around to see Olivia gripping my arm, looking furious and red in the face. I allow myself a moment of satisfaction at how her polite mask is shattered in this moment, then give her a cool look right back.

"Let go of me," I say. "Or I promise you, you'll regret it."

It's a sign of how much things have shifted between us that she actually does what I tell her to, snatching her hand back as though she's been burned. But she takes a step closer to me, glaring me down.

"What the hell was that in there?" she hisses.

I cock my head. "What? You didn't like it? You're the one who was so desperate for me to marry Troy. Are you having regrets now? I'm just using the power given to me by marriage."

"You're fucking with something that has nothing to do with you," she fires back.

That stokes the rage inside me that always seems to be simmering these days, and my eyes go wide with disbelief. "Nothing to do with me? Are you kidding?"

"The arrangement for the Oberon deal was between me and Troy!"

"With *me* caught in the middle," I bite out. "You sold me to him like a piece of livestock just so you could get richer. But now Troy's gone, so you'll have to deal with me instead." My lips twist

167

into a bitter smile. "And I'm not feeling very generous toward you at the moment."

Olivia steps back, looking like she wants nothing more than to hit me in the face the way she has before. But we're still in public, and she probably knows I won't just take it anymore, so she finally manages to arrange her face back into the socially acceptable mask she's so good at wearing.

"This was supposed to help me better our family estate," she whispers, her voice harsh. "The Oberon contract would've been instrumental in that. You are completely *ruining* what I set out to do."

I hold her gaze, lifting one shoulder in a shrug. "You should have listened to me when you had the chance."

Something flashes in Olivia's eyes, but I know her well enough by now that I don't mistake it for regret or remorse. She's not capable of those emotions. No, this is more like the furious rage of a trapped animal.

"You're making a big mistake," she says, drawing each word out.

There's a threat clear in her voice, but if she's expecting me to cower and back down, she's in for a disappointment. I'm done with that. I'm done being a pawn for her to use.

So I just gaze into her horribly familiar eyes and let a smile curve my lips. "I would have thought you'd be proud, Grandma," I tell her. "After all, you're the one who taught me how to play this game."

With that, I turn on my heel and walk off down the hall. I don't look back to see if Olivia is following me or watching me leave, because it doesn't matter.

Instead, I just keep going, getting into the elevator and taking it all the way back down to the lobby.

The guys are waiting for me outside the way they promised they would be, talking amongst themselves. Every so often, one of them will look in the direction of the building's doors, and I smile, knowing they're anxious for me to return to them.

When I step out of the cool, air-conditioned building and back into the sunlight, the warmth feels good on my face. All three of the brothers start moving toward me immediately, meeting me halfway as I cross the sidewalk toward them.

"How did it go?" Malice asks, his gaze tracking over my face as if looking for clues.

"Are you kidding? She totally crushed it, I'm sure," Ransom cuts in.

Vic just sighs, keeping his eyes on me. "Let her talk."

I smile at them all, a rush of leftover adrenaline making me feel giddy. "It worked. I fucked up the Oberon deal, and Olivia is pissed. I have a bunch of stuff to tell you later, Vic. I don't understand most of what they talked about in the meeting, but I know you will."

Before I can say anything else, Malice is scooping me up into his arms. He spins me around once and then holds me close, burying his face between my neck and shoulder.

"I knew you could do it," he murmurs, his lips ghosting over my skin. "You can do anything, Solnyshka."

I lean into his solid, muscled body, shivering at the way his touch sends electricity dancing down my spine. It's the closest we've been since he and the others got me back from Troy, and even though my head always seems to ruin things, my body definitely knows what it wants.

I cling to his shoulders a little, swallowing hard as my mouth goes dry. Malice skims his nose over my pulse point and inhales deeply, like he's been craving the scent of me.

His hands are so firm and warm on my back, and when one slides down lower, hovering just over my ass, I gasp softly. It feels good to be this close to him, and since he's not pushing anything, it's not setting off the part of me that's not okay with being touched just yet.

If anything, it's catering to the part of me that is *really* okay with being touched and *really* wants more.

For a moment, there's nothing but the two of us. Nothing but this bubble of heat and approval and want. I'm distantly aware of his brothers, in the way that if they stepped in, the bubble would extend to them as well.

But neither of us push for more, even as the tension cranks up a notch between us. We stay locked in this hug, and Malice presses his body a bit closer, letting me feel that I'm not the only one affected by being this close.

Then he sets me down and steps away, giving me space once again.

I feel bereft at the loss of him, and I'm half tempted to reach out and pull him back toward me... but I don't.

One step at a time, Willow. You'll get there.

As if he can read my thoughts, Ransom moves closer, tugging a lock of my hair between his fingers. The dark color is starting to fade a bit, leaving it a lighter brown, and he tucks it behind my ear, his fingers trailing lightly down my jaw.

"This was a big step," he says. "We're on our way. Now come on, pretty girl. Let's go home."

I nod, and he and Vic each slip a hand into mine. Then we all pile into the car and head back to the condo we've claimed as ours.

19

WILLOW

Buoyed by my success at the board meeting, we spend the rest of the day continuing to work on the plan to take Olivia down. Sabotaging that contract she was counting on was a good start, but it wasn't enough. If I want to truly neutralize her as a threat, we need to absolutely ruin her.

Her estate was already weakened, but we need to make that even worse. She still has a lot of resources, but now that I'm on an even playing field, our goal is to systematically destroy Olivia's business holdings until she has nothing left.

She made the mistake of tying herself to me when she made that deal with Troy... and now that Troy is dead, I can use those ties to fuck with my grandmother in a big way.

I sit in Vic's office, using one of the new computers he brought in as I pore over information about Olivia. This is more research than I've done in a while, but it feels good to be able to do something to contribute to all this. Of course, the guys all have their own grudges against Olivia, but I know that I'm at the center of this for them.

Plus I need to be as prepared as possible for what's to come and what I need to do. But after several hours of staring at the screen, trying to absorb as much information as I can, my eyes are burning and begging for a break.

I sit back from the monitor and rub my eyes a bit, getting up out of the chair and deciding that it's finally time to start using some of the amenities that came with this place.

Namely, that swanky-ass bathtub.

I head out of the office and down the hall. Ransom is in the living room playing something on the TV, and he hits pause when he sees me.

"What are you up to?" he asks, leaning over the couch to give me a smile.

"I need a break," I tell him. "I don't know how Vic manages to stare at screens all day without going a little insane. Or having his eyeballs melt out of their sockets."

He laughs. "It's his super power, I think. That, or he's just immune to the normal burnout shit the rest of us have to deal with. Do you want me to make you a snack or something?"

I shake my head. "Nah, I'm going to break in that bathtub. It's been tempting me ever since we moved in here."

I hesitate for a moment, biting my lip—torn between the thing I want and still being held back by my fears and traumas. I hate that I feel this way, because it makes me feel like the old version of myself, the one I thought I had left behind. The one who was drawn to these brothers so deeply but wasn't brave enough to let herself have them. I've come so far since then, but it feels like I've lost so much progress because of what Troy did to me.

But maybe taking baby steps will help me get it back. Or at least not make things worse.

So I swallow hard and smile at Ransom. "Will you... join me?"

He blinks, his brows climbing up his forehead with surprise, making his piercing glint. "Really? You're sure?"

"Yes."

He gets up so fast that it's like he's been launched off the couch, all thoughts of his game clearly forgotten, and I laugh at how eager he seems.

I lead the way into the bathroom, pleased with how we redeco-rated it.

The tub and separate shower are the same, but we ruined Troy's monochrome nightmare with colorful towels and candles to add some life to the place. It feels much better to be in here now, even if my heart is beating faster than usual.

I'm keenly aware of Ransom as I sit on the edge of the huge tub and start the water running, adding some of the bath oils I picked up on a whim and filling the bathroom with a light citrusy scent.

His eyes are on me, and even though this bathroom is so much bigger than any one we've been in before, it's like his presence makes it feel smaller. And not in a bad way. I can just feel so much of him.

It also brings back memories of the last time we took a bath together—the morning after he and Malice fucked me.

It feels so long ago now, but standing there thinking about it makes it feel like I can feel their hands ghosting over my skin. I shiver agreeably as steam rises up, and then get up to start undressing.

Ransom doesn't take his eyes off of me as I pull my shirt over my head.

I changed into more comfortable clothes when we got back from the board meeting, so it's easy enough to take off the oversized shirt that probably belonged to Malice first, and then shimmy out of the soft cotton shorts and my underwear.

I can't help but look as Ransom takes his clothes off too.

He's so fucking handsome, his tattoos on display as he shucks off the shirt and starts going for his jeans.

Neither of us speak, but we don't have to. We're both too caught up in this moment and everything it's loaded with. The tension cranks up another notch or two as Ransom drags his jeans down, revealing that he wasn't wearing underwear at all.

It's very him, but my cheeks still flare with heat at the sight of it, and I have to swallow hard when I realize he's already hard.

The metal studs in his cock catch the light from the window

over the tub, and it makes my pulse race just that much faster to see it.

Ransom catches me looking and quirks a grin at me. "Sorry. I can't really help it. My dick just likes you a lot."

That makes me laugh, and my cheeks are flushed as the compliment settles over me. We haven't even done anything, but the sight of me naked is still enough to get Ransom hard.

Finally, I tear my eyes away from his naked body and move to get into the tub. Ransom helps me, steadying me as I step in, and then he gets in as well, sitting down with his back against the edge of the tub, leaving room for me to settle against him if I want to.

The tub is large enough that I wouldn't have to, if I wanted my space. I could lean against the opposite edge, and only our legs would be tangled together.

But instead of doing that, I move to lean against his chest, settling between his legs.

The minute my bare back touches his bare chest, something in me seizes up. There's a moment of a tension as the world narrows down to just the feeling of his skin on mine and awful memories of Troy try to break through to the forefront of my mind.

But I remind myself that I'm safe.

I'm not with Troy. I'm with Ransom, and he would never hurt me.

That thought goes a long way toward calming me down, and I take a few deep breaths, relaxing every muscle in turn as I sink into the warm water.

Ransom doesn't rush me. He doesn't move away or move to touch me more, just letting me find my comfort zone. Once I'm no longer stiff and tense, he wraps his arms around me, holding me loosely enough that I don't feel held down, but tight enough that I feel the comfort in it.

I inhale the lemony air around us and then let out that breath, closing my eyes and drifting a bit.

"You were starting to remind me of Vic," Ransom murmurs. "With all that research you were doing in his office."

"There's so much to sift through," I reply, my eyes still closed. "Olivia has her fingers in so many pies, and I need to know about all of it. I understand why rich people have to hire people to handle all their affairs and stuff. There's just so much."

He nods, humming thoughtfully. "It does make a lot of sense. I know Vic would probably volunteer to go through everything and just tell you what you need to know. He likes this kind of stuff."

"I know he does. And I know he would. But it feels like something I need to know myself. She made this so personal when she dragged me into it and tried to take away my life. When she came for you guys. I want it to be personal right back when we ruin her."

He laughs at that, and the sound is low and deep. It sends a shiver down my spine, and this close, I can feel the vibrations in his chest.

"I love how savage you're being about this," he tells me. "She deserves every fucking bit of it. And then some."

"She does." I open my eyes, biting my lip. "And I want her to suffer for everything she did to us. But at the same time..."

"Yeah?" Ransom asks, nudging me a little when I trail off.

"At the same time, I'm just ready for all of this to be over. I'm on her level now, I can play in her world, and I have the resources to take this fight to her, which is great. But I'm so ready to just be done with it. To be free of her, you know? It's nice to not be on the run anymore, but she's still a threat."

Ransom runs a wet hand down my arm, and I can feel him nodding behind me. "Yeah, I get what you mean. We have more leverage, a firmer place to stand than we did before, but it's not the same as not having to deal with her at all."

"Exactly. I guess at least we have a home now."

"There is that. I wasn't gonna complain, but living out of that hotel was so fucking shitty. It was too small, Malice snores like a fucking freight train, and Vic is so particular about where you put your shoes."

I giggle at that, relaxing against him even further. "I hate to break it to you, but the massive bed we got means that you're still going to have to listen to Malice snoring."

He sighs dramatically, but there's such an edge of humor to it that it makes me laugh. "Clearly, I was born just to suffer. Ah, well. Getting to curl up with you makes it worth it."

"Remember you said that."

"I definitely will."

We fall silent for a while, just soaking in the moment. The water is the perfect temperature, and the scent of lemon around us is fresh and soothing. The light streaming in through the window makes patterns on the tiled floor, and I let myself fully relax.

"Do you have ideas for what you want to do once this is all over?" Ransom asks after a bit. "We're not on the run anymore, and we have a place where we can put down roots. At least, for as long as we want to."

I hum, thinking it over. "I'm not really sure. For so long, my plan was just to go to school and get a degree and try to make something of myself. But then I met Olivia, and everything changed." I snort softly. "Well, I guess meeting you three changed things first."

"In a much better way, I hope."

"Definitely. Well, at first, I was convinced you three were going to ruin my life. Or kill me. But instead, it turned into something amazing. I guess my point was that ever since Olivia came along, I haven't really had a chance to think about the next thing. I was dealing with her offering me money and a place in the family. Then she wanted me to get married. Then Misty died. Then Olivia showed her true colors, and everything after that has just been us running from one thing to the next. This feels like the first chance we've had to catch our breaths in a while."

"Mm," Ransom agrees. "It's kind of weird, honestly. But after being chased down and shot at, I'll take a break any way I can get one."

"Hell, yes," I murmur. "What about you? Have you and your brothers talked about what you might want to do once this is all

176

said and done? Without Olivia making your lives difficult as X, you'll have a lot more freedom."

"We're all definitely looking forward to not having to do odd jobs for her anymore, that's for sure. Other than that, I don't know if we have a plan yet. I'm sure Vic has the beginnings of one, at least, because that's how he is, but Malice and I are more in the moment. Just trying to get Olivia off our backs completely before we start planning anything else."

"That makes sense," I whisper, nodding. "I think it would be good if you guys had the chance to mess with cars again. I don't know if that was something you started just because you needed the money at the time, but I know you in particular miss it."

There's a warm huff of laughter, and Ransom's breath ghosts over my skin. His hands move over my sides, making the water ripple around us.

"You know me so well," he murmurs, and I can hear warmth in his tone.

I shrug. "I just remember that it was like your happy place. Where you went when you needed a break. You'd be in the garage messing with your bike or with a car, and you always seemed to enjoy it. I want you to have that again."

"One day," he promises. "And I'll teach you all about it too if you want. You'll be able to rebuild an engine in no time."

A little laugh bursts out of me. "I'm not so sure about that."

"Well, before we ran away to Mexico, you would've said you weren't sure you could ride a motorcycle, right? But you did great."

He does have a point there. I can remember the wind in my hair and the way Ransom rewarded me for learning to ride on my own.

"It was more fun than I thought it would be," I admit. "And less scary."

"See? I know what I'm talking about. When we have room, we'll get bikes. I'll pick out a really nice one for you and teach you more about riding."

I can tell he's excited about that prospect from the way his tone has picked up. He's also touching me more than he was before. His hands glide over my skin, wet and leaving a trail of heat as they go.

His thumb skates over the inside of my elbow, and I shiver a little at the sensation. Somehow over the course of the conversation, he went from barely touching me to letting his hands roam over me in slow, easy patterns. It's old habit, his natural instinct when he's around me.

At first, I didn't really notice it all that much, caught up in the conversation, but now it's like it's all I can focus on, and I swallow hard as his touch starts to affect me, turning me on.

There's still that haze of unease that settles over me, but I don't give it any oxygen, focusing instead on how good his fingers and palms feel on my skin. His touch has always comforted me, even when I didn't want it to, and now it's making me feel wet between my legs in a way that I've missed.

"Ransom," I whisper, his name spilling from my lips.

"Hm?" He sounds languid and content, but then seems to notice what he's doing. "Oh, shit. Sorry, angel. It's just habit. I'll—"

He starts to move his hand away from me, but I reach up and stop him before he can.

I fit my hand over his, and it feels right.

At first, I just leave my hand there, letting it press over his, feeling his touch against my skin. Then I slowly and tentatively start moving his hand downward a bit. I guide it in a caress down my arm and then back up, over my shoulder. I let his fingers feather over my neck and then move them down to my chest.

My tongue darts out, licking my lips, and I pull his hand downward even more, letting it rest against my breast for a second.

"Willow..." Ransom breathes. "You don't—"

"Shhh," I murmur back.

He falls silent, but I can hear the way his breaths are coming faster now, and I can feel the way his heart is racing a little, where his chest is still pressed against my back. His cock twitches, and I'm aware of it against my back, thick and hot.

I guide him to cup one breast and then the other, brushing the calloused pad of his thumb over my nipple. The roughness against that sensitive, damp skin makes my breath catch, and a moan pours out of me before I can help it.

I push his hand harder over my chest, arching as my breast presses into the fullness of his hand.

"Fuck," I whisper, my nipples hardening even more.

Ransom seems content to let me direct this, not pushing for more or letting his hand go anywhere I don't lead it. He groans when I urge his hand down lower, sliding it over the planes of my stomach and then to my thighs.

His cock is rock hard against the small of my back, and I feel it when his hips twitch upward. He doesn't move more than that, and I let out a breath, closing my eyes, focusing on how his hand feels on me.

I let his fingers drag over the scarring on my thighs, not even a little self-conscious about what it must feel like to him. We're past that in every way we can be, and I know my scars don't bother any of my men. They've seen all of me, everything I have and everything I am, and they keep choosing me. They keep wanting me.

"Goddamn," Ransom hisses, and his fingers tighten slightly on my thigh before relaxing. "You have no idea how good you feel, pretty girl. You're so—"

He cuts himself off with a groan, and I swear I can *feel* that noise against my back and between my legs.

My pussy is throbbing now, desperate for attention.

It's been a while since I felt this kind of need, this kind of desire. Those first couple of days after being rescued from Troy's cabin, I wasn't sure if I ever would again. But my body hums with a current of desire, and I slide Ransom's hand down between my legs, letting it press against the heat of my crotch.

He groans again, cursing under his breath, and this time, my hips push up, grinding against his hand.

The friction feels good, but it's not quite enough. Carefully, I press one of his fingers into me, and my head falls back against

Ransom's shoulder when it breaches my entrance. It feels so famil-iar, so right, and I have to remember how to breathe.

"You're so fucking wet," Ransom pants. "You feel so fucking good. I wanna make you feel good, angel."

"You always do," I gasp back.

I work my hips, grinding against his hand for a bit before drawing those fingers up to circle around my clit. I press his hand there, silently urging him to keep going, and then work my own fingers into my soaking wet pussy.

"*Ah!*" My breathy cry echoes around us in the bathroom, and water splashes a bit as I thrust my hips up. It's so good and not enough all at the same time.

"There you go," Ransom murmurs. He buries his face against my neck, breathing hard against my skin. "Take what you need. Did you miss this? Does it feel good?"

I nod, breathless. My fingers work deeper into my pussy, and I add another one, trying to fill myself up to the brim. Ransom's fingers keep drawing circles around my clit, and I gasp in pleasure as it rocks through me.

Slowly, I slide my fingers out of myself and then replace them with Ransom's. His hands are bigger, rougher than mine, and two of his fingers fill me up enough that I'm writhing and bucking in place against him.

My breath comes in short pants, and I can feel the orgasm growing. It's slower than usual, as if it's had to be coaxed out of hiding, but that heat is there, building in my gut and spreading out through me.

Powerful. Undeniable. *Inevitable.*

I moan, gasping Ransom's name, grinding against our hands as he thrusts his fingers deeper, curling them against my g-spot.

"You wanna come?" he whispers. "Then come. You can do it. You're so close. I can feel it. You're safe, pretty girl. I've got you. You can let go."

When the orgasm hits me, I bite down on my lip hard, shaking and arching through it. Ransom lets me keep his hand where it is, and his fingers stroke against my inner walls as they ripple and spasm around him.

A low chant of, "Fuck, fuck, fuck, *fuck*," spills from his mouth, and I can feel his cock throbbing against the small of my back.

Then there's a rush of wetness and heat against my back as his cum jets out beneath the water, his cock pulsing over and over with each spurt. The feel of him coming, even if it's not inside me, is enough to draw out my climax, making me moan roughly as the rush of pleasure crests again.

We're both breathless in the aftermath, leaning against each other while our hearts thud in unison.

After a drawn out moment, Ransom presses a kiss to my bare shoulder.

"Shit. I'm sorry," he murmurs.

My brows furrow as I blink. "For what?"

"For coming like that. This was supposed to be about *you* getting what you needed. I wasn't trying to make it about me or me getting off."

I smile, touched by the way he always finds a way to put me first, to take care of me in big and small ways.

"Don't be sorry," I tell him quietly, wrapping my hand around his. His fingers are still buried inside me, like he's not ready to lose that connection yet. "I liked it. I like that you could get off just from feeling me come. It makes me feel... I don't know. Good. Seen."

I can feel him smile against my skin, and when I tip my head back to meet his lips in a kiss, he meets me halfway.

For once, there's no rush of discomfort, just the warm haze of the afterglow, and I savor this moment. It's like being wrapped up in a cocoon of warmth and safety, and it feels like some of the jagged shards in my heart fall away.

WILLOW

It's several days later when I make my next move against Olivia.

I'm in the living room of the penthouse with Vic, going over all of Troy's assets and his business dealings. Now that I have access to them, it's important that I know what everything is—even if trying to absorb all of this information leaves my head spinning.

Troy's parents have been trying to cut me out a little, but there's only so much they can do when Troy himself set this in motion. Under duress, true. But fortunately, there's no proof of that, and I have witnesses who will say it was all completely voluntary.

"Look at this," Vic says, drawing my attention to the screen of his laptop.

"What am I looking at?" I ask, grimacing as I stare blankly at the figures and charts in front of me.

"I've found another weak spot you can use to kneecap Olivia. See this number here?" He points, and I nod. "That's capital that Troy funneled into one of her businesses. Judging from the date, it looks like it was a part of the agreement when he married you."

I make a face. "So what do we do with it?"

Vic smiles at me, his blue eyes gleaming brightly. He really does thrive when it comes to things like this, and I love to see it.

"You withdraw it. Because Troy's assets are your assets now, you can say where they go. If you don't want them invested in Olivia's business, you only need to pull them out."

I smile back. "What would happen if I did pull them out?"

"Considering these numbers for the last few years, her business isn't doing so great," he explains. "More than likely, the money went to this business in particular to keep it from going under. If you were to remove that support..."

"It would topple like a house of cards?"

He grins. "And quickly, from what I can tell."

"Do it," I tell him, feeling that same surge of savage glee that I felt when I shut Olivia down at the board meeting.

Vic starts the withdrawal process, and I fill in the necessary information on my end. I have to take a breath as I do, my heart racing a little. This is a playing field I've never fought on before, but with Vic's help, I'm doing battle with Olivia in a way that will hit her right at the heart of everything she thinks is important.

"I can't believe I'm doing this," I murmur, shaking my head.

"It's what she deserves," he points out, his voice turning hard.

"No, I know. It's just... I used to not even be able to afford decent food every week once I took care of all the bills that needed to be paid. Now I'm fucking with someone's business to the tune of millions of dollars. It's just wild."

"And I'll keep looking for ways that you can ruin her even more," he promises. "You may as well put all this wealth and status to good use, right?"

I nod, leaning back against the couch. "Right. Thanks, Vic. I'm so glad to have you on my side in all of this."

He flushes a little at that, his face going slightly pink. There's a pleased smile playing around his mouth, and he drops his gaze back to the keyboard of his computer.

"It's nice to be using my skills against her for once," he says. "She exploited them for her own gain for a long time, and it's much more enjoyable to do it this way."

I like seeing this side of him so much. Getting to see all of him.

He's so much more comfortable around me these days, and it makes me feel good to know that he trusts me.

The feeling is mutual.

I would trust Vic with my life.

Once the withdrawal process is started, we turn to the next order of business. My conversation with Ransom in the tub reminded me all over again how important getting my college degree has always been to me. For a long time, it was the only real goal I even had. My desire to stick it out and graduate instead of quitting to help Olivia run her estate was part of what made her reveal her true colors, forcing my hand and blackmailing me into agreeing to marry Troy.

Now that we've decided to stay in Detroit, I want to follow through on that goal—partly for my own satisfaction, and partly as a giant *fuck you* to Olivia, a reminder that she doesn't control my life anymore.

I definitely don't want to continue at Wayne State though. There's just so much baggage at that school for me to ever really feel comfortable there again.

I told the guys my plan to transfer to another school and continue my studies, and they were on board with it. So now all that's left is going to campus to pick up my transcripts so I can apply somewhere else.

All three of the brothers insist on coming with me. None of them are eager to have me out of their sights for long, and I honestly prefer it that way too. We were forced apart for far too long, and it left invisible wounds on all of us. Staying together now helps heal those wounds, at least a little.

We head out after lunch, and they fall into place around me as we head down the hall and to the elevator.

"This will be new," I say, casting a teasing glance at them. "For once, you'll be coming to campus *with* me, not just showing up there because you're basically stalking me."

Ransom belts out a laugh, draping an arm around my shoulder.

Malice snorts and rolls his eyes, but I can see amusement in their gray depths.

It doesn't take long to collect my transcripts once we get to the Wayne State campus, and although the woman behind the desk in the admin office keeps shooting glances at my men, I'm glad they're with me. I don't have many fond memories of this school, and it settles my nerves to feel them at my back.

As we leave the building and head back across campus, Ransom entertains us all by pointing out the various places where I had run-ins with the men, and I'm laughing as we pile inside the car.

But the light mood evaporates when we get back to my inherited condo... and find Olivia waiting for us.

She's standing outside the building, and her eyes lock with mine before Malice even stops the car. My heart starts to beat harder as we get out, and she strides up to us, red in the face and eyes blazing with fury.

Usually, even when she's angry as hell, she looks put together and composed, completely in charge. But now she looks more unkempt than I've ever seen her before.

Her hair is escaping from the neat updo she pulled it into, and one of the buttons on her blouse isn't done up. She's clutching at her purse like a lifeline, and there are dark circles under her eyes that even her expensive makeup can't cover.

Good, I think savagely. *It's about time she found out what it's like to feel helpless and out of control.*

"Olivia." I give her my best fake smile as the men all close ranks around me, Malice and Ransom on either side and Vic right behind me. "What are you doing here?"

"I know what you did," she hisses as soon as she reaches me.

She jabs a finger at me, then jumps when Malice smacks her arm away. I realize as he does that her hand is trembling. Whether from stress or from anger, I'm not sure, but it's another slip of that untouchable armor she usually surrounds herself with.

"You'll have to be more specific," I tell her, doing my best to sound composed and unbothered.

"You removed the money Troy put into my business," she snaps. "You had no right."

"I think you'll find I have every right," I shoot back. "Because that money is mine now."

Olivia's eyes narrow as she glares at me, hatred clear in every line of her body. "I'm warning you. Stop fucking with me. You have no idea what you're doing here."

"I have a pretty good idea what I'm doing, actually," I tell her, letting my lips curve upward on one side. "And every time you confront me like this..." I let my gaze linger on her rumpled clothing and her messy hair. "It just makes me more certain that I'm on the right path."

Even more of Olivia's facade slips when I say that. Her face morphs into something filled with anger and hate, and she doesn't try to hide it at all anymore. She looks vicious and cruel, almost inhuman, as if a monster has possessed the body of an old woman.

"I knew it," she spits, lowering her voice. "I knew the moment my son met that *slut* that she was going to be the ruin of this family. That she wouldn't rest until she'd dragged the Stanton name into the mud. And then they had you." She takes a step closer to me, her mouth curling into a sneer. "Your mother was a gold-digging whore. My son tried to tell me they were in love, as if that was supposed to mean something, but I saw her for what she was. She was trash, and in the end, that's all you are too."

All three of my men react to the insult, tense and angry. I can feel it growing behind me, bubbling up inside them like it's about to explode outward.

"You watch your fucking—" Malice starts, taking a step forward.

Before he can move too far, I reach out, putting a hand on his arm. I look away from Olivia for long enough to lock eyes with him and shake my head. I try to communicate silently that we have a plan for Olivia, and that him getting thrown in jail for assaulting

186

her right here in the open is not a part of it. Just because we got Judge Bailey to recall the warrants that were out for the guys, it doesn't mean they couldn't be arrested for a new crime.

Malice curls his hands into fists. I can feel the strength of his muscles under my hand, as if he's a predator on a very short leash, wanting to bite. But he takes a deep breath and nods, stepping back, letting me handle it.

I turn back to Olivia, and she looks just as sour as ever.

"You keep talking about the Stanton name and the Stanton estate like it's this big, grand thing," I tell her. "But you want to know the truth, Olivia? It's nothing more than a house of cards, waiting to fall apart."

For one tense moment, my grandmother just glares at me. Her lips twitch like she wants to say something, but instead, she just turns on her heel, striding back toward the black car that's parked at the side of the road. Her driver watches impassively as she gets into the back seat, and I can see what look like two bodyguards in the vehicle as well.

She snaps something to the driver, and her car peels away.

"Fucking bitch," Malice snarls, breaking the silence as she disappears around a corner. "Who the fuck does she think she is?"

"She's used to being the one holding all the cards," Vic says. He sounds calm and collected as ever, but when I turn my head, I can see anger simmering in his eyes. "Being on the other end of things has put her in a bad place, clearly."

"Wow, poor her," Ransom says, rolling his eyes. "My heart just bleeds for how hard this must be for her."

"At the end of the day, this was a good thing," Vic points out. "It means we've got her on her heels. She's stressed and pissed off, which means everything we're doing to her is having the desired effect."

He's right, and I hold on to that thought as we head inside and take the elevator up to the penthouse. Olivia isn't so smug anymore, and it felt really nice to wipe that self-satisfied look off her face.

187

Hopefully forever.

Not long after we get back, Ransom and Vic head out again to take care of some errands. They've been slowly rebuilding their supply of tech, weaponry, and ammo, since they left so much behind when they fled Detroit and then Mexico.

I pace around the condo, feeling strangely agitated, as if there are ants crawling under my skin. Every time we confront Olivia, I feel a simultaneous rush of excitement and fear, the same mixture I might feel if I passed my hand through an open flame, dancing too close to a bonfire.

Between Troy and Olivia, so much has been taken from me, but bit by bit, I've been clawing back those pieces of myself that they tried to destroy.

It's not enough though.

I want more.

My pulse picks up as I stride into the kitchen, stopping short when I see Malice. He's standing near the sink—*looming* over it, really—his muscular, tattooed frame looking out of place in the sleek, modern room as he drinks a glass of water.

Something lights inside my belly, the spark of a flame that once used to burn like an inferno. He's so solid and real, so darkly handsome and powerful. And he's *mine*. I'm sick of anything holding me back from him. I'm sick of feeling like I've been locked away in a glass case by my trauma.

He puts the glass down on the counter, and I stride forward before I even register making the decision to do it. The movement catches his attention, and he looks over at me as if he's about to say something, but I don't give him the chance.

I put my hands on either side of his face as soon as I reach him, going up onto my tiptoes. Then I practically attack him with a hard kiss.

MALICE

FUCKING HELL.

One second, I'm about to ask Willow if she wants to order dinner in tonight, and the next, she's launching herself at me and kissing me hard.

The intensity of it catches me off-guard, but it's fucking instinct at this point. My arms go around her, and my mouth responds ravenously, even as my brain scrambles to catch up to whatever the hell is going on.

Right now, my body is more concerned with the feeling of her against me and the way her mouth moves with mine. Heat surges through me, and I feel that hunger that I always feel for her, urging me to kiss her harder and deeper.

But then my brain does catch up, and I can feel that this isn't the same kind of desperation that she usually kisses me with. Or that she used to before Troy took her and broke her down. This feels more like she's trying to force herself into it, trying to ignore how much she must still be struggling with shit like this.

As much as I want her—and I really fucking do—I know this kind of thing can't be rushed. And I don't want to risk pushing her too far or doing something she's gonna regret later.

So I pull away from her, breaking the kiss.

Willow's large brown eyes are wild, and her face is flushed. She reaches for me again, breathing hard. She makes a needy sound, but it's not the kind I like, so I put a hand on her chest, gently holding her back.

"Solnyshka," I warn gruffly. "You don't wanna do this."

"Yes, I *do*." She pushes against my hold on her. "I do want to."

"Okay, maybe you do. But I don't know if you're ready for it, and I don't wanna—"

"I am ready. I'm so fucking ready, and I'm so fucking tired of not being able to have this, Malice." Her voice is thick with emotion, and she looks like she's on the verge of tears.

My body roars with its own need, my cock rock hard already and pressing against the front of my jeans. It's fucking begging to just take her and fuck her, to bend her over the kitchen island and claim her again right here and now.

I drag in a deep breath and then another, trying to clear my head enough to think past all of that.

"Willow." I use her real name this time instead of my nickname for her, speaking more firmly this time.

She takes a deep breath of her own, stepping back and wrapping her arms around herself. She shakes her head, making the tousled mane of her dyed brown hair shift around her shoulders.

"I've been reading those books you got me," she whispers. "And every time I read them, I think of the men in my life that I love... and I want to be with them. I think of all the things we used to do, and the way you used to make me feel. I get turned on reading those books, caught up in the sex scenes, and I'm so fucking sick of whatever fucked up shit is in my mind, holding me back from experiencing that myself."

I swallow hard, taking in how intense she sounds. She's serious about this, and my head is flooded with images of her reading those books and getting wet and needy.

My cock is hard enough to punch through a wall right now, but I keep myself under control. This isn't about me and my needs.

190

This is about Willow. So as much as I do want to just bend her over and fuck her, raw and dirty like I used to, I have to take a different approach.

"Go get one of those books," I tell her, my voice coming out husky with need. "One of your favorite ones that you've read."

Willow blinks, her brows pinching together. But she doesn't argue, turning and leaving the room.

She comes back a few minutes later with the book, and I look at it, then back up at her as I nod. "Good girl. Now go sit on the couch."

She does, looking at me in confusion as I follow her into the living room.

"Did you touch yourself when you were reading these books?" I ask, my gaze locked on her as she settles on one end of the large leather couch.

She sucks in a breath. Just a tiny inhalation of air, but it's enough to make desire pulse through me like a caged animal. Then she shakes her head, her cheeks going pink. "No."

"Did you want to?"

"Yes," she admits, dragging her bottom lip between her teeth.

I grit my teeth, reaching down to palm my cock just to keep myself from exploding. "Do it, then. Let me see it."

Her eyebrows shoot upward. "You want me to read... now?"

I shake my head and hold out my hand for the book. "No. I'm gonna read to you, and I want you to get yourself off."

Willow sucks in a surprised breath. I know she wasn't expecting me to say that, but I recognize the look in her eyes as she nods slowly, her tongue darting out to wet her lips. She likes this idea.

Her gaze tracks every movement as I take the book from her and then sit down on the other end of the couch. It's big enough that there's still some space between us, but we're close enough that I can see the way her pupils have dilated slightly.

I take my time, kicking out my legs and leaning back a little before I open the book and flip through it. I got Willow a mix of newer books and some that I remembered my mom reading back when my brothers and I were younger. This is one of the newer ones, and I'm surprised to see that some of the scenes look hot as hell.

"You dirty little girl," I murmur, glancing over at Willow as I hold the book open to a particularly sexy scene. "You've been reading these at night, picturing all of this shit happening to you, haven't you? Do you like to imagine you're her?"

"Yes." She shifts on the cushion a little, turning to face me more fully. "Except I..."

"You what?"

"I imagine that the guy is you. Or Ransom, or Vic. Or all three of you."

Fuck.

My cock just about punches a hole through my pants, and I make a noise low in my throat. Sharing Willow with my brothers is one of the hottest fucking things in the world. Seeing them make her fall apart is almost as good as doing it myself.

Memories of working together to get her off flood my mind, and I'm suddenly not so sure this was a good idea. I wanted to give Willow a chance to get off on her own terms, to take back some of the power that Troy stole from her... but it just might kill me before she even gets there.

"Good girl," I rasp, gripping the book so tightly it's a miracle I don't end up tearing the pages. "Picture that while I read. Imagine it's one of us touching you. Let yourself be as filthy as you want inside your own head, yeah? Because you're in charge up there. It's all up to you."

Willow nods, her eyes darkening even more as she watches me.

"Read that scene," she instructs, lifting her chin a little as she cranes her neck to read the words across the distance that separates us. "It's... it's a good one."

"I can tell."

And I can. Not just from the little snippet I just read, but because of the way I can already sense the change in her. Her breathing is getting a little faster, the flush in her cheeks deepening. She's already turned on just thinking about it, and I can't wait to see what happens when she listens to me read it out loud.

It takes a monumental effort to drag my attention away from Willow so that I can focus on the page, but I manage to do it, clearing my throat and starting to read.

In this scene, the hero and heroine are in a car, with a driver up front, separated from them by a partition. The hero tells the heroine to suck his cock, and the author of the book doesn't shy away from describing every detail as she leans over and takes him into her mouth.

He's not gentle with her, and as I describe the way he wraps a fist around her hair, thrusting into her mouth as he showers her with filthy praise, my voice turns to gravel.

After several passages, I glance up at Willow, watching as her lips part. She's staring at the book in my hands, but her gaze is unfocused, as if she's lost inside her own mind—and I can't help but wonder which one of me or my brothers she's imagining doing that with. I don't even care which one of us it is, to be honest, as long as she's losing herself in the fantasy of it.

I keep reading, my own cock throbbing as I describe how deep the heroine takes him, how even when her body is pushed to its limits, she works to take even more. At first, Willow just listens, but after another minute or so, she lets herself move. Her hands roam over her chest, cupping her tits, rolling her nipples through her shirt the way I know she likes.

"Mmm," she hums, resting her head against the back of the couch and squeezing her thighs together.

She darts a glance over at me, and I keep my attention divided between the book and her, letting her know I'm watching every fucking thing she's doing. That just seems to turn her on even more, and she hikes up the hem of her shirt, baring her bra-covered tits.

"You're turned on," I rasp. "Your nipples are so fucking hard.

Play with them for me, Solnyshka. I won't let myself touch them yet, so do it for me. Remind me how you like it."

"Fuck, Malice," she whimpers, and I grit my teeth, shaking my head.

"Nope. No fucking Malice," I say, an almost teasing tone to my voice as I repeat her words back at her with a new meaning. It's not really funny enough to be a joke though, not with the tension filling the air between us and the uncomfortable pressure of my cock against my pants. "If you want to come, you'll have to take care of that yourself. You'll have to use your own fingers to toy with your nipples or fuck that sweet pussy." I smirk as I add, "You can pretend they're mine if you like. I won't mind."

"Fine."

Fire flares in her eyes and she sits up a little, grabbing her shirt and lifting her arms.

My mouth goes dry, and I forget to read at all for a few seconds as I watch her pull the shirt all the way off. Her bra goes next, and her delicate hands go back to her breasts, pinching and tugging roughly at her nipples.

My balls tighten, precum leaking into the front of my boxers as my entire body goes taut with leashed tension.

Fuck, I want to cross the distance between us and take one of those little pink nubs in my mouth. I wanna bite down on it and make Willow cry out, feel her grinding against my body as she gets lost in the pleasure and pain, riding that fine line the way only she can.

Her eyes dart up to me again, as if she can sense the way my thoughts are going. She licks her lips and then pinches her nipple harder, arching into it.

"Feels good," she whispers, and this time, I swear she's the one teasing me.

I let out a rough breath at the sight, the way her neck arches back, the look of pleasure and tentative surrender on her face. It's so fucking gorgeous, and I don't think I'll ever get enough of this. Not ever. Not when it hits so fucking good every time.

My chest heaves as if I've been running at a sprint, and my voice is strained as I keep going. In the book, the hero spills his load down the heroine's throat, pressing even deeper as she swallows around him. Then he pulls her up to kiss her, driving his tongue into her mouth to taste himself. They arrive at their destination, and I grin as I read the part where he carries her inside, so desperate to taste her that he can't wait another second.

I can fucking relate to that.

The hero throws the heroine down on the bed, pulls her clothes off and then his own, and then wrenches her legs apart, baring her to him completely. As I describe it in vivid detail, Willow whimpers.

"You like that?" I ask, unable to keep myself from tempting her. "I still won't touch you, Solnyshka. But if you want your legs open, you can do it yourself. You want to spread them wide? Show me how wet you are?"

On the couch beside me, she slowly opens her legs. Even though no one is touching her, I can tell that she spreads them almost wider than is comfortable, as if she's trying to mimic the feel of what I just described.

"It's okay to still want it rough," I tell her, my voice dropping low as I ignore the book for the moment. "There was nothing wrong with you for liking it that way before, and there's nothing wrong with you for wanting it that way now. No one can take that from you. No one can tell you how to feel."

She swallows hard, the blush on her cheeks going even darker. "I do want it. I don't understand why, but... I do."

"Then show me."

I watch her as she lets go of her tits and slides one hand down her chest and stomach. Her body undulates as she moves against her touch, her breathing ragged now.

She touches herself through her pants at first, not removing them yet. She grinds against her own hand, cupping her fingers to give herself the most room to work with. But it's clear it's not enough. She makes a face and then undoes the button and zipper, sliding her hand beneath the waistband.

My fingers twitch as she does, wishing it was my own hand right where hers is. Wanting to know how soaked through she is just from this. Judging from the way she moans as she bucks against her hand, she's already so fucking worked up.

In the book, the hero drags his tongue over the heroine's pussy, beginning to eat her out. A whimper spills from Willow as she starts touching herself for real, and she bites down on her bottom lip as if she's trying to keep the sounds muffled.

I cut off mid-sentence, looking at her sharply.

"No. Let me hear you, Solnyshka," I rasp. "Don't hold anything back. There's no one here but you and me, and I wanna hear you fall apart."

She glances at me, her nipples peaked and stiff as our gazes lock. And the next time she moans, it comes out loud and clear. Like music to my fucking ears.

"Good girl," I say, smirking hungrily. "That's what I wanna hear. I've always loved it when you get loud for me. When you forget to even *pretend* to be a good girl and let yourself get filthy."

"Fuck," she gasps. "Malice."

"I'm right here, Solnyshka." My gaze roves over her as I speak, soaking in the sight of her like this. Wild and messy and free. "You're doing so fucking well. Tell me how it feels."

"Good," she pants out. Her hips roll up in a sharp arch, and I have to wonder what those fingers of hers are doing to make her feel that good. "It feels good."

I clench my jaw so hard my teeth ache as my cock twitches in my pants. It wants more than this, but I hold on to the book a little harder, dropping my eyes back down to the pages in front of me. I take a breath and then another one, focusing on the point of all this.

I want Willow to let go. I want her to just *feel* without the fear or the trauma closing in. I've got to keep my mind on that for right now.

"Fuck," she breathes again, this time on more of a light sob than a moan. Her hand is working so fast in her pants now, and I can see the way her chest heaves as she fights to breathe.

"Slow down," I urge her.

Her eyes snap to me, and they're nearly completely dark with lust. It's hot as fuck to see her like this, especially after watching her walk through life like a zombie in those first days after we got her back from Troy.

"I can't. I—"

"You can," I tell her. "Listen to me, Solnyshka. There's no need to rush. No one's going to stop you. Just let yourself feel it. Let yourself enjoy it. How wet are you right now?"

She swallows again. "So wet. It's so... god, I can feel it soaking my fingers."

"Good. Rub your clit for me, yeah? Slow circles."

She nods shakily, and I can see the movements of her hand slow as she follows my instructions. It's fucking torture to just watch this, to direct her from the other side of the couch, but it's what she needs right now. That's the most important thing.

I keep reading, slowing my words to match the pace of her fingers as I describe every filthy detail of the hero eating the heroine out in the book. He fucks her with his tongue, making her gush on his face, and she's still coming when he pulls her legs open even wider and drags her in to meet his deep thrust as he impales her hard enough to make her scream.

Willow's hips buck forward again when I get to that part, and she moans, a low, filthy sound.

"Jesus Christ," I mutter, the pages blurring in front of my eyes as I drag in a ragged breath. "*Kogda ty tak stonesh', jeto svodit menja s uma. Ja mogu konchit', prosto slushaja, kak ty izdaesh' jetot zvuk.*"

I'm on the edge of losing control entirely. I can feel my cock pulsing, the tip leaking even more precum from the need I feel right now. It seems like it should be impossible for one woman to be so fucking sexy without even really trying, but Willow does it. She manages to make me feel things no one else ever has before.

My blood rushes in my ears, and the next time I look over at Willow, I can't take my eyes off her, caught up in the sight of her pleasure.

She was slow and tentative at first, but she's more confident now. That, or she's just more lost in the feelings and sensations, not caring about me watching. Or at least not letting it stop her. She definitely cares, and the way she darts little glances up at me every so often proves that.

Me watching her, reading to her, being here as a part of this? She wants all of it, and I love knowing that.

I love knowing that she's this fucking needy. Just for me.

"You don't have to tell me how wet you are anymore," I tell her. "I can *hear* it. I can fucking smell it, Solnyshka. The way you smell when you're this turned on is my favorite goddamned thing in the world. Sinful and sweet at the same time. I would lap you up if I could."

"You would?"

"Fuck, yes." The hopeful edge to her voice nearly snaps my restraint, but I manage to answer with words instead of just showing her what I want to do. "I'd spear my tongue into you and gather up every single drop. I'd drink you down like the finest fucking wine. Until my entire chin was soaked. I'd make you come on my face, and then I'd do it all over again."

"I..." Her voice breaks off, turning into a whimper. "I miss that."

Fuck.

With the way my cock is throbbing, I'm almost certain I'm about to come in my fucking pants, but I don't even care. Willow is about to come too, and getting her over the edge is all I care about right now. It takes a monumental act of will, but I rip my gaze away from her and keep reading. The hero is fucking the heroine now, rough and dirty, a carnal meeting of bodies that's born of nothing but raw need.

"Please," Willow moans, and I look at her again. She's working her hips against her hand as the other hand plays with her tits again. She's flushed all over and covered in a fine sheen of sweat, tendrils of her hair sticking to her temples. "Please, please, please."

"What do you want?" I ask, and I have to clear my throat to get my words to come out. The air is thick with the scent of sex, and it's shredding my already strained control.

"I'm so close, Malice," she manages to get out. "I'm so close, please. Please, I wanna come. Oh my god."

The way her voice sounds so wrecked goes straight to my cock, and I groan, closing my eyes and sucking in another few deep breaths.

When I look at her again, she's staring right at me, her eyes boring into mine, the need clear on her face.

"There you go. Such a good girl," I murmur gruffly, egging her on. Praising her and encouraging her. "That's right. Let go. Come for me. I wanna see it. I wanna see you lose it for me. Ride your fucking hand, Solnyshka, like the dirty, perfect girl you are."

She whines in response to my words, a breathy, desperate sound. It's as if my permission is exactly what she's been waiting for. There's less of the wild desperation from a few minutes ago—she's still following my directions to go slower—but I can tell when she plunges her fingers into herself again. The wet noise is loud in the quiet of the living room, and she shakes and writhes on the couch.

Her other hand pinches and twists at her nipple, and she digs those fingers in, moaning from the pleasure and the pain. "I'm... oh fuck!"

It's such a fucking beautiful sight, and I keep watching, breathless, as she shivers and then comes on her own hand with a soft cry.

My mouth is so dry that I couldn't go back to reading if I wanted to. Not with *this* in front of me. I've never been so close to coming without anyone touching my cock before, but it makes sense that if anyone was going to drive me to the edge like this, it would be Willow. My cock is so hard it's painful, and I feel like I could explode if she breathed on it right.

"Goddamn," I croak. "No one has ever wrecked me like you do,

Solnyshka. I haven't even touched you, and you just fucking ruined me."

On the couch, Willow shudders through her aftershocks. They seem to go on forever, wracking her body from head to toe at first before finally fading into small little tremors. When the last of them passes through her, she blinks her eyes open, finally pulling her hand out of her pants.

She looks at me across the length of the couch, her brown eyes dark and liquid.

"Thank you," she whispers.

Those two words hit me harder than anything she's spoken up to this point.

In a heartbeat, I toss the book to the side and surge to my feet, finally closing the distance between us. Leaning over her, I cage her in a little with my arms as I drop a firm kiss to her forehead. When she tilts her head up, leaning into my touch, I follow her lead and kiss her lips next, feeling protective over her—the way I always do—but also so many other things that I can barely name them all.

Possessive.

Hungry.

So full of love that my entire body is bursting with it.

It's a struggle to pull away, to make myself draw back from her, but before I can get anywhere, Willow reaches up and wraps her arms around me.

"Wait. Don't go," she whispers. "I want more. Please."

Her words set off a war inside me.

I told myself when I started this that I was just doing it to help her get off. It was never supposed to be more than that. I wanted to give her the orgasm I knew she needed, but I'm still not sure she's ready for more.

As if she can sense the internal battle raging beneath my skin, Willow slides her fingers through the hair at the nape of my neck, digging her fingernails into my scalp. I hiss out a breath, the beast that I've kept locked in its cage rattling at the bars.

I need her.

Dammit, I need her so much.

And my Solnyshka needs me too.

"Fuck it," I mutter under my breath.

Then I'm kissing her again, climbing up onto the couch with her.

WILLOW

I'M FLOATING on a high of orgasmic bliss, my entire body looser and more relaxed than it's been in a long time.

And all I want is to keep chasing this high.

All I want is exactly what I asked Malice for. *More.*

My hands roam over his back, feeling the muscles flex under his clothes and under his skin. I've gotten glimpses of him—and all the guys, really—without their shirts in the time since we moved into the penthouse, but not like this. I haven't touched them or kissed them the way I've wanted to.

Malice's hands skate up my sides, making me shiver. His calloused palms feel good everywhere, and when they come up to cover my breasts, I arch against him, pressing myself harder into his hands.

"Fuck," he grates out against my mouth. "Solnyshka, you—"

He breaks off suddenly, letting go of my breasts and leaning back so that he can take me in. His eyes drink in the sight of me, and I can feel myself blushing. Even now, there's something about the way he looks at me that always makes me feel just a little shy.

But in a good way.

In a way that makes me desperate for him to keep going.

"You really want more?" he asks, narrowing his eyes a little.

"Yes." I nod emphatically.

Without taking his gaze off me, he reaches over to retrieve the book from where he dropped it. He holds it out to me, his inked forearms rippling as he presses it into my hands.

"Your turn then," he says. "You read this time. Pick any scene you like. But if you stop, I stop."

I'm about to ask him what he means, but before I can, he drops his head and presses a light kiss to my nipple. I hiss out a breath, almost dropping the book, and he immediately draws back a couple inches, going still.

Fuck, that's what he means. He means he won't touch me unless I'm reading.

My hands tremble as I skim the pages quickly, searching for another good scene to read. I find one where the hero takes the heroine out onto a private balcony, then bends her over the railing high above the city and fucks her. Starting from the beginning of the scene, I read out loud in a shaky voice.

It's harder than I thought it would be. I have no idea how Malice managed to read coherently when he was doing this. I keep losing my place as he presses his lips to my skin again, working his way down in a winding path. He hesitates when he gets to the spot where my pants hang open, and the sound of him dragging in a long breath through his nose makes goosebumps pop out on my skin.

I know he said he loves the way I smell when I'm turned on, and there's something filthy in the best way about the way he's inhaling me.

"Keep going," he orders, and I realize I've gone silent.

"S-sorry."

Clearing my throat, I dive back in... and so does Malice. He tugs my pants down, along with my panties, sliding them down my legs and discarding them somewhere.

My breath comes harder, faster, every nerve in my body quivering on a knife's edge of need. It feels like it's been so long since I've done this with him, and every part of me is anticipating it.

The words on the page seem to blur as his hands grip my thighs, and his tongue finds my clit a second later. It's not as forceful as the way he usually eats me out, but it's been so long and I'm already so sensitive that it hits me like a ton of bricks anyway.

I almost stop reading but force myself to keep going. In the book, he's got her bent over, her hands placed just where he wants them as he shoves her dress up, and my thighs clench as I describe it in a halting voice.

Malice swipes his tongue over me in long, languid licks, savoring the arousal that's gathered there.

"You taste so goddamned good," he groans when he comes up for air. "Missed this. Missed having you like this."

"Me—me too," I manage to stammer out.

"The book, Solnyshka. Keep reading."

He goes back to it as I rasp out words that barely make sense to me anymore. All of my brain cells are focused on how good his tongue feels as it rolls over my clit. If it wasn't for his big hands holding me down, I'd be grinding all over his face, bucking and trying to get more of that delicious, slippery friction.

"'He gripped her cheeks, pulling them apart and baring everything to him,'" I read, my throat dry. "Oh god, Malice, please..."

"Is that part of the book?" he demands, lifting his head so that the pressure of his tongue disappears.

"No, but—"

"Then keep reading."

I can feel the orgasm building, just out of reach, and I lick my lips and find my place again. I describe the way he drives into her on the balcony, making her back arch as he wraps a hand around her hair.

"'She could feel him...'" I whimper. "Oh fuck. 'She could feel him—'"

I can't get the words out any longer, and every time I stop, Malice does too. He teases me like that, pulling away each time my words break off, until finally I blurt out, "'She could feel him *everywhere.*'"

"Good girl," he growls.

His tongue moves faster, relentless, hot, and wet, and I'm help-less to do anything but fall apart for him. I shudder through it, practically screaming the words from the book, so desperate to make sure he doesn't stop that I keep reading even after my orgasm crests and finally starts to recede.

I'm basically just babbling now, and Malice chuckles as he draws back, wiping his hand over his mouth.

"That was pretty good," he tells me. "Maybe we'll try it again sometime. I like hearing you read dirty things, Solnyshka. Filthy words always sound better coming from your sweet lips."

He plucks the book from my hands and sets it on the coffee table. Then he leans down and presses a kiss to my cheek.

When he starts to draw away, my eyes open wide.

"Wait," I ask. "Is that it?"

"That's enough."

"But you didn't come yet."

He chuckles, wincing a little as he reaches down to squeeze his dick. "But you did. Twice. So that's enough."

No. No, this is all wrong.

Even though he ate me out until I practically soaked his chin, he's not kissing me or touching me the way he usually would. Malice Voronin is a man who takes what he wants, and even when it was my very first time, he didn't hold back. He fucked me like I was his own personal whore... and I want that right now. I want everything he can give me.

I don't want him to handle me like I'm fragile. Like I'm breakable.

I don't want to feel breakable. I want to feel strong and powerful like I used to when he fucked me.

"*No*," I say, an edge of frustration creeping into my voice. "I don't want you to handle me gently like this. You once told me that you don't fuck gentle. That you don't *do* gentle. I want that. I want you to fuck me the way you used to."

"Willow—"

"Please, Malice. You don't have to hold back. Please. Fuck me the way you did when you trusted that I could take it."

Malice's nostrils flare wide, his cheek muscles jumping as he clenches his jaw. He's breathing hard, and his fingers grip my arm tightly. He seems to realize what he's doing, and he jerks his hand back, curling his fingers into a fist instead. I can almost see the struggle in his eyes, the way he's fighting with himself. His body clearly wants one thing, but he's trying to convince himself of something else.

He's holding himself back, restraining himself, almost like a leashed beast. Like one move could snap his self-imposed chains and let his most primal desires take over.

I lick my lips, my chest heaving as I hold his gaze.

"Please, Malice," I whisper again. "I know you love me. I feel it every day. But I don't need you to fuck me like you love me. I just need you to fuck me like you *need* me. Like you'll die if you don't get inside me. Like nothing else exists right now except you and me."

I can see the effect my words have on him, his entire body shuddering as his fists tighten even more, turning his knuckles white.

"Pick a word," he says after a long moment, his voice gruff and strained.

"What?"

"A word," he bites out. "That'll let me know if you need me to stop."

Oh. I blink a few times, thinking it over. A thrill goes through me as I realize that this means he's going to give me what I want— just with a simple precaution. And a safe word is a good idea. As much as I want this now, it will give me an escape if things change for me later.

It gives me the power, and that's exactly what I need right now.

"Pineapple," I say finally, not even sure where that word came from. It just popped into my head, and it's not like it's something I'd accidentally say while having sex, so it works.

Malice nods. "Pineapple. You have to use it. If you want me to stop, you have to use the word."

"Okay."

"Promise me." His eyes sear into me, full of heat and intention, and I swallow hard, nodding.

"I promise. I'll use it."

There's something so sweet in the gesture. It's such a *Malice* thing, wanting to show he cares in his own way, even as he's planning to let himself go, to be as rough with me as he wants.

But that's what we both want right now, and my heart races as I watch his face.

It's like I'm finally seeing the last of his control snap right in front of me.

There's no more holding back, and when he reaches for me this time, he yanks me hard against his body.

I gasp, going eagerly, melting against him as he kisses me. This time, it isn't a brush of his lips or a tease. This is all rabid heat and hunger. This is Malice kissing me like he wants to devour me. Like he's about to consume me the way a wildfire consumes a forest, transforming me entirely with the force of his desire. His teeth snag my lower lip, biting down hard, and I taste the faint hint of blood between us as I gasp into his mouth.

"I would give you anything," he mutters. "There's not a single thing you could ask me for that I would deny you, Solnyshka."

One of his hands fists my hair, making sparks scatter from my scalp all the way through my body. Then he jerks my head back hard enough to make me cry out before attacking my neck next. It's as if all the need that he's been holding back since he and his brothers saved me is finally pouring out, and he can't stop himself.

He leaves a trail of biting kisses from under my jaw down to my shoulder, and I squirm against him, gasping for breath.

"Oh my god," I moan, shifting, trying to find something to grind against. My body is humming as if it's channeling a surge of electricity. As if the orgasms from moments ago were nothing more than an appetizer before the main course.

"Fuck," Malice groans, his breath hot against my neck. "You're impossible to resist. Can't get enough of you."

I drag my nails down his back, pressing against him. "I need more," I gasp out. "I need you."

He growls, and when he pulls back, there's something intense and almost feral in his eyes. His fingers find their way between my legs, and he touches me roughly, rubbing along my wet slit.

"You're so fucking wet," he groans. "You know what I was thinking about the whole time you touched yourself?"

I shake my head, gripping one of the couch cushions like an anchor as I spread my legs wider, relishing the burn in my inner thighs. "What?"

"How badly I wanted to come over here and touch you myself. I wanted to bite down on your tits, really make you scream. I wanted to pull your hand out of the way and fuck you myself. To impale you on my fingers and then my cock, until I was all you were thinking about."

"You already *were* all I was thinking about," I pant. "I wanted that so much. Fuck, please. Show me how it would've been. Please."

I don't have to ask twice.

We're past that by now.

The time for begging this man to touch me is fully in the rearview mirror.

Faster than I can blink, Malice is moving. He presses me down so my back is against the smooth, cool leather of the couch, kneeling on the cushions between my legs. He looms over me, broad-shouldered and so much bigger than I am, but I don't feel afraid.

Let *other* people fear this man. I never will.

In this moment, all I feel is desperately turned on and hungry for more.

His mouth descends on my chest, and I whimper as he starts nipping at my breasts, biting and sucking on them like he wanted to earlier. He mimics the way I was pinching my own nipples, trapping them between his teeth, and the sharp bites of pain just add to the fire building in my veins.

I writhe on the couch, my hips bucking up against his body, holding on to his arms just to have something to ground me.

"Malice," I moan, his name spilling from my lips like a prayer. "Malice, Malice, Malice."

He licks one nipple, soothing the ache left behind from his teeth, and then goes to the other one, giving it the same treatment. By the time he raises his head from my chest, my skin is covered in bite marks, and my pussy is dripping.

"Keep your legs spread," he commands. "Just like that. I want that pussy ready and waiting for me."

He doesn't look away from me for a second as he gets up just enough to start taking off his pants.

Even though I've already come twice, it's like my body is making up for lost time, trying to overwrite every bad thing that's happened to me since the last time Malice touched me by imprinting him on every inch of my skin.

He tears his shirt over his head, then shoves his jeans down and off, and the sight of it is enough to make my mouth water. His tattooed cock juts out from his body, rock hard and wet at the tip. It's flushed, the veins standing out from the shaft, proof of just how close he is to exploding. How long he's been waiting for this.

My pussy clenches, making another gush of wetness drip from my slit.

"You're so hard," I whisper, dragging my lip between my teeth.

Malice snorts, a hint of amusement sparking in his dark eyes.

"I've been hard since the first second you kissed me. This is what you do to me, Solnyshka. You and your body and your unbreakable spirit. Your heart and your fucking *soul*. Your gorgeous tits, covered in our marks, and that perfect pink pussy. You fucking drive me wild. All I want—all I'll *ever* want—is you."

"You can have me," I tell him, raw honesty infusing my voice. "Please. I want you."

"I know," he says, laughing quietly. It's low and dark, and the seductive edge of it climbs up my spine and leaves me shivering. "I believe you, and I know what you need. You've made that clear enough. I'm gonna fuck you just the way you want. Gonna fill you up with my cock until you can't even remember your own fucking name. Until all you can say is mine."

I whimper at the promise in his words, and when he puts his hands on me again, every nerve ending in my body reacts to his touch, lighting up like the finale of a fireworks show.

"Turn over for me. Face down and ass up. Good girl."

He flips me over and then guides me up onto my elbows and knees on the couch. With my back arched and my ass up in the air like this, I'm completely exposed to him. There's nowhere to hide, and he can see everything.

But that's what I want. I want him to see it... and I want him to take it.

As if he can read my mind, Malice grabs my ass, squeezing hard enough that I know he's going to leave fingerprints behind. "I like that you don't hide from me, Solnyshka. It only makes me crave you more."

He doesn't waste time, doesn't tease me. One second, I feel him moving behind me, and then the next, he's slamming his cock right into my pussy.

I cry out, my body shaking from the force of it.

I'm so wet that it's not hard for him to work himself inside me in one go, but his tattooed cock is so thick that I can still feel the burn of the stretch as he goes in deep. My pussy wraps around him, my inner walls clinging to his hard shaft like I'm trying to keep him from ever moving.

But he manages to draw himself out, only to slam right back in, setting a hard, furious pace.

His fingers dig into the skin of my hips, and the sound of our skin slapping together echoes through the living room. The couch creaks and groans under us as Malice plows into me, and eventually my arms give out entirely, leaving me face down and ass up on the couch.

"*This* is how we're supposed to be," Malice growls, dragging me back by the hips into each deliciously deep thrust. "Bound together like this. You full of my cock. Taking it like you were made for me. Fuck, you *were* made for me, weren't you? Weren't you?"

He punctuates that question with another hard punch of his hips, and I cry out, my fingers scrabbling against the leather of the couch.

"Yes," I practically sob. "God, yes. I was made for you. For you and your brothers. Please!"

"Please, what? What do you want? More? You want me to fuck you harder?"

I nod, too overcome to force the words out. I can already feel a perfect, indescribable ache building deep inside me, but I want more of him. I want all he can give me.

He drives himself in deeper and harder, and each thrust feels like it's wringing pleasure out of my body. I'm drowning in it, struggling to remember to breathe, wailing with each slam of his hips.

Malice hauls me up at some point, wrapping his hand around my throat. I gasp against the force of it, my back arched, crying out his name on a broken moan as he fucks into my body so deep that I swear I can feel it in my belly.

The sound of skin on skin is almost deafening in the living room, and the couch creaks and groans under us. But all that really matters is the way his cock feels buried in me, slamming up into my body, leaving me a soaking, swollen mess.

I can feel myself hurtling toward the edge of pleasure, almost ready to topple over it and fly headfirst into another orgasm.

"Oh my god," I gasp out. "Oh—oh my—"

"Are you close?" Malice demands. He slams his cock in harder, and I nearly sob with the pleasure it sparks in me.

"Yes," I blurt, nodding as if the words might not be enough. "I'm so close, please—"

"Touch yourself," he orders. "Rub that clit while I fuck your pretty cunt. Get yourself off."

I obey him immediately. My hand flies up between my legs,

and I let Malice's body support me, keeping me from toppling face first onto the leather of the couch.

My pussy is soaking wet by now, and my fingers slip and slide around as I touch myself. I can feel where Malice is buried in me, feel the way he slams in and out, forcing my body to accommodate his large size.

It makes my breath catch to *feel* him fucking me like this, to have his cock brush against my fingers as they work their way up to the sensitive nub of my clit.

As soon as the tips of my fingers touch it, I bite down hard on my lip. I'm so sensitive, so overstimulated, and I know this isn't going to take long.

I rub the little bundle of nerves in quick, small circles, almost matching the pace of Malice's cock as he bottoms out inside me again and again.

"That's it," he pants, his voice like gravel. He drops his head, his raspy growl falling right into my ear. "That's it. Touch yourself. Feel how fucking wet you are. How needy you are for this. I wanna feel you come on my cock, Solnyshka. I wanna feel your pretty pussy milk me dry."

I sob my pleasure as he speaks, each sentence punctuated by another hard thrust of his cock.

My fingers fly over my clit, and my hips buck wildly, trying to ride out the pleasure that's threatening to drown me the longer this goes on. It's like a rubber band, stretching tighter and tighter, filling my belly with that impossibly hot fire until it snaps, letting it all rush forth.

I scream Malice's name as I come, shaking and gasping for air. The force of my climax makes it hard to breathe, and Malice holds me through it, working his cock in and out with long, deep thrusts.

It's so intense that it's almost too much, and I snatch my hand away from my clit, writhing against Malice as the orgasm rolls through me. Every nerve in my body is firing all at once, it feels like, and everything is electric and white hot. My vision goes dull around the edges, and I have to take huge gulps of air, trying to stay afloat.

"Good girl," he growls. He bites down on my shoulder, hard enough that I feel it even through the haze of pleasure and disorientation. "You're so fucking beautiful like this."

He pulls out suddenly, and my body immediately mourns the loss of his hot cock inside it. I let out a pitiful whimper, and he chuckles as he kisses my shoulder.

His hands are rough and gentle at the same time as he flips me over, laying me down with my back against the leather of the couch. I stare up at him, lost in the burning heat of his gaze, and he stares right back at me.

"I need to fuck you like this," he says roughly, emotions churning in his eyes. "Face to face. I need to see you."

I swallow hard as he lifts my hips up with one hand and then guides his cock right back into my sopping pussy.

It's just this side of too sensitive, and I shiver at the feeling, squirming in his hold.

"I can't come again," I tell him, sounding breathless and wrecked. "I can't."

"Say the safe word if you wanna stop."

Malice freezes, going completely still, his cock only half buried inside me as he waits to see if I'm going to say it.

But I don't.

I want this. I want him. I want to be pushed right up to the edge of what I can take, just so that I *know* I can take it. And more than anything, I want to feel this man come inside me.

He waits for another few seconds, and when I shake my head, my lips tilting up in a challenging grin, fierce pride rises up alongside the desire in his expression. His answering grin is sinful, and he dips his head down to kiss me hard. His teeth graze my lower lip, and his tongue delves into my mouth, intense and almost furious with need.

I can taste it in him, and I whimper into the kiss as he starts moving again.

When he pulls back, that heat is still in his eyes, but it's tempered by something warm and possessive.

"I want you to come again for me," he says lowly.

"I—"

"You can. Don't think about anything else, Solnyshka. Just *feel*. Just let yourself have everything you deserve."

He doesn't look away from me for a second, rolling his hips and thrusting into me all the way to the root. It's such a contrast to the hard, almost brutal way he was fucking me before. This is slow and deep, our gazes locked together.

I can feel every inch of him as he works his cock into me, and when he pulls out, my inner walls seem to cling to him, making the resulting drag of skin on skin so spine-tinglingly good.

Each time he buries himself in me, it's a hard, penetrating feeling, and it rocks me to my core. I clutch at him, needing an anchor, needing to feel grounded, as I stare into his dark eyes.

He stares right back into mine, and it almost feels like we're speaking without words.

I can feel the love coming from Malice. The protectiveness. The desire. All the things he's willing to do for me and to me, just to keep me safe and happy. There's no difference in the way he looks at me now, compared to how he looked at me before I got taken by Troy.

Nothing that happened has changed anything for him, except for making him more determined to keep me safe. But the feelings are the same. The love is the same.

All of a sudden, it's so much. The emotions are filling me up, expanding inside my chest until there's no more room to contain them. I gasp softly, overwhelmed and overcome, and tears well in my eyes and start to spill over.

"Willow?" Malice freezes again, alarm crossing his harsh features. He moves likes he's going to pull out, but I wrap my legs around his waist and shake my head.

"Don't stop," I whisper. "You're not hurting me. Please don't stop."

"Solnyshka," he murmurs, but he doesn't stop.

He keeps going, moving in steady strokes that somehow seem to match the waves of emotion coursing through me. He dips his head, kissing away the tears, his lips finding each one as they track down my cheeks.

"I love you," he breathes. "Never gonna let anyone hurt you again. I swear it on my life. On my fucking soul. Never, Solnyshka. Never."

My fingers slide over his heated skin, memorizing every line and curve of his muscled frame. He's gotten a little sweaty just like I have, and I feel as if we've both been reduced to our most basic, raw state. We couldn't hide anything from each other in this moment even if we tried.

Every atom in my body is attuned to him, and slowly, something hot begins to build low in my belly. The spark is muted at first, from me being oversensitive and emotional, but it's there all the same.

And the deeper Malice fucks me, the more it grows.

Finally, I'm gasping his name, riding it out as the heat builds, taking over everything. When my fourth orgasm hits, I sob my way through it, writhing against him.

"That's it," he grunts. His hips stutter, and I know he's close too. My pussy ripples around his cock, spasming with my pleasure, and he lets out a choked noise. "Fuck, just like that. Oh fuck, I'm—"

He breaks off with a growl as he follows me over the edge, coming hard. His arms tremble with the effort of holding himself up, and once he's ridden out his own orgasm, he collapses on top of me.

My chest heaves as I try to get air into my lungs, my head spinning. My body tingles in a good way, feeling sore and overworked, but... better than before. Every muscle in me is loose and light, my skin slowly cooling from the exertion as I lie beneath him with my eyes closed.

I know I'm a mess, covered in sweat and tears and cum, but

Malice finally lifts his head from the crook of my neck, he gazes at me like I'm the most beautiful thing he's ever seen.

"What?" I ask, smiling a little.

He just shakes his head, shoving his dark hair back with one hand before leaning down to kiss me. "You good?"

"Yeah." I nod, letting out a soft, shaky breath. "I'm good."

Malice searches my face, as if he's trying to figure out if I'm telling the truth or not, but whatever he sees must give him some comfort. There's none of the anxious light in his eyes that was there before, and its absence bolsters me even more.

"I needed that," I tell him, tracing my fingers up and down his arm.

"Seemed like it might have been the opposite of what you needed," he says, shifting his weight on top of me a little, although he makes no move to pull out yet.

I bite my lip, trying to figure out how to put it into words for him so he'll understand.

"It's been hard, since you guys saved me. I felt like a stranger in my own skin, almost. There were all these things I wanted, all these things I'd been working so hard to accept that I was into, and suddenly, I couldn't handle them anymore. It made me feel broken."

Malice frowns, reaching up to brush hair back from my face. "You're *not* broken. And that's not all we want from you, Solnyshka. Even if you never wanted those things again, it's not like we would stop caring about you."

"I know." I nod, gripping his forearm lightly. "You've all been so patient with me. But I missed this. I missed *you*. And to be honest, almost nothing in the world has ever made me feel as strong as being fucked by you does. I wanted to reclaim that."

He's quiet for a moment, as if he's processing my words. Then he snorts. "So that's why you jumped me after we got home."

I chuckle at his phrasing, but I nod, because he's not wrong. "Yeah. I just really needed to do something with the way I was feeling. So thank you. For letting me get that out. For giving me what I

216

needed and taking care of me the way I needed to be taken care of."

His hard features soften a little as he smiles. "I always will, you know. I'm always gonna be there for you when you need me."

He leans down, pressing his forehead to mine. It's such a tender gesture, one I would've once thought Malice was incapable of, but now I know better. He's got so much more inside him than I realized at first, and I feel lucky to be one of the few people in the world he lets in like this.

I reach up and thread my fingers through his thick dark hair, savoring the moment. The closeness.

Malice pulls out after a while, and I wince at the rush of cum and the soreness in my pussy. I'm a complete mess, and when he looks down at me as he tugs his pants back on, a possessive grin splits his face.

"Proud of yourself?" I ask teasingly.

"Always when it comes to wrecking you." He smirks, his gaze darkening all over again. "I'll be right back."

He heads to the bathroom and comes back with a damp cloth, and I lie still, letting him clean me up. There's only so much he can do with the cloth, considering how messy I am, but it feels good to let him take care of me like this.

His fingers follow the path of the cloth in the aftermath, sliding tenderly over the tattoos that he etched onto my chest and shoulder. He studies them intently, and then something glints in his eyes.

"I'll be right back," he says again.

I push myself up onto my elbows, watching in confusion as he strides out of the room. I half expect him to come back with snacks or water or something, since we definitely worked up an appetite. But instead, he returns with his tattooing gear in hand.

It's brand new. He bought it to replace the kit he left behind in Mexico when we had to flee in the middle of the night, and my stomach flutters at the sight of it.

"Are you going to give me another tattoo?" I ask, anticipation already making goosebumps spread over my skin.

He shakes his head, cocking one dark eyebrow in something almost like a challenge.

"Not this time, Solnyshka. You've got my mark on you. Three of them, actually. Now I want your mark on me."

23

WILLOW

My jaw falls open in surprise, and I'm suddenly filled with a rush of nerves.

"You want me to tattoo you?" I ask, incredulous. "I've never done that before. I wouldn't even know how. I'm definitely going to mess it up, and you take such pride in your tattoos."

I look at the ones I can see on his skin, the ones I've practically memorized by now. The last thing I want is for him to have something wonky and ugly there, standing out from the good work he's done on himself, or had done in prison.

But Malice just chuckles, coming over and cupping my face in both hands. He draws me up into a kiss, and I can't help but melt into it. It's possessive and messy, all teeth and tongue and sharp edges. If I wasn't already so fucked out, it would have me tingling with the need for more.

As it is, it leaves me breathless, and I have to stare at him for a second to get my brain back online after we break apart.

"I don't care," he says, the rough edge in his voice making it sound deeper than it usually does. "You could tattoo a stick figure or a blob on me, and I'd still love it. I want to wear your mark."

I laugh, shaking my head. "You're crazy."

But I can tell he's serious. He means it unequivocally, and it makes my stomach turn over with nerves. At the same time, something about the idea is so appealing. Malice is marked up in so many ways, from his tattoos to all the scars that litter his body, and the thought of having something permanent on him, something that I put there, is thrilling in a way I didn't expect it to be.

Maybe some of his possessiveness has rubbed off on me.

I take a deep breath, then nod. "Okay. I'll see what I can do. But you can't get mad if it looks like shit."

He grins, kissing my forehead before stepping back. "I promise. Now come here." He purses his lips before he adds, "And don't get dressed yet. I want you naked while you tattoo me."

My nipples harden, my thighs unconsciously squeezing together. Leaving my scattered clothes where they are, I scoot to the edge of the couch as he sits down beside me.

He shoves the coffee table out of the way a bit and then sets the tattoo equipment down on it, and I listen attentively as he gives me a rundown on how the gear all works. I have a basic understanding of it from watching him, but it's impressive how much he knows, and how easily he explains it.

There's still an anxious rumble in my stomach, but the more Malice talks, the more excited I get to tattoo him. It's a huge show of trust—and knowing Malice the way I do, I understand it's a big deal for him. He doesn't trust easily at all.

Once he finishes his lesson, I stand up and run my gaze over him, struck as always by how unfairly hot he is.

He might not be model gorgeous the way Ransom is, but there's something about his dark intensity that's so striking. The way he carries himself, the way his muscles stand out. It's all very appealing, and there's so much of him to work with. Even though he has a lot of tattoos already, there are some empty spaces, and I look at him the way he looked at me the first time he tattooed me, like a canvas to be evaluated.

Malice just lets me get on with it, one eyebrow raised, heat flickering in his eyes while I take him in.

"See something you like?" he asks, a teasing note in his voice.

I roll my eyes. "You already know the answer to that."

"Maybe I just like hearing it from you."

"Vain," I tease back. "I'm checking out what I have to work with."

He nods, letting me look my fill, but I know we're both aware of the heat building between us. It's bright and undeniable, and I swallow hard, letting my fingers trail over the skin of his shoulders and upper arms.

Finally, I pick a spot on his chest. It's not a large spot, just a bit of open space between his other tattoos. But I don't want to do anything big anyway, and I like the idea of him having my mark near his heart, just like the first one he gave me.

"Okay," I say, taking a deep breath. "I'm ready."

Malice nods. He wraps my fingers around the tattoo gun. "Remember what I told you, and you'll be fine. Even pressure, don't go too deep."

"Right," I murmur.

I flick the gun on, and the loud buzz makes me jump at first, but I settle into it. My heart races as I touch the needle to Malice's skin, but he doesn't flinch, and nothing terrible happens.

There's just a clean line of ink, and that gives me more confidence.

"Wipe the spot every few passes," he instructs. "So you can see what you're doing without ink everywhere."

I nod and do as he suggests, cleaning away the ink that smears over his skin.

"Good. Don't be afraid to go back over a line if you think it's going to be patchy. Just keep a light hand."

His tips help a lot, and I adjust as necessary, trying to keep my main focus on the needle and his skin.

"You're doing great," he praises after a few moments. "I knew you would."

"You have a lot of faith in me," I murmur back.

He shrugs lightly, barely moving his shoulder so as not to disturb the skin I'm tattooing. "I've seen what you're capable of.

221

Working a tattoo gun is easy compared to some of the shit you've done."

That makes me smile, and I keep working, going over a line a second time just to make sure it's dark enough. I remember how much the shading hurt when Malice was giving me my last tattoo, but he barely seems to be feeling the needle at all.

"Does this even feel like anything to you?" I ask. "You're not even flinching."

He shoots me a savage grin. "Oh, I can feel it, but maybe I just like it."

I grin back, knowing he's telling the truth. Malice is just like that, and honestly, I guess I am too.

It's easier than I thought it would be, but it does take a good amount of focus. The tattoo gun is an unfamiliar weight and thickness in my hand, and it takes me some time to get used to it. I go slow, taking my time and visualizing what I want each line to look like before I draw it.

"It gets easier every time you get one too," Malice continues. "Well, maybe not easier, but you get more used to it. You sat better for your second one, remember?"

I nod, because I do remember that. The first tattoo was a surprising amount of pain. The needle felt like it was branding me, burning into my skin. The second time, I had more of an idea what to expect.

I blush, remembering how his brothers helped me with the pain of the first tattoo. With Ransom's hand between my legs, working my clit, pleasure and pain mingled into something so different than anything I'd ever felt before.

The flush on my cheeks draws Malice's attention, or maybe he just likes looking at me. But his eyes are on me, and even though I'm trying to keep my focus on the tattoo I'm giving him, I can feel him looking.

"What?" I huff. "You're staring."

"You just look hot as fuck doing this. Especially naked."

"I have no idea what I'm doing," I protest.

He shrugs. "You still look hot."

Even though we literally just had sex, the tension between us is growing again. Malice's skin is warm where my free hand is braced against his chest, and I can feel the beat of his heart.

"What are you thinking about?" he murmurs, his gaze locked on my face.

"The first tattoo you gave me. And how I needed help handling the pain."

He chuckles, and I can feel the vibrations of that sound too. "You moved around more than I would've liked, but it worked like a charm in the end."

"Too bad I can't tattoo you and help you through the pain you're *not* feeling at the same time," I reply, grinning.

He laughs, and it's a nice sound. This feels good, comfortable and easy, and even the nerves about possibly fucking up Malice's tattoo have mostly faded.

"I remember when you were pissed at us." Malice's voice drops a little. "And you said you were going to get the tattoo removed."

I make a face at that memory. Like a lot of stuff near the beginning of all of this, it feels like it happened a very long time ago. We've been through so much since then, both good and bad—but all of it has clarified how we feel about each other.

"I did think about it," I murmur, chewing on my lip. "But... in the end, there was no way I could've done it. I didn't want to lose you guys, even when I thought that was the right thing to do. And you were right. The outward mark is just a signifier of something deeper. Something I couldn't have erased even if I wanted to."

He hums his approval at that, and when I sneak a glance up at his face, his gray eyes are fierce. His expression is full of love, Malice-style, and it makes me feel so treasured to bask under the warmth of it.

"Even if you had gotten it removed, I would've just given you another one when you came back," he tells me. "Because yeah, it's about the feeling, but I like to see the marks there too."

"Possessive bastard," I mutter, but I'm smiling.

"You know it. There are only two other people in the entire world who are allowed to touch you, and everyone else needs to know that you're already ours. That you've been claimed by me and my brothers."

My heart races at the conviction in his words, and my sore pussy clenches around nothing as my body reacts. Even though I'm not the one getting tattooed this time, I can still feel myself getting turned on, and I have to pull the tattoo gun away from Malice's skin for a bit to take a breath.

He looks a little smug, as if he knows exactly why I needed to take a break, but judging from the way his pants are tenting again, I'm not the only one who's been affected.

Luckily, there's not much more to do on the tattoo. I pull back, eyeing it a bit, and then go back in, adding a line here or darkening a section there. It's simple, nowhere near as ornate as some of the tattoos he's given me, but I'm proud of it all the same.

I wipe away the extra ink and blood one last time, and then stand back, switching off the gun.

"Okay, I'm done."

Malice looks down at his chest to see what I've put on him, and suddenly, a rush of nerves rise up again. I know what he said before, but what if he decides it was a bad idea to let someone with no experience put something permanent on his body?

I did the best I could, but I'm no expert. I don't even think I would qualify as a novice.

But then Malice smiles, and when he looks up at me, his eyes are molten and proud.

"It's fucking perfect," he says gruffly.

Finally, I let out a breath. "I'm glad you like it."

It doesn't look that bad, if I do say so myself. It's not crooked, at least, and it seems to fit in on his chest, nestled between all the other stark black lines and curves and angles of his other tattoos.

Just above his heart, I've drawn the letter W in smooth lines.

My initial, just like he tattooed his and his brothers' initials on me.

"Why just the W?" Malice asks, his gaze dropping to the tattoo again.

I shrug a shoulder. "I was raised as Willow Hayes because that was Misty's last name, but... that doesn't really feel right anymore. Then I found out I was a Stanton, but there's no way in hell I'm taking that name after everything that's happened. Then I was forced to marry Troy, but even though I'm leveraging being his widow to make moves against my grandmother, I'm never going to consider myself a Copeland. So it's just W for Willow. That's the simplest, purest part of me, I guess. The part I've always been no matter what else has changed. Just me. That's the mark I wanted to put on you."

Malice's jaw tightens when I bring up the Stanton name and Troy, but by the time I finish speaking, his expression has cleared.

"*Moja dusha prinadlezhit Tebe,*" he murmurs.

Before I can ask what he said, he's pulling me closer, threading his fingers into my hair and dragging me into a messy kiss. With his lips on mine, I lose track of everything else, gripping his shoulders and trying to keep myself afloat.

So when the door opens and Ransom and Vic come in, I jump in surprise.

Malice keeps a hold on me, not letting me go anywhere, and his brothers immediately pick up on what's going on. The air in the room seems to thicken as they take in the fact that I'm completely naked, and my hair is probably still a mess from getting fucked on the couch.

"Well, well," Ransom drawls. "What have you two been up to?"

"Sex," Vic answers, and I'm honestly not sure if he's teasing us, or if he's just such a literal person that he's answering his brother's question.

"Damn, I see how it is. Let us go do all the work while you stay home and fuck Willow."

Ransom is *definitely* teasing us, but I can hear something else in his voice too. Relief and pride. All of the brothers are aware of what a

225

big step this is for me, and I'm grateful all over again that they've never been the types to get jealous of each other or the time each of them spends with me. They know I love them all, and I know they love me.

Malice flips them both off, deepening our kiss in what I'm sure is meant to be a show for his brothers as his hands grope roughly at my body. Then he finally releases me, stretching a little as I step back.

Now that I'm no longer in front of him, his brothers can see the tattoo on his chest. They both seem to put the pieces together at the same time, looking from Malice to the tattoo gun and then to me.

"You let Willow give you a tattoo?" Ransom asks, sounding surprised.

"Yeah. And?" Malice shoots back. "She did a great job. And it wasn't about what the tattoo looked like anyway."

Vic sets down the bag he was carrying when they entered and moves closer, examining the W that's marked on his brother's chest in fresh ink. "Quite good for your first time, honestly," he murmurs.

I smile at him, the praise going straight to my head and mixing with all the other endorphins floating around in my system.

"You know what has to happen now, right?" Ransom sets his own bag down, then folds his arms.

"What?"

"You have to tattoo me and Vic too. Keep it even. Malice can't be the only one going around with your initial on his chest."

I chuckle ruefully. "You sure you want that? You see how wonky the one I did for Malice is." It's only half a joke, despite Vic's confirmation that it looks pretty good for my first time. "You should run far away from this."

"No." Vic shakes his head, surprising me by immediately taking Ransom's side. "We want you to do it."

"Yeah, we don't care if it's professional quality. It being your work is what makes it special," Ransom agrees.

I look to Malice, since it's his equipment, and he just raises an

226

eyebrow at me. It's pure challenge, like he wants to see if I can do it, and there's no hesitation in him at all.

"Okay." I nod, grinning in spite of myself. "If you really want me to, I can mark you both too."

Malice shows me how to change out the needles in the gun and get new ink, and Ransom takes off his shirt first. He sits on the couch with his legs spread, leaving room for me to kneel between them.

"In the same spot as I did for Malice?" I ask him, glancing up at his face.

His blue-green eyes gleam as he looks down at me. "If you can fit it in, yeah."

He doesn't have as many tattoos as Malice, so it's easier to find space for it, and I get to work.

It's easier the second time, which shouldn't be a surprise, I guess. I'm more used to the weight of the gun and the way it moves, so I can control it more, making more even lines as I start to tattoo Ransom's chest.

I can feel Vic and Malice watching me, and the thick feeling of tension in the room doesn't abate. It makes the air seem so hot that it practically sears my skin, warming me from the outside in, and I have to fight the urge to look over at them.

Ransom doesn't flinch from the pain either, taking it with the good grace and easy humor he takes most things in life.

"You know, I feel kind of like an idiot, but I didn't expect this to be so hot," he says after a few minutes.

"Which part?" I ask, pausing to wipe away some of the ink.

"You doing tattoos. You've got this look of concentration on your face, like you're trying to make sure you do a good job, and it's sexy as fuck."

Vic makes a noise of agreement, and I find myself smiling.

"That's just the endorphins talking. All of you lunatics seem to get off on pain."

"As if you don't," Ransom fires back, and the weight of knowledge in his voice makes my pussy clench. He's seen firsthand what the perfect mix of pain and pleasure can do to me.

This tattoo goes a bit quicker, and after several more minutes, I sit back, wiping away the last of the ink and blood to reveal the fresh W on Ransom's chest. He smiles when he looks down at it, that same warm, fond look on his face that Malice wore.

"Amazing job, angel. I'll wear this with pride."

He puts his hands on my face and draws me up so he can kiss me. It's slow and deep, but there's heat there all the same. Ransom pours his feelings into it, and I gasp a little against his lips, kissing him right back.

"How are you so perfect?" he murmurs against my lips.

My lips curve upward, and I know he can feel my grin. "I'm not really perfect." He starts to speak, probably to tell me I'm wrong, but before he can, I add, "But I *am* perfect for the three of you. Just like you're perfect for me."

His voice drops low as he groans, "Fuck, yes. You have no idea."

He kisses me again, and I get the feeling that if Vic wasn't waiting for his turn to be tattooed, there's a good chance I'd end up on my back on the couch again. But after a few more heartbeats, he reluctantly releases me, then gets up to make room for Vic.

Vic already has his shirt off, and I know without even checking that his shirt will be folded neatly on the coffee table instead of tossed to the side like Ransom's and Malice's shirts.

He smiles when he sits down, and I smile back, taking a moment to check out the canvas of his body the way I did with his brothers.

It's different with Vic, of course. He has some tattoos that he got willingly, but so many of them are marks left behind by his asshole father. I wonder what he thinks of when he sees them, and if he ever thinks of getting them removed. Maybe he wears them like badges of honor, the same way I've decided to wear my scars. A reminder to himself of what he's been through and what he survived.

Either way, I want the tattoo I give him to be a reminder of something so much better than that.

After prepping the gun one more time with Malice's help, I grab it and rest one hand on Vic's chest to balance myself.

"Okay?" I ask, glancing at him.

His blue eyes are dark, and he does seem a bit on edge. Still, he nods, giving me his approval to keep going.

The third time is even easier, even if my hand is starting to cramp up a little from holding the gun. I move the needle in neat lines, the design of my initial already burned into my brain by now.

Vic takes deep, even breaths, and his fingers tap out a steady rhythm on his thigh as he counts to himself, riding out the sensations.

I know he's using his counting techniques to get through the pain, but I can tell from the way his face is flushed that there's pleasure too. When I go over a line to make it a little darker, a noise spills out of Vic's mouth, and I have to wonder if he let it slip on purpose, or if it was involuntary.

Either way, it sounded closer to a moan than a sound of distress, and the sexual tension in the air kicks up another notch.

I can feel Malice and Ransom off to the side, their attention locked on me intently. Ransom's breathing is loud, and Malice makes a noise low in his throat, similar to the sound his twin just made.

Vic jerks a little in his seat, and I glance up at him, pausing for a second. He's hard in his pants, and he stops tapping his fingers on his leg and palms his cock instead, squeezing his hard-on as if trying to master himself.

I lick my lips, my heart racing a little.

"You could take care of yourself the same way you guys took care of me when I got my first tattoo," I whisper.

The way his eyes immediately flare with heat and then go even darker lets me know that he remembers exactly what happened when I got my first tattoo, and his fingers fumble for his waistband without hesitation.

I watch, keeping the needle away from his skin as he drags his cock out and takes it in hand.

It's thick and hard, flushed at the tip and leaking slightly. My stomach flutters at the sight, and I lean closer and spit directly onto the head, giving him some lube to work with.

"Do that again," he rasps, so I do, watching him smear it over the smooth, veiny skin of his cock.

It's almost mesmerizing, and it takes a few seconds for me to wrench my attention back to the tattoo I'm giving him and away from how Vic strokes himself in slow movements.

Out of the corner of my eye, I catch more motion, and when I shoot a quick glance in that direction, I see Ransom lick his palm before wrapping his fist around his own cock. Beside him, Malice is hard again, stroking himself as he watches me.

If the room didn't smell like sex before, it definitely does now, and the scent of it is like a fucking aphrodisiac, making me crave more. My body is exhausted, but my clit still throbs a little, weak little pulses that urge me on.

"Fuck..." Vic tips his head back on another groan, and I'm positive by now that each noise he makes is intended to be audible.

He wants me to hear what I'm doing to him, how much he's getting off on this. There's still that fine control, his usual precision in how he keeps his strokes even, not letting his hand fly over his cock to bring him to completion too soon... but he's getting close.

"I'm almost done," I murmur, going back in to touch up a few places.

"Me too," he rasps with a sound that's almost a laugh.

The strain in his voice makes a shiver run through me, and I finish up the tattoo before setting the gun aside for good.

When I give my full attention to Vic, I can tell he's about to lose it. His breath comes in harsh pants, and his hips buck up in little jerks, meeting the movement of his fist. On my other side, I can hear the wet, filthy sounds of his two brothers jerking off as well—and suddenly, there's only one thing in the world that I want.

"Come on me," I blurt, the words spilling out of my mouth. "All of you. Please."

Vic's gaze locks with mine, his nostrils flaring. "Are you sure?"

"God, yes," I gasp out. "I want you to. Paint me with your cum. Make me filthy for you. Mark me as yours."

"Shit," Vic curses.

"See?" Ransom groans. "Like I said, you're perfect. Such a good fucking girl."

"Such a *dirty* fucking girl," Malice adds. "You want us to make you even dirtier? We can do that."

He and Ransom step closer, and Vic surges to his feet. All three of them are surrounding me now in front of the couch, with me still on my knees. That puts their cocks level with my face, and I bite my lip hard, watching with hungry anticipation as they stroke themselves. The room is filled with the sound of slick skin on skin, their harsh breathing, and the noises that pour from their lips.

Vic comes first, going tense and rigid as pleasure rips through him. He grunts and juts his hips forward, letting the hot, sticky ropes of his cum splatter over my face and chest.

I moan low in my throat, enjoying the feeling of it.

Malice and Ransom follow in quick succession. They jack themselves off until they explode, squeezing out every drop of cum, painting my face, neck, and chest with the hot, pearly liquid.

I shudder, pleasure rocking through me, and even though it's not an orgasm, it's almost as good.

It's everything I needed... and then some.

24

WILLOW

IN THE NEXT FEW DAYS, I seek out more opportunities to use my new position and wealth to fuck with Olivia. It's just small things here and there, things Vic recommends from his research, but it does feel really good to be doing something against her. To be making consistent moves and making sure my grandmother knows we're not backing down.

On top of that, I feel better than I have since the guys got me back.

It's not an overnight fix, but the knowledge that I've made progress seems to set off a kind of domino effect. It reminds me that I'm not hopelessly broken, so on those mornings when I wake up in tears or a cold sweat from a nightmare, it doesn't feel like the end of the world.

I'm still struggling in some ways, and there are still times when I wake up in the middle of the night gasping for breath, so sure that I'm still in that tiny little hole in the floor Troy used to force me into. But then one of the guys will wake up and soothe me back to sleep, or Malice will snore, and it'll remind me that I'm safe. That I'm with them, and they're not going to abandon me because I'm not fixed yet.

It feels like being on more solid footing, and I'm so fucking grateful for that. I'm no longer anyone's victim. Troy got what was coming to him, and I'm not just a pawn in Olivia's games. I'm playing in her world, making moves that force her to see me as an equal, and I'm doing it on my own terms. I stole the wealth of the man I was forced to marry, and now I'm using it to build the life for myself I always wanted. Not the one I thought I wanted or the life I assumed I should want, but the one I truly want.

A life where I get to call the shots and do things that make me happy. A life surrounded by three men who love me unconditionally, whose support and unwavering love make me feel like I could do anything.

I'm finally starting to feel that strength that they always say they see in me, and it makes me feel good.

So I'm smiling as I take the elevator down to the building's garage, humming a little under my breath.

Ransom has been down here for the last couple of hours, working on his new bike. It's a shiny blue Ducati, and I can tell he's thrilled to have replaced his old one.

He glances up when he sees me approach, wiping grease off his hands on a dirty rag.

"What are you grinning about, pretty girl?" he asks.

That just makes my smile stretch wider as I come over. "Nothing, really. Just in a good mood."

"I like to see you smiling." He reaches out and pulls me closer, kissing me lightly.

His lips feel good against mine, the way they always do. Soft and tender, with just that edge of desire that promises it could be something more if we both wanted it to turn into that. I savor it, enjoying the way I can melt against him now more easily than before.

"How's it going down here?" I ask him, pulling back and trailing a hand over the shiny surface of the bike.

"Good. It's coming along well. I was gonna go pick up a part for the bike soon."

"Isn't it new?"

"Yeah, but I mostly wanted it for the shell, if that makes sense. I always fiddle with the guts of a bike to make everything a little better. I'm overhauling this one to really open it up."

I nod along with him, even though I'm only sort of following what he means. "Ah, right. That makes sense."

Ransom grins, seeing right through me. "Do you wanna come along for the ride?" He waggles his eyebrows at me.

"Yes," I say immediately. It's been a while since I've been on the back of a bike with Ransom, and it's one of my favorite things in the world.

He flicks his tongue piercing between his teeth as he grins wider, clearly pleased with that response. "Cool. When we get back, I'll show you how to install the part."

"I like the sound of that."

He puts away his tools and closes up the panel in the bike he had opened, then swings his leg over the seat. He pats the spot behind him.

"Hop on, angel."

A flutter of excitement fills my stomach as I climb onto the motorcycle, wrapping my arms around his waist. Ransom revs the bike a few times and then peels out of the garage, taking us out onto the road.

I'm sure no one who lives in this section of the city is used to motorcycles tearing down the road, but Ransom doesn't seem to care. He speeds along, and the wind rushing by feels amazing, whipping my hair around my face. It takes me back to the first time he took me out, after I showed up at their warehouse late one night. I was so nervous about it then, but the exhilaration won me over.

We don't head to an auto parts shop, but instead go farther into the city, closer to where the guys used to live. We pull up to an old, worn looking garage, and Ransom cuts the engine and helps me off the bike.

"Stick close," he murmurs to me.

I was already planning on it, but I take a step even closer, and he wraps an arm around me, tugging me against his side. As soon as we walk in, it's clear that the people who hang around this place know Ransom well.

"Voronin. Haven't seen you around here in a while," a burly man in his mid-forties says, shoving back his shoulder length hair as he strides over. "You been getting parts from somewhere else?"

Ransom snorts. "Never, Luis. We've just been busy. Haven't been doing much bodywork or chopping lately."

Luis grunts in response. His gaze flicks to me, but it darts away when Ransom stiffens slightly, his arm tightening around me in a possessive gesture. It's clear he's staked his claim, and Luis clearly doesn't want to piss him off, because he doesn't look at me again as the two of them talk shop.

"I'm working on a new Ducati, and I need some forks," Ransom says. "I'm going for high-performance, so I need something with adjustable damping and preload settings. What've you got for me?"

Everything he said sounded like gibberish to me, but Luis nods. "Yeah, I think I can help you with that. We've got some new forks we pulled off a shiny red thing we brought in last week." He brings us into the back of the shop, where he digs out a few parts and shows them to Ransom. "Will those do the trick?"

Ransom nods. "Yeah, this'll be great. How much?"

They haggle over the price, going back and forth. It's not heated, but it's clear both of them know what they're doing and what they're willing to give.

"Deal," Luis finally says. He holds out a hand, and instead of shaking it, Ransom finally releases his hold on me long enough to pull out several large bills and slap them into Luis's palm.

"A pleasure as always," Ransom tells the man with a nod. "Come on, angel."

He takes the parts the man offers him, then jerks his head toward the door, and we head out.

"That was... interesting," I tell him as we go.

He snorts. "That's business. Well, business on this side of the tracks, at least. Luis gets parts in from chop shops—or wherever, really—and then he sells them for his own prices. Or trades them for other things. We worked with him a lot, back in the day. But he's right. It's been a while."

He leads the way back to his bike, popping open the under-seat storage compartment so he can stow the parts he just bought. Off to the side of the garage, I hear several men laughing, followed by the sound of shattering glass. It makes me jump, and I half turn to see if I can figure out where the noise is coming from.

Bang!

A loud shot rings out, and I feel something graze past my arm.

Time almost seems to slow down. It only takes me a second to figure out that the sound I just heard was a gunshot, but Ransom is faster than me. He wraps his fingers around my arm, yanking me out of the way of the next shot.

"Motherfucker! Get down, angel!"

We use the bike for cover, huddling behind it, and I can see a car speeding by down the street, more gunshots echoing as it goes past.

The bullets ping into the bike, hitting the metal with loud sounds, popping the tires, leaving it a mess.

My heart is going a mile a minute, my entire body tense and on edge as my fight-or-flight response kicks in. The car peels off down the street, rounding a corner with a screech of tires. As soon as it's out of sight, Ransom leaps into action.

"Stay close," he mutters, and this time, it sounds much more serious than when he said it just a few minutes ago. "They could come back for another shot at us."

Luis and his men are emerging from the garage, all armed with weapons, but Ransom doesn't stop to talk to them. Pulling out his own gun from the under-seat compartment, he shoves it into the waistband of his pants and then grabs my arm, standing up and dragging me behind him.

We dart between buildings and down alleyways, staying off the main streets, and my stomach swoops sickeningly as vivid memories of sprinting to try to evade Troy's Jeep in Mexico fill my mind.

By the time Ransom finally stops running, I've lost track of where we are entirely. He pulls me into the doorway alcove of an abandoned looking building, glancing up and down the street before pulling out his phone to make a call.

"Vic," he says as soon as his brother picks up. "I'm with Willow, down by Luis's place. Someone just fucking shot at us." He grimaces, baring his teeth. "I don't know who. I didn't get a good look at them. But my bike is fucked, and we need to get out of —" He breaks off, listening to something Vic is saying. "Yeah, alright. That works."

He sounds pissed as he talks to Vic, one hand still wrapped around my forearm. It's a good thing he hasn't let go, really. His almost bruising grip on me is keeping me grounded, holding the fluttery feelings of panic at bay.

It's not even the first time someone has shot at me or around me, but that was a close call. A bullet grazed my arm, and if it hadn't been for Ransom's quick reaction...

I don't want to think about that.

Ransom's face is pinched when he hangs up the call, shoving his phone into his pocket.

"Motherfucking cocksuckers," he mutters under his breath.

"I'm sorry," I murmur.

"What? What do you have to be sorry for?"

"Your bike. It was brand new, and now—"

Before I can finish, Ransom lets go of my arm. His face is intense as he reaches up, gripping my chin and looking right into my eyes.

"Fuck the bike," he says firmly. "I don't give a shit about the bike."

"But—"

"Willow. No bike, nothing in the world, will ever matter more to me than you. You're safe, and that's all that fucking matters. Okay?"

I swallow hard, then nod shakily. The last several minutes feel a little surreal. We went from just running a simple errand to

237

getting shot at, and I'm still reeling from it a little. But I force my muscles to stop shaking, reminding myself that there's no room for fear right now. I can't let it cloud my thoughts or slow me down.

"We're getting a ride out of here, since my bike is fucked," Ransom explains. "Stay behind me as much as you can."

He positions his body in front of mine, his fingers wrapped around the grip of his gun as he watches the street warily. We stay like that for what feels like forever, and when Vic and Malice pull up in the car, my heart leaps at the sight of them.

Keeping his gun drawn and his head low, Ransom wraps an arm around my shoulders and hustles me into the car. We jump into the back, and Malice cranks the wheel to pull away from the curb.

"Did you see anything on the way over?" Ransom asks, peering out the back window as he shoves his gun back into his waistband.

Vic shakes his head. "Nothing." He looks to me, craning his neck from where he sits in the front passenger seat. "You're alright?"

I nod. "Yeah. Ransom pulled me down before anything could happen."

"Good."

Malice adjusts his grip on the wheel as he growls, "What the fuck happened?"

"We were leaving the garage when I heard gunshots," I tell him. "I think a bullet grazed my arm—"

As soon as the words are out of my mouth, Vic twists around in the front seat, reaching back to take my arm in his hands. He inspects the spot, running his fingers over the raised mark.

"No bleeding, at least," he murmurs. "You're sure it was just a graze? You didn't get hit anywhere else?"

"No." I swallow. "It's okay. It doesn't even really hurt."

"What else did you see?" Malice wants to know.

Ransom takes over, answering his brother as Vic finally releases my arm. "They were in a car, whoever they were. Speeding down

238

the street. I know shit goes down at Luis's place sometimes, but this wasn't like that. It didn't feel... random."

"Was anyone else around?"

"There were some of Luis's guys hanging around like usual, but no one gave us any trouble. I got the part I needed, and we were about to head out when it happened."

"And you didn't see who it was?" Malice asks.

Ransom shakes his head. "I was a little busy trying to get us down behind the bike. But the windows were tinted, and they were going too fast anyway."

"Fuck," Malice snarls, pounding the wheel with his fist. "This can't just be about Luis or his suppliers. That's too big a fucking coincidence. There's no fucking way."

I twist my fingers together, my heart racing all over again. "So you think this was about me? About us?"

Malice's gray eyes flick to mine in the rearview mirror. "I think we have to go forward assuming it was. We take no chances."

I nod, feeling sick. But Malice is right. There are plenty of people in Detroit who hate me—who hate all of us—so it would be foolish to assume that an attempted drive-by was just a random act of violence. The more likely scenario is that it was targeted. Someone is trying to take us out.

We get back to the penthouse, and the guys surround me again as we get out of the car. Ransom's head is on a swivel as Malice locks the car, and all of us are tense and quiet on the elevator ride up. Once we reach the top floor, Vic holds me back from going inside the penthouse until Malice and Ransom can do a sweep inside.

The thought that someone might be in there, lying in wait for us, ready to kill any or all of us, is enough to make nausea roil my stomach.

"Okay, it's clear," Malice says after a minute, beckoning us inside.

As I step over the threshold, my phone rings in my back pocket. The sound is startlingly loud in the silence of the condo, and it makes me jump. I scramble to dig it out of my pocket, and when I see the name on the caller ID, my heart clenches.

Olivia.

Malice is standing close enough to me that he can read her name on the screen, and he looks up from the phone, his gaze locking with mine.

"There are no coincidences," he says grimly, his jaw tight.

He's right. There's no way it doesn't mean anything that Olivia is calling me less than an hour after someone shot at me.

My throat is tight with anger and worry as I slide my finger across the screen to answer the call. I lift the phone and put it on speaker, forcing words out as Ransom and Vic come to stand close beside me too.

"Were those your people?" I demand, skipping over any pretense of niceties. "Did you hire someone try to gun me down in the street?"

Her laugh is cool and calm in my ear. "I don't know what you're talking about, of course," she says evenly. "I wouldn't even know how to begin doing something like that. I don't dabble in crime, unlike your filthy little boyfriends."

My fingers curl around the phone, irritation pricking at me. Of course she won't admit it. Not on the phone, where I could be recording her words. She's smarter than that, which is why she's managed to 'dabble in crime,' as she put it, for years without getting caught.

"It sounds like you must be having a rough afternoon," she continues, and I can practically hear the smirk in her voice. "Someone shot at you, you say? That's terrible."

"Cut the shit, Olivia," I bite out. "I know you sent them."

"And I'm telling you I didn't." She chuckles. "But if someone shot at you, my dear, I wouldn't act so surprised. After all, you painted a target on your back when you became Troy Copeland's widow and inherited his entire estate. Just like you said, you've leveled up in this world. And that comes with its own set of risks. Do you understand?"

My brows pinch together tightly, and I glance at the men around me. *What the hell is she getting at?*

"Don't act like you care about me," I spit. "You're a fucking cunt, and even if the rest of the world can't see it, I can."

She makes a disapproving noise. "Such foul language. Clearly none of my efforts to teach you how to behave like a lady had an effect. But I just wanted to warn you to be careful. You're my only living relative, after all, just like I'm yours. It would be such a shame if you died."

"What the fuck are you talking about?" I demand in a hard voice, sick of her falsely sweet tone. "What do you want?"

"I've had my lawyers looking into it, and they've found a way to ensure that I will be the benefactor of everything you own in the event of your death," she says, a note of triumph in her voice. "I just wanted to make you aware of that."

My stomach drops. "What?"

"Don't sound so surprised, dear. I just took a page out of your book. You were clever enough to have Troy sign everything over to you before he died tragically. And now it turns out that if the same fate befalls you, *I'll* get everything Troy once had. Funny how life works out, isn't it?"

Malice makes a low, angry noise, and I stare down at the screen of my phone as her words wash over me.

"You're crazy," I hiss. "You can't do this."

She clicks her tongue against her teeth. "You know, I was starting to think you understood, but you keep underestimating what I'll do to preserve my legacy. I will not sit idly by and let you ruin what I have dedicated my life to building up. So here are your options. You can either sign everything over to me willingly now, or I'll get all of it anyway when you die. It's really quite simple."

For a horrible moment, I have a flash of being back in that graveyard. Of having just buried Misty, standing over my adoptive mother's grave as Olivia levied her ultimatum.

I was so helpless then, shocked and without a leg to stand on. The only thing I could do was give in. I can remember her cool,

241

cruel tone, the way she didn't seem to care at all that she was playing with my life, using me like a puppet just to increase her wealth.

It's the same now. The fraying edges I saw when she confronted me last are completely gone.

She hasn't just been struggling to plug the leaks in her business that we've been poking over the past weeks. All that time, even as I made moves against her, she was preparing her counterstrike.

And now she's delivered a warning shot.

"I'll give you some time to make your choice," she says coolly. "But I won't wait forever. You've always said you don't want any part of this life, Willow. That you don't care about the money. Now's your chance to prove whether that's really true. Sign everything over to me, and you can have the peace you want so badly."

Then she hangs up the call, leaving me standing in stillness, clutching my phone in a death grip.

I blink, looking up to meet the faces of my men as they huddle around me. They look pissed as hell, but I'm just... reeling.

For as long as I've known Olivia, she's tried to use me. She's seen me as a pawn in her game. It's still true, I guess, that she wants me to be useful to her.

But now there's only one way I can do that.

By being dead.

25

VICTOR

WATCHING the fear spread across Willow's face makes anger rise up in me. I can feel it, hot and sharp, bubbling in my stomach and spreading through my body.

I usually have a much better handle on things like this, but where Willow and her safety are concerned, it's hard not to get pissed off. Especially about something like this.

There's still a lot of baggage that I carry around because of my piece of shit father. Because of the way he treated me—used me. And seeing Willow used in a similar way makes my blood boil. Olivia treats her like a means to an end, an object. Something she would willingly destroy to get what she wants. Like a chess piece to be sacrificed when it's no longer useful on the board.

There's pain in Willow's eyes as she puts down her phone. She looks shell-shocked, like she can't quite believe that her grandmother is willing to put a hit out on her, to outright have her assassinated to get what she wants.

For so long when we were on the run, there was at least some comfort in knowing that Olivia wanted Willow *alive*.

But that's no longer the case.

"I don't—" She breaks off, swallowing. "I should've seen this coming. She killed Misty. She either killed my birth mother or paid someone to start the fire. And now she's going to try to kill me too."

"She fucking won't," Malice says fiercely. He steps in and grabs Willow's arm, taking her phone from her. He puts it down on the table beside the door with more force than necessary and pulls her close. "Do you hear me? She's not gonna fucking touch you."

"I... she already tried. She already got so close. If it wasn't for Ransom being there today, then whoever was in that car would've succeeded in shooting me."

"Yeah, and I'll be there the next time too. And the next. Or my brothers will." Ransom's voice is hard. "No one's going to get a clear shot at you, angel. Ever. It's not gonna happen."

She nods, but I can tell she's not really hearing what they're saying. She's caught in her own head, thinking about Olivia's words and what happened this afternoon.

"If I give her what she wants and sign everything over to her, it *won't* be over," she mutters, her voice thick. "All I'll have done is give up every resource I have, and I guarantee she won't truly stop trying to come after me. Or she'll leave me alone and go after you three instead. It's not a real offer. I can't win. Either way, no matter what I do, she's not going to stop until I'm dead."

I step in closer, reaching out to touch her shoulder lightly. It makes her jump, but she at least looks up at me.

"She's told us her plan now," I say, keeping my voice low. "So we know what to be on the look out for. She's not going to be able to harm a hair on your head. I promise."

If our words are reaching Willow, they don't seem to be providing any comfort. She shakes her head, pulling away from us, wrapping her arms around herself. There's an almost wild look in her eyes, and I can see that she's spiraling a little, the shock of what happened giving way to anxiety and fear.

"How?" she demands, her voice thready. "How can you even promise that?"

"What the fuck do you mean, 'how'?" Malice growls. "You think we can't keep you safe?"

"It's not about that! It's not about you keeping me safe. It's about Olivia. She's always one step ahead! Even when we have the upper hand, she manages to tip the scales in her favor. Nothing we've done has stopped her. Maybe we've slowed her down some, we've put some bumps in the road for her, but she's unstoppable."

Malice shakes his head, his dark hair glinting. "No. No one is unstoppable."

"Then how do we stop her?" Willow cries. "Because nothing we've tried has worked. She just keeps coming back and hitting harder every time. First she wanted me to get married, then she forced me to marry Troy, and now she wants me dead! You can't rescue me from being dead!"

Her voice rings out in the penthouse, and we all kind of stop short at the note of panic in her voice. Ransom looks stricken, as if he doesn't even want to think about Willow being dead, and I know how he feels. Just hearing her say the words felt like a knife to my chest.

Malice balls his hands into fists and shakes his head, his jaw tight.

"Well, there's one way to make sure she stops for good. She's copying your playbook, so now we copy hers right back. We take her out."

That seems to cut through Willow's panic, at least for a moment. She stares at Malice, her face paling a little. "What, you mean... kill her?"

My twin meets her gaze steadily, not backing down. "You said yourself that nothing else we've tried has worked. So why the fuck shouldn't we kill her?"

"I..." Willow shakes her head.

I can see the conflict in her face, and it hits me right in the chest. It's beautiful, how even after everything that's happened to her, everything she's seen, she's still such a good person. A person who wouldn't choose to kill someone even to save her own skin. Unfortunately, sometimes that's the only option, which my brothers and I know well.

"She doesn't deserve your mercy," Ransom points out, his tone more serious than I've heard in a while. "She's perfectly willing to kill you or have someone else do it for her. She's a monster, Willow. Don't forget that."

"I haven't forgotten. I *can't*. But... I don't know if I can kill her."

"You won't have to," Malice assures her. "You don't have to get any blood on your hands. We'll do it. We'd be fucking happy to do it. After all this bitch has done, she deserves a slow, painful death."

Willow shakes her head again, still looking like she's processing all of this. It has to be a lot for her, to move from the idea of ruining Olivia financially to outright killing her. But she did have a point that Olivia keeps raising the stakes. So we have to be willing to do the same.

We have to go all in.

Gloves off.

Fighting dirty.

Willow licks her lips, looking down at her hands. "How would you even do it, anyway? I know you said it would be dangerous to attack her, and it's not like she walks around unprotected. She has security with her all the time. And now that she's made her threat, she's probably going to beef up the security she already has. Do you really think you can take her on?"

Malice bristles, looking almost offended, as if Willow is doubting us. But I know it's not about that. She's worried about us.

"We wouldn't just run in, guns blazing," I promise her. "We would need a plan."

"A damned good one too," Ransom admits, shoving a hand through his hair. "Even in a weakened state, Olivia is well-connected and well-protected."

"There are ways past both of those issues," I remind him. "We didn't go after her when Willow was with Troy because if we'd been arrested or killed, Willow would've been stuck with Troy, with no one left to find her. But the stakes are different now. Which means we can play the game differently."

Malice starts pacing, cracking his knuckles as he stalks across the living room floor. He practically radiates furious energy, but the same could be said for all of us. Ransom's eyes glitter with anger, and that same unsettled agitation is there in me too.

But I push it back for now, because I need to focus. I need to be able to think past the raw emotions that grip me. My mind moves a mile a minute, putting together plans and discarding them just as fast.

Whatever we attempt against Olivia, the plan has to be airtight. It has to leave no room for error or surprise. Willow's grandmother has proven that she's very good at exploiting any opening we give her and operating in our blind spots. Manipulating them, even—like when she let us believe that Troy was dead, so he could come out of nowhere to ambush us and take Willow.

We can't afford a mistake like that again.

"We've been hitting her financially," Malice says finally. "How's she paying for all this security?"

"We haven't been able to hit her hard enough," Willow replies. "We can hurt her investments and take away the expansions she wants to make to restore her estate, but she's still incredibly rich."

"Do you think we could try to outbid her?" Ransom asks. "Like, pay some of her security to just... take a little break and let us get in there?"

"That's risky as hell," Malice grunts. "What's to stop them from just taking the money and then fucking us over? Then we'd be trapped with no backup."

Ransom makes a face. "Yeah, there is that. But we took out Troy and his bodyguards. There's got to be a way."

"Troy wasn't expecting us. He had guards around, sure. But they were overconfident, thinking no one would find them in his cabin. Counting on Olivia to underestimate the threat is a mistake. And she can always hire more guards, while there will only ever be just four of us."

"Wait," I say, cutting into their conversation as something sparks in my mind. "I have an idea."

"What?" Willow asks, a flicker of hope lighting in her expression.

"Those jobs we used to do for her. All the stuff she blackmailed us into doing when we only knew her as X."

Willow's face crumples. "We already tried that route, remember? I couldn't get enough information connecting her to being X and all the illegal shit she made you do. She's kept her footprint too clean."

"No, you're right about that, but that's not what I mean," I say. I start pacing a little, letting the idea grow in my mind. "We won't use those jobs for blackmail against her. Instead, we can use them to find people who have reason to be enemies with Olivia. Every job she sent us on, she was fucking someone over, right? So we follow those breadcrumbs, and we find someone who hates her just as much as we do. One of them might be able to help us take her down. Even the odds, so that there are more than just four of us to pull off this attack."

Ransom and Malice nod, both looking thoughtful.

"That's a place to start, at least," Ransom says, scrubbing at the back of his head. "Getting outside help with this might be our best bet."

"Are you sure that's a good idea?" Willow asks, chewing her lip.

She still seems uncertain and worried, and I wish I could take that away from her. I know what it's like to feel as if the rug has been ripped out from under you entirely.

"It's the best idea we have right now," I tell her, reaching out to squeeze her hand. "And it's relatively low-risk, all things considered. Olivia already knows we won't take this lying down, so she's going to be expecting something to happen. The only way we'll have a chance is if we do something she's *not* expecting. We just have to hope we can find someone with a big enough grudge against her."

"Olivia Stanton is a heartless cunt," Malice spits. "We'll find someone who hates her. Shouldn't be too hard. She's probably fucked over countless people to get what she wants."

"So that's the plan?" Ransom asks, practically bouncing on his toes like he can't wait to get started.

"Yes." Malice nods immediately.

I do too, and when we all turn to look at Willow, she dips her chin once in agreement.

"Okay," she whispers. "Let's do it."

I turn, heading for my office to start sifting through information. As I go, I call over my shoulder to Ransom.

"You and Malice work on upping the security of this place. We have to be on our guard. Olivia gave Willow time to make her decision, but we can't trust that she'll actually uphold her word. I'll go see what I can find from the jobs we've done for her."

Ransom nods grimly, and we split up, each moving quickly to handle our respective tasks.

IT'S NOT AN EASY SEARCH.

A lot of the jobs we've done for Olivia were crimes against white collar businesses or up and comers in the Detroit business world. And although some of those people might be pissed as hell to find out that Olivia Stanton sabotaged them, they're not exactly the types who'd be most likely to want to help people like us—or to *be* much help, even if they wanted to.

We need to find someone more like us.

Someone familiar with violence, who's lived and breathed it and has it in their bones.

We're looking for a needle in a haystack here, and there's plenty to sift through.

It takes more than a few days of constant work to go through our previous correspondences with X and cross reference them with my notes and recon for each job we did. Ransom and Malice work to reinforce security on the condo, and we keep Willow close

249

the whole time, refusing to let her leave our little hideout. Just to be safe.

She bears it well enough for the first couple of days, but by the time we're closing in on day five, I can tell she's starting to get antsy.

She feels trapped, I'm sure, and I get that. But there's no way around it. We can't let anything happen to her. Because none of us can live without her, and it's obvious that the gloves are completely off with Olivia now.

I've set up my command center in the room I've taken over as my office. It's barely furnished except for a desk and a nice office chair, along with the multiple computers and screens that I use to get shit done.

I've been in here almost all day every day since we made the decision to try to eliminate Olivia. The last time I spent this much uninterrupted time at my computers was when we were trying to find Willow after Troy stole her from us, and pulling long hours now brings back uncomfortable memories of that time. My side has healed up well, but the scar from the bullet wound twinges sometimes as I work, as if my entire body is being transported back to those awful, soul-crushing days of searching for the woman we love.

After closing the most recent file I've been studying, I lean back in my chair and roll my neck. I blink a few times, feeling the strain in my eyes, then rest my hand on the mouse again. As I open another file, Willow wanders into the room.

The door is off to one side, so I barely pick up the movement in my periphery, but I'm instantly aware of her presence. It seems to fill the room, and I look over at her.

"What's up?"

"Nothing," she says, shaking her head. "I just miss you. You've been in here so much lately."

I smile, feeling the curl of pleasure in my stomach. I like that she missed me. I like that she's been thinking of me.

And she's right. I have been spending almost every waking

hour in here, so I turn in my chair, putting the monitors at my back. I can take a small break to give her all my focus.

Seeing that makes her brighten, a little bit of color returning to her pale cheeks. She's been strung-out and on edge, small circles growing under her eyes, and it makes me worry about her.

"How are you holding up?" I ask. "I know this can't be easy for you."

She sighs, scrunching up her nose. "Is it that obvious?"

"If you know how to look for it, yes."

"And you know how to look for everything," she murmurs, but she doesn't sound put out about it. "You read me so well. You see everything."

"I still want to hear it from you," I tell her.

She seems to think about it for a moment, and then sighs again. "I don't know. I just... I was just starting to feel like I was in control, you know? Like I was getting my strength back and feeling more like myself after... everything."

I nod, not needing her to elaborate on what she means by that. None of us are likely to forget anytime soon. "And now this is a setback."

"Yeah. The steady footing I had, it feels like it's slipping away. Like I'm losing control of my own life, and I hate it. I was supposed to be getting better, but this is like three steps back. I'm always looking over my shoulder, jittery all the time, worried about what might happen."

I nod, understanding where she's coming from. After all, maintaining tight, unbending control of my life and my emotions is something I worked on really fucking hard over the years. So I get what it feels like to feel that slip away. Even though I've let go of some of that when it comes to Willow, there are other parts that I'll probably always need, just to keep myself from falling back into the darkness that tries to claim me sometimes.

"You haven't lost that progress," I promise her. "Recovery isn't a switch you can flip. It's an ongoing process. Even when you were feeling better, you still had nightmares, right?"

"Yeah," she murmurs.

"But you still felt like you were getting somewhere. You were making progress despite the setbacks."

She nods.

I tap my fingers on my leg, ordering my thoughts. "You know how I've struggled with things. I struggled for years with the baggage from what happened to me. Even after I met you, and I wanted to open up and wanted to touch you and everything else, I couldn't for a long time."

"I know," she murmurs. "But you still made a lot of progress. You worked up to it."

"Exactly," I tell her, nodding.

She blinks, seeming to get my point. Her smile is tentative, but so beautiful. "Thank you," she whispers. "For trying so hard. For working to get where you are. So we can be where we are now."

"Of course. I would do anything for you."

I mean it. There's no hesitation or doubt in my words. And as I speak, a thought sparks in the back of my mind.

I hesitate for a second, working it over in my mind. It's a good idea, I'm pretty sure, and although it's something new to me, I *did* just tell Willow that I'd do anything for her. This is a small thing in the grand scheme of it all.

So I get up from my chair and start to head for the door. "Come with me."

Willow frowns, clearly confused, but she follows me to the bedroom where the massive bed we've all been sharing sits against one wall.

"What are we doing in here?" she wants to know.

"I'll be right back," I tell her, then stride out and head for another room that's become a sort of storage room. Our growing collection of gear and weaponry is stashed in this room, and I go to a bin where I remember Ransom tossing a coil of rope.

I pull it out and return to the bedroom, and when Willow sees me walk in with the rope held in my hands, her eyebrows shoot upward. I see a flicker of recognition in her eyes, and I'm sure she's thinking of the last time the two of us used a rope in a bedroom.

It was the first time I fucked her.

When she let me tie her up.

But instead of telling her to get on the bed, I hand her the rope and then crawl onto the firm mattress myself. I lie down on the middle of it, then look over at her expectantly.

Her mouth falls open, a tiny gasp falling from her lips.

"Vic, are you saying..."

I nod at her. "I want you to tie me up, just like you had me do to you once. It's a small thing, but maybe it will help you take back your control right now. It helped me."

Her eyes go wide, and I can tell she's shocked that I'm offering. Honestly, a part of me is surprised by it too. There was definitely a time when this would've been the last thing I would have given to anyone. But it's different with Willow. I know her. I *trust* her. And this might help.

"Are you sure?" she breathes, sliding the soft rope through her hands. "You don't have to do this, Vic.."

"I'm sure," I tell her. "I trust you with my life. So I trust you with this too."

Willow gazes at me for a moment, emotions I've never quite seen before crossing her face. I wish I was better at naming them, because they make something in my own chest ache, and she swallows before she nods once. She shifts the rope in her hands, testing the heft of it, and then climbs onto the bed with me.

Before doing anything else, she kisses me, her mouth soft and warm against mine. I lean up into it, letting her press me down to the bed as she goes.

Her touch is gentle when she grabs my wrists, drawing them up and toward the headboard. There's a look of concentration on her face, as if she wants to be sure she does this right, and it's endearing to see.

Her knots aren't as good as someone like Malice's would be, but they hold as she starts to bind my wrists to the headboard.

I test the knot work when she's done, and something flares through me when I realize she's tied them well enough that I'm not going anywhere until she releases me. Not without a good deal of effort, at least. My heart pounds in my chest, and I have to lick my lips.

"Okay?" she murmurs.

I nod, my voice hoarse. "Yeah. It's okay."

Finally, she smiles, and it's a more genuine smile than I've seen on her face in days. Heat and something like mischief light in her eyes, and she traps her bottom lip between her teeth. Her hands move down my body slowly, going from my arms to my chest, and she lets herself explore.

The glint of desire in her luminous brown eyes grows brighter with every second, and I can tell that she's turned on not just by the situation, but also by the show of trust. Or at least, I think she is. That's how I felt when she let me tie her up, and she seems to feel the same way.

It's a heady thing, to have absolute control over someone, and to know that it doesn't make them fear you.

My heart pounds in my chest as she touches me, and I groan when her fingers skate over my nipples through my shirt. Willow picks up on that, of course, and she teases with them a bit more, pushing my shirt up so she can have unfettered access.

"Fuck," I groan. "I didn't think this was going to be so intense so soon."

Her eyes flash to my face, like she's trying to check in and make sure I'm alright, and I nod to let her know I am.

"Don't stop."

"Does it feel good?" she asks, and although her voice is soft, there's something ravenous in her eyes.

I grit my teeth, tugging on the ropes a little.

"It feels so fucking good," I rasp. "Your hands on me are the best thing I've ever felt. You make me feel... god, butterfly, you make me want..."

"What?" Willow breathes. "Tell me."

"More," I manage to say. "Give me more. Keep touching me. Fuck, don't ever stop."

"I never want to."

As if to prove the truth of her words, she drops her head, letting her mouth follow where her hands just were. They start at my neck, and she licks and sucks there, her teeth nipping lightly at sensitive spots.

And *every* spot seems sensitive right now. My entire body is primed to react to her touch, and to want so much more. Every brush of her lips or scrape of her teeth just adds to the desire building up in me, and I have to remind myself to breathe as she moves down to my chest, counting upward slowly in my head.

Her eyes flash up to meet mine as she drags her tongue down my sternum, her hands holding on to my hips, and I groan her name, my jaw clenching.

"Fuck, that's so good. Your mouth, butterfly. What are you doing to me?"

"Making you feel good," she murmurs back. "It's one of my favorite things in the entire world, Vic. I love making you come undone for me. Love when you lose all that control you hold on to so tightly, just for me. Just so you can fuck me the way you want, holding nothing back."

Her tongue dips and swirls around my nipple, and I hiss as pleasure shoots through me. My cock is fully hard now, pressed painfully against the inside of my jeans, but Willow seems to be taking her time getting there.

And even though it's pure torture, part of me doesn't even mind. I don't want to rush her as she explores my entire torso with her lips and tongue, tracing my tattoos, my ribs, the muscles of my pecs and abs.

"I can never get enough of you," I mutter breathlessly. The words just spill out of me, and I don't bother to hold them back. "Never enough. Everything you do just makes me want you more. I want to feel you, butterfly. *Always.* I want to be buried inside you so deep that I can't feel anything other than you."

Willow moans softly from the torrent of words, her eyes darkening with arousal. She reaches over to grab the knife that Malice keeps on the bedside table and uses it to cut my shirt all the way off, getting it out of the way.

I can't even be upset about the waste of clothes or the fact that she tosses the scraps onto the floor rather than folding them up neatly. Right now, the only thing I can focus on is how much I want her. How good this feels.

She kisses her way down to my stomach, and once she's there, she finally stops teasing. Her hand presses against the bulge in my pants, and I grunt in pleasure, arching up to try to rub against her small, soft palm, wanting more friction.

Willow allows it, her pupils blown wide as she watches me move, practically humping her hand.

"You want me so much," she whispers. "Don't you?"

"You have no idea," I tell her. "I don't just want. I need you, butterfly."

She licks her lips and removes her hand, but just long enough to get my pants undone. With quick movements, she drags them and my boxers down, tossing them off to the side with the remnants of my shirt.

My cock springs up, hard and flushed, already damp at the tip. It's not so much different from when she was tattooing me. Something about this beautiful, soft, incredible woman affects me like nothing else ever has. I never really watched porn, never really even thought about sex that much until I met Willow. I would take care of my needs when they built up quickly and perfunctorily, only jerking off on set days of the week as a way of keeping my body regulated.

Willow is the only person who has ever made me *need*. Who's made me need something so much that I would break every single one of my habits and rules.

Only for her. And I prefer it that way.

I want her to be the only one who can make me like this.

"Please," I groan, my cock pulsing as if it's straining to reach her. "Touch me, butterfly. Fuck, *please*."

"Yes," she breathes, licking her palm.

Her hand is soft and warm as she wraps it around my shaft, and I exhale hard, almost like the breath has been punched out of me.

She strokes me slowly, working my length up and down, rubbing her palm over the head as she comes back down. The precum leaking out of my cock helps slick the way even more, and each movement makes sparks shoot down my spine.

It's a little embarrassing, although my stamina is much better than it used to be... but I could come just from this. Just from her touching me a little, just from watching the way her face transforms with desire as she watches my cock slip between her fingers.

She squeezes a little, and my breath catches as the pleasure rushes over me.

"Willow, I—" The words get caught in my throat, and I moan again, bucking up into her touch even more. "Fuck."

"Not yet," she tells me, slowing her hand down a bit. "I want to see how much you can take. Is that okay?"

Truthfully, I feel like I'm already wound so tight I'm about to snap. But this is about her taking back her power.

Letting her have control over me was the whole point.

So I nod, giving her the green light, and she grins, starting to stroke me faster again.

Her hand flies over my cock, working me up, building the heat in my veins into a raging fire. Then she suddenly slows down again, making my entire body lurch with shock of the change. It's almost too much, and there's something about the uneven way she's jacking me off that makes my pulse race, keeping me off balance.

But it's not bad. It feels too incredible for that.

"There you go," Willow murmurs, looking almost transfixed as she watches me. "Your cock is so beautiful, Vic. I swear I've never seen you this hard. I love how you feel in my hand, velvety soft and so thick."

Even her words turn me on. I can feel myself getting closer to the edge, barreling toward it—

And then she stops again.

I make a low noise of frustration, breathing hard now. My cock aches, dripping freely, and my balls are tight as my thigh muscles clench.

"Fuck," I gasp out. "Fuck, fuck, *fuck*. You're... diabolical."

"How badly do you want to come?" she whispers, and I can tell she's enjoying this. I am too, even if it also feels like I'm about to die.

"I'm so close. I'm so—fuck, butterfly, I need—"

"I'm going to give it to you," she promises, her voice raspy in a way that tells me she's just as worked up as I am. "Your cock is so hard, Vic. I can feel how bad you want it. I'm gonna make you feel so good."

"I already—"

My voice breaks off in a choked grunt as she starts to jerk me off again.

It's such a fucking gorgeous sight, watching her take control like this. She looks intent as she works me up, watching my face, listening to the sounds I'm making. She takes it all in, observing every detail just like I would if I were in her place, so that she'll know when to pull back and keep me on the edge.

It goes on for a couple more rounds, and each time she denies me, my need just ratchets up higher. I can't hold back the groans spilling from me, and my words come out rough-edged and jagged, so desperate for her to finish it. To let me come.

I've never begged before, but I'm fucking *pleading* now. The words fall from my lips easily as my body arches and bucks, my wrists twisting in the ropes.

Willow is breathing hard, and she makes a low, needy noise herself. Finally, she lets go of my cock, and I pant, my entire body screaming in protest at the loss of her touch.

She gets off the bed, and I open my mouth to ask what she's doing, but then she starts stripping off her clothes.

"Fuck," I groan. "You're so gorgeous. You're perfect, butterfly. I need you. Please, I need—"

"I know," she says soothingly. "I need you too. I promised I'd make you feel good, remember?"

I nod, watching as she climbs back onto the bed, her dyed brown hair falling over her shoulders to brush her breasts. Her pussy is wet, and I can see her arousal glistening between her thighs as she comes over and straddles me.

She grips the base, lowering herself down onto my cock, and as soon as my crown breaches her tight, wet heat, I groan, bucking up into her even deeper.

"Yes," I grit out. "Fuck yes."

She moans in response, still in control, taking her time seating herself fully on my shaft. Once I'm all the way in, she braces her hands on my chest and starts riding me, no longer teasing at all.

This is everything I've been craving, and I think I could die happy like this. She promised she'd give me what I needed, and she has, but it's clear she's chasing her own pleasure too. Her hips roll in undulating circles, and her breasts bounce invitingly as she moves, making me wish my hands were free to touch her.

She tips her head back, moaning my name as she rides me, and it's the most beautiful sight I've ever seen.

"I wish you could see yourself like this," I tell her, panting. "How fucking beautiful you look. Like a goddess. Taking what you want, doing it just how you want to. It's amazing. It's so good."

She bends down, capturing my lips in a searing kiss as she keeps going, lifting her hips and slamming them back down to bury me inside her over and over. Our breaths mingle, almost animalistic sounds spilling into each other's mouths as she rides me.

"Fuck, Vic," she moans. "I love you."

And after all of it, after everything she did to tease me and drive me wild, those three words are what break me.

The orgasm that's been threatening to spill over since Willow first tied me to the bed suddenly surges through me. The muscles in my neck go tense with the strain as I growl out, "Fuck. I'm coming. Come with me. Please."

"Uh huh," Willow whimpers. "Right there. Right... fucking... *there.*"

I'm already filling her up as she comes on my cock, and the feel of her squeezing around me almost makes me black out. She keeps riding me, then finally goes limp, collapsing onto my chest.

It takes a while for us to catch our breath, but eventually, Willow climbs off me. Just like I did the night my brothers tied her up for me, she unties me from the bed and helps me rub at my wrists, returning circulation to them.

Now that I can move freely, I can't resist wrapping my arms around her. I pull her down so that she's draped on top of me as I lie back, kissing her forehead and smoothing her messy hair.

"Thank you for that," she whispers. "I don't know how you guys always know what I need when I need it, but... that was perfect."

"I told you I'd do anything for you," I reply. "And I meant it."

26

MALICE

THE THING about leaving the penthouse lately is that it makes me feel like there's ants under my skin. Itchy and restless, on edge. I feel like I'm waiting for an attack to come, always looking over my shoulder, trying to be ready for whatever happens.

I wouldn't have left at all, but we need some shit if we want to be both protected and ready for our mission.

If Olivia fucking Stanton thinks we're gonna let her kill Willow, then she's out of her fucking mind.

We've been rebuilding our stock of gear ever since we got back to Detroit, but now that we know what we're up against, we need more. Vic's done some things to increase our surveillance capabilities around the penthouse, doing what he can there, but it's not enough. I trust my twin with my life, but I always have a backup plan, and it's usually the more old-fashioned way, I guess.

Weapons, bullets, a few good knives. We've gotta be ready to throw down with whoever thinks they can come for what's ours, and that means we have to have the firepower to do the job.

I grab several bulletproof vests, adding them to the stash of gear I've already picked out, then take my haul to the counter, going through a mental list in my head. My brothers and I have had plenty of occasions where we needed to buy weapons over the years, and there are plenty of places in Detroit to get them discreetly if you know where to look.

The place that's become our go-to is in the back of a pawn shop. A whole under-the-table business is run behind the scenes here by a greasy fucker named Smith. He's too fucking chatty, usually, and he's missing two fingers on his left hand. Ransom and I have an ongoing bet over how he lost them, although for all his talk, he has yet to spill that particular story. He also prices his merchandise high, but money isn't an object anymore, and his shit is usually the best.

The best is what we need right now.

Smith takes a look at the pile I put on the dented chrome counter he stands behind and whistles.

"You don't usually get so much all at once," he says, scratching at his pock-marked cheek with the two remaining fingers on his left hand. "But then, I haven't seen you or your brothers around much lately. Run into some trouble?"

"Something like that," I grunt back. "How much?"

He rifles through the pile. "Five grand."

"You're out of your fucking mind, Smith. I could go out to the pawn shop up front and get this shit for less than that."

"Not the vest," he points out. "You won't find that up there. Those aren't standard issue. This is cop grade. Nothing's getting through that unless it's a point blank spray or a bullet made specifically to pierce through Kevlar."

Smith always does drive a hard bargain, but that's just part of the process when you go to places like this. We used to deal with him all the time when we had our chop shop, sometimes even trading him car work in exchange for weapons when we needed to.

It's weird how that feels like it was so long ago, when it really wasn't, in the grand scheme of things. It feels like it was a different lifetime, in a way. As if I could divide my life into two parts— before Willow and after Willow.

Almost as if he can read my thoughts, Smith purses his thin

lips thoughtfully. "You know, I'd almost wondered if you and your brothers had gotten out of the game. Used to be I could rely on one of you coming in here like clockwork to get supplies. Then nothing for a while. You guys going straight?"

"Not exactly," I tell him. "We've just had other shit going on."

Her arches a brow and chuckles. "Must be a woman. That's the only thing that could ever get me to drop everything I had going on. Gave up a lot of promising work for a nice pair of legs and a sweet ass. Hell, I gave up two fingers for a woman who was all that and more."

I roll my eyes, not reacting much to his words, even though I make a note to tell Ransom about it later. I'm not going to admit out loud that I've got anything in common with Smith, but he's not wrong.

Our lives are completely unrecognizable from what they once were. The three of us had a system, a routine. We did our chop work, we did jobs for X, and we tried to find time to do our own shit while we could, making plans for some distant, vague future when we weren't gonna be under anyone's thumb.

Then Willow came along and turned all of that on its head.

But I'm not complaining at all.

All the shit we were doing before seems unimportant compared to protecting the woman we all love.

Determination fills my chest, rising up like a wave.

I've fucking failed in the past, and I know it. I wasn't able to protect our mother, no matter how hard I tried to. I wasn't able to keep Vic from being brutalized by our father before that. But I refuse to fail this time. I will protect Willow, no matter what it takes. I'll die for her if it comes to it. Just as long as her light doesn't go out. Just as long as my Solnyshka keeps shining her light on the world.

"Fine. Five grand," I tell Smith, nodding sharply.

He looks me over and then smirks. "Yup. Definitely a woman. Pleasure doing business with you. Watch your back out there."

I make a noise of acknowledgement and pay him, then gather up the gear, heading out the back way with everything.

The gun in my waistband, hidden beneath my shirt, is a familiar and comforting weight as I glance around, checking the alley to make sure it's clear. I keep an eye out, wary and alert, as I drive back to our homebase, and I don't drop my guard until I get back to the penthouse.

As I take the elevator up, I shift my weight impatiently, the agitation inside me ramping up higher and higher. I've been gone less than two hours, but that's two hours too long with the way shit has been going lately.

I need to see my Solnyshka. I need to touch her and hear her voice.

Willow is in the living room with Vic, who's working on the couch for once instead of in his office. They both glance up when I enter the condo, but I only have eyes for her in this moment. She stands up to greet me, but before the words even pass her lips, I drop the gear by the door and stride toward her, hauling her into my arms and pulling her close.

"What—"

That's all she manages to get out before I'm kissing her, hard and hungry. Everything in me needs this right now. Needs to touch her and worship her, to show her how much she means. How far I'm willing to go for her.

There's a moment where she stiffens with surprise, but then she melts into it, making a low, pleased noise as she kisses me back.

When the need to breathe makes my lungs burn, I draw back just enough to look down at her. Her brown eyes shine like rich chocolate, and I find myself speaking before I can even think about it, the words pouring out before I can stop them.

"I already told you I love you," I say roughly. "But that's not fucking good enough."

"Not good enough for what?" she asks, frowning a little.

"To make you understand how I feel. How fucking deep this

shit goes. I'd do anything to keep you safe. I don't care who I have to kill, or how many people I have to lay out. I don't care if I have to die for it. No one is *ever* gonna lay a finger on you again. You deserve so much more than the bullshit life has handed to you, and I'm gonna make sure you get it. You're just... you're everything, Solnyshka. You're so fucking beautiful and strong. You've been through so much, and you never give up. You never let anything break you, and I love that so goddamned much. You're the light to all my darkness."

At first, Willow seems speechless. She stares up at me, her full lips parted and kiss bruised.

"Malice," she murmurs softly. Then she reaches up, cupping my face in both of her hands.

I lean into the touch, letting her cool, soft palms soothe my heated skin.

"And you're the darkness I need," she whispers. "My perfect dark knight."

A small movement in my periphery reminds me that my brother is watching. He's abandoned his computer for once, leaning against the back of the couch, his gaze locked on the two of us.

Glancing over at him, I jerk my chin just slightly.

I don't need to do more than that. The two of us have always been able to communicate without words, to let each other know things with looks and gestures. Mom always called it our twin telepathy.

He gets to his feet, accepting my silent invitation. When he comes up behind Willow, sandwiching her between our bodies, her breath catches.

"*Oh.*"

Her mouth falls open as she leans back against him, letting her hands slide down to rest against my chest.

"Vic needs you too. Just as much as I do. Do you want us to show you?" I ask her, and it comes out on a low growl.

Willow swallows, and she's pinned so tightly between us that I can feel the way her body shivers against mine. She holds my gaze, but I know her words are meant for both me and my twin when she whispers her answer.

"Yes."

27

WILLOW

My heart is racing a mile a minute. Part of me can't believe this is happening.

I've been dreaming about this for a lot longer than I'd like to admit—being fucked by the Voronin twins together. Even when we were all together, there was a part of me that wondered what it would be like to be sandwiched between the two of them, contending with Malice's fiery intensity and Vic's cool intentionality.

Now that I'm here, my head is already spinning.

They're keeping me pinned between them, and I can feel the solidness of their bodies as they hold me in place. Malice kisses me again, rougher this time, more full of intent, and Vic's lips find their way to my neck.

I groan into Malice's mouth, squirming between them as they work me up.

Vic's mouth finds a patch of scar tissue on my neck, leading down to my shoulder, and he licks and nips at it, practically worshiping it.

The physical sensation is dulled there, the nerves damaged and buried under the thick patches of scars, but it still sends sparks of electric heat shooting down my spine all the same.

His hands splay over my stomach, fingers dipping just a bit below my waistband. It's enough that when I buck forward, seeking out friction while my body throbs with need, I end up grinding against Malice instead.

"Whatever you're doing, Vic," he growls, "she likes it."

Then he kisses me with so much heat and intensity that I forget to breathe. His mouth is an inferno, and he grazes my lips with his teeth before plunging his tongue into my mouth and groaning like he's devouring his favorite meal.

"*I* like it," Vic murmurs, letting his hands wander.

His fingers slide under my shirt, finding more scars and tracing the patterns they make. When I arch back against him, I can feel that he's hard in his pants, his cock pressed against my ass through the layers of our clothes.

I moan again, and Malice pulls away from the kiss, but only enough so that he can rip my shirt down the middle and start attacking my breasts with his mouth.

"Oh my god," I hiss out, shivering between them, not sure who I should try to get closer to.

They're both working individually here, but also in tandem. Each thing one of them does just makes me more sensitive for the other, and I'm caught in their push and pull, trying to stay afloat.

Malice ends up grabbing my ass, using his big hands to lift me up. I have to wrap my legs around his waist, and that just puts me even closer to the heat of his body.

I practically grind against him, my body crying out for more as he kisses me again.

Vic moves in closer behind me, and I put my arms around his neck, leaning back some so he has more access to my neck.

I could probably come like this eventually, held up between the two of them, lost in the haze of how good their mouths and hands feel on me.

But I want more than that. I want the chance to live out this fantasy, wholly and completely.

"Bedroom," I manage to gasp out.

Vic steps back, but Malice doesn't even put me down as we head for the bedroom.

"I hope you're fucking ready, Solnyshka," Malice growls, his hands digging into my ass as he holds me up. "Because I'm not in the mood to be gentle."

"Are you ever?" I can't help but tease, fisting *his* hair for once and tugging at the strands.

He makes a warning noise in his throat. "No. And you love it."

"I love *you*," I correct. "Both of you."

I can feel Vic's eyes on us as he follows, and as soon as we get to the bedroom, Malice lays me out on the bed. He stands back as the two of them gaze down at me. There's heat in their eyes, twin hungers that burn like hot steel and blue flame.

In this moment, they seem even more alike than ever. They've both got their sharp edges, and it's like they're mirroring each other now.

The thought of what they might do to me together is enough to make me shiver, and my legs fall open almost unconsciously.

"Look at you," Malice murmurs. "You're a fucking vision. So innocent on the outside, but we know better than that by now, don't we, Vic? I bet our girl is wet for us already."

Victor swallows, his gaze dropping downward before returning to my face. "Are you?"

"Yes," I whisper, because there's no reason to deny it. "I can feel it soaking my panties. The second you both touched me, I couldn't stop it."

Malice peels his shirt off, revealing his inked torso, and Victor does the same. My eyes zero in on the tattoos I gave them, healing well and standing out on their skin, proving my claim on them both.

The shock of possessiveness that shoots through me is so intense it almost surprises me, although it shouldn't.

They're mine. And I'm never letting them go.

"Would you let Vic fuck you?" Malice asks, balling up his shirt and tossing it to the floor.

I frown, not sure why that's even a question. "Of course."

He smirks. "Would you let him fuck you while I take your ass?"

I suck in a breath, surprised and turned on all at once. I've done something like this once before, with Ransom and Malice, and it was so intense that I almost blacked out. It'll be a lot to take both of them, but there's no denying that my panties just got a whole lot wetter at the suggestion.

Malice grins as he reads my expression. "You want it, don't you? You wanna feel both of us inside you, filling you up. Taking you apart. Me and my twin, claiming you entirely for our own."

"I'm already yours," I tell him. "Every part of me. There isn't a hole in my body I wouldn't let you fuck. Let you claim."

Malice's eyes glint with heated approval. "Good girl."

I glance over at Vic, who's been mostly quiet so far. That's not rare for him, since he's usually the one more likely to sit back and observe, but I want to make sure we're all on the same page.

"Do you want that?" I whisper. "To fuck my pussy while Malice takes my ass?"

His expression is tight, like he's about to lose control. I know this is new territory for him. It's pushing past his old boundaries in a big way, and I hope he'll take the chance. It takes a few seconds, but the blazing desire in his eyes wins out against everything else. He glances at his brother and then back to me, nodding.

"Yes," he rasps. "I want it."

"Good." Malice chuckles roughly. "Now that we're all in agreement, let's do this shit."

He takes over in that way he has, sharing a glance with his twin before they both climb onto the bed. The mattress dips beneath their weight, and suddenly, their hands are everywhere.

Malice starts working to get the shredded remnants of my shirt all the way off, sliding my arms free of the sleeves, and Vic goes for my pants. I start to lose track of whose hands are whose, just going with the feelings and sensations of it. Fingers brush over my breasts, teasing and tweaking my nipples, and my breath catches as I moan softly, arching into the touch. More fingers slide over my pussy as my panties are tugged off, pressing against the wetness there but not pushing in.

"Please," I groan, trying to grind against that hand, and Malice smirks, pressing down harder before pulling his hand away.

"We're gonna give you all that you can take in a bit, Solnysh-ka," he promises. "For now, you've got to be patient."

I make a face at him that could definitely be described as a pout. "I can never be patient. Not when it comes to you guys."

"Here," Vic murmurs, and suddenly there are hands on my face, drawing my attention and my gaze to him. "Focus on me."

His voice is soft and deep, and I let myself do as he says, focusing on him. I can tell that his usual control is frayed, coming apart at the edges a bit, but he's going with it, allowing himself to feel and do and be the way he wants to in the moment.

It looks good on him, that hint of wildness, and when he lowers his head to kiss me, I meet him eagerly, groaning as our lips touch. He cradles my face, deepening the kiss, and then his hands start to wander.

"So soft," he murmurs. "Your skin is so fucking soft. And then... this. This beautiful, addictive chaos."

He slides his hands down my neck and to my shoulders, and I can feel it when his fingers start to trace the edges of my scars. He's always been so fascinated by them, turned on by their random shapes and patterns where others might find them ugly.

I've learned to enjoy it, so when he moves to kiss and lick his way down the thick patch on my side, I just breathe into it, enjoying being savored like this.

My eyes slide back to Malice while Vic maps out my body, watching the broad-shouldered man shuck off the rest of his clothes. His tattooed cock springs free, already hard, and he strokes it a little, like he's tiding it over before it can be buried inside me.

My pussy throbs at the thought, even though that's not the part of me that Malice is going to be filling up. Not today, anyway.

"Oh god!" I hiss out a breath as Vic sets the edge of his teeth

271

against a sensitive patch of scars, drawing my attention back to him. "Fuck, Vic."

He hums softly, soothing the sting with the flat of his tongue.

"Incredible," he murmurs, his lips moving against my skin. "You taste so good."

When he pulls away, I want to beg him to come back and keep going. But then he kicks off his pants and boxer briefs, and I suck in a breath at the sight of his cock, which is already flushed and hard.

Almost side by side, it's interesting to see the twins like this. Malice is more ripped, his cock a bit longer, and Vic is still muscled but in a leaner way, his cock thicker around the shaft.

My heart skips a beat, and I feel like the greediest, luckiest woman in the world, because I don't have to choose between these two men. I get to have them both.

Both of their cocks filling me up at the same time.

"Ride Vic first," Malice instructs, giving my thigh a squeeze. "To warm you up."

I swallow hard and nod, rolling to the side a little to make room so that Vic can take his place on his back. When I get back on top of him, it feels so right, reminding me of the way I rode him the day he let me tie him up. His hands come to my hips, his fingers immediately slotting into place, touching the edges of the scars that extend down that far.

"The first time I was inside you, I thought I might die from how fucking good it felt," he groans. "It still feels that way. Every fucking time."

"Don't die," I whisper. "Just fuck me."

I lick my lips and take a breath before sitting down more, impaling myself on his cock.

It's so thick that even with how wet I am, it's a stretch to take it. My body clenches tightly around him before it adjusts, and with a few more strokes, I'm able to sink all the way down, burying Vic inside me to the hilt.

"Shit," Malice groans. I can feel his eyes boring into me as he watches the whole thing. "I wish you could see yourself right now.

How fucking good you look. He's a lot to take, isn't he? But you don't let that stop you. He waited for you for years, you know, Solnyshka. All that time, whether we knew it or not, we were all waiting for you. For our fucking queen. You're taking Vic's cock so damned well. Sitting on him like he's your throne."

His words hit me in a tender place. They fill up my chest and send emotions expanding outward, making my pussy clench around the hard length inside me. Vic hisses at the feeling, and I rest my hands on his chest, starting slow as I draw myself up and down to ride him.

"Just like that," Malice praises. "Take every inch of him. Let him fill you up. You look like a fucking siren riding my brother's dick, Solnyshka."

All I can do is moan in response as sensations crash through me. I can feel every vein and ridge in Vic's cock, the way the thickness of him presses against my inner walls, working me up as I move.

When I look down at Vic, he's hazy eyed and blissed out. I drag my hands down his chest, lightly touching the still healing bullet wound in his side before looking at the tattoo I put on his chest. Marks he wears either for or because of me—but he wears them both with so much pride.

Something hot and intense wells up in me, and it's not just the pleasure from how good this feels. It's possessive energy, the feeling of being proud to have claimed a man like this. Someone so devoted and clever, so haunted and rough around the edges. We fought hard to get here, to this place where I'm sitting astride his cock while Malice watches and directs, and that makes it even better.

"Tell me how it feels," Malice demands, and that draws my attention back to him. He's kneeling on the bed now, and the heat of his body sears into me when he presses himself closer behind me.

"So good," I gasp. "He's so fucking big. So thick. I'll never get used to how much he stretches me."

"You're gonna get even more than that in a minute," he murmurs. "I want you soaked and ready for me. Vic, help her out. Play with her clit a little. Her tits. You know what drives her wild. I know you've been taking notes since the very first time you watched her come."

Vic's tongue flashes out as he licks his lips and then obeys his brother's urging. His hands come up first, playing with my breasts, cupping them in his palms before he tweaks at my nipples.

The sharp sting sends a jolt through me, and I whimper softly.

"Ransom has all those piercings," Vic says, pinching my nipples harder. "Should we give you one someday, butterfly? Maybe right here."

I gush over his cock at the rush of sensation. Malice was right about his brother knowing what drives me crazy. He's spent more time than any of them watching, memorizing the way my body responds to each and every touch. I'm pretty sure he could get me off in a hundred different ways without ever even touching my clit.

"I'd be into that," I whisper back. "But only if all of you are there when I get it done. I'll need someone to—*ah!*—to help distract me from the pain."

One of Vic's hands slides downward, making my breath catch. His fingers touch the place where our bodies are joined together, sliding over the slippery skin as if he wants to feel for himself how much I'm stretching around him, the way my body opens for him just because it feels so good. There's a look on his face that's almost reverent, and I slow my movements so that he can feel all of it, my gaze locked with his.

"We'll be there," he promises. "We'll help you decorate this gorgeous body. Color and ink and piercings that catch the light. You'll be chaos all over."

His fingertips find my clit as he speaks, and my mind goes blank. Vic's fingers are so precise and skilled. The same attention he gives to everything is being applied here, and he rubs my clit in slow circles, working me up even more.

"Fuck, oh my god. That feels so good," I moan. "Fuck, please."

"I love how you don't hold anything back when you beg," Malice says. "We'll give you everything you want, Solnyshka."

I open my mouth to tell him that there's so much I want right now, but before I can say anything, I feel something cool and slick touch my ass. My muscles tense instinctively, my stomach fluttering.

"Breathe," Vic instructs. He reaches up with his free hand to touch my face. "Remember when Malice and Ransom did this? Just breathe with me the way you did then. Stay with me."

I nod and drag in a shaky breath and then another.

"Good girl," Malice praises. "Just like that."

Vic keeps his fingers moving, working my clit as I ride his dick slowly. The intrusion in my ass as Malice works me open is a less familiar sensation than having something filling my pussy, but I'm learning to love it. It's another kind of stretch, different and pleasurable in a totally new way.

And still, when an orgasm starts to build, it catches me almost completely by surprise.

I barely have time to wrap my head around it before I'm being swept up in a wave of pleasure so intense it threatens to take my breath away. I cry out, trembling on top of Vic, going tight around his cock.

Vic pulls his hand away from my clit, gripping my hips tightly. I can tell from his hold on me that he's fighting for control, and that war plays out over his face as well.

"Fuck," he hisses, his fingertips digging into my skin. "You feel too fucking good."

My pussy spasms around his cock, and it's clearly enough for him to be right there on the edge himself. He's holding himself back by a thread, so close to falling apart, but refusing to let go just yet.

I stop moving, catching my breath and giving Vic a chance to back away from his climax and calm himself down.

Without the movement of riding Vic to distract me, I can feel Malice's progress behind me even more. The pleasure still cascading through me from my orgasm puts my nerves on high alert, and everything feels even more intense than it did before.

So when Malice pulls his fingers out of my ass, I gasp, suddenly feeling empty, even though Vic is still buried to the hilt inside me.

But then something else presses against my stretched hole, and I groan at the feel of Malice's cock. He's always been big, always been a stretch to take, but pressing into this smaller, tighter hole, he feels even bigger.

"Oh god," I groan. "Oh fuck."

"You've got this," Malice grits out. "I could feel your ass clenching around my fingers, trying to drag them in even deeper. Your body wants this, Solnyshka. It's ready for my cock."

I breathe in and out slowly, squirming between him and Victor to open myself up even more. That lets him start working his way in, the head of his cock popping past that tight ring of muscle. The next couple of inches of him follow, pressing inside, and I hiss at how intense it feels.

"Use your safe word if you need to," Malice pants, fisting my hair with one hand. "You remember it."

I nod shakily, my fingers biting into Vic's chest where my hands are braced there.

"Good girl. Do you want me to stop?"

I shake my head. I want this. I want everything they do to me. The pleasure and the pain, and especially when those two sensations merge into one. Everything about them is intense, but it's always worth it, and I know this won't be any different.

Malice curses behind me, pressing himself in just a bit deeper. His fingers are rough when he grabs my chin and turns my head so he can kiss me.

It's not the best angle, but that doesn't matter. Our lips clash, messy and desperate, and I whimper into his mouth as he bites down on my lower lip, adding another layer of slight pain to the mix.

"Let me in," Malice breathes. "Let me fill you up."

I nod again, feeling almost boneless from everything coursing through me right now. Vic's hands lose some of their death grip on my hips, and he strokes my skin gently, helping me to find my breath and calm down enough to relax even more.

Malice works his way in deeper, and even though I know how big his cock is because I've seen it and touched it and had it inside me, it seems impossibly larger right now. Like no matter how much he pushes in, there's still more of him to go.

Once he's in enough that I can really feel it, the fact that there's two cocks buried in me starts to hit hard. Vic is still filling my pussy, thick and hard and throbbing, and when his hips jerk upward, I swear I feel it everywhere.

It's so much, and every little shift, every movement, only adds to the sensation. I'm intensely aware of the fact that I'm pinned between them, that there's nowhere for me to go.

And I love it.

"Well, this is my new favorite thing to come home to," an amused, heated voice comments from the doorway. "The woman I love, stuffed full of my brothers' cocks. Malice is almost all the way in, angel. Can you take all of him?"

Ransom's words make my heart skip a beat, and I look over to see him leaning against the door frame. His eyes are already going dark with lust from the sight I must make, and he drags his gaze over my body, taking in all the places where I'm touching his brothers.

I lift my head, barely able to speak right now. "Are you—fuck—are you gonna join us?"

He smiles and shakes his head, playing with his tongue piercing. "Nah. Vic always made watching seem so fun, so now it's my turn. I'm gonna watch you get fucked by my brothers. I want to hear them make you scream."

He moves to sit in the nice arm chair by the window, and I shiver at the knowledge that we have an audience now. We're putting on a show for him, and it makes me feel debauched and sexy.

Vic's fingers start to dig into my hips again, and a groan

rumbles beneath my palms where they rest on his chest. That's all the warning I get before he's moving, pressing his hips up, making his cock push impossibly deeper into me.

My mouth falls open, because that already felt good before, but now with Malice also filling me up, it's way more intense.

And then Malice starts to move too.

"Goddamn, your ass is so tight," he grunts. "I couldn't pick a favorite hole of yours if I tried. They're all so fucking good."

I rock between the two men, my movements mostly controlled by theirs as they find a rhythm, one drawing out while the other plunges back in, each stroke growing harder and harder.

"*Fuck,*" I sob. "I'm so close."

"You've got Vic about to bust a nut already." Malice's voice is gruff in my ear. "But he's holding back for you. Because he wants to make you feel good. He won't come until you do, Solnyshka. That's how much he fucking loves you. Are you gonna come for him? Gonna come on both of our cocks and scream our names when you do?"

I nod almost frantically. It's all pleasure now, the lines between the pain and the searing heat blurring until they don't exist. Until it's just me, trying to breathe through it, trying to hold all of this in my body even though it's too big and too much, and I feel like I'm going to burst at any second.

"Please, Vic," I gasp out, looking down at his face. I can see that his control is completely lost, and he's right there, about to give himself over to this sensation. "Please. Come with me. Let me feel it."

He curses under his breath, but that's all it takes.

His hips punch upward one last time, his eyes falling closed. I can feel the first jet of his cum as it bathes my insides, and it's like a spark to tinder. Everything that's been building inside me—the pleasure, the pain, that delicious tension and friction—all explodes in a rush that nearly shatters me.

I scream, first Vic's name and then Malice's, and then no words at all, just a ragged, desperate sound. My body shakes and shudders as I writhe between Malice and Vic, riding out the heat of my orgasm as it claims me.

"Such a good girl for us. Take my cum. I want you fucking *dripping*."

Malice grabs on to my waist and thrusts in deep, leaving no space between our bodies as he explodes inside me. His hips grind against me with every pulse of his cock until he's emptied himself completely.

In the aftermath, I collapse on top of Vic. Malice just manages to catch himself before he crushes both of us under his weight. For a long moment, none of us seem capable of moving. All we can do is fight to catch our breaths, our sweaty skin sticking together as our chests rise and fall.

Eventually, Malice lifts his head up, kissing the tip of my ear. "*That's* how much we need you, Solnyshka. And if you ever forget, we'll be happy to remind you anytime."

He starts to ease himself out of my body, going slowly. Now that some of the endorphins have calmed down, there's a twinge of pain as he pulls out, leaving me a gaping mess.

He flops onto his back off to the side, still breathing hard. That leaves Vic to pull out, and he does it just as carefully, groaning when the movement shows just how sensitive we both still are.

"Holy fuck, angel," Ransom says, drawing my attention back to him. "You're a mess. You like leaking from both holes? Because it's a good goddamned look on you."

His cock is out now, and he's fisting it in his hand, working himself over as he watches with heated eyes. I want him to be a part of this too, more than just an observer, but there's no way I can take him now, not as sore and worn out as I am from his brothers fucking me.

So I clamber off the bed, almost toppling right over with how wobbly my legs are. Cum drips down my thighs, but that doesn't stop me from dropping to my knees and crawling over to where Ransom sits.

His nostrils flare, and arousal burns even hotter in his eyes as he tracks my movement. "What are you doing?"

"Taking care of you too," I tell him. I grab his wrist, pulling his hand away from his cock. The head is shiny with precum, and the shaft is flushed. It makes the rows of neat piercings stand out even more, and I take the base of him in my hand before closing my mouth over the head.

"Jesus Christ," Ransom moans. He tips his head back as I suck him off, working my mouth over his heated flesh.

In this moment, I feel so fucking powerful. I just fucked both of the twins at the same time, and now they're watching from the bed as I take Ransom apart with my mouth. I can feel their gazes, still heated even after we all just came so hard together.

I'm the center of their attention, the one they all revolve around like planets in orbit, and it makes me feel bold. It makes me feel like I can do anything.

I tuck my hair behind my ear and keep working Ransom, sucking him all the way down until he hits the back of my throat. My tongue rubs against the underside of his cock, playing with the metal of his piercings, letting him feel every part of my mouth.

He groans, his hips bucking as the pleasure rises, and I don't stop. When I need to come up for air, I keep my hand moving over his shaft, squeezing a little.

This is what I love. Having all three of them at the same time. Their love, their attention, their pleasure. I love taking everything they can give me and then some, not held back by my trauma anymore.

Nothing Troy ever did to me can compare to this. To the feeling of being on top of the world and the way Ransom shudders when I take his cock back into my mouth. To the way I can feel Malice and Vic watching, pride and approval and desire in their eyes.

It feels so good, and there's no shame in it at all.

"I'm close," Ransom grits out. "Shit, you're so good at that. I'm gonna—"

I swallow him down, wanting him to come, wanting him to finish in my mouth.

He does in a few short bursts, pumping his load down my throat as he comes undone. His low growl shivers through me, and even though I couldn't come again right now if I wanted to, it's still its own kind of pleasure.

I lick Ransom clean until there isn't a single drop left, and then he pulls me up, hauling me onto his lap. I have just enough time to breathe before he's kissing me hard, his pierced tongue swiping through my mouth. He must taste himself on my lips, and I know he likes it.

He kisses me until we're both breathless, and his ocean blue eyes glimmer as he looks down at me.

"I fucking love you," he says.

I grin at him, exhausted but thrilled at the same time. "Ditto."

WILLOW

For once, I don't have any bad dreams.

I wake up, warm and comfortable, not drenched in sweat or feeling like my heart is going a mile a minute. I'm surrounded by three male bodies, and the smell of sex still hangs in the air.

When I shift, I can feel everything that happened yesterday. The soreness in my ass, and the stretch of my muscles from the exertion. But I also feel a contentment that goes bone-deep, and I like the physical reminders, the marks they left on me. It's proof that what happened was real, and I love that.

Judging from the light filtering into the room, it's pretty early in the morning. We all got dressed again after our marathon sex session and ate some dinner before passing out. The guys are still asleep, Malice snoring softly. The sound makes me smile, and I prop myself up in bed so I can look at all of them.

They're all so different, even if they're pretty similar too. Each of them is so beautiful in their own way. Malice with his scars and tattoos and muscles, the gruff look that he usually wears, and the rare moments when it falls away to reveal something softer underneath. He's sleeping on his stomach, half his face pressed into the pillow, arm tucked underneath it while he's out cold.

Vic is curled on his side toward me, his face soft and

unbothered in sleep. It's probably the only time he really slows down, and with how hard he's been working lately, it's good to see him take a rest. He's just as handsome, sharp in a different way from Malice, but just as deadly when he wants to be.

And then there's Ransom. He's tucked on my other side, one arm thrown over me, brown hair a mess over the pillows. He's the most classically handsome of the three of them, the one who has the model good looks and the easy smiles, but he's just as dangerous as his brothers.

His long eyelashes flutter against his cheeks, his pierced eyebrow rising as he smiles slowly, clearly not as asleep as I thought he was.

"See something you like?" he whispers, his voice rough from sleep.

"Maybe," I whisper back. "One of the benefits of having the three of you all sleep in bed with me is being able to look at you, after all."

He snorts, opening his eyes. "Yeah, I feel the same way. You're beautiful first thing in the morning."

I make a face at him, reaching up to touch the matted mess of my dyed hair. "I need a shower, and the back of my head is one big tangle. I'm sure I've looked better."

"Nah." Ransom shakes his head. "You've looked different, or more dressed up, but there's nothing better than seeing you fresh off a good night of sleep after you were fucked to within an inch of your life the day before. It looks damn good on you."

My cheeks flush as I chuckle, and he reaches over to run his fingertips over my cheekbone.

"Still so sweet and innocent even now," he murmurs. "How do you do that?"

"I don't know. I don't feel innocent anymore. I feel... powerful most of the time. Dirty in a good way."

That makes him grin warmly, and he tips my chin up a little. "Good. That's how you deserve to feel. It's not just anyone who could have three men like us at her beck and call. You've tamed us pretty well."

"I wouldn't say any of you are tame. And I wouldn't want you to be."

Ransom draws me closer, pulling me into a kiss, and I go happily. But as his hands start to wander over my body, I'm suddenly struck with a wave of nausea. It isn't the same as the panicky feeling I used to get after they first got me back from Troy, but it hits me just as hard.

Bile lurches up my throat, and I pull back from Ransom quickly, scrambling out of bed as quickly as I can. I run to the attached bathroom, one hand over my mouth as my stomach clenches. There's barely enough time for me to kneel in front of the toilet before I'm throwing up, the sour taste of it burning my tongue.

It comes in waves, leaving me heaving for a few seconds, and I breathe through my mouth, feeling ill and shaky.

Ransom appears in the bathroom door a second later, and he's quick to come over and wrap his fingers around my hair, rubbing my back with his other hand while I try to breathe through it.

"What's wrong?" he asks, and I can hear the concern in his voice. "Is it... was last night too much?"

I shake my head, bracing my forearm on the toilet seat so that I can rest my forehead against it. "No, I don't think so. I felt fine in the moment. Overwhelmed, but in a way that felt good. And then this morning when I woke up, I felt a little sore, but I expected that. This has to be something different."

"What did you eat yesterday?"

"I don't know. The usual?" I try to think back. Vic made me lunch, a neatly cut sandwich and a bowl of fruit, and before that, I had cereal for breakfast. Nothing out of the ordinary.

"You didn't order out at all?" he presses.

I shake my head, and then instantly regret the movement when my stomach gurgles unhappily. "No, it was all stuff we had here."

"So probably not food poisoning." He stops, as if something

284

just occurred to him. "Or regular poisoning." I glance up at him in alarm, and he shrugs. "I mean, Olivia is trying to have you killed. We have to consider—"

As if just the thought of that is enough to turn my stomach, I cut Ransom off by throwing up again, this time clutching on to the toilet as I heave violently.

Ransom helps me through it, and then gets me a glass of water.

I gulp it down gratefully, even if my stomach is still unhappy.

I know he's got a point about the possibility of me being poisoned, but I don't even want to think about that. And most likely, if Olivia was going to have someone poison me, it would be with something fast-acting. Something I wouldn't have a chance to recover from.

There used to be times before I met the guys, where the combination of working long hours, dealing with school work, and barely eating anything because I couldn't afford too much would leave me feeling sick sometimes, but it was never anything like this.

Never anything that came on so suddenly in the morning—

I suck in a breath as soon as I have that thought, my chest going tight. Hopefully it's just a coincidence that I'm feeling this sick out of nowhere first thing in the morning, but...

With shaky fingers, I reach over to rub at my left arm, feeling for the place where my birth control implant is supposed to be.

But the usual bump of it isn't there.

It's gone.

My stomach drops out.

"Oh my god," I whisper. "Oh my god. Oh fuck."

I wrap my arms around myself, trying to take deep breaths, trying to calm down, but it's no good.

When Troy abducted me in Mexico, I was drugged, barely conscious for an unknown amount of time as he transported me back to his safe house outside Detroit. I've never had any real idea what he or his men did to me during that time, although I was well aware that at some point, they stripped me and changed my clothes. I didn't want to think about it too much, since every time I did, it just made me feel more horrified and helpless.

But the truth is, he had the perfect opportunity to remove my birth control implant during that time. After the men got me back from Troy, I was beat up and bruised, with cuts and lacerations all over. It didn't even occur to me to check for it, partly because it never occurred to me that Troy might *want* to get me pregnant.

"Oh god," I murmur again, the words thick and choked.

"Willow?" Ransom comes over and crouches on the floor beside me, but I barely notice him, caught up in my own panic.

He strokes his fingers through my hair, brushing it back from my face. His hands are gentle, but I feel like I'm removed from the moment. Like everything is happening to someone else, and I'm watching it from behind a pane of glass. It's all muted and distorted, and I have enough of a handle on things to recognize that I'm in some sort of shock.

"You're scaring me, angel. Please talk to me. What's wrong?"

The concern in Ransom's voice cuts through the fog in my head a little, and I blink up at him.

"I..."

My voice sounds wrecked, half from the panic and half from my throat being raw from throwing up. I shake my head, not even sure how to begin to get something like this out.

How can I tell him?

How can I even come to terms with something like this?

A part of my mind casts around for some other explanation. Some other reason that I might be feeling sick. If I am pregnant, maybe the father is one of the brothers and not Troy.

But I know it doesn't line up like that. Up until Troy captured me, I was on birth control. The implant was safely tucked away in my arm, doing the work of keeping me from getting knocked up. There was no real chance of me getting pregnant.

And now...

I cover my face, pressing the heels of my hands against my eyes as if I could block out everything if I just try hard enough. My head is spinning out of control, and my heart is racing so fast it feels like it might beat out of my chest.

"Shit," Ransom murmurs. "You're pale as a fucking ghost. I need you to tell me what's wrong. *Was* it poison? Do you feel worse? If we need to get you to a hospital or something, then we have to move—"

"No. That's not it," I manage to choke out.

"Then what is it?"

My entire body rebels at the idea of saying it out loud, but I know I have to tell him. I can't do this on my own, and they'll all find out soon enough if I'm right.

"It's not poison making me sick. And it's not something I ate. My period is a bit late, but I didn't really think much of it. I thought it was just stress from dealing with Olivia and moving here and everything, but..." I shake my head. "The timing lines up a little too well. I think... I think I'm pregnant."

Ransom's eyes light up for a second, and I realize that he doesn't understand yet. He thinks it might be his baby, or one of his brothers'. Before he can get too excited, I shake my head.

"No, Ransom."

That makes him stop and think about it, and I can see the moment all the pieces come together in his mind. Pain takes the place of excitement in his eyes, and I know it's pain for me. Because he realizes what this means.

"I think... I think Troy had my birth control implant removed," I whisper, my voice shaking. "I didn't even think about it while I was there or in the aftermath because there were so many other things to worry about. And I didn't notice the pain or the bruising from the removal because I had so many other bruises. Other marks. I should've checked. I should've known he would—"

I break off, the pain in my chest becoming too much to bear.

"Fuck," Ransom breathes. Before I can say anything else, he's pulling me into his arms, crushing me to his chest in a tight hug. He's on his knees and so am I, his strong arms wrapped around me.

It's enough to make the dam inside me overflow, and I let myself cry into his chest.

"What the hell is going on? What's wrong?"

Malice's voice comes from behind Ransom, and I look up to see him and Vic standing side by side in the bathroom doorway. They must've realized something was wrong when we didn't come back to bed.

I can see the worry on their faces at finding us like this, and I swallow hard, brushing a hand over my face to wipe away my tears.

Silence fills the bathroom for a long moment. The thought of repeating those awful words makes my stomach turn for an entirely different reason than the nausea that brought me in here in the first place, but when Ransom shoots me a questioning look, I shake my head.

I know he would take this burden from me if he could, but I have to be the one to say it.

Wiping my eyes again, I take a shuddering breath, trying to steady myself. My limbs feel heavy and numb, and I glance from Malice to Vic, almost as if I'm trying to memorize the way they look before they hear the awful news I'm about to deliver.

"I think I'm pregnant," I tell them, the words halting and stiff. "And it's... it's probably Troy's."

Vic makes a noise low in his throat, his shoulders going tense. Malice's jaw clenches immediately, fury snapping in his eyes.

"Are you sure?" he demands.

I shake my head. "No. Not entirely. I woke up feeling sick, and my period is late. But I don't know for sure."

Vic and Malice share a look, and without a word being spoken between them, Vic nods and then leaves.

As soon as his twin disappears, Malice comes into the bathroom and puts the lid down on the toilet, sitting there with us. Ransom keeps stroking my hair, letting me lean against him, and Malice wraps his large hand around mine, threading our fingers together.

"Vic will get a test," he says. "We've gotta be sure."

288

I nod, because he's right about that. Even if I don't want to know the truth, I can't avoid it forever. And I have to be sure.

We sit in silence for what feels like an eternity, and by the time Vic comes back with the test, I'm not shaking quite as much. It still doesn't feel completely real, and my mind sort of refuses to latch on to this new crisis.

Vic presses the test into my hands when he comes back, and I let out a shaky breath. He and his brothers clear out, giving me some space to deal with it. Part of me wants them to stay, to hold my hands while I figure out just how fucked I am, but a larger part of me wants to do this alone.

I can hear them right outside the door though, too protective to go very far even now.

It's pretty simple to pee on the stick, although it takes a little maneuvering to get it right. I have a memory of being pretty young and sitting outside the bathroom door while Misty did this, trying to see if she felt shitty that morning because she'd been partying too much or because she was pregnant.

It turned out okay for her in the end, and I silently hope that it'll be the same for me.

The minutes until the test will reveal the result crawl by, and I pace the bathroom, hugging myself tightly, everything in me practically begging for it to be negative.

But when I finally look, I see a little plus sign staring back at me, sealing my fate.

It's positive.

I'm pregnant.

For a second, I just stare at it, overcome. Then I open the door and hold it out wordlessly, letting the three men see it.

Tears well in my eyes, and I blink them back, trying not to fall apart. But it's almost impossible not to. My fate is written right there, in damning pink lines. I'm going to have Troy's baby.

It takes several agonizing heartbeats before I'm able to look up at the guys, my stomach twisting with nerves. Part of me expects to see disgust on their faces, or anger. I'm carrying the child of one of their worst enemies, and I almost expect them to look at me like I'm tainted. I wouldn't blame them. I *feel* tainted.

But instead, they all reach for me at nearly the same time. They step forward to surround me, and I'm pulled into the circle of their bodies and held close.

"It's not his," Ransom says softly. "Not in any way that counts. Troy is dead, so this is *your* kid."

"I wish I could kill him again," Malice mutters. "And make it hurt even worse this time. But Ransom is right. We're gonna love and protect you and any baby you have. No matter who the father is."

A tiny sob escapes my lips, and I feel their arms tighten around me in response.

"But... why?" I ask, my voice shredded. "How can you promise that, knowing that Troy... knowing that the baby will be part his?"

"Because it doesn't matter." Vic's voice rumbles in my ear. "DNA isn't what decides who a person will become. Our father was a piece of shit, remember? And none of us turned out like him."

My tears soak Malice's shirt. "I know. I just..."

"And look at you," Ransom adds, stroking my hair again. "Your grandmother is the biggest fucking bitch in the whole state. And you're nothing like her. That should be pretty good proof right there of how little someone's family tree matters."

"Your kid will decide who they want to be, no matter who their father is," Malice says, his hands splaying over my back. "Troy is gone from this fucking earth, so he won't be an influence."

What they're saying makes sense, logically. And I want to believe them, to cling to the conviction in their voices and let myself hope that everything could still be okay. But in this moment, it's hard to imagine that *anything* that's a part of Troy Copeland could ever be good, even this baby.

More tears leak from my eyes, and I squeeze my lids shut as the men continue to hold me, murmuring soft, soothing words. Finally, as if he can sense the conflict still raging inside me, Ransom pulls back a little. The other men loosen their holds on me as well, and he rests two knuckles under my chin, catching my gaze.

"Do you remember what I told you on my bike that day, angel?" he asks quietly. "Right before Misty died?"

My heart stutters. Of course I remember. Every minute of that day is burned into my memory, including the part of it where Ransom took me for a ride on his motorcycle. That was the first time he ever made me come on his bike, revving the engine to help me get off... and in the aftermath, as we sat talking in the quiet stillness, he told me a secret he'd never told anyone else.

He doesn't have the same mother as Malice and Vic.

His blue-green eyes are somber as he watches me now, taking in the look on my face as I process his words. I'm aware of his brothers watching us, confusion pinching Malice's brows together, but I keep my focus on Ransom as I nod, the lump in my throat growing.

"Yes," I whisper. "I remember."

RANSOM

I HOLD WILLOW'S GAZE, seeing all the emotions in her beautiful eyes. She knows what it means for me to be saying this out loud in front of my own brothers, but I want to prove a point to her. I need her to understand that just because Troy is the father of her kid, that doesn't mean her child is going to be anything like him.

Blood only goes so far.

I know she probably already grasps that truth, deep down. But right now, she's got all of this fear, anger, and anxiety eating at her. And this admission is the only way I can think of to remind her that family is what we make it, not what's forced upon us by our DNA.

In all honesty, I never really thought about how I'd tell my brothers the truth about this. How, or if, I would reveal that I'm only their half-brother. I definitely wouldn't have imagined it would be in a moment like this, but Willow needs to hear me say it.

Stepping back from the circle a bit, I take a deep breath.

Malice and Vic look between Willow and me, clearly understanding that something is going on here.

"What is it?" Vic asks. "What did you tell her?"

"So, the thing is..." I clear my throat. "I know a lot about how blood isn't the only thing that can make someone family. Because of our shitty dad, but also because... we don't have the same mom."

Malice's eyebrows shoot up, and Vic's furrow as they take that in. I run a hand through my hair and press on, needing to get it out.

"My mom was different from yours, someone else our dear old dad treated like shit. But in the end, that woman died, and Diana offered to raise me." I clear my throat. "I've known for a long time, but I just never wanted to bring it up. I guess I didn't want you to see me as anything other than your true brother. Your *full* brother."

I shrug a little awkwardly, waiting for their response. Luckily, the thing about Malice is that he doesn't hide his emotions well at all. He looks confused for a second and then surprised.

"What the fuck would that matter?" he asks finally. "You've been with us forever, and that's more important than anything else."

Vic nods. "And Mom loved you, so that's what counts. We could see how much she cared, even if you weren't her son by blood."

Something aches in my chest at the memory of the woman I'll always consider my mother. "She was a fucking saint," I murmur.

Malice nods, his jaw clenching. His eyes burn in the way they always do when we talk about our mom, gleaming with love and fierce devotion. Vic makes a sound of affirmation, and when I glance over at him, he holds my gaze, speaking in a low voice.

"You're our *brother*," he says. "No matter if we share two parents or one. Family doesn't have to mean blood. It's about who loves you."

"A-fucking-men," Malice agrees. "And about who you can trust to have your back. That's always been you, Ransom."

Willow lets out a soft sob, stepping forward and burying her head against my chest. I wrap my arms around her, feeling her tears soak into my shirt.

"I told you," she whispers. "I told you they wouldn't care."

"I know." My voice turns raspy as my throat goes tight. "You were right, angel. Of course you were."

Something I didn't realize I'd been carrying falls away from my shoulders as I tangle my fingers in my beautiful girl's hair, holding my brother's gazes over her head.

I know my father only told me the truth about my real mother as a way to fuck with me, a way to get into my head and make me doubt myself. And for years, I tried to tell myself that there was a good reason not to share this knowledge with my brothers. I told myself it didn't matter, or that I didn't want to burden them with it.

But the truth is, I was scared.

Some part of me, however small, always feared that they would see me differently or treat me differently if they knew I was only their half-brother.

I'm relieved to have it out in the open now though. And I'm even more relieved that they don't care. I didn't really think they would, but there was always a part of me that felt a little 'less than' because I wasn't as closely connected to them as they thought I was.

But after hearing Willow worry that we would turn on her or her unborn baby because the father was a monster, it clarified everything for me.

Parentage truly doesn't matter.

Leaning back a little, I brush Willow's cheeks with my thumbs, wiping away the tears there. Her brown eyes are swollen and bloodshot from crying, but just like I told her when we woke up earlier, she still looks beautiful to me. She always fucking will.

"No matter what you decide to do, we'll support you," I tell her, tucking her tangled hair behind her ears. "We'll love you. And if you decide to keep this baby, we'll love it too."

"Truly?" Her lower lip quavers, and she traps it between her teeth.

"Of course." I chuckle, and although there's no humor in it, there *is* warmth. "My brothers and I had a terrible father, I don't remember my actual mother, and your grandmother is one of the most god-awful people I've ever met. But all of us turned out okay. Hell, you turned out so much better than okay. You're the best person I know, angel. We love every damn thing about you, and we definitely don't hold Olivia against you. So why would we hold Troy against your baby? Your blood family may be fucked up, but you have a real family." I jerk my chin, encompassing myself and my brothers in a single gesture. "Us. We're right here with you, and we always will be."

She leans her face into my palm, closing her eyes like she's trying to ground herself through that touch. Some of the tension slides out of her shoulders, and as they slump a little, I share a look with my brothers over her head.

We can't fix this in one day, and we definitely can't heal her trauma with one conversation.

But no matter what happens, our family will stick together.

AFTER WE FINALLY BREAK APART, we take our time getting cleaned up and properly dressed. My brothers and I all watch Willow like hawks to make sure she doesn't suffer another bout of morning sickness or seem to be falling back into a panic.

Once we've gotten some breakfast in our systems, we decide that Willow has had enough excitement for one day. She insists she doesn't need to be coddled, putting her foot down and refusing to go back to bed when there's still planning to do.

"We can't take a break. Not even for this. We can't let this slow us down," she says, looking at us defiantly. "The sooner we find an enemy of Olivia's that we can recruit to help us, the sooner we can end this. For good, this time."

Her voice drops low on those last words, and the determination in her voice is hot as hell.

Still, Malice looks about ready to throw her over his shoulder and cart her off to bed himself, until Vic slides in smoothly with a compromise.

He sets up a nest of blankets and pillows on the couch in the living room for Willow to curl up in, getting her water and snacks, making sure she has what she needs before he goes and gets his laptop to set up near her and work at the coffee table.

She gives him a grateful smile, and then we get back to the planning.

It all comes down to being able to find someone who can help us against Olivia. Without that, it's going to be hard to find a way to take her out before she gets to Willow.

"We need a backup plan," Malice says, pacing in front of the massive TV. "Just in case."

"You're starting to sound like me," Vic replies. But he nods. "I'm working on it. It's just difficult because there's a lot of information we don't have. Nothing that's publicly available about Olivia is going to get us what we need."

"We should just take a hit out on her," Malice mutters. "Give the old bitch a taste of her own medicine."

Vic types something on his computer. "I'm adding that to the list, just in case."

We go back and forth for the rest of the day, hashing out what we can and coming up with contingencies for what we can't control. Which is most of it.

Between bouts of planning, we take care of Willow. The three of us trade off getting her things to eat and refilling her water. One of us is touching her at all times, stroking her hair, holding her hand, just making sure that she knows we're here.

She seems better than she was this morning, but I know it's still going to take a while for her to truly come to terms with it. So we're all focused on making sure she doesn't have a reason to doubt our love and support for a second.

Later that night, when she starts to nod off on the couch, Malice does pick her up and carry her to bed, tucking her in despite her protests that's she fine.

I head into the kitchen, rummaging through the cabinets for a bottle of whiskey.

"Fuck it," I mutter under my breath, going to sit down at the table without getting a glass. It's been one of those drink it straight from the bottle kind of days.

Malice comes in and sits down across from me, putting his elbows on the table.

"How long did it take for her to fall asleep?" I ask.

He snorts. "About thirty seconds after her head hit the pillow. She was worn the fuck out."

"Can't blame her for that. It's been a hell of a day."

"Yeah."

I swig from the bottle and then pass it across to Malice, who does the same. We sit in silence for a bit, both of us lost in our own thoughts. There's something nostalgic about it, reminding me of those days when we would do this back at the warehouse. Sitting in the kitchen sharing a bottle or some food. Or when the three of us would congregate in the living room to drink and hash out our latest plan. Or just shoot the shit.

I'm glad that some things haven't changed, even though so much is different now.

"So, how long have you known about your real mom?" Malice asks after a while, breaking the silence.

"A while," I admit. "Dad told me. A few months before we killed him."

"Fucking bastard," my brother mutters. "I bet he did that shit on purpose."

"Yeah, I think he did. I was too young to remember my real mom, and I guess he just wanted me to know that as much as I loved the woman who raised me, she wasn't actually my mother by birth."

Vic comes walking into the kitchen as I finish speaking, shaking his head.

"Emotional abuse was his specialty," he says dryly.

He sits down at the table, accepting the whiskey when Malice passes it to him. He glances toward the cabinet as if he's considering grabbing a glass, but then settles on wiping the neck of the bottle clean before taking a sip.

I laugh, but there's not much humor in it. "Yeah. It definitely fucked me up for a while, thinking about it. He told me that he was just going to fucking abandon me when my real mom died, but Diana told him she would raise me."

Malice nods, looking down at the table as his fingertips drum across the surface. "That sounds like her."

"She loved you," Vic adds quietly. "That was obvious to all of us."

"I know. Knowing she did all that and raised me as her own, even though I was the product of our shit stain dad cheating on her? It just made me love her even more. Made me want to kill that bastard even more than I already did."

"He got what he deserved." Malice clenches his hand into a fist, banging it lightly against the table, and we all drink to that, passing the whiskey around again.

"You kept it to yourself for a long time," Vic observes as he sets the bottle down.

I shrug. "I didn't know how to say it. And I guess I had to deal with my own shitty feelings about it first. I mean, you two are twins, so you've got this connection, and I already felt weird being the youngest for a while. Add onto that that I wasn't even your full brother..." I shake my head. "It was a lot."

"Like we said before, we don't give a shit if you had a different mom," Malice tells me. He grins, the same one I recognize from when we were growing up and he would tease me about something. "You're still our annoying little brother."

I roll my eyes at that, reaching over the table to punch him in the arm. He chuckles, but then grows serious.

"Our mom loved you," he says. "We love you. That's good enough. It's all that matters."

"Yeah, I know." I settle back into my chair. "I love you assholes too. I'm not messed up about it anymore. I just wish it was that easy for Willow, you know?"

Malice's lip curls back in a snarl. "Death was too easy an

escape for the fucker who did this to her," he grits out. "Fucking piece of shit."

I take a deep swig from the bottle, letting the whiskey burn down my throat. "I was happy to let the two of you torture him at the time, but goddammit, I regret not getting in a few shots of my own now. We could've kept him alive for days, dragging it out, and it *still* wouldn't have been enough."

Vic taps his fingers together, glancing in the direction of the bedroom. "You're not wrong. But we need to focus on Willow now. Bringing up Troy, even to say we wish we'd tortured him more, is just going to make her keep thinking about him. And she's having a hard enough time with this already."

"I can't even imagine how she must feel," I mutter, raking a hand through my hair.

My brothers both nod, the atmosphere in the kitchen turning grim. When Vic plucks the bottle from my hand, and I can tell how agitated he is, because he doesn't even bother to wipe the neck before taking a swig.

"The good news is, we made good progress today," he says. "I've got a list of potential allies, people who have reason to hate Olivia and also have the skills to back us up when we go after her. We can start reaching out to them tomorrow."

"Good," Malice mutters. "Because knowing that Willow is pregnant raises the stakes on all of this. If her bitch of a grandmother finds out about it, that will probably only give her more reason to want Willow and the baby dead. We have to end this... before Olivia does."

30

WILLOW

THE NEXT MORNING, I wake up to an empty bed.

I know the guys came to sleep last night because I half remember waking up in the middle of the night to them coming in, whispering amongst themselves.

Which means that they're already up and getting started for the day.

I curse under my breath, throwing the blankets back and shuffling out of bed. I don't want to be the weak link in the team just because I'm pregnant. I don't want them to think I'm too weak to help out now.

There's a little nausea as I get dressed, but I take some deep breaths, pushing it down. I don't have time to be sick right now.

When I step into the kitchen, Vic is already there, and it smells like he's been cooking. I wait, wanting to see if the smell is going to turn my stomach, but surprisingly, it doesn't.

"What's all this?" I ask him.

He smiles a little. "I did some research on foods that are supposed to be good for settling morning sickness. And healthy for pregnant women. You'll have to let me know if it helps."

I can't help but grin at that, taking in the small spread he's laid out. There's a fruit plate laid out, each piece of fruit cut into neat, equal pieces. Toast with peanut butter on another plate, next to more toast, smeared with what looks like avocado. Next to all that is a steaming cup of tea that smells gingery when I pick it up.

"Thank you, Vic," I tell him, taking a small sip of the tea.

I sit and start eating some of everything, relieved when it all stays down and the tea helps settle my stomach.

Ransom and Malice come in a bit later, already dressed as well.

"Are you ready?" Malice asks Vic, who is loading the dishwasher in his precise way.

"Five minutes."

"Wait, where are you going?" I ask.

"I made a list of people who might be able to help us with the Olivia situation," Vic says. "We're going to try to recruit them today."

"Then I want to come," I say, stuffing a piece of toast in my mouth. "Just let me—"

"No," Malice cuts in. "You're staying here."

"But—"

"No buts. You're not coming." He folds his arms, and I glare up at him.

"I can still do stuff, you know. I'm not some helpless flower just because I'm pregnant. We didn't even know I was before, and I was still doing stuff. It's not like I'm that far along yet."

"It's not safe," Malice insists.

"Are you just worried I'll slow you down?"

He shakes his head. "No, it's not about that. It's about the fact that your fucking crazy grandma wants you dead. We were trying to keep you safe before we found out about the baby, and that hasn't fucking changed. Olivia is still out there, planning to kill you."

I hate that he's right, and I sit back in my chair, trying not to pout about it. Because he is right. And I can tell that he's not going to budge. As much as I hate feeling coddled and cooped up, I do like the fact that he cares so much.

"Fine," I mutter. "I'll stay here."

"Good girl," Malice says. He comes over and threads his fingers into my hair, pulling me up to my feet so he can kiss me. It's not a soft goodbye kiss either. It's hard and biting, the way Malice always seems to be. The heat of it washes through me, and I have to swallow hard when he pulls away.

"We'll be back before you know it," he whispers in my ear. "You behave."

I give him a little shrug when he draws back, and he slaps my ass lightly in warning, making me grin.

Once he and Vic are gone, it's just me and Ransom left in the penthouse.

"If it makes you feel better, they're going to be insufferable out there together," Ransom says when he catches me staring at the door after them. "Vic's going to want to do it his way, and Malice is going to be Malice, and they'll be bickering constantly."

I laugh, finishing the last of my tea. "That does sound like them, you're right."

"I know my brothers," he replies with a shrug.

With everything that's been going on lately, I've turned into a stage five clinger. I really hate having any of my men out of my sight, the same way I know they feel about me, so time seems to move extra slow while Malice and Vic are gone.

Ransom spends some time maintaining their weapons, cleaning guns and sharpening knives, and after checking the programs Vic has running to alert him to any unusual movement or activity from Olivia—monitoring her bank accounts and the security feeds around her place, things like that—I kill time reading one of the romance novels from the pile I've been working through.

"Is it a good part?" Ransom asks, waggling his eyebrows when he comes back into the living room a while later and sees me with my nose buried in the book. "What's the brooding hero up to now? Has he ripped his shirt off yet?"

"I don't know what you think I'm reading," I say, shaking my head. "No one's ripping any shirts." Then I reconsider and add, "Although he did rip her panties off once."

Amused approval gleams in his eyes. "Fuck, yes. Now I see why you like these books so much."

Leaning on the back of the couch, he reads over my shoulder. I wait for more teasing to come, but instead, he actually seems to be intrigued by it.

"Okay, this is actually better than I was expecting it to be," he admits.

I smile, putting the book down. "Come over here for a minute."

Ransom grins, half vaulting over the couch so he can settle in next to me. "Hi."

"Hi." I reach up and run my hands through his hair, searching his face. He looks more comfortable and collected than he did yesterday, his ocean-colored eyes clear and untroubled. "How are you doing?"

Turning his head a little, he kisses my palm. "I should be asking you that. You're the one going through a lot right now."

I just smile, shaking my head. "I'm asking you though."

He blows out a messy breath. "I'm okay. I'm glad I talked about it all yesterday. Glad I told Malice and Vic the truth. The part of me that knows them and trusts them knew it wasn't going to go badly, but I guess I just needed the nudge. It feels good to have it off my chest."

"I'm glad you did it. And I'm glad they reminded you they'll love you no matter what. You deserve to hear that."

Ransom reaches up and touches my face, stroking his fingers over my cheek.

"My sweet, beautiful angel. How the fuck did we get so lucky to have you fall into our lives?" he murmurs, then pulls me in for a kiss.

It starts out soft and a little chaste, mostly just him kissing me because he wants to. His mouth is warm, his lips firm and sure as he brushes them over mine.

But then his tongue flicks out, teasing and exploratory, and that makes me smile into the kiss, parting my lips for him. There's a second of hesitation, like he's not sure yet what he wants to do, and then he goes for it, pressing his tongue into my mouth, sweeping it through like he's been dying to taste me.

His hands roam over my body, sliding over my clothes at first before slipping under them. I can feel the callouses on his palms as he drags them over my hips, and the feeling makes me shiver against him.

When we break apart to breathe, his mouth finds my neck, nipping at my pulse point and licking along the sensitive line of my throat.

"Ransom," I moan, squirming on the couch. "Please."

He chuckles, and the sound is low and deep, enough to have my body tightening with need.

"I know what you want," he murmurs, lips brushing over my skin. "Don't worry, I've got you, angel."

I moan again as he bites down on my neck and then pulls the collar of my shirt out of the way so he can do the same to my shoulder. It hurts just the right amount, and I can feel my pussy throbbing.

But when I start to clamber onto his lap, desperate to grind against him and get all the friction I need, he stops me. I give him a quizzical look, panting slightly, and he chuckles.

"Don't worry, pretty girl. I've got a better idea."

"As long as it involves your cock in me, I'm all ears."

He tweaks my nipple, making me hiss. "Listen to you and your dirty mouth. I fucking love it."

I smirk, because every filthy thing I know, I learned from him and his brothers. And they've been extremely good teachers.

"Then fill me up with your cock," I tell him. "I want to feel every piercing. I want to feel you every time I move tomorrow."

He groans. "Oh, I'll make sure you do."

I can tell my words have gotten him fully hard, ready to grab me and drive into me—but instead of doing that, he gets up from the couch. I scrunch up my nose, tracking him with my gaze as I try to figure out what he's up to.

But it all becomes clear when he pulls me up to stand and then pushes me down until I'm draped over the arm of the couch from one side.

My heart races at the confident, commanding way he positions me, my pulse picking up even more as I realize how exposed I am for him like this. My feet are on the floor, and I'm hinged at the waist over the couch arm, my ass perfectly presented to Ransom. If he pushed my face down, I'd be muffled by the couch, but everything else would be there, open and ready for him.

Behind me, Ransom drags my pants and panties down. He doesn't even bother to take them all the way off, leaving them bunched around my ankles. That just adds to the delicious feeling of vulnerability in a way, and I moan when he slides his hands up my thighs and then squeezes my ass.

"You have no idea how good you look like this," he whispers huskily. "Fuck, angel."

"Show me," I beg, arching back as much as I can. "Show me how much you like it."

He presses his crotch against the seam of my ass, letting me feel how his dick is hard as steel for me. The roughness of his pants against my skin and the hot brand of his cock behind the fabric makes my clit throb. He gropes my ass thoroughly and then pulls back, and I can hear him shoving his pants down to fetch out his cock.

"You gonna be a good girl and take my dick like you were begging for?"

The bare head of his dick works its way into me, and it feels amazing. My body is still a little sore from the other night, but it immediately stretches to accommodate him, the slick wetness of my arousal easing his way in.

"Please," I groan, my fingernails digging into the leather of the couch. "Please, I need it. I need you."

Ransom doesn't make me wait. He bottoms out quickly, then sets a hard, fast rhythm, pounding into me like he can't get enough of it. His hands go to my hips, holding on tightly, and I gasp his name when his piercing hits a spot inside me that makes pleasure shoot through my body like a bolt of lightning.

I try to spread my legs wider for him, but I'm brought up short by the pants and panties still around my ankles, trapping me. Something about being restrained like this turns me on even more, and I whimper, sliding one hand downward to play with my clit.

"Fuck," I gasp. "Fuck, fuck, fuck."

"I can't get enough of you," Ransom says. "Fuck, never enough. You're so fucking good. You feel so fucking good."

His voice is strained as he fucks into me deeper, each thrust making his piercings rub against my inner walls.

It's enough to drive me crazy, to have me spiraling, closer and closer to detonating for him... .

And then, out of nowhere, his phone rings.

Ransom curses under his breath, and he doesn't stop fucking me. Instead, he buries himself deep inside me, gripping my hip tightly with one hand to hold me still as he reaches over to grab his cell from where he set it on the back of the couch.

"Hey," he says into the phone, his fingers digging into my flesh as he picks up the call. "Hold on."

I try to stifle my moans, to keep myself quiet so that whoever is on the other end of this call can't hear me—but with his cock filling up every inch of me, that's one of those 'easier said than done' kind of things.

Ransom puts the phone on the back of the couch again, and I can hear from the background noise that he put it on speaker.

"Okay, go ahead," he says. Now that both of his hands are free again, he grabs my hips even tighter, fucking into me with a long, deep stroke.

I bite my lip, dragging in a breath through my nose as Malice's voice emerges from the phone speaker.

"We got one possible lead," he says. "No one else was lining up to help us though. Probably all afraid of that bitch and not wanting to get involved."

"Or they just didn't have anything to offer," Vic adds. "Not everyone in the criminal world has the resources or guts to go up against someone like Olivia, and we don't need any dead weight."

"Point is, we've got something to follow up on," Malice says.

"Better than nothing," Ransom tells him. Then he thrusts into me so sharply that it makes my mouth fall open, allowing a whimper to escape.

"What was that?" Malice asks. "Was that Willow?"

Ransom laughs and does it again, snapping his hips forward and burying his cock all the way to the hilt. "Say hi, pretty girl."

I moan, shaking against the arm of the couch. "Fuck. Hi, Malice. Hi, Vic."

There's no way they can't tell what we're doing right now, and even if they couldn't hear the moaning or the sound of Ransom's hips hitting my ass, the wrecked sound of my voice would do it.

"Motherfucker," Malice curses. "We're out here doing the work, and you're at home getting off."

"I've earned it," Ransom counters, laughing breathlessly.

"The fuck you have."

Ransom squeezes my hip, bending down lower over my body. That presses his cock even deeper into me, and I whimper again, writhing under him.

"They're on their way home now," he says to me. "Should we show them what they're missing here?"

All I can do is nod, breathless and too turned on to make coherent words come out right now. Something about knowing they're listening to this, hearing the way Ransom fucks me so good, drives me crazy.

"Good girl," he growls softly. "Let them hear you. Moan for them so they know how good I'm making you feel."

Then he starts fucking me harder, setting an almost brutal pace and filling the room with the sounds of skin on skin.

The moans spill from my lips with ease as each hard thrust pushes me that much higher. It's a garbled mix of gasps and cries and moans and pleas, and the sound of tires screeching from the phone proves that Malice has started driving faster.

I can't help but laugh at that, adrenaline and desire rushing through me.

"Oh, you think it's funny to torture us, Solnyshka? You won't be laughing when we get there," Malice promises, his voice husky. "You're gonna be face down and ass up with my cock so deep in you that you'll feel it for the next week. You're gonna take it so good for me, aren't you?"

"Yes," I moan. "Fuck, yes. Anything you want."

Vic chuckles. "That's a dangerous promise, butterfly. You know how Malice gets. And maybe while he's fucking you, I'll take my turn with your mouth."

Dirty talk from Vic is always one of my favorite things in the world, and it sparks more heat inside me as I picture it. Malice buried in my pussy, his cock splitting me open in the best way. And Vic in my mouth, my lips wrapped around his thick cock, sucking him down.

"Please," I beg, my body trembling as Ransom grabs my wrists and pins them against my lower back. "Please, I want that so much. I want you so much. All of you."

"Goddammit, move," Malice snarls, and it registers that he's probably talking to someone on the road and not to us. "We're gonna make it happen. We're gonna give you all you can take, Solnyshka—and then some. But you like that, don't you? When we push you. When we take you right to the edge and then a little over it."

A strangled sound falls from my lips. "Yes."

"She does." Pride fills Ransom's voice. "You should see how fucking good she looks right now. Her ass is red from the pounding I've been giving her, her back arched so perfectly, hair all splayed out on the couch cushions. Like a dirty angel."

He adjusts our positions a little as he speaks, and now my clit grinds against the arm of the couch every time he drives into me.

"Fuck!" I cry out. "Oh my god, I'm so close. I'm gonna—"

Before I can get another word out, the pleasure is slamming through me. It steals my breath as wave after wave of sensation hits me hard. All I can do is scream, twisting and arching on the couch, bucking back against Ransom and dragging his cock even deeper.

Ransom ends the call with a curse of his own, focusing on his own pleasure now. He grabs my hips hard and drags me back into each thrust, not giving me even a second to breathe.

"God," he groans. "You feel so fucking good. So fucking tight. I can't get enough of you and this perfect pussy. Fuck!"

He hits his peak and spills inside me, filling me up with a hot rush. His hips press tight to my ass, and he's as deep as he can go, riding out the wave of his orgasm. Every pulse of his pierced cock feels incredible, and I whimper wordlessly when I feel a little trail of cum sliding down my thigh.

He releases my wrists and then pulls out, leaving me sprawled over the edge of the couch like a melting popsicle.

I lie there, too worn out to move yet, trying to catch my breath. For the first time since yesterday morning, I feel happy and sated, content that even if things are spiraling out of control in some ways, at least I still have this.

Ransom presses a kiss to my shoulder. "Malice is gonna fucking kill me for that. But it was so damn worth it."

I chuckle. "Yeah, it definitely wa—"

My voice breaks off as a shrill alarm rises up from the other room.

The office.

Ransom straightens, his entire demeanor changing in an instant. All the loose, sated energy is gone, replaced by the man who can be just as deadly as his brothers.

"Fuck," he curses. "That's one of Vic's alarms." In a smooth motion, he reaches under the coffee table, where they've stashed a gun in case of emergencies. "Get in the bedroom, angel, and lock the door. *Now!*"

I scramble off the couch, but before I can move any further than that, the sound of footsteps echoes in the hall outside.

Then the door explodes inward, kicked off its hinges.

"Fuck," Ransom curses.

He reacts immediately, shoving me down behind the couch as he levels his gun at them. He fires off two shots, diving out of the way as they return fire. He ends up behind the large chair set off to one side of the couch, taking cover behind it and shooting toward the intruders again, trying to keep them pinned down near the doorway.

My pulse jackhammers as I struggle against my clothes, which are still twisted up around my ankles.

We're under attack.

The men haven't let me leave the penthouse in days, and Olivia clearly got tired of waiting for me to emerge and sent someone in after us. More than *one* someone. There are three of them, which means we're outnumbered.

"Willow, stay down!" Ransom calls, firing again. I can't see what's happening near the door, since my view is obscured by the couch, but I hear a crash and then heavy footsteps. Two more shots cut through the air, and then a masked man appears around the edge of the couch.

He raises his weapon, pointing it right at me.

Time seems to freeze for a second as I look down the barrel of the gun—and then another shot rings out.

I flinch, braced for the pain and the impact... but there's nothing. His gun falls to the floor, landing with a heavy thud, and he follows it a second later, crumpling to the carpet like a sack of rocks.

More gunshots are punctuated by shouting voices, and then the room goes quiet, leaving only the sound of my blood rushing in my ears.

"Motherfucker," someone curses.

I almost weep with relief at the familiar voice.

Malice. He and Vic are back.

31

VICTOR

As MALICE BITES OUT several more curses beside me, I glance around the room, taking in the scene quickly.

Willow is partially obscured by the couch, with the man who was about to shoot her lying dead in a heap a few feet away. Blood spreads across the cream colored carpet, staining it a deep crimson.

The other two men are down too. Ransom got one of them, and Malice took out the other while I shot the bastard who was gunning to kill Willow. Fury lances through me at the memory of him standing over her, and even though I know it's pointless and will only make more of a mess, I stride forward quickly, put my gun right to his temple, and spatter his brains across the floor—just to be goddamned sure he never gets the chance to touch her again.

"Shit," Ransom says, panting hard as he tugs his pants back into place. "Thank fucking god you two got back when you did. Guess it was a good thing you were speeding."

It's almost a joke, since we all know exactly why Malice was driving so fast. He drove like a maniac because he wanted to get home and fuck her senseless, not because he thought he'd show up to find Ransom and Willow fighting for their lives.

But nothing about this is funny, so no one laughs.

Instead, Malice kicks the body of one of the downed men,

clearly needing to let out his extra adrenaline and aggression somehow.

"What the fuck happened?" he snarls.

His anger is bright and fierce, and even though I'm usually more collected than he is, I feel an answering rage in my chest. This place was supposed to be safe. We increased security, set up alarms. But three people got in and almost managed to kill Ransom and Willow.

"Your alarm worked, Vic," Ransom says, flicking a glance my way. "They got into the building, but we had warning before they reached the penthouse. It was enough to keep us alive. We would've been sitting ducks otherwise."

"Olivia. This has to be her doing. She got impatient when Willow wasn't coming out, so she sent these fuckers to do her dirty work and break in here. This bitch wants her money that bad." Malice shakes his head, scowling down at the body of the attacker nearest to him.

I step over the man I just shot and go to Willow, reaching out a hand to help her up.

"Are you okay?" I ask softly.

She swallows hard, nodding. I'm glad my alarm system gave them some advance warning, but it's clear that the whole thing happened fast. She and Ransom didn't even have time to get dressed before these assholes came bursting in on them. Her pants are around her ankles, and I reach down to tug them up, helping her get dressed as she clings to me. I can feel her hands shaking, and when she exhales, the breath seems to shudder out of her lungs.

"I... he was just..." She tightens her grip, staring at my face as I deftly zip up and button her pants. "He almost killed me, Vic. He would have if you hadn't..."

"I know," I tell her, my voice tight. "But he's dead now."

She came close to dying, honestly. Too fucking close. She was unarmed, staring down the barrel of that gun, and if we hadn't gotten here when we did...

I shake my head, not wanting to finish that thought. I can't focus on it, or I'll lose every scrap of control I have.

Willow seems to be of the same mind, because she stiffens her shoulders and takes another deep breath. I can see the fear and worry edging out of her eyes, leaving behind conviction and determination. She's gathering her strength, letting this incident firm her resolve against her grandmother instead of breaking her down.

That's one of the things I love most about her.

Nothing can break this woman.

"Get his mask off," Malice tells Ransom, gesturing to the body closest to our brother. They each take a body, tugging the masks off, and I release Willow so that I can reach down and do the same to the man leaking blood and brain matter into the carpet.

I have to maneuver the mask a little to get it off his mangled head, and as soon as I do, I let out a harsh breath.

Across the room, Ransom makes a noise of displeasure, and Malice explodes to his feet, hurling the mask in his hand against the wall.

"Ethan fucking Donovan!" he rages, kicking the body again.

I look from the man at my feet—whom I recognize as one of Donovan's men—and look over to see the familiar face of Donovan himself. He's the one sprawled out near Malice, and another one of his seconds lies near Ransom.

"Still in Olivia's pocket, I guess," Ransom mutters, his lips curling with disgust. "She either offered him a lot of money, or she had something she was holding over him the same way she did to us. Hell, if he didn't hate us so fucking much—and if he weren't dead—he almost would've been a good candidate to help us go up against her."

"Well, he's not helping us with shit now," Malice bites out.

He kicks Ethan's body again, harder this time, and I wince. It's not because I object to violence against a dead body, especially not a slimy asshole like Ethan Donovan. But every time Malice jars his body, more blood leaks out of him.

The living room is a complete mess. Bodies and blood every-

313

where, the couch all shot up, glass broken and bullet holes in the walls. I hate it.

"We should get out of here before someone calls the cops," I say, glancing between my brothers. "We increased security as much as we could, but obviously, it wasn't enough. In a building like this, with multiple ways in and out, I couldn't tighten things up enough. We need to go somewhere else. Someplace Olivia will have a harder time finding us."

"You think moving will keep us safer?" Ransom asks, crouching by the body of Donovan's second and rifling through his pockets.

"It's all relative at this point. She's getting impatient and closing in. Nothing will make us *safe*, but we just need to buy ourselves enough time to make our move against her and take her out of the picture. Even if we're only one step ahead of her, we need to stay one step ahead until this is over."

Willow wraps her arms around herself, her gaze darting around the living room. I know this place once belonged to Troy, so it's not like she's emotionally attached to it in that sense. But it's also the place where the four of us created a small, makeshift version of a home for ourselves.

It's not Troy's any longer. It's *ours*.

And I hate that once again, Olivia is forcing us out.

"Okay." Malice rubs a hand over his jaw, leaving a small streak of blood. "Ten minutes. That's all we've got. Grab all the shit we're gonna need, and let's clean this place up. We've gotta get these bodies out of here too. And Vic, I want a full perimeter check. Make sure there isn't an ambush waiting outside for us."

I nod, and we all spring into action. Ransom grabs the spare duffel bags we bought and starts packing up weapons and ammo first, then goes through and gets clothes and basic toiletries, anything we might need. Malice strips the sheets from the bed and comes back to roll the bodies of the dead men in them for us to take down to the car.

I clean up as much as I can, making a face at all the blood. The carpet is probably ruined, and I make a mental note that if we ever do come back here, I want it all ripped out anyway.

Willow grabs her things, quiet and withdrawn, and I find myself hoping that this will be the last time she'll have to vacate an apartment where someone died.

We take everything down to the car, stuffing the bodies into the trunk and throwing our shit into the back seat. It's a tight fit, the vehicle so crammed full that Willow has to crawl onto Ransom's lap in the back seat, where he wraps his arms around her protectively. I take my usual spot in the front passenger seat as Malice gets behind the wheel.

As we peel out, I wipe the security footage from the penthouse and the surrounding areas, just in case Olivia tries to use that to find out where we went.

"Keep your eye out for a tail," I murmur to Malice. "Anyone following us."

"On it." He nods, already glancing in the rearview mirror. "We're clean."

"She's probably expecting Ethan to check in at some point. When he doesn't, she'll figure out that the hit went sideways."

"Fuck, I wish I could see the look on her face when she finds out her pet goon is dead," Ransom says bitterly. "And with their leader out of the picture, dead thanks to Olivia's bullshit, I bet she won't be able to keep the rest of the Donovan crew under her thumb. They weren't that tight of a gang in the first place, and without Donovan to hold them together, they'll fall apart like leaves in the wind"

I nod, my fingers flying over the keys as sidewalks and buildings whiz past us outside. "Good point. That's one threat gone, at least. But we don't know how long that will last, so we can't get comfortable. She could have other gangs or hired mercenaries on deck."

"Where are we going?" Willow asks, craning her neck to look around the seat. "Another hotel?"

I shake my head. "No, that won't be safe enough either. We need a place away from people."

"I made a call while we were packing up," Malice informs her. "We still have some contacts from the chop shop days who owe us for work we did on an IOU. One of them set us up with a safe house. It's off the beaten path, so hopefully that'll help keep us off the radar. It's nothing fancy, but it'll do."

Willow nods, falling silent again.

When we reach the safe house, it's exactly like Malice said. It's a small place, just two bedrooms, a kitchen, a small living area, and a bathroom. After the time we spent in the penthouse, this is definitely a downgrade, but that's not what matters right now.

We unload the car, and then Malice and Ransom go to drop the bodies. I stay behind, getting my computers set up and keeping an eye on Willow.

She doesn't say much at first, but there's an agitation in her that's almost palpable. She paces around the small living room almost like she's Malice, walking the perimeter to keep an eye out for threats.

"Willow," I say, dragging her out of her thoughts and making her look at me. "Are you alright?"

She sighs and finally comes to a stop. "Yeah. I mean... I just kind of hate this, honestly."

"The house?"

"No, just... all of it. I hate that we have to keep leaving places behind in a hurry. I hate that this feels like we're on the run again. We were doing so well. We had the high ground for one goddamned *second*—and now Olivia has us running again."

"I know it must feel like that," I tell her. "But this isn't the same. We're in a much different situation than we were last time. We had to run today, yes, but this isn't a step backward, even if it feels like it is."

"I guess so. I just hate that it feels like no matter what we do, she always wins. She always holds all the cards. No one has ever been able to make me feel as... helpless as she does."

"You are not helpless," I say firmly. "Listen to me. You are so much stronger than you know, butterfly."

"When that man came at me with that gun, I froze," she admits, swallowing. "In that split second, it was like my body just went numb. I didn't know what to do. I definitely felt helpless then."

"We're always going to protect you," I vow. "But would it help if I taught you some ways to defend yourself?"

She licks her lips, considering. "Okay."

We push the dusty couch out of the way to give us more space, and I run Willow through some basic self-defense drills. We keep it light, considering she's pregnant, but I give her the information she can use if she needs it. I point out all the sensitive places on a person that she can go for, showing her how to jab someone in the throat or the solar plexus.

"And if it's a person with a dick, I'm sure I don't need to tell you how to incapacitate them for long enough to get away."

She laughs at that, and even if the sound is a bit strained, it feels like progress.

I show her how to get out of a headlock and how to keep someone from choking her out.

When I wrap my arm around her throat to demonstrate a move, her hair tickles my skin, her scent invading my nostrils as I inhale. Being pressed up behind her makes my body respond, my cock going half hard just from this proximity to her. It's not as intense as it used to be, like the time I kissed her in the kitchen and couldn't help but come in my pants, but I don't think I'll ever be able to touch her and not have a reaction.

My cheeks flush when I realize she can probably feel my cock twitching against her ass.

"Sorry," I murmur. "It's... an automatic response at this point."

"It's okay." She makes no move to pull away, reaching up instead to grip my forearm. "I don't mind. I've never minded, Vic. I like that you react this way to me."

"No one else has ever done this to me," I admit. "I've always been so good at controlling my reactions. There's just something about you that makes that impossible."

She sighs, turning in my arms and leaning up to kiss me lightly. It's just a brush of lips, but it still makes my heart rate speed up and my cock harden even more. If we had time, if things weren't so tense right now, I'd be tempted to follow the sensation, to press Willow against my body again and let her feel exactly how much I want her.

But there are other things to focus on right now.

"We're going to live through this," I say, my voice low. "Someday, we won't have to worry so much about just staying alive. And then I'm going to fuck you every single day, just because I can."

"Is that a promise?"

She smiles, hope lighting in her eyes, and I nod. "It's a vow."

32

WILLOW

Vic shows me a few more moves, then gives me a quick rundown on how to load and shoot a gun, and by the time we've wrapped up our impromptu lesson, Malice and Ransom get back.

"Any trouble?" Vic asks, glancing up as they walk through the door.

Malice shakes his head. "Nah. Dumped the bodies and got out of there."

He still has a streak of blood on his jaw, dried to a dark color now, and the sight of it makes my stomach turn. Death seems to hover over us all the time now, like an uninvited fifth member of our little family, and I hate it.

"How did it go this afternoon?" I ask, glancing between Malice and Vic. "Did you get any leads?"

I would have tried to get more information sooner, but being almost killed put a damper on that.

Malice sighs, rubbing at his face with one hand. "Maybe. It wasn't as useful as we wanted it to be, but..."

"...we talked to a man who has a few criminal connections, and he knew of a gang leader who hates Olivia Stanton," Vic finishes, picking up the thread of the thought. "Jonah Kent."

"Someone she had you go after for a job?" I ask.

319

Vic shakes his head. "No, but it's still worth reaching out to see if he can help. We're looking for someone who hates Olivia and will want to put her in the ground the same way we do, and it sounds like this guy is just the type we're after."

"How are we going to get in touch with him?"

"We've got a connection," Ransom answers. "Apparently, he's done some business with the Kings of Chaos before."

"Who?"

"Do you remember when we took you to that club, Sin and Salvation?"

I frown, thinking back. It feels like it happened fucking ages ago, but I have a sudden flashback of being fucked by them in the bathroom of that club. Heat rushes through me at the memory, and my cheeks flush as I nod.

"The people who run that club should be able to put us in touch with the leader of the Enigma gang."

"Can we go now?" I ask eagerly. "And try to get the info from them?"

Malice's face hardens. "Vic and I will go again. Just the two of us. You almost just got killed, Solnyshka. You should stay here. With Ransom."

A ripple of panic washes through me at that thought.

"No!" I shake my head. "We're not splitting up again. It's more dangerous to be separate than together. And besides, I want to be a part of this. I'm the one she's after. I want to help bring her down. I've *earned* that."

"You don't have to earn it," Ransom cuts in. "You've already proven yourself, angel. We're just trying to keep you safe."

"And I think we'd be safer if we stuck together."

"She has a point," Vic says quietly. Malice turns to glare at him, and he just shrugs. "It'll be easier to protect her if we're all together. If one of us goes down, there will still be two more bodies between an attacker and Willow."

I don't like the sound of that at all, and that's not what I meant about being safer together. But Malice actually seems swayed by his twin's argument, so I keep my lips pressed together instead of arguing that none of them should be throwing themselves in front of bullets for me. Vic already did that once, and the memory still haunts me.

Finally, Malice nods curtly. "Fine. But we stick close together, and if I tell you to run, Solnyshka, you fucking run. No hesitation. No questions. You get me?"

"Yes," I say, my heart thudding unevenly.

"Good."

We head to the car and then hit the road, Malice driving and Vic up front as usual. We make it to the club without incident, and all three men cluster around me like a phalanx of bodyguards as we head inside, surrounding me and keeping their eyes peeled for trouble.

It's getting to be late evening by now, and the club looks pretty much the same as it did the last time we were here. The dance floor is packed with people, a sweaty mass of bodies that grope and grind against each other. The atmosphere is thick with smoke and the scent of sweat, but we ignore all of that.

We're not here for fun tonight, so we head right up to the bar.

There's no sign of the men we met before, so Ransom flashes his charming smile at the bartender. He leans in over the bar to speak to her, having to get close to be heard over the music.

She shakes her head at first, seeming to brush him off, but then Ransom's face goes serious and he says something else. The bartender's eyes widen, and she nods, holding up a hand in the universal sign to wait.

She slips through a door that must lead to the back of the club, and it's only a couple minutes before she comes back.

"Okay," she says, raising her voice so we can all hear her. "You can come on back to the office."

We go around the bar and then through the same door, and once it closes behind us, the sounds from the club are muffled. The bass still thumps through the walls, but it feels more distant than being out in the mix of it. It's easier to hear myself think.

We walk down a short hallway and then knock on a closed door.

"Come in," someone calls from inside.

Malice opens the door, and we all file into the office.

I recognize one of the men inside from the last time we were here. He's got glasses, laughing amber eyes, and model good looks, and he gives us a curious look as we enter the small space. The other two are more serious looking, one with icy blue eyes and harsh features, and the other with green eyes that seem to pierce through us as he looks us over.

There's a scar on his upper lip, and he looks relaxed and at ease as he sits behind the desk on one side of the office, but it's pretty obvious that if we made a wrong move, he'd be ready to put a bullet through our heads in a heartbeat.

Ransom takes over the introductions, the most personable of the brothers as always.

"Willow, I think you met Ash before, right?" He nods to the man with the glasses.

"Right," I answer. "Nice to see you again."

Ash grins and gives me a little salute.

"And this is Priest and Gage," Ransom continues. "This is Willow. She's with us."

The three of them look me over, but it's not the same way other men do it. There's nothing predatory or lecherous in it, and I remember that they have their own partner, a woman that all of them apparently love. They're just looking at me to get the measure of me, and I have to wonder what they see.

"What can we do for you?" Gage asks. He looks at Malice, and I can tell that they're both the leaders of their respective groups. They both have that air of carrying the burden of making the tough calls and expecting their orders to be followed.

"What do you know about the Enigma gang?" Malice asks.

Gage raises an eyebrow. "I can't answer that until you tell me why you want to know."

"We need a way to get in touch with their leader."

There's a beat of silence while Gage sizes Malice up, and Malice doesn't flinch away from that perceptive gaze for a second. He lets Gage look, but the impatience is there in his posture, the way he folds his arms.

"Why should we get involved with whatever shit you've got going on?" Gage asks. "I can tell you have some kind of problem, but that has nothing to do with us."

"Oh, come on, Gage," Ash says. He lounges on the couch off to the side, spinning a pen idly between his fingers. "Where's your sense of community?"

Gage makes a face. "We're not in a community. And we're not running a charity."

"It's not charity. Consider it... payback. They've helped us out a lot, remember?" Ash gives him a significant look.

"There's no debt there," Gage argues. "They got something out of that too. It was an equal exchange."

Ash rolls his eyes, and it's pretty clear that this is a common thing for the two of them. They have a dynamic, much like the Voronin brothers do, and if Priest, Ash, and Gage didn't all look so different, I'd almost think they were brothers as well.

Priest, who's been mostly quiet through all of this, finally speaks up. "I think Ash is right."

That catches Gage's attention, and he glances over at the blond man with a sigh. "He'll never let you forget you said that, you know."

Priest doesn't quite smile, but his lips turn up at the corners a little. "I know. I'm just saying that it can't hurt to have a friendly exchange here and there. We help them out now, and then maybe they'll help us out later if we need it. More connections don't hurt. I know you don't trust anyone but us. But the Voronins have proved themselves. And we know what it's like to need help in a tight spot. They're not even asking for that much, all things considered."

As the leader, Gage could easily tell the two of them to shut up and that his word is law or whatever, but he doesn't do that.

He listens to them and seems to be weighing their words carefully.

There's respect there, a closeness that goes beyond family. I remember the silver haired woman who was with them the last time we were here. River. They have to be close to be sharing one woman, I suppose. And I remember how that was the first time I felt less alone in falling for multiple men.

Finally, Gage turns his gaze back to us, looking at each of us in turn.

"How do I know this isn't going to come back and bite us in the ass?" he wants to know. "If we're going to do you a favor, I need to know why."

My men all look at each other, as if they're silently debating how much they should say. But I step forward, clearing my throat.

"We don't want to start any trouble," I tell Gage, glancing from him to the other two. "Especially not for you. But we're in trouble ourselves. We need to talk to the leader of the Enigma gang because he might be our only chance to keep my grandmother from killing me. We just want to end this. I want a chance to not have to live in fear for myself and my men all the time. Please."

I can hear the emotion in my voice, but I don't try to hold it back. If Jonah can truly be an ally against Olivia, then we *need* him. And I need Gage to know that this is important.

He and the other two Kings of Chaos exchange looks, and Ash gives me a little smile. "Yeah, I think we can relate to that. Not wanting to live in fear is a damned good goal. Gage?"

He and Priest both look to the man behind the desk, and finally, he nods.

"Alright. We know the Enigma gang from some business we did with them this past year. Their leader is Jonah Kent. Their territory is on the east side of the city." He gives us a cross street, as well as the name of the tattoo parlor that apparently serves as their legitimate front and base of operations. "You're looking for a tall man, dark hair, weirdly light colored eyes."

I breathe a sigh of relief, a rush of gratitude filling me. There's still no guarantee that Jonah will help us, but at least we can ask him face to face.

"Thank you," Ransom says. "That's a huge help."

We turn to leave, but Gage's voice stops us before we can go. "Hey."

I glance back to see him staring right at me, and something in his eyes makes me think he understands what we're up against better than I'll probably ever know. He dips his chin, his expression serious.

"Good luck," he tells me.

I nod, offering him a smile that I hope looks less terrified than I feel.

I hope like hell that we'll have that luck. Because we definitely need it.

33

WILLOW

WE ACT on the new lead immediately, getting back in the car and heading out to the east side of Detroit where Gage told us to go.

When we reach the tattoo parlor, Malice pulls the car up to the curb as his brothers scan the street for any obvious threats.

Although it's after hours, a group of people are clustered around outside the tattoo shop. One of them stands at least a head taller than the others, and Ransom nods in his direction.

"That must be Jonah."

We get out and walk over, the three men once again keeping me between them, not taking any chances. The conversation the group was having dies as we near them, and they eye us warily.

"Can we help you?" one of them asks. "Do you have an appointment?"

She jerks her head in the direction of the tattoo parlor.

Malice ignores her and looks at the man we think is the Enigma leader.

"Jonah Kent?" he asks.

The tall man sizes us up for a second, looking extra hard at Malice. I can't blame him for that. Malice can't help but look intimidating on a good day, and after the week we've had, that aura of violence that surrounds him is stronger than ever.

"Yeah," the man finally says. He's got a gravelly voice, as if he's been smoking his whole life. "Why d'you wanna know?"

He takes a drag from his cigarette and then blows the smoke in our direction carelessly. I can feel the guys shifting around me, not appreciating the disrespect.

Everyone is on edge, and the tension in the air climbs up another few notches. Jonah is on his guard, and the people with him are too. I have no doubt that they're all armed, and if we make a wrong move, this could turn bad.

"What do you want?" Jonah asks, cocking his head to the side and narrowing his eyes.

There's a beat, and then Malice gives a little. "We have a proposition for you."

"Nah." Jonah chuckles, arching an eyebrow. "Not looking for work. You'd have to have a hell of a good ask to get me to move from this spot."

"It involves Olivia Stanton."

As if those are the magic words, Jonah's whole demeanor changes. He goes from slouching against the front of the building to standing up straight, eyes serious. He takes one final drag off his cigarette and then stamps it out on the sidewalk.

"Come with me," he says.

He leads us into the tattoo parlor and then straight through to the back.

The back room here isn't as nice as the one at Sin and Salvation, but the vibes are different too. There's a lumpy couch with cracked leather shoved into a corner, and a scratched and scarred wooden desk against a wall.

None of us go for any of the furniture.

As soon as the door is closed, Jonah turns to stare at us. "What the hell do you want?" he asks again. "And what does it have to do with Olivia Stanton?"

"We're trying to take her out," Malice explains.

"Why?" Jonah demands. "You don't just go after a bitch like her for shits and giggles. What's your angle?"

Malice gives him the quick version of the story. "She's after one of ours. She's already sent people after us twice, and she's not gonna stop until she gets what she wants."

"And what is it she wants?" Jonah asks.

"Me, dead," I tell him. "She knows she won't get what she wants from me if I'm still alive, so." I shrug.

Jonah listens intently, and I can see anger burning in his eyes. It's definitely anger directed at Olivia, but I have no idea what the story is there. It doesn't seem like a good idea to ask.

"We heard you have beef with Olivia," Malice continues. "And we could use your help bringing her down."

Jonah rubs at his face, looking tempted. It looks like he's about to say something, but before he can, the door to the office opens and a girl who looks about my age comes walking in.

"Oh there you are," she says, cutting into the conversation. "I was—"

She stops short when she sees us all standing there, glancing around.

We might be about the same age, but that's where the similarities probably end. This girl is badass looking, with tattoos up and down both arms and teal colored hair. She moves like she owns the place, and there's something protective in her gaze as she takes the four of us in.

"What's going on?" she asks.

"Quinn, I told you to knock when I have people back here," Jonah says.

The girl—Quinn—shrugs. "Didn't know you had people back here. But you could cut this tension with a knife. What's up?"

"It's nothing," he says, giving her a look.

It's pretty clear from their similar facial features and the way they hold themselves that these two are related, probably father and daughter if I had to guess.

She gives him a look right back, folding her arms and not budging.

Jonah sighs. "They're here looking for help taking down Olivia Stanton," he grumbles.

Quinn's eyes go wide at that. "The one who... ?"

Jonah just nods.

With that kind of reaction, I can't help myself anymore. "I'm sorry if this is a weird question, but... what happened?" I ask. "What did Olivia do?"

They both glance at me, and Jonah's expression goes hard. At first, I think he's going to refuse to answer, but then he starts speaking, his tone bitter. "Olivia tried to blackmail me," he says. "Using my brother Casey as leverage. She had dirt on him, and she held it over his head. I didn't want to do her bullshit, but I tried anyway. When I couldn't make it happen, she had my brother put in prison, and he died there."

The anger is clear in his voice, and this is definitely a personal grudge. One that's not far off from the grudge we have against her.

I suck in a breath because yeah, I can relate very much to the anger of having Olivia hold people you care about over your head.

"She did something like that to us too," I tell him. "So we get it. And if we don't stop her, she'll probably kill me and then do it to other people so she can keep getting what she wants. Nothing's going to stop her because she doesn't care about people's lives. All she cares about is getting what she wants."

Jonah nods, his hand curling into fists at his side. "She's a bitch. She plays with people, treats them like chess pieces to be used, and then when she's done, she just throws them away. Or leaves them somewhere to rot."

"Help us stop her," Vic says. "We can end this, but we need help."

"Alright," Jonah agrees finally. "Okay. I want nothing more than to see that cunt die for what she did to my family, so I'll help you."

"Thank you," I breathe, relief surging through me.

"One thing, though. I'm not gonna bring my gang into this. They can provide support or work as a diversion, but I won't volunteer them for the actual fight. It's a personal thing for me, and I'm not putting them in danger for it."

Quinn puts her hands on her hips, cutting in before we can say anything. "Except me. Of course you'll let me help, even if you won't ask anyone else to."

Jonah turns to her, face already set in disapproving lines. "Quinn, no. You can't be involved in this either."

"Fucking hell, Dad. You need to start trusting me. I've trained. You've seen me in action. You *know* I can handle myself. I get that you want to protect me, but you have to cut the cord a little. Seriously. I've been asking for months for you to give me more responsibilities—"

"Going up against a woman with no morals and no problems killing anyone in her way isn't the way to prove yourself, Quinn."

She rolls her eyes. "No, according to you, the way to prove myself is to sit around doing nothing. I don't need you to protect me all the time. I can handle myself."

"I'm going to want to protect you forever," Jonah shoots back. "Sorry. Just the way it is."

The two of them face off, and it seems like this is an old argument. Jonah wants his daughter to be safe, and she just wants a chance to prove herself and to get to show that she can be a badass too.

"Dad—"

"You're supposed to be working anyway," he cuts in. "You're needed out in the shop, so get to it."

There's a finality to his tone, and Quinn groans, rolling her eyes again. "Fine. But we're not done talking about this," she says and heads back out.

Once she's gone, Malice leans forward, ready to get back to business.

"We can't fuck around when it comes to Olivia," he says. "We've gone up against her a few times before, and she always manages to come out on top. That can't happen this time."

"What do you know about her?" Jonah asks. "How well protected is she?"

Vic takes over then. "We have some information. Willow's been inside her home and has seen her resources. We know she has security, even though we don't know how many people she has on hand. We know that she's trusting her station to make her untouchable. That's why we can't just kill her in broad daylight or something. This has to be low profile."

"We have proved that there are ways around that, though," Ransom points out. "Her being well connected and influential doesn't make her immortal."

"No, but it means we have to be more careful than we would otherwise."

Jonah paces a little, clearly deep in thought. "My men and I have done a few jobs like that. Tight security with a need to lie low and make sure we don't get fucked over. We managed to isolate the mark and take them out that way."

"That would be ideal," Vic says. "Her main strength is her resources. At the end of the day, she couldn't take us in a one on one fight, but she'd never let it get that close if she had the choice. Do you think we could do that here?"

"I have a few ideas. But first we'll need to learn her schedule, her habits. It has to be air tight if we're gonna manage to pull this off."

Vic starts taking notes, and hope blooms in my chest as we hash out a plan. Olivia has treated everyone she meets like a pawn, and it's finally coming around to bite her in the ass. It's what she deserves after everything she's done.

She's hurt more people than just me.

And now the fact that she's so heartless is going to be the thing that brings her down.

34

RANSOM

I⊤'s late at night by the time we leave the tattoo parlor after our meeting with Jonah. The three of us gather around Willow to escort her back to the car, feeling the eyes of Jonah's people on us as we go.

Any of us are willing to take a bullet for her if we have to, but hopefully it won't come to that.

We get back to the car without incident and start making our way back to the safe house, talking about the plan and the meeting we just had.

"Can we really trust him?" Vic asks. "We made a lot of progress tonight, but it could be a trap."

I shake my head. "I don't think it was. Unless Jonah's the best actor in the world, he definitely hates Olivia and would probably rather die than help her in any way."

"I agree," Willow says. "He could double cross us in the end, but I really don't think he will."

"She could try to pay him off," Malice points out. "That seems like her kind of shit."

"I can't say Jonah has integrity because I don't know him, but he never played Olivia's games. Plus, the kind of anger and grief that comes from losing someone you love is a more powerful motivator than any amount of money. Working with Olivia would just put him and his daughter in danger if Olivia decided to betray him to clean up loose ends."

Vic nods. "You're probably right. Then we'll trust him until he gives us a reason not to."

"And hopefully he won't," I add. "It'd be nice to actually have something work out for once."

We get back to the safe house, and Malice and I do a sweep to make sure nothing was compromised while we were gone. Once we know it's clear, we all head inside, ready to decompress.

Willow drops down onto the dusty couch with a sigh, and it's clear she's exhausted. It feels like the attack this afternoon happened a long time ago now, but the stress of the day is probably still weighing on her.

I go over and lean over the back of the couch, running my fingers through her hair. "How're you holding up?"

She opens her mouth to answer and ends up yawning instead, covering her mouth and blushing a little. "Sorry. I've been getting tired a lot easier these days."

"No one can blame you for that. Shit's been crazy."

"Yeah. But I think it's also because of the baby."

She puts a hand on her stomach, and it hits me all over again that she's pregnant. It's easy to forget sometimes, since she's not showing yet, and she hasn't let it slow her down, but her sitting there with her hand on her belly definitely is a stark reminder.

And I can't lie, the idea of her swollen and round with a baby turns me the fuck on.

But on the flip side of that, knowing that Troy is the father still makes me furious. At least he's no longer alive to fuck things up or use his kid as leverage. That's the best case scenario right now.

As I gaze down at Willow, I make a silent vow to love the hell out of this baby as an extra 'fuck you' to Troy. We'll make sure his kid turns out nothing like him, treating him or her better than Troy ever would have. Considering that people from his world seem to exclusively think of their kids as bargaining chips and chess pieces to move around, it shouldn't be hard to do.

"Alright, come on," I say to Willow.

She looks at me, confused. "Where are we going?"

Instead of answering, I scoop her up from the couch, sweeping her into my arms so I can carry her to the bedroom.

"Oh my god." She squeals, half laughing as she bats at my shoulders. "I'm too heavy for this. And I can walk just fine."

"No, you're not. And I know you can," I tell her. "But I want to carry you. Let me have this."

Willow blushes a little, but she doesn't argue, instead leaning against me as we head for the bedroom. It's not as nice as the one we left behind in the penthouse, and the bed definitely isn't as big, but that's not going to stop us all from cramming into it so that we can sleep close to our girl.

I set Willow down, watching as she takes off her shoes and changes into her pajamas. After popping into the small, dingy bathroom, she gets into bed. I tuck her in, leaning down to kiss her forehead as I do.

"Are you guys going to join me soon?" she asks, looking up at me with hopeful eyes.

"Yeah, we will. We've just got to start getting shit rolling on this plan to take down Olivia. The sooner we find an opening to make our move, the better."

Willow starts to push herself up onto her elbows, trying to get up. "Then I should be out there planning with you," she protests. "I want to help."

"You've done your part for the day. Now you need to rest."

"I didn't even do anything."

"Sure you did. You got Gage to listen to you and give us the information we needed, and you talking to Jonah definitely helped tip the scale on him helping us. We probably wouldn't have been able to get them on board without you."

Her mouth twists in a little frown that makes me want to kiss it off her face. "I guess so. It just feels wrong for me to be in bed while you're doing all the work."

"I think I can speak for all of us when I say we'd rather you be resting than worrying about this. It's fine, angel."

She makes a face but finally lies back down, snuggling up in the bed. With a smile, I turn to leave, but Willow catches my hand before I can.

"What's up?" I ask.

"I... you know how Malice said before that I wouldn't have to be the one to kill Olivia? That you guys would do it so I won't have to?"

"Yeah, I remember. What about it?"

"Is it bad that I kind of *want* to be the one to do it?" she whispers.

I chuckle, shaking my head. "I'm definitely not the right person to ask that question, seeing as I helped my brothers kill our own father. But I don't think it's bad. It's you being human and finding your strength. Olivia has put you through hell over and over again, and it's not wrong to want to end that yourself. You've kept your heart open for so long, and I'm proud of you for that, but it's okay to close it sometimes. To close off people who will only reach inside and make it bleed."

Willow nods, smothering another yawn. "Thank you, Ransom."

"Anytime, pretty girl." I lean in and kiss her again before leaving her to rest so I can go plan with my brothers.

OVER THE NEXT SEVERAL DAYS, we kick shit into high gear.

We talk to Jonah a few times and basically spend every waking moment planning how to take down Olivia. We're looking for the perfect opening, which has meant that we had to learn more about her schedule and her routine.

And that shit has not been easy. Vic has managed to use his

hacking skills to find out a little, watching her through cameras and finding her name on guests lists at various upcoming events, but it's not enough. Olivia still has a good amount of resources, and she basically always has some kind of security with her. That's making it difficult.

But Vic never gives up when it comes to stuff like this. Especially where Willow is involved.

He's got a few ins, and he's been chipping away at it piece by piece. Working to find out what she's got coming up and also working on figuring out the details of her security. How many people she has, who goes with her where, the kind of car she drives, and on and on.

Willow's still been battling morning sickness, and every time she throws up in the morning, I can tell it brings up a lot of conflicting, weird emotions as she grapples with her pregnancy all over again. But at least one of us is always there to hold her hair back, to rub her shoulders, and to listen as she processes it all, and I think that's helping.

It's probably also helping in a way that we've got so much other shit on our plate right now. She can deal with her feelings in small increments in between planning sessions, rather than having to sort through all of them right away.

One evening, the four of us are gathered in the small living room of the safe house, working on things. Vic is buried in his laptop, fingers flying across the keyboard as he looks things up and sifts through information.

Malice is on another laptop, taking info he's being given by Vic, cross referencing shit and just serving as an extra pair of eyes on some of it.

I'm piecing together a schedule with Willow on an honest to god calendar, trying to put together a visual of Olivia's movements so we can figure out the best time to catch her off-guard.

We're all focused and intent on what we're doing. It's been like that ever since we met with Jonah that first time. There's been a cloud of urgency hanging over us for the past several days, and I can tell it's been wearing on us all. Willow looks tired and drawn, and Malice and Vic are at their most intense and serious, both of them twin pillars of stony-faced intention.

And I know this is important, and that time is of the essence because if we miss a window or give Olivia enough time to make another attempt on Willow's life, it might be the last chance we get... but at the same time, it feels like we could all use a little break. Or at least a moment of lightness in the midst of all this shit.

The silence in the room is starting to feel oppressive, so I do something to break it, reaching over and poking Willow lightly in the side.

She glances over at me, and I smooth my face into neutral lines, looking down at the calendar we're working on. Once she looks away, going back to her work, I poke her again, this time tickling her a little in her side.

She squirms and giggles, batting my hand away, but I tickle her more intently, running my fingers over her ribs.

"What are you doing?" she asks.

"Lightening the mood a little," I tell her with a grin.

She laughs, both from the comment and the tickling, but she doesn't tell me to stop. So I keep going until she's breathless and squirming away from me.

Willow ends up leaning back on her elbows on the floor, and I can see the lines of her body and the flushed color of her face. She's so fucking beautiful like this. She always is, but right now with that smile on her face and her shirt riding up, the shorts she's wearing showing off her legs... it's like she's a perfect vision.

I can't help myself. I lean over her, dipping my head to press a kiss to the soft, warm skin of her inner thigh.

Her brown eyes flare dark with heat, and she swallows hard, her legs spreading just a little wider for me.

"Fuck," I groan. "I love doing this to you."

"Tickling me?" she asks, arching an eyebrow.

"No. Getting you all turned on like this. The way you smell

when you're all worked up is my favorite fucking thing. I knew I'd get addicted the first time I tasted you."

"Oh," she breathes. She licks her lips, and the urge to chase her tongue back into her mouth is strong, but I hold back, watching her instead.

"I didn't know I would like it so much," she continues. "Having your mouth on me. I think I'm addicted to how it feels. You're really good at eating me out."

"Would you say I'm the best at it?" I ask, cocking a brow at her.

A throat clears nearby.

"Excuse the fuck outta me," Malice butts in, his attention on us now. When I look up, he and Vic both are staring in our direction, their work seemingly forgotten for the moment. "You know there's only one acceptable answer to that, right, Solnyshka?"

"And that answer is 'no,'" Vic adds, nodding firmly.

I smirk. Even though I'm the youngest, Vic has less experience with sex than me or Malice. But I love that he's gotten confident enough with Willow to be highly incensed by the suggestion that I might be better at eating her out than he is.

"Are you saying we need to be working harder?" Vic presses when Willow doesn't answer right away.

"No!" She quickly shakes her head, speaking in a rush. "No, I love being eaten out by all of you. It always feels so good. Don't worry."

Malice looks mildly appeased and definitely turned on by the course of this conversation.

"That's better," he mutters, only grumbling a little bit.

"But it's different with all three of you," Willow adds. "I think that's what I like the best. You all bring something different to it, and it's all good."

"Different how?" Vic asks, his analytical mind clearly intrigued by that.

Willow frowns as if she's thinking. "I'm not sure. It's just... different. In a good way, I mean. I just think I could tell each of you apart by your different styles, even if I couldn't see you."

338

"Even if you were blindfolded?" I ask, a challenge sparking in my mind.

"Sure." She lifts one delicate shoulder in a shrug.

"Well, that's good enough for me." I scoop Willow up from the floor and get to my feet.

She yelps in surprise, holding on to me. "What are you doing?"

I tighten my hold on her, looking down at her as if the answer should be obvious.

"Come on now, pretty girl. You can't just throw down a challenge like that without being prepared to prove it. So my brothers and I are going to have an eating contest."

35

WILLOW

My heart skips a beat as I realize what Ransom has in mind here.

My arousal spikes, my pussy clenching with anticipation. Ransom sets me on the bed and then rummages through one of the bags on the floor, coming up with a tie that one of them stuffed into their duffel before we left the condo the other day.

He comes over and drags it along my skin, letting me feel the silky material, then he holds it up.

"Ready?" he asks, heat shining in his blue-green eyes.

I nod. "Bring it on."

His answering grin is the last thing I see before he ties the makeshift blindfold around my head, blocking out my sight and plunging me into darkness.

Having my sight restricted definitely amplifies everything else. For a second, I feel disoriented, even though I know I'm still sitting on the bed, but then I hear movement. Hands descend on me, and each touch feels electric.

They skate over my hair and down my neck and arms. Another pair works its way up my legs and thighs. More fingers caress my face and then move down to grope at my chest.

I moan, my lips parted as I try to arch into each touch, seeking out more.

"Love how greedy you are for us," Malice mutters appreciatively.

The three of them start to remove my clothes, stripping me down to nothing. My shirt gets pulled over my head and my shorts and panties are discarded somewhere. The cool air in the room rushes over my skin, and even that feels more intense than it ordinarily would.

I can feel them watching me too, their gazes settling on my naked body like physical touches. Something about knowing they can see me while I can't see them makes me squirm, my pussy getting even wetter.

They're probably all still dressed too, and that image in my mind's eye is hot as hell.

"Okay." Ransom's smooth, deep voice makes me jump a little. "Here's how we'll do this. We'll each take a turn going down on you, and you have to guess who it is as we switch out. If you guess wrong, we get to do whatever we want to you."

There's so much promise in his tone, and I know that whether I guess them all right or not, there's no real way I can lose here. My blood heats with desire and approval, and I have to clear my throat before I can speak.

"Okay."

I curl my fingers into the soft material of the blanket I'm lying on, waiting with anticipation. I can't hear them talking, but I can imagine that they're working out the order they want to do this in, communicating without speaking out loud.

Then I hear some soft rustling noises, and a second later, strong hands close around my thighs. I gasp softly as those hands spread me open wider, and a warm, firm body settles between them.

The first touch of a wet tongue to my pussy makes me jump, and then I moan as that tongue starts to lick and lap at me, not even giving me a moment to adjust.

That's what tips me off that this is Malice. His licks are

demanding, each stroke of his tongue exuding power. His fingers dig into my thighs, and I grind against his face, heat coursing through me.

"Malice," I moan, pressing into him, trying to get more.

There's no answer in response, but he does draw away, leaving me wet and needy.

After another few seconds, another mouth is on me.

It takes even less time for me to realize that it's Ransom, and that's partly because of the piercing in his tongue, although he tries to hide it. But the way he licks me gives it away too. He laps at me like he wants to savor it, swirling his tongue around my clit and giving little teasing flicks over the sensitive nub.

"Ransom," I guess, my toes curling.

There's a muffled curse, and then his tongue spears its way into my pussy, fucking me shallowly before retreating.

The next mouth is even more obvious. I'm positive it's Vic. His way is a little more shy than his brothers'. He's newer at it, but there's a hunger behind it all the same. It's so perfectly him, the way he dives in and then tries to figure out the best way to please me, his tongue dipping and lapping and working me up even more.

"Vic," I gasp.

Pride rushes through me as he makes a noise of confirmation.

"That's it, then." I lift my head as I grin in the men's general direction, still unable to see them. "I won."

Ransom chuckles. "Ah, but I never said we only got one turn with you, angel. We're not done yet."

Huh. I guess that's true.

So the game keeps going.

Another mouth comes back to my pussy, a tongue working its way deep inside me. It fucks me, alternating between deep thrusts and licking my clit, keeping me on the edge. Before I can get too into how that feels, they switch out again, and this time, teeth graze my clit, giving me that edge of pain that enhances everything else so much. Then they switch again.

As it keeps going, I get more and more worked up. The

changing styles keep me on edge, none of them letting me get used to it enough to chase the pleasure that's building under my skin.

The more turned on I get, the harder it is to keep track of who's who. The little things that distinguish them from each other start to blend together, but I keep guessing names.

"Ransom."

"Vic."

"Malice."

"Malice again."

It comes out breathier and breathier, and I tremble and shake on the bed, my thighs quivering with the sensations.

"Ransom," I guess, and then I hear the man in question laugh.

"Wrong guess, pretty girl."

Someone pinches my nipples hard enough to make me gasp and gush, and I cry out. Then another mouth is on me, lapping up the surge of arousal that trickles down my inner thighs before latching on to my clit.

"She's getting close," Vic observes, his voice somehow clinical and heated at the same time. "Keep doing that, and she'll come for you."

This time, it *is* Ransom between my legs. I can feel his tongue piercing as he sucks hard on my clit, making my back bow.

"Fuck!"

I clutch at his hair, tugging on the strands as I fly apart just like Vic said I would.

Even as I tremble in the aftermath of the orgasm, the men don't stop. My body feels sensitive and overstimulated—and that, combined with the blindfold, cranks everything up another notch. It's almost too much when that tongue presses into me, and I whimper, not sure whether I want to grind closer or squirm away.

"Malice," I guess, and someone makes a buzzer sound.

Wrong again.

A hand comes down, slapping my pussy lightly once the mouth moves away, and I cry out as pleasure and pain merge inside me.

It keeps going like that, getting more and more intense. The three of them wring two more orgasms out of me, and I guess wrong a few more times. They keep working me up, pinching my nipples, pulling my hair, biting down on my inner thighs, and by the time I'm coming apart for a fourth time, I don't even care who's who.

I cry out all of their names like a litany, because all that matters is that they're there.

"Well, I think we *all* won here," Ransom says hoarsely as I finally start to float down from the high.

"Agreed." Malice's voice comes from closer to my head as my blindfold is tugged off.

I blink past the sudden rush of light, breathing hard. All three of the men are surrounding me on the mattress, and it's clear they all enjoyed taking turns between my legs. Malice grips a handful of my hair, tilting my face up so I have to look him in the eye.

"Do you want more?"

I pant and nod, trying to find my breath. "Yes. Please. Please, I want you to fuck me. To use me. Take what you want from me."

Vic curses, a muted sound behind Malice, and I can see Ransom palming his cock through his jeans.

"Do you know what I want?" Malice asks, drawing my attention back to him.

I shake my head, my heart thudding.

"I want you to take all of our cocks at once," he tells me in a rough voice. "I want you stuffed full of me and my brothers."

Adrenaline spikes through me, and I'm nodding before he even finishes speaking. "Fuck... yes!"

"Good girl."

Victor helps me get into position on the bed, and my limbs are so loose and wobbly that I definitely need the assistance. They shuck off their clothes, and the sight of all three of their cocks, hard and throbbing and ready for me, goes right to my head—and to my pussy.

Ransom ends up being underneath me, his hands finding their way to my hips to hold on to me. I'm so wet and relaxed from coming so many times that he slides in with ease, and the feeling of his piercings rubbing against my insides stokes the heat inside me.

He starts to move his hips, and I move mine too, meeting him in the middle as I ride him slowly.

I look down into his eyes, so close to the color of the ocean on a clear day, and he gazes back up at me with a crooked smile on his face.

"Fucking gorgeous," he murmurs, reaching up to brush hair back behind my ear. "You ready for Vic?"

"Always," I breathe, and he grins in approval.

Victor climbs up onto the bed behind me. I feel his careful, precise hands as he runs them down my back and then grips my ass, and my breath catches at the thought that he'll be the one to fuck me there this time.

Malice is right there at the side of the bed, talking him through it since he's done this before.

"Use more lube than you think you need," he instructs in his gruff tone. "There's not really such a thing as too much."

I feel the cool, slick press of his finger as Vic starts to work me open, and I relax even more, letting him in.

Malice talks him through adding another finger and stretching me, telling him to go slow and when to add a third finger.

"Breathe," he says to me. "Relax and let him in."

It's easy to follow those instructions like this, and I moan at the sensation of having fingers in my ass and Ransom's cock in my pussy. Ransom thrusts shallowly, letting Vic have this moment.

Eventually, Malice declares it good enough, and I'm trembling with need by now.

Vic slicks his cock up and starts to work it inside me, and my mouth falls open. This man does *not* have a small cock, and feeling him breaching my ass really drives that reality home.

He presses in a couple of inches and then stops, his breath catching. It seems like it might almost be too much for him, and I can feel his body trembling as he works to hold himself back.

I crane my neck so I can look up at him, holding his gaze.

345

"Breathe," I remind him, my own voice shaky. "You can do this."

He stares down at me, and I can see emotion and desire swirling in his eyes. He drags in a deep breath, and his fingers start tapping out a rhythm on my back. I watch as his lips move in a silent count, mastering himself as he tries to calm down so he can keep going.

Feeling the way he grounds himself, being a part of it in this intimate way, makes me feel closer to him than ever. It makes warmth swell within me, and I keep watching until he's calmed down and can keep going.

Then I have to remind *myself* to breathe, sucking in desperate breaths of air as he keeps sliding into me.

Somehow, my body stretches to fit. Inch by inch, Vic fills me up, and combined with the feeling of Ransom already in me, it's so overwhelming. I swallow hard, trembling already just from the sensation of being so full, and then Malice comes over to me.

"The first time you sucked my cock, I should've known it would end up like this. You were inexperienced but so fucking hungry. So eager. Ready for more, even when you weren't sure you could take it. A part of me realized right then and there that you're the only woman for me and my brothers."

"I'd fucking better be," I say, and he smiles at the possessive edge in my voice.

"You know the safe word," he murmurs.

I nod, the movement jerky. "Yeah. I remember."

"Good. Actually..." He seems to consider something. "Since your mouth is about to be busy, if you wanna stop, just tap my thigh three times. Can you do that?"

"Yes."

"Such a good fucking girl." His fingers thread through my hair, and I nuzzle into the touch, then moan when he grabs a handful of my hair and holds me still. "You said you like it when I don't hold back. Is that what you want?"

I nod again. "Give me everything."

346

I know what it means to say that to Malice of all people, so I understand what I'm getting myself into, but I crave it all the same. I want to feel the full force of him. I don't want him to hold anything back as he takes me, completing this loop of me with all three of the men I love.

Malice looks down at me, looking like some kind of ancient warrior god, a creature so beautiful and dark it can't possibly be real. He runs his thumb across my lips, then presses it into my mouth.

"Open," he demands.

I do it without hesitation, and he grabs my chin, bringing his cock to my mouth.

I moan at the taste of his skin as his shaft slides past my lips, and just like that, all three of them are inside me. I can feel each of them, and it's just like when they were taking turns eating me out. Each of them have their own distinct feel, and I could pick them out easily, just by the way they feel inside me.

"Fucking hell. You take us so well, pretty girl."

Ransom starts to move, his hips bucking up as he thrusts as much as he can. A second later, Vic finds his own rhythm, starting to move as well.

I gasp around Malice's cock, and he keeps his hand tight around my hair as he starts to fuck my face, living up to his promise to not take it easy on me.

"There you go, Solnyshka. Open your throat for me. I want to feel you gagging on my cock."

His cock works into my mouth with the same amount of force his brothers use as they drive into my pussy and ass, and I do gag a little, tears gathering at the corners of my eyes. Drool drips down my chin, and my mouth fills with saliva, making it even easier for Malice to use it.

It's so much to handle, the intensity of it making me feel like my body is on fire. Each push and pull sends sparks of pleasure shooting through my gut, and I drag my nails down Ransom's chest, making him hiss.

Malice jerks my hair sharply as he pushes his cock in even farther, hitting the back of my throat. That makes me choke and splutter, and he pulls back just enough for me to snatch a breath of air before driving in again.

"Fuck," Ransom groans, his fingers digging into my hips. "I'm not gonna last long."

"You're so fucking *tight*," Vic mutters, and I can tell from the way his voice is shaking that he's not going to hold out much longer either.

Malice is holding my head with both hands now, controlling me completely as he thrusts all the way down my throat, and I choke a bit, trying to swallow around him. Sweat dampens my skin, every one of my limbs shaking from the effort and exertion.

"Eyes on me, Solnyshka," he growls, and when I peer up at him through my lashes, he smiles approvingly. "There you are. Look at you taking us. All of us. Like you can't get enough. You're a whore just for the three of us, aren't you? Our perfect little slut."

I moan around his cock, and even if I wanted to move between the brothers, I don't think I could. I'm pinned and impaled from all sides, and if they weren't all holding me up, I probably would've collapsed by now.

Another orgasm is swelling inside me. I can already feel the edges of it, that pleasurable heat threatening to spark out of control.

"You want it, don't you?" Malice pants. "You want us to fill you up. You want Ransom and Vic to fill your pretty little holes with their cum and for me to bust all over your face."

All I can do is whimper, doing my best to nod despite the iron grip he has on my head.

"Yeah, I knew it. Our little cum slut. Our Willow. So filthy..." Thrust. "And perfect..." Thrust. "And *ours*."

Each word hits me hard, and as if they can feel my response in the way I clench around them, Ransom and Vic start to fuck into me harder and faster.

When my orgasm crests, it rushes through me in a burst of hot sensation. My breath catches, and I cry out around my mouthful of

348

Malice's dick, shaking and writhing as I come apart. My nails bite into Ransom's chest, my entire body locking up as wave after wave of pleasure hit me one after the other.

It's the hardest I've ever come in my life, and I forget to breathe at one point, gasping for air around Malice as I come back to myself.

As if he's been waiting for me, that's enough to spark Vic to finally let go. He curses loudly behind me, biting down on my shoulder as he comes, filling my ass with pulses of his hot cum.

"Shit," Ransom gasps, right on Vic's heels as he spills inside my pussy. "Oh fuck, goddammit. *Fuck.*"

That just leaves Malice, still fucking my face, holding me up by the hair as he shoves his cock down my throat again and again.

"*Mne nravitsja, kak ty pozvoljaesh' mne ispol'zovat' tebja,*" he grits out.

Then he comes, spurting in hot jets down my throat before he pulls back and lets the rest go all over my face.

I hold my tongue out, mouth open, feeling the droplets spatter my skin. Malice's hand grips my jaw again, and he drags his tongue over my cheeks and nose, gathering the remnants of his release. Then he kisses me, feeding it to me through our kiss, pressing it into my mouth as I lick against his tongue.

Ransom and Vic ease their way out of me as Malice and I finally break apart. Without them to hold me up, I collapse on the bed, spent and worn out. They all lie down around me, pulling me into their arms, each one of them trying to touch me in some way.

I float in a haze of contentment, blinking blearily as my pulse starts to slow. After a few minutes, Malice goes up on one elbow, leaning over me.

"You okay?" he asks.

"Well, I think I forgot my own name," I joke. "But other than that, I'm peachy." My brows pinch together, and I look up at him as I add, "Why do I like it so much when you call me a slut?"

Malice's eyes blaze, and he drops his head to kiss me one more time.

349

"Because you're more than that to us, and you know it," he murmurs against my lips, pride and possessiveness in his voice. "When we fuck you like this, sharing you and using you, you're our beautiful little slut. But out there in the world, you're our fucking queen. Our partner. Our *everything*."

MALICE

A DAY LATER, we're all sitting in the living room again. It's just like old times, gathering together to work on our plans and make sure we have everything ready. We've been operating on the idea that we might have to leap into action at a moment's notice, so we wanna be ready.

Vic is doing his usual thing, and Ransom and I are taking care of the weapons and gear. Thanks to Willow's newfound wealth, we have better shit than we ever used to be able to afford, which is good. None of us are stupid enough to think we're gonna end this without it coming to a fight.

It's pretty quiet, all of us absorbed in our tasks, so when Vic looks up suddenly, sucking in a breath, it catches my attention immediately.

"What's up?" I ask, glancing over.

"We've got an opening coming up. A chance to go after Olivia."

That gets everyone's attention, all of us looking at Vic. He turns his computer screen to face us, highlighting the relevant information.

"I've been watching her and also keeping an eye out for her name popping up on any guest lists for important events in the city. High priced charity dinners, galas, that kind of thing."

Ransom rolls his eyes. "Fucking typical."

"Yeah, but in this case, it helps us," Vic says. "She's going to be attending an event outside of Detroit in a few days, and she'll be driving there."

"How far outside the city?" I want to know, already snapping into tactical mode.

"An hour or two, depending on traffic."

"What's the event?" Willow wants to know.

"A viewing of a private art collection. Some reclusive billionaire is opening up his collection for a single evening only."

"Oh, for fuck's sake," Ransom grumbles. "That's the most bougie goddamned thing I've ever heard. Who even cares about shit like that? Go to a fucking museum."

Vic shrugs. "Rich people care. And like I keep saying, it works to our advantage here."

"I don't know..." Willow chews on her lip. "Even if it's a private showing, that still seems too public. Too many possible witnesses."

I watch Vic's face, and I can already tell what he's planning, so I shake my head.

"We won't go after her at the event," I tell Willow. "That *would* be too public. Instead, we'll hit her while she's on the way there. Vic, what's the security rundown?"

"She's on the alert," he answers, turning his computer back toward himself and typing a bit. "She's upped her security. Usually, she has at least two bodyguards with her at all times, plus extra security in an additional vehicle that follows her main car."

"So we separate them with Jonah's help. She'll have a driver for sure, who may or may not be trained as a bodyguard also, as well as the usual two guards. But we can handle that. We'll take out the driver and force the car off the road. Then we'll handle Olivia."

Vic nods, his eyes riveted to the screen. "Yes. Luckily, this man with the art collection is reclusive. His estate is basically in the middle of nowhere—almost as far off the grid as Troy's hideout was. It won't be hard to make this happen off the beaten path to cut down on the possibility of witnesses."

Willow takes all of that in, idly shredding a little scrap of paper as she listens. She still looks nervous about all of it, but when she nods, there's determination in her eyes.

Ransom nods too, slapping a hand on the coffee table. "It's as good a chance as any. And we need to move soon. We don't have time to wait for a better opening. Either Olivia will get more members of Ethan's old crew to come after us, or she'll find someone else she can pay to do it."

"Or blackmail," Willow mutters darkly. "That seems to be her MO."

"Right." Ransom snorts a breath. "Either way, we can't risk it. We don't want to give her the chance to attack you again."

"We'll take two cars. One to take out the security vehicle, or at least keep it occupied, and one to go for Olivia's car," Vic says, in hardcore planning mode now.

"I want to be in the one that goes after Olivia," Willow declares.

"No," I say immediately.

"What do you mean, no? Why not? I won't be much help taking out the other car."

"I mean you're not going at all. You need to stay someplace where it's safe."

Anger and stubbornness flare in Willow's eyes, and she folds her arms, looking right at me without a trace of fear or hesitation. It's pure defiance, and it's hot as hell, even though it's also frustrating.

"I'm. Going," she says firmly. "And you can't stop me. She's my grandmother. It's *me* she's been trying to kill. I'm going to be there when it all ends."

There's a war raging inside me. Everything in me is screaming that this is a fucking bad idea. She needs to be somewhere safe, someplace her evil bitch of a grandma can't get to her. The protectiveness I feel toward her is strong, but just as strong is the fact that this is the shit I love most about Willow.

How fierce she is. How brave she is. How she doesn't back down, no matter how much bullshit gets thrown her way.

If I'm being honest with myself, I think I fell in love with her the day she pressed her forehead to the barrel of my gun and basically dared me to shoot her.

I know she won't cave on this. It's too big and too important to her.

And I don't actually want to let her out of my sight. In theory, she'd be safer away from the action, but there's no one I trust to keep an eye on her besides me and my brothers, and leaving her alone in the safe house comes with its own set of risks.

"Fuck," I groan, dragging a hand down my face. "Fine. You can come. But you're going to stay in the car that takes out the extra security."

"Why?" she demands.

"Because that's safer. Going after Olivia is more dangerous, and I know you don't believe for a second that she's going to go down without a fight. I don't want you involved in that."

I can tell that she's not happy with that arrangement, but this is something I won't fucking budge on.

I tug her onto my lap, the movement so sudden that it makes her yelp.

"That's how it's gonna be, Solnyshka," I say in a low voice, running my nose along her neck. "You can either do that or you can stay behind."

"Alright," she mumbles. "I'll go in that car."

"Good girl." I press a kiss to the sensitive spot just behind her ear.

Ransom shoves his sleeves up on his forearms, grinning. "Okay, then we've got a plan. I'll get in touch with Jonah and let him know what's going on. Olivia Stanton's days are fucking numbered."

354

ONCE THE TIME is set and Jonah is on board, everything else starts to fall into place. The next few days go by quickly as we get ready, making sure we have everything ironed out.

It feels like we're on a track barreling toward the future, and for the first time in a long time, I'll admit I'm afraid. Afraid in a way I never really have been before.

It's not the thought of dying. I don't fear death. I've brushed up against it plenty of times before, and that fear has lost its edge.

But that's just when it comes to my *own* death.

Thinking about Willow getting hurt? About her possibly dying? That shit fucks me up in a way that nothing else does. I can't let it happen. I can't let her die. I'd gladly give up my own life before I'd let anything happen to her.

Worry twists in my gut, feeling like a sort of omen of something terrible. But I do my best to shove it aside. I don't have time to get trapped in an endless spiral of worries. That kind of shit becomes a self-fulfilling prophecy sometimes, and it's better for me to focus on making sure we're ready for this.

My brothers and I have pulled off jobs before, plenty of times, and now we have Jonah on our side. I don't trust him the same way I do my brothers or Willow, but it's clear he's skilled, and we'll benefit from the added power in numbers.

Soon enough, the day of the event—and the attack—arrives.

I prowl around the safe house like a caged animal, all restless energy with no outlet just yet. On my third or fourth pass by the living room, Willow huffs and comes over to me, grabbing my upper arms to hold me still.

"You're going to wear a hole in the carpet," she says. "It might be an improvement on the decor, but you need to calm down."

I make a face at her, my lips pinched tight, and she makes one right back before leaning up to kiss me lightly.

It's barely enough to help calm my nerves, even when I pull her in close and deepen the kiss, pressing my tongue into her mouth. She makes a soft noise into it and arches against me, and I lick my way inside her mouth, laying claim to it like I want to devour her.

And maybe I do.

Maybe I want to consume her whole, just so that no one can ever take her from me.

Part of me feels like I'm clinging to her to keep her from slipping away.

"*Ya by umer za tebja*," I murmur when our lips break apart.

"What does that mean?"

"I would die for you."

Her eyes fly wide, her breath catching. Then she shakes her head, huffing a quiet laugh.

"What?" I ask.

She blinks, her brown eyes shimmering. "It's just... the one time I ask you what you just said in Russian, and you hit me with that."

I can tell she's a little overwhelmed by my statement, and I don't want to make her worry any more than I'm sure she already is, so I don't repeat it. I just kiss her one last time before passing her over to my brothers.

They pull her into their arms one after the other, and I leave them to it, giving them privacy as they kiss her and murmur quiet words. I fucking love the times when we all surround her, sharing her between us—but some moments are meant to be more intimate than that, shared between two people alone, and this is one of those.

Once it's finally time, the first thing we do is meet up with Jonah, driving across Detroit to the tattoo parlor that serves as his base of operations.

His daughter is there with him when we pull up, glaring at him with her hands on her hips, her teal colored hair drawn back into a tight ponytail.

"I can't believe you're really not going to let me come with you," she says. "A job this big, and you really expect me to just sit here and wait for you to get back?"

356

Jonah closes his eyes and sighs. "That's exactly what I expect you to do, Quinn. We've already been over this. I'm not letting you get wrapped up in this shit. And besides, I need you here. With half of the Enigma crew being sent out to serve as a diversion and keep the road clear, we'll have fewer people protecting our territory. I need you in charge of the men who stay behind."

She scowls at him darkly, looking a whole lot like Willow in her stubborn defiance. She and her father have a silent standoff that goes on for at least a minute, a whole debate being played out without words.

Finally, Quinn gives in, breaking eye contact. "Fine. But you'd better bring your ass back here in one piece, old man. Or you'll hear about it from me."

He snorts under his breath and pulls her into a one armed hug, squeezing her for a second before letting her go. "Get out of here. You have work to do."

She glances at the rest of us and then goes, heading into the tattoo parlor.

Once she's gone, Jonah turns his attention to us, his demeanor hardening. "I'm ready. Let's bring this bitch down."

From there, we split up into two teams. Willow, Ransom, and Jonah go in one car, and Vic and I go in the other. I get behind the wheel, leaving Vic free to coordinate and check things, planning any recalibrations to the plan as needed. If Olivia's car makes a detour or doesn't leave on time, he'll know about it.

Several members of Jonah's crew are spread out around Detroit as well, ready to distract and delay the other wealthy society members who were invited to the art showing tonight. We can't have any of them driving the same route Olivia will be taking and witnessing what goes down. We need her completely isolated and alone.

The car Jonah, Ransom, and Willow are in will tail her backup vehicle at a distance, waiting for their moment to take that car out. Vic and I will speed ahead to get into position on the stretch of road that we've determined will be best for the attack.

We'll lie in wait for her, and once her backup guards are out of the picture, Vic and I will move in on her.

We keep in touch via earpieces, the kind of expensive shit we could never afford before, checking in every so often to make sure things are going according to plan.

This really is the perfect area for something like this. Forty-five minutes or so outside the city, we're on long stretches of two lane roads where there's almost no traffic. No one comes out here without a reason, so there's not much chance of interference.

The drive would be peaceful if it wasn't for the clattering of my nerves in my head and the adrenaline pumping through me. It ratchets up a notch the closer we get to where we need to be, and once we're in place, I'm barely sitting still at all.

Vic glances over at me from his laptop, raising an eyebrow. He doesn't say anything, but I don't really need him to.

I just shake my head, curling my fingers around the steering wheel as I pull over and position us just off the road, partially obscured behind the brush. There's too much to say, and it feels like saying this shit out loud might jinx it and make all my worst fears come to life.

I glance at the clock. We're coming up on the time when Olivia should be getting close.

There's no time to be anything but ruthless and focused now. We have to be ready.

"We're trailing her backup vehicle." Ransom's voice comes through in my ear. "They're getting close now. Almost go time."

"Wait for the right moment," Vic advises. "We're only going to get one shot at this."

"Got it."

The atmosphere grows even more tense as we wait. I can hear some murmured conversation from the other car, Ransom and Jonah discussing something, and Willow adding her input.

Just hearing her voice makes me feel a bit better. I know that no matter what happens, Ransom will do his damnedest to keep her safe.

"Now!" Ransom says suddenly, and I can hear tires screech in the background as the car they're in accelerates.

The sound of gunshots rings through my earpiece, but I can't focus on that anymore. I have to assume Ransom and Jonah are doing what they need to do, because less than a minute later, the car carrying Olivia in it comes zooming up ahead, right toward where we're waiting.

"Let's go," Vic says.

He stows his laptop and grabs his gun, and I roll down the window, moving almost on instinct. Before the sleek black SUV can get too far past us, I shoot out the two back tires, sending it into a tailspin, weaving across the road.

It does a complete three-sixty before it screeches to a halt, and almost as soon as it stops, the doors of the car burst open. Two men in suits emerge from the front of the car, armed and shooting right at us.

Vic opens the door on his side of the car and uses it for cover, popping up at strategic moments to fire back at the guards. I do the same on my side, using the anticipation burning through my veins to keep moving.

I clip one of the guards in the leg, and he goes down, only to be shot through the head by Vic a second later.

The back passenger door of the car opens, and Olivia's third guard pokes an arm out, shooting toward us and giving cover to his partner. That man takes advantage of the cover and rushes toward us, clearly trying to reach us so he can take us out at close range.

He barrels into the car door Vic is hiding behind, shoving my twin backward. Vic grunts, shooting toward him again. He clips the guard, who grunts and launches himself at my brother. More bullets fly from the guard inside the car, and I curse under my breath.

Fuck. I've got to take that one down.

Steadying my hand as Vic grapples with the guard who went after him, I wait for the other guard's arm to emerge around the SUV's door again, and the moment it does, I take my shot. My bullet connects with the man's forearm, making him drop the gun clutched in his grip. He pitches sideways a little, giving me just the barest glimpse of his face, but that's all I need.

I squeeze the trigger again, and blood sprays as I hit the side of his head. I'm not sure it's enough to take him down at first, but then he topples from the car and lies next to the half open door, going still.

Beside me, two muffled gunshots ring out, and I hear the sound of heavy breathing. A second later, Vic stands up. Blood spatter crosses his face, making him look unhinged and dangerous, but I don't bother pointing it out. I'm sure he's aware of it, but he has a more important mission right now than getting cleaned up.

The two of us share a quick nod and then move as one, crossing the road with our weapons drawn and pointed at the car.

"Go around to the other side," Vic tells me. "We'll box her in so she can't run."

I nod, crossing around the car to the other passenger door. At the same exact moment, we both yank our doors open.

I raise my gun, ready to put a fucking bullet in Olivia's skull—

But the back seat of the car is empty.

"What the fuck?" I snarl.

"Check for any possible hiding compartments," Vic directs quickly. "Maybe she got spooked and hid."

My heart is beating in overtime as we search the car, but there's no goddamned sign of her. Slamming my fist against the metal siding of the SUV, I step away from it, my gun gripped tightly in my hand.

"Ransom. Jonah. Abort," I bite out. "Get Willow the fuck out of here. Olivia isn't in this car. I don't know where the fuck she is, but she's not—"

A screech of tires from my right cuts me off. I don't even have time to look up before the sound of more gunshots are echoing through the trees around me. Something punches my chest, two bullets slamming into my vest and knocking all the air out of my lungs.

For a second, I can't breathe at all, my entire chest seizing up from the force of the blow. Then something hits the back of my head, and I go down hard, hitting the asphalt with a heavy thud.

The last thing I see before I black out is Vic hitting the ground beside me.

37

WILLOW

My heart is racing so fast, I'm sure everyone in the car can hear it trying to beat out of my chest.

Malice was saying something about how Olivia wasn't in the car... then there were gunshots, and the sound of some kind of scuffle.

And now nothing. The transmission is totally dead

"Malice?" Ransom shouts, holding a hand to his ear as if that will help. "Malice, what the fuck?"

"Vic!" I call, my voice shaking. "What happened?"

No response from him either.

"Gun it," Ransom tells Jonah grimly. "They need backup. *Now.*"

The man we recruited to help us is behind the wheel, and he nods once and steps on the gas. We managed to run Olivia's second security team off the road, although they gave us a run for our money. The side of the car we're currently in is scraped all to hell, and there are bullet holes in the siding.

We speed past the destroyed black SUV that holds Olivia's backup security team, leaving it to burn by the side of the road as we race toward where Malice and Vic were supposed to intercept her in the main car. It's only about a half mile away from where we took out her backup, so it doesn't take us long to reach the spot.

"Stay on your fucking guard," Ransom mutters to Jonah as an SUV sitting in the middle of the road comes into view up ahead. "It could be a trap."

Jonah grunts in response, slowing our car as both men hold weapons at the ready. I have a gun too, as well as a vest, but I didn't have to shoot anyone during our attack on Olivia's other guards. Still, I curl my fingers around the grip of my weapon, feeling sick from the overload of adrenaline.

There are three bodies on the ground, but it only takes a quick glance to confirm that none of them are Malice or Vic.

"Fucking... *fuck!*"

Ransom bellows the curse, shoving his door open as soon as we roll to a stop. Jonah gets out too, the two of them doing a sweep of the area with their weapons drawn. But even before Ransom shakes his head, some part of me already knows.

There's no one else here.

No Olivia.

No Malice or Vic.

They're gone.

"Fuck," Ransom repeats, staring down at the bodies of the guards. "She had to have known we were coming. That's why she wasn't in the fucking car. It was a trap." He whirls around to face Jonah, gun raised in his hand. "You sold us out."

Jonah's eyes go wide, and he raises his own gun in a heartbeat, the two men standing off.

"I didn't," he insists, his voice hard. "Listen, I want that bitch dead as much as you do. Maybe even more, because I already lost the person she was holding over my fucking head. I wouldn't help her. Not for any price. I'd die first."

"Why the hell should I believe that?" Ransom growls, adding a second hand to steady his gun. His eyes are wild with worry and grief and anger. I've never seen him like this before, but I recognize all the emotions on his face—because I feel them too.

We can't let this be the end. We can't lose Malice and Vic.

"Believe me, or don't." Jonah keeps his gaze locked on Ransom, his weapon steady and his eyes narrowed. "But I'd think twice before pulling that trigger, because I'm a good fucking shot. You shoot, and I shoot back. Best case, we both die. Is that what you want?"

"Maybe I fucking do. If you betrayed us, there's nothing that could keep me from killing you."

Jonah snorts, his top lip pulling back in a snarl. "If Olivia Stanton knew we were coming, it's because one of *you* told her, or she found some way to surveil you and figured out what your plan was. Hell, maybe this whole art show she was supposedly going to was a lie, something meant to draw you out."

Ransom's handsome face contorts with fury at Jonah's words, and he shakes his head, his Adam's apple bobbing as he swallows. "Fuck. *Fuck.*"

"Ransom." I swallow, taking a small step forward, desperate to defuse this situation. I've already lost two of my men, I can't bear to see another shot right in front of me. "I believe him. I don't think he'd sell us out."

Ransom is breathing hard, and I can see indecision in his features as he fights some sort of internal battle. But finally, he lowers the gun just a little. Jonah mirrors the movement, the two of them slowly ending their standoff.

There's a sudden noise in my ear, and I jump, slapping a hand to the earpiece situated there.

"Malice?" I blurt. "Vic! Are you there?"

There's a quiet laugh in response, feminine and almost dainty, and my stomach curls.

Olivia.

"I'm sorry, darling. Your two little fuckboys are indisposed at the moment."

Her voice filters into my ear like poison, and I know Ransom and Jonah must be able to hear her too, because they both stiffen.

"Where are they?" I demand, my throat going tight.

364

She just laughs again, ignoring my question as she continues. "You thought the four of you could take me on by yourselves? Did you really think I'd open myself up to an ambush like that? Your men should have been more creative. Did you all forget that I'm X? The Voronin brothers worked for me for *years*. I've seen their handiwork. They've done enough jobs for me that I know how they operate. So all it took to lure all of you out into the open was the perfect opportunity to attack me. Except, silly me, I forgot to get into my car."

My stomach is in knots, and her taunting tone grates on my frayed nerves as terror skates through me.

"Did you kill them?" I hiss. "Are Malice and Victor dead?"

"No," she replies smoothly. "I'm not a fool. That would be like breaking a very expensive tool before I even got a chance to use it. They're alive. But they won't be for long unless I get what I want."

"Fuck you," I choke out, my hand tightening around the grip of my gun.

"Sorry, that isn't one of the options here, Willow," she says coolly. "There are only two options you have right now." She sighs, clicking her tongue against her teeth. "Since you've clearly decided not to take me up on my offer to spare your life if you signed everything over to me, I've decided to take a different tack. All of Troy's holdings in exchange for your two men. Give me what I want, and they'll live. Or you can keep playing this game and lose everyone you love, one by one."

I stare at Ransom as we both listen to Olivia speak, our gazes locked, the sound of my own pulse loud in my own head. Anger and fear and heartache war inside me. Every time I think it couldn't be possible to hate Olivia more than I already do, she proves me wrong.

"You're a heartless bitch!" I spit at her. "A fucking monster. You—"

Olivia sighs, cutting me off with a sharp voice. "And *you* are wasting time. Make your choice, Willow." She rattles off an address, then adds, "I will be waiting there. Tonight at eight o'clock sharp. If you want your men back alive, you'll come—unarmed—with the paperwork necessary to sign everything you stole from Troy over to me."

She cuts the transmission before I can say anything else, and the earpiece goes dead again.

I stand rooted to the spot, trying to breathe through the panic that's clutching me.

Jonah looks from Ransom to me, the lines of his face deepening as he frowns. "What are you going to do?"

My mind races, and I drag in a breath as I try to think. Numbness and clarity burn away the fear as the course of action lays itself out in front of me. There's only one thing that matters right now.

I can't let Olivia kill Vic and Malice. I just can't.

"I'm going to give her everything she wants," I tell him.

At eight p.m., Ransom and I approach the building Olivia told us to come to, alone and unarmed.

At first, the address didn't make much sense, but when we looked it up, I understood immediately why she had chosen this location.

It's a building that's under construction, and the company in charge of the project is Oberon—the same corporation Olivia has a large stake in. She probably chose this as her ideal meeting place because it's guaranteed to be empty since it's still being built. There will be no one around to witness the handoff, and she can control the environment since her company owns the site.

So far, just the foundation and scaffolding have been put up, and in the dusky gloom, it looks like a twisted skeleton.

I have the paperwork with me, everything I'll need in order to sign everything over to Olivia, and my heart beats a furious rhythm in my chest.

Ransom looks down at me, his blue-green eyes glinting in the light of a few nearby streetlamps. This building is in a part of Detroit that's being redeveloped, so there are several other construction projects nearby. The area is quiet at this time of night, making it feel like a ghost town.

"Are you sure about this?" he asks.

I nod. "Yeah. I'm sure. It's what any of you would do for me."

He looks like he's about to say something, but then he just shakes his head and pulls me into a kiss. The last few hours have been hell for him, I know, worried about his brothers and not being able to do anything about it. I can feel the anxiety and concern in him when he kisses me.

I wrap my arms around him tightly, and we hold on for a moment, breathing each other in.

"We're going to get them back," I murmur against his chest. "We have to do this. It's the only way."

"I know." His voice is thick. "Just... be careful. Okay?"

"I will. You too."

He holds me for another moment and then drops a kiss to the top of my head. Letting go of him is one of the hardest things I've ever done. Without Malice and Victor by my side, I feel like I'm missing an essential part of myself, and the thought that I could lose Ransom too—could lose all three of them—makes terror shoot through me, so sharp and violent that it almost steals my breath.

But I meant what I said. This is the only way.

The skeletal frame of the building looks empty, but I can see a dim light shining inside as we approach, and there are two men with guns standing near a doorway that's probably meant to be the main entrance.

"We're unarmed," I say as we approach, raising my hands. Beside me, Ransom does the same. "Just like Olivia told us to be. And I have what she wants."

One of the men steps forward to check us for weapons while his buddy keeps his gun trained on us. The guard patting us down finishes checking Ransom first, then huffs out a grunt. There's a ripping sound as he jerks the Velcro fastenings of the bullet proof vest off and tosses it aside, and my stomach flips over with nerves. Of course Olivia wouldn't allow us inside with that kind of protection on.

When the guard turns his attention to me, sliding his hands over my body, I can hear Ransom make a noise low in his throat. He hates seeing this man grope me, even if there's nothing sexual about it, and my skin prickles with an unpleasant awareness. I've overcome a lot of my fear of being touched in the aftermath of my abduction, but it's really only where my men are concerned. Being touched by a stranger like this still makes nausea churn in my stomach.

But we need to get inside that building, and we'll never make it if Ransom gets into a fight with the guards out here, so I catch his gaze and give him a subtle shake of my head, letting him know I'm okay and silently urging him not to do anything.

He clenches his jaw, glaring at the guard as the burly man rips my Kevlar vest off too. Then Olivia's hired muscle nods.

"Alright, they're clean. Let's bring 'em in."

His friend steps forward, and they grab our wrists and zip tie them together before marching us deeper into the building. I twist my wrists a little as we go, subtly testing the strength of my bonds, but these men clearly know what they're doing. There's no chance I'll be able to slip these.

The guards lead us down a series of hallways and through a few half-finished rooms. The building will eventually be at least twelves stories tall, but most of the floors above us aren't finished yet. All that's there is the framework, looming above us as I glance upward. It looks like only the first two floors have had any substantial work done on them, and even down here, the walls are unfinished and the foundation is showing.

"Through here," one of the guards grunts, giving me a little shove. "Keep going."

He and his friend usher us into a large empty space. There are several pillars spaced around it, and the ceiling is mostly open, revealing the framework above us. The floor is cement, rough and unfinished, and there's a gaping hole on one side of the space, wide and deep. A cement mixer with a spout is situated near the hole, as if one of the next things the contractors will do is pour concrete to fill the hole.

A muffled sound comes from the depths of the hole, and my heart lurches. We step closer to it, and a voice calls out from below.

"Willow?"

"Vic!"

The hole is at least nine feet deep, and it's even darker down there than it is in the rest of the space, which is dimly lit by a floodlight attached to a large extension cord. But even in the shadows, I can see Vic's face, and Malice's beside it.

Relief floods my body, despite the fact that they're trapped down there. At least they're actually alive. Olivia wasn't lying about that.

I suck in a breath, but before I can say anything else, Olivia steps out of the shadows, flanked by several more hired bodyguards.

She looks out of place in this dim, unfinished building littered with construction materials. She's dressed in a pale gray pantsuit, her hands clasped in front of her, not a hair is out of place.

Her chin lifts, giving her a look of superiority as she meets my gaze and smiles. "I knew that, one way or another, your attachment to these men was going to be your downfall."

"Loving people who love me back was never a mistake." I square my shoulders, my arms unconsciously straining against the zip ties. "Your mistake was believing that blood matters more than that. That blood means anything at all. It doesn't."

Olivia snorts, and her expression shifts from that cool smile to something bored and a little disgusted. She snaps her fingers. "Show me the paperwork."

I look down at my bound hands and then back up at her as if she's stupid. My grandmother huffs a breath before gesturing to one of the guards who escorted us in. Stepping around me, he grabs the papers from my jacket and brings them over to Olivia.

There's a metal table near the floodlight with some blueprints laid out on it, and the guard spreads the papers out there for Olivia to go over. She reads through them quickly, muttering under her breath as she does. Then she looks up.

"Good. It all looks to be in order. Thank you for this, Willow." She nods at her guards. "Take care of them both."

Before I know what's happening, rough hands shove at me. I stumble, losing my footing as I'm pushed into the hole.

There's a sickening feeling of falling, waiting for the hard concrete to rush up to meet me, and I hear Ransom cursing as he falls in too.

Luckily, Vic moves fast, managing to use his body to cushion my fall so I don't go straight into the concrete. Malice does the same for Ransom, keeping him from landing too hard.

"Are you okay?" Vic murmurs, setting me on my feet.

I nod quickly, looking up to where my grandmother stands at the edge of the pit gazing down on us.

She smirks. "See? I told you they would be your downfall. But you wanted to be with them so badly, so now you can be. All four of you can rot together forever in the foundation of this place once that hole is filled in."

Malice growls, looking like he wants to throw himself out of the hole so he can wring Olivia's neck.

My heart is in my throat, fear and dread climbing up in the form of sour bile.

Olivia moves as if she's going to go make good on her threat, but before she can take more than a step, a gunshot rings out.

The guard standing nearest to her goes down.

38

WILLOW

My heart lurches in my chest as my grandmother's remaining bodyguards shout to each other, all of them scrambling to figure out where the attack came from.

He made it. Jonah is here.

"What the fuck is going on?" Malice growls, staring up toward the top of the pit. It's hard to see what's going on above us, but I can hear footsteps and more shots as my grandmother's hired men do their best to secure her and keep her safe.

"Jonah," Ransom replies quickly, turning to face his brothers. "He came with us as backup. He snuck into the building after us. Come on, we need to get the fuck out of this pit before the guards regroup. Give me a boost."

Victor and Malice share a look, processing all of that information in a heartbeat. The trust the brothers all have for each other is evident in the way they spring into action immediately. The two of them are bound just like we are, their wrists secured in front of their bodies with zip ties, and their bulletproof vests have been stripped off. But they link hands, providing a platform for Ransom to step onto before heaving him toward the top of the pit. He throws his body over the edge and hauls himself out, immediately grabbing a gun from the downed guard.

Crouching by the edge of the pit, he helps Jonah—wherever he is—lay down more cover fire for us as Malice boosts Vic out of the hole in the cement. I'm next, and I emerge just in time to see Ransom almost get taken out by a shot from a guard who's hiding behind a pillar on the other side of the room.

"Fuck! We're sitting ducks out here!" he bellows, returning fire and glancing around wildly. "The table, Vic!"

Vic is already moving, flipping the nearby table onto its side and positioning it in front of us so that there's some physical barrier between us and Olivia's guards. Vaguely, I'm aware of the sounds of a scuffle above us, and I realize that must be where Jonah is. He went up to the second floor to get a better vantage, but it sounds like at least one of Olivia's guards has found him.

With the table blocking us a bit, Vic reaches down into the pit and grabs Malice's hands. He hauls his twin up and out, and the four of us crouch behind the table that's barely big enough to cover all of us.

"How many?" Malice asks.

"Four down here. One already taken out, three with Olivia." Ransom pops up and fires off another shot. "And at least one up top with Jonah."

"That means no more cover from Jonah," Malice mutters. "But at least he got us out of that fucking pit."

"We need to—"

Whatever Vic was about to say breaks off in a curse as the three guards on the first floor rush us. We scatter, Ransom using his entire body to shove me to one side as his brothers break the other way, darting into the shadowy darkness outside the perimeter of the floodlight. I run toward an area of half-finished walls and exposed piping, with Ransom right behind me. It's awkward and difficult to sprint with my arms bound, and I almost trip and go down once before I catch my footing again.

We end up in what will probably be a storage room or something at some point, a small five by five space with only two walls completed.

Pushing me down in the corner of the room, Ransom turns to face the open doorway we just came through. One of the guards followed us, and Ransom raises his gun to fire—but nothing happens. With a furious roar, he throws himself forward, bum-rushing the guard and grappling for his gun as two shots pop off.

I've rarely seen Ransom fight the way Malice does, but he's relentless now, fighting skillfully even with his wrists bound. He throws elbows, headbutts that guard, and slams him into the wall. They're still fighting for control of the gun, and as the guard inches it sideways, trying to break Ransom's grip and get a good angle for a shot, Ransom slams his foot into the side of the guard's knee.

The man grunts and stumbles a little, and Ransom follows up with another headbutt, this time to the wind-pipe. He presses his advantage, twisting the gun out of the guard's hand.

The guard recovers quickly—but it's too late.

He moves to make another attack, but before he can, Ransom raises the weapon quickly and puts a single bullet between his eyes.

The man drops instantly, and Ransom stands over him, breathing hard and disheveled. Crouching beside the downed guard, he drops the gun and pats the man down quickly, finally finding what he's after—a small butterfly knife.

He brings the gun and knife both over to me as the muffled sounds of fighting filter to us from elsewhere in the building. "Hold out your hands," he pants.

I do it immediately, and he cuts the binds on my wrists, then hands the knife to me. I cut through the zip ties holding his wrists together, and he plucks the knife from my hand, replacing it with the gun.

"Stay here," he tells me, glancing toward the doorway. "If anybody but one of us comes through that door, shoot them."

"Where are you going?" I whisper, my heart pounding a frantic rhythm in my chest.

"I'm gonna go find my brothers and help them."

"I'm coming with you!"

He shakes his head. "No."

"Then take the gun."

I try to press it into his hands, but he won't take it, stepping back. "Not a chance, angel. You need it."

He leans in to press a hard kiss to my lips, and before I can even find my voice to protest again, he's gone, slipping out the door into the rest of the building.

I wrap my fingers around the grip of the gun, my hands shaking. I can still hear the distant sounds of a fight, so I know it isn't over yet. I'm glad Ransom is going to help Malice and Vic, who may still be bound at the wrists and unarmed, trying to take down or evade Olivia's guards at a huge disadvantage. But I hate being stuck in this room by myself. It's terrifying and unsettling, and even though I know he wanted to keep me safe, it feels wrong to be here.

"Fuck," I mutter, my gaze darting toward the doorway.

The shouts in the distance increase in volume, growing more urgent—and it snaps something inside me. Pressing to my feet, I creep toward the door, the gun held tightly in both hands.

The floodlight has either been shot out or unplugged in the scuffle, because the space is darker now. I can still see, but every shadow seems to loom like a threat, and my heart thuds wildly against my ribs as I move toward the sound of the fight.

"Fuck, Ransom, watch out!"

That's Malice's voice, and it makes it clear that Ransom found them. There's a scuffling sound, a deep grunt, and then Ransom curses.

"On your left!"

More noises, a heavy thud, and a gunshot. I pick up my pace, fear curling in my gut as Ransom calls out, "We've got this one. Malice, he's trying to get Olivia out of here! Stop him!"

I turn a corner just in time to see one of Olivia's bodyguards shove her behind him several yards away, moving her toward an exit. Ransom and Victor are working together to take down her other man as Malice—whose wrists are still bound—hurls a bucket of tools toward the guard trying to evacuate her. The guard ducks, and Malice moves, barreling toward him.

Then two things happen at once, so fast that I almost can't track them both.

Victor wraps his zip tied wrists around the neck of the guard he and Ransom are fighting, yanking backward as Ransom darts in and jams his knife between the man's ribs. On the other side of the room, Malice hits Olivia's remaining guard in the face with both fists just as the guard swings his gun to pistol whip Malice.

Both blows connect, but Malice's is harder. The guard's head snaps to the side, and he goes down... but as Malice reels from the blow to his head, Olivia darts forward. She has a gun of her own, and she jams it up beneath his chin, standing behind Malice to use him as a shield.

"Stop!" she shrieks, and there's nothing even remotely like the calm, cool woman I've seen at fancy parties in her now. She looks disheveled, almost crazed, her expensive clothes torn and stained, and her hair pulled out of its neat updo. "I'll kill him! I will!"

As if to prove her point, she half curls her finger on the trigger, making my heart leap in my throat. Malice stiffens, and Victor and Ransom, who are standing over the body of her other fallen guard, go still.

"That's right." She bares her teeth, breathing hard. "I'm gonna walk out of here, and if you try anything, if you move a single goddamned muscle, I'll blow his brains out!"

She's smaller than Malice, but with his hands bound and the gun where it is, she's got an advantage that makes up for her size. She gives a tug, urging him to move, and he takes a few slow steps backward as she digs the barrel of the gun harder into his skin.

Ransom and Vic are watching Malice and my grandmother, clearly looking for any kind of opening, but Malice's gaze darts around quickly—and lands on me in the shadows.

Our eyes lock, and surprise registers on his face for a split second. Then his gaze drops to the gun in my hand, and he gives the tiniest, almost imperceptible nod.

Fear floods me, making my entire body go cold all over.

I never emerged into the room, so no one knows I'm here. No one but Malice.

And he wants me to shoot Olivia.

Oh god.

I don't have a clear shot. Her body is mostly obscured behind his, and if I miss by even an inch, I'll end up putting a bullet in the man I love instead of my grandmother. How does he possibly think I can do this?

Unbidden, the words he spoke to me earlier filter through my mind.

Ja by umer za tebja.

I would die for you.

He doesn't care if I hit him too, as long as I take Olivia out. He's willing to die to make sure that happens. To protect me. To protect his brothers.

My palms are sweaty as I grip the gun tighter. I don't have much time. Olivia is walking Malice slowly backward, and if I let them get much farther, I'll have to step out of the shadows to take the shot.

I feel sick, bile climbing up my throat as I raise the gun. Malice's gaze flicks toward me one more time, and I have to blink furiously, refusing to let tears cloud my vision. My hands shake, but I grit my teeth and force them to stop, locking my arms out as I take aim.

Please don't let me kill him.

My finger caresses the trigger for a second, I adjust my hands just a little... and then I fire. The kickback from the gun ripples up my arms, and a heartbeat later, blood sprays from Olivia's neck. She lets out a choked sound, and Malice shoves her backward just as she pulls the trigger of her own weapon. The bullet flies upward, missing him by a hair, and Olivia staggers and falls, blood pouring from a hole in her neck.

Instantly, Malice goes for her gun, grabbing it and unloading the clip into her chest. Her body jerks with the impact, and as the last shot rings out, the room goes quiet.

Then Malice drops the gun on her chest and turns to stride toward me, nearly knocking me off my feet as our bodies collide. He wraps his bound arms around me, pulling me close in a bear hug.

"You did it," he breathes. "I fucking knew you could."

I can't breathe at all, and it's not just because of how tightly he's holding me. My lungs seem to have seized up as all the latent fear I wouldn't let myself feel before I pulled the trigger rushes through me.

"Angel." Ransom's voice comes from one side, and when Malice releases me, his brother is right there. Fear and relief seem to battle in his expression, and he cups my face in his hands, his fingers digging into my hair. "You were supposed to stay put. Stay hidden."

He doesn't chastise me any more than that though, crushing his lips to mine instead. He must've cut Vic's binds already, because Vic's hands come to my shoulders as he turns me around. There's an almost haunted expression on his face, and I know he's probably grappling with the same overwhelming emotions I am at having almost had to watch people he loves die.

"That was a good shot," he tells me.

I nod, although his words only make my stomach clench all over again.

When Vic releases me, I glance toward his twin. Ransom is cutting the zip ties off his wrists, and my breath hitches as I catch sight of a raw patch of skin on Malice's arm, a red line that cuts across his tattooed flesh.

It's from the bullet, I realize.

That's how close I came to missing.

He notices me staring at him in horror and glances down at the wound, then shakes his head.

"I'm fine," he tells me, his voice firm. "I'm alive because you took the shot, Solnyshka. We all are. I'm gonna have a hell of a bruise from where a couple bullets hit my vest before Olivia's men ambushed us, but this?" He gestures to the raw wound on his arm. "This is nothing. I'll wear the scar with pride."

A noise from nearby draws our attention, all of the men tensing up as if ready to fight again. But when Jonah limps into the room, holding his hands up, we relax a bit.

"Everything clear?" Ransom asks. "Her other bodyguard is down?"

"There were two of 'em," Jonah informs us, grimacing. "But yeah, they're down."

"Fuck." Ransom looks him over. "Are you okay?"

"I'm fine," he grunts.

The tall, lanky man has blood on his face, arms, and knuckles, but he doesn't seem to care. His gaze scans the room we're in, taking in the scene before landing on Olivia's body.

He steps closer to her, and I follow, shivering a little as I take in the pool of blood beneath her still form. She doesn't look peaceful in death. Her face is contorted, her jaw hanging open a little and her eyes wide. It's gruesome and unsettling, but I don't look away. Because there's something fitting about it too. At least in death, she can't hide behind the façade of civility. She looks just like the monster she is.

And with a bullet hole in her neck and several in her chest, she's definitely not getting up again.

Jonah spits on her body, glaring down at it. "I hope you rot in hell, you foul bitch. Finally, my brother can rest in peace."

He curls his fingers into fists, and I let out a breath, leaning against Vic as we stand gathered around the body. I wonder if my mother—both of them, actually—will be resting easier now that Olivia is dead.

Silence reigns as the five of us stare down at the corpse for a long moment, and then Ransom clears his throat.

"We should get the fuck out of here," he says. "This area is pretty dead after five o'clock, which I'm sure is part of why Olivia picked it. So I'm not sure anyone would've heard us, but we need to clean up the scene and clear out."

Before we can make a move to go, Jonah makes a low, pained sound. Then his legs buckle beneath him, and he collapses to the floor.

"Shit," Malice hisses. "Goddammit."

We all rush over to him, crouching down to check him out. He's the only one of us that still has a Kevlar vest on, but when Vic and Malice undo the Velcro and tug it off, I suck in a breath. That fight with two of Olivia's guards ended worse than he let us think. His shirt is sticky with blood, and he has several deep wounds in his chest that look like they came from a knife.

"Oh god," I breathe. "Is there anything we can do? We have to help him."

"Ransom, bring the car closer. Maybe if we keep pressure on it —" Vic tears a strip from Jonah's shirt and presses it to the wound, trying to staunch the flow of blood.

"Too fucking late for that." Jonah shakes his head, letting out a humorless, pained laugh. "Don't bother."

His face is ashy and gray in the darkness, and he takes a deep breath that rattles in his lungs. He looked beat up and exhausted when he stepped into the room a few moments ago, but I realize now that it was so much more than that. My stomach flips over as it hits me that this isn't a wound he can shrug off.

He's dying.

"Listen," he says, and it comes out raspy. "Listen to me."

"Don't try to talk," Vic urges him. "We have to get you stabilized."

"No. *Listen.*" Jonah's eyes find mine, and they catch and hold. I lean closer, staring down at him. "Tell Quinn... tell her I love her," he manages, a trickle of blood spilling past his lips.

I nod, my throat going tight.

His body shudders, and he drags in another ragged breath. Then another.

And then he goes still.

39

WILLOW

I STAND over Jonah's body, and my heart breaks for him.

I'm glad he got to see his brother avenged before he died, but this isn't how I wanted it to end. We would have been completely fucked without his help, probably already dead under a couple tons of concrete in that hole.

"Thank you," I whisper, even though I know he can't hear me anymore.

Tears well in my eyes as Ransom comes over, wrapping an arm around me. He kisses the top of my head, holding me close, and I let myself lean against him.

"He was a good man," Ransom murmurs. "And he got his revenge in the end."

Malice nods. "Some people don't even get that."

I know they're right, but it still hurts to think that he's never going to get to go home to his daughter. *Fuck. Poor Quinn.*

"We need to go," Vic finally says, breaking the silence that's settled over us. "There's a lot of cleanup to do here."

"What the fuck are we even going to do with all these bodies?" Ransom grimaces. "I'm pretty sure burning this building down would attract way more attention than we want. Besides, it's bigger than the places we normally torch, and it's all concrete.

We brought cleanup stuff, but we don't have any accelerant either."

"We'll do what Olivia was planning to do to us." Vic tilts his chin toward the pit where Olivia had us all trapped earlier. "We'll dump them in that hole and cover them up with cement."

Malice lets out a savage sort of growl. "Fuck, yes. It's what these fuckers deserve."

Ransom grabs the bleach and other cleanup equipment we stashed in the trunk of the car before coming to meet Olivia, and then the guys start hauling bodies to the pit. I do my best to help them clean up, standing the equipment that was overturned back upright and gathering a few stray weapons.

They leave Jonah's body where it is, coming for Olivia's corpse last.

I look down at her one last time, almost as if I'm trying to memorize the stillness on her face. She wore so many expressions in the time I knew her. So many of them were fake, just masks to make people see what she wanted them to see. Polished and polite, just a kind, rich old woman. But something so monstrous and evil lurked underneath.

She was nothing more than a cold-hearted manipulator.

A murderer.

A monster.

"You did well, butterfly," Victor tells me in a low voice.

"You did," Ransom agrees. "That shot was clean as hell."

My hands, so steady when I took the shot that killed Olivia, shake a little now. But the truth is, I don't regret being the one to take her down. I know Malice promised me I wouldn't have to be, but when it came down to a choice between her life and his, the decision was incredibly easy.

Relief washes through me when her body gets tossed into the hole, and I watch as Ransom and Malice start filling it with concrete, covering everything up.

Vic and I walk the space, wiping away fingerprints and making sure there's nothing left behind that could tie us to this scene. He does a few other things as well, and when he's satisfied, he gives me a nod. I gather the papers Olivia wanted so badly and keep them with me, leaving nothing behind.

Once we're done, there's still the matter of Jonah's body.

"We should take him back to his people," Malice says. "We can't leave him here, and they deserve to know what happened."

We're all in agreement, even though I'm dreading delivering the news to his crew. Especially Quinn.

Malice and Ransom carry him outside, and Vic's head swivels back and forth as we leave the unfinished construction site. The street is dark and quiet as they load Jonah's body gently into the trunk, and we all slip into the car.

Ransom hands Vic his computer, which we brought with us, and the look on Vic's face almost brings a smile to my lips. He looks like he's being reunited with a long-lost friend, and he gets to work immediately, scrubbing traffic footage and anything else that could link us to the Oberon construction site as we drive.

Even though it's late at night by now, there's a group of men hanging around outside the tattoo parlor when we pull up into the alley, and they eye us warily as we get out of the car.

I can tell they're looking for their leader, since even though he refused to involve his gang in his personal vendetta, they knew about his arrangement with us.

"Where's Jonah?" one of them asks.

Malice opens the trunk and steps back, and a couple of Jonah's men come forward to glance inside. It only takes one look for them to understand what's happening here, and they go tense, looking at Malice with angry eyes.

"What the fuck?" the taller man demands. "You son of a bitch!"

Before Malice can say anything, the two of them are pulling out guns, aiming right at Malice. That kicks the others off, even if they don't know why yet, and they draw on the rest of us, cranking the tension up even more.

Malice lifts his hands, his jaw clenched.

"We didn't do this," he says in a low voice. "It was—"

"Why the fuck should we listen to anything you have to say? You show up here and talk Jonah into taking on this job, and now he's dead."

Malice's jaw works, every line of his body taut. Defusing situations like this isn't his strong point, and I can tell he's getting tired of having a gun pointed at him. My stomach ties itself into several tight knots as I glance between the brothers and the Enigma gang.

Fuck. Please don't let this end badly. Not after everything else that's happened tonight.

Malice glances at Ransom, and the younger Voronin brother steps up as much as he can without getting shot.

"It's not what it looks like," he begins. "You know he agreed to help us, and we didn't betray him. It was—"

The back door to the tattoo shop swings open before he can finish, and Quinn comes out. She takes in the scene and then comes over to the car, looking down into the trunk.

My breath catches, a lump growing in my throat. I wait for her to fall apart or start screaming at us, accusing us of killing her father, but instead, she takes a deep breath. When she looks up, there's pain in her eyes, but there's something like resolve there too.

Her entire demeanor changes, her expression hardening as if she's aged several years in just the space of a few seconds, and there's a commanding glint in her eye as she turns to face her father's men.

"Stand down," she says quietly.

"But, Quinn, they—"

"I said stand down!" she barks, her voice cracking like a whip. "They didn't do this. My father..." She falters for just a second, then starts again, her voice gaining strength. "My father went of his own free will. He had a chance to take down his enemy, the woman responsible for Casey's death, and he took it. He knew the risks before he went. It was important enough to him to go anyway."

There's a moment of loaded silence, but Quinn doesn't blink.

She doesn't waver or back down at all. Finally, the first man who spoke to us drops his head, a gesture of both acquiescence and respect. He shoves his gun back in to the waistband of his pants, and one by one, the rest of the gang members put their weapons away too.

I exhale a shaky breath, glancing quickly at my men before stepping forward. They usually take the lead when we deal with groups like the Enigma gang and the Kings of Chaos, but in this moment, I feel like I should be the one to speak to Quinn.

"I'm sorry," I say quietly. "I can never express our gratitude enough. He saved our lives. We'll always owe that to him. We owe *you.*"

She nods, her eyes glinting in the light that filters into the alley. She's tall too, just like her dad, and I have to tilt my head a little to meet her gaze.

"Thank you." With a tiny gesture of one hand, she motions for the two men who first looked into the trunk to approach. "Bring him inside," she instructs. "We'll deal with funeral arrangements tomorrow."

The men nod and carefully remove Jonah's body, supporting it between them as they bring it inside. The remaining gang members fade back a little at another gesture from Quinn, and it strikes me in a rush that she's just become their leader, stepping into her father's shoes. I haven't heard it confirmed with words, but I can see it in the way she acts and in the way they treat her.

"What happened?" Quinn asks now that we have more privacy. "How did he..."

"He saved our asses," Ransom tells her, his voice solemn. "The plan was fucked from the beginning, but we didn't know that. We were caught flat-footed, and if it hadn't been for him, we'd all be dead right now."

She swallows, running a hand over one of her tattooed arms as if trying to banish the goosebumps scattered across her skin. "So he got his revenge in the end? Olivia Stanton is dead?"

Vic nods. "Yes. Dead and unable to hurt anyone else again. He was instrumental in that, and he got a chance to spit on her corpse before he fell. He got his closure, for whatever that's worth."

"Good," Quinn murmurs. "He hated her so much for what happened to my uncle, so... so at least I know he got to see her die before the end."

It's impressive, how good she is at keeping her shit together. She has to be hurting inside, feeling the grief of losing her dad, but she's keeping her tough façade up. Even still, there's so much pain in her eyes, and it breaks my heart to see it.

I lower my voice a little, wanting these words to be just for her. "He told us to tell you something. Right before he... died."

She swallows. "What was it?"

"That he loves you. Those were his last words."

That seems to be the thing that breaks through the new mantle of leadership she's wearing. Tears glisten in her eyes, and she closes them for a second, dragging in a few deep breaths.

"Thank you," she whispers.

Unable to help myself, I take a tentative step toward her, wrapping my arms around her in a hug. It's awkward at first, and I almost expect her to shove me away, since several of her father's men—*her* men—are still watching. She's stiff for a second, but then her arms tighten around me, squeezing tightly as if she needed this more than words could express. I feel her body shudder against mine, and then she releases me and steps back, squaring her shoulders.

"Are you going to be alright?" I murmur.

"Yeah." She nods, and I can already see her compartmentalizing her emotions again. "I always am. I have to be, so I will be."

To my surprise, Malice steps forward, offering her his hand. She takes it, and they shake once.

"Jonah helped us more than we can say," he tells her. "So if you ever need something from us, we owe you one."

I've learned enough about the world my men inhabit by now to know that offering an open-ended favor like that is rare. The Voronin brothers spent years under X's thumb, doing jobs for my grandmother in exchange for Malice's early release from prison. So owing anyone for anything, having that sort of thing hanging over them, is the kind of thing they would normally avoid at all costs. But for what Jonah did for us, they're clearly willing to do it.

There's not much more to say after that. I have a feeling Quinn and her people want to be left alone to start dealing with the realities of her father's death and figuring out what comes next, so with a final nod, my men and I get back into the car.

I look back once as we pull away, watching Quinn gesture as she gives orders to the gathered men and wondering when—or if—our paths might cross again.

The drive back to the safe house feels long.

I keep replaying everything that happened today over and over in my head, reliving all the moments that we could all have died. Everything that could've gone wrong with our plan seemed to go wrong, and if it weren't for Jonah being on our side...

I don't even want to think about it.

Somehow, we all made it out alive. My grandmother is dead and buried under several tons of concrete, unable to ever hurt us again. That's hard to wrap my head around, but I keep repeating it in my mind, trying to make it feel real.

The guys are mostly quiet as we head back into the safe house, lost in their own thoughts. I want to leave them to it, to let them decompress after the night we've had, but there's something building inside me that I can't ignore.

So as soon as we get back and step through the door, I turn to them, my heart thudding.

"Take off your shirts," I demand, surprising even myself with the fierceness of my tone.

Ransom raises his pierced eyebrow, almost smirking at me. "Not wasting any time, huh?"

Clearly he thinks I want sex, but this isn't even about that.

"No, I just... I need to see."

I keep thinking about Jonah and the way he walked up to my grandmother's body, spit on her corpse, and then just... collapsed.

386

He looked okay before that, hiding his injury well enough that I didn't even know it was a lethal wound until he went down.

The thought that one of my men might have a hidden injury like that makes me feel sick to my stomach. I need to see with my own eyes that they're alright. That they're whole. It's the only thing that will make my heart calm down.

They seem to understand, because one by one, they start taking their shirts off.

I go to Vic first, running my hands over his chest and torso. His muscles tense beneath my hands, and I can feel it when he takes a shuddering breath. It makes me swallow hard, knowing that just feeling me touch him like this is enough to get him to react this way.

I run my fingers over the scar from the last time he got shot for me, and the bruise that must be left from him getting shot this time, even with his vest on.

Thank fuck for bulletproof vests.

Vic lets me touch my fill, and when I'm finally satisfied that there are no life-threatening injuries, I move on to Ransom.

I feel as if I know all of these men's scars by heart now, having cataloged them with my hands and mouth since we've been together. There's nothing new on Ransom, and the dried blood on his arm turns out to be from someone else, to my relief.

"I'm all good," he murmurs to me, lifting one of my hands and kissing my knuckles. "I promise."

I nod, my heart thumping in my chest.

Last, I turn to Malice. The most reckless of the group, the one most likely to be trying to hide a bullet wound and shrug it off. I take my time, making sure all the scars on him are the usual ones, and that none of the blood is his. There are bruises on his chest from being shot, blood that probably belongs to Olivia, and a shit-load of scrapes and bruises that can be explained by being kidnapped and thrown in a hole, but nothing else.

The invisible vise around my lungs finally releases its grip, and I feel like I can breathe normally again.

"Thank you," I whisper to Malice, staring at his tattooed, bruised chest. "For not dying."

He grabs my hand and then uses his free hand to tip my face up to his so that I'm looking him in the eye.

"I meant what I said, Solnyshka," he murmurs. "I wouldn't have hesitated to die for you, if that's what it took."

"Neither would I," Vic agrees instantly, and when I glance at Ransom, he's nodding too. Something flutters in my stomach, and I swallow hard.

Malice's fingers draw my face back to him. The hardness of his features softens a little as a smile pulls at his lips.

"But I'd rather *live* for you," he tells me. "I'd rather spend the rest of my life making you happy."

"A-fucking-men," Ransom adds.

Emotions swell inside me, and I'm suddenly overwhelmed by how much I love these three men. Tears well in my eyes, spilling down my cheeks, but for the first time in a long time, they're not sad tears. They're tears of joy and love and relief.

"That sounds perfect," I breathe.

The room tilts around me as Victor picks me up, cradling me in his arms. He carries me into the bedroom with his brothers close on our heels.

Between the three of them, they get me undressed, doing their own checks to make sure I'm okay. Other than some bruises and scrapes like they have, I'm fine, and the three of them kiss each mark on my body.

They kiss every bruise and all of my scars, making me feel so loved and cherished that I start crying all over again. Then they kiss my tears away too.

There's going to be a lot to do going forward, but for now, there's just this moment.

Me and the three of them, celebrating the one thing that matters most.

We're alive.

And we have each other.

WILLOW

A FEW DAYS LATER, we go to meet with the Copeland family.

Just like the last time I saw them, I'm dressed well, and my men have echoed that. All three of them are in dark pants and blazers, looking somehow professional and dangerous all at the same time.

We meet Alexander and Stella at their company headquarters, which is sterile and beautiful. White marble gleams everywhere, and there are flower arrangements on strategic surfaces. The glass of the doors and windows is so shiny we can see ourselves in it, and there's nothing out of place or a speck of dust or dirt to be seen.

But like everything in this world, I know it's a facade. Just a pretty veneer to hide the ugliness underneath.

There was a time when I would have felt small, walking into this boardroom and trying to speak to people like this. I would have seen their expensive clothes and the way they hold themselves and thought they were better than me. That I had no business here.

I know so much better now.

So I sit across the table from them, chin lifted and shoulders squared.

Malice, Vic, and Ransom stand behind me, backing me up but letting me handle this.

Alexander and Stella Copeland are as unpleasant and bitter as ever, and they glare at me with raw hatred in their expressions. I've earned it, I guess, since I'm the reason the Voronin brothers killed their son. But I hate them too, for raising their son to be a monster, so I guess we're even.

"What do you want?" Stella asks stiffly, her hands laced together on the table.

"I want to offer you a deal," I tell her. "You can buy me out of Troy's shares of your company and get me out of your lives. You won't have to deal with me fucking with you or abusing the power I have as his widow, sitting in his seat at the table." I pause for a moment, letting that sink in. "Or, you can refuse, and I'll use my power as a shareholder to make shit difficult for you every chance I get."

Alexander sends me a look so full of anger and hate that it would have frightened me if I wasn't the one calling the shots here. Whatever option they choose, I can't lose.

"Someone should have taught you your place a long time ago," he hisses, contempt in every word.

I don't even flinch.

"People have tried," I say lightly. "Your son, most notably. And look what happened to him. My grandmother also thought she could decide for me what my place was and what my life should be like. I hope she's reflecting on how well that worked out for her, wherever she is."

Stella puts a hand over her mouth, and she and her husband both eye me with suspicion. Olivia Stanton has officially been reported missing, and since there hasn't been any sign of her body, no one can say for sure what happened. Vic wiped our tracks clean, and only the four of us know that she's buried under seven feet of straight concrete.

But I let the threat be what it is.

Holding their gazes, I slide a piece of paper across the table with the amount I'm willing to accept as a buyout written on it. Vic and I went over everything yesterday, deciding what I should ask for. And it's not a small amount.

The Copelands look at the paper and then glare at me, hatred intensifying in their eyes, but I have no sympathy for them. If their son had just left me alone, then this wouldn't be an issue. And I'll use the money to make sure their grandchild—whose existence they'll never know about—is taken care of.

When it's clear I'm not going to back down, they have a whispered conversation between themselves. The men and I wait, still and silent. We're not in any rush.

Finally, the Copelands turn back to us, and Alexander nods.

"Alright. If this is what it will take to get you out of our lives forever, then we accept your offer."

I smile at them both, nodding. "Good. I thought you might."

Vic steps forward then, ready to handle the logistics of the buyout. We brought contracts with us, and he's prepared with an account number for them to wire the money to. My stomach flutters a little as the wire transfer goes through. The amount is actually a bit less than the total value of Troy's shares, but instead of being tied up in the company, it's now cash sitting in our bank account.

It takes a bit of time, and I'm a bit antsy by the time it's finally all completed, eager to get out of this too bright, too sleek office.

Vic gives me a nod, and I slide the paperwork across the table to the Copelands, then push my chair back and rise.

"I would say it's a pleasure doing business with you, but that would be a lie," I tell them bluntly.

With that, I turn and leave, surrounded by my men. As the door closes behind us, I can hear Alexander and Stella arguing in hushed voices, taking out their anger on each other and each pointing the blame at anyone but themselves.

I smirk. *Assholes will always be assholes.*

We leave the building, striding across the large lobby and then stepping out into the fresh air. As we make our way to the car, I glance over at Ransom to find him grinning broadly. The sight of it is so beautiful and infectious that it makes me grin too, and I nudge him with my shoulder.

"How pissed do you think they're going to be when the feds come knocking on their door tonight, and they realize we not only took their money but framed them for Olivia's murder too?" I whisper.

His smile grows impossibly bigger, ruthless glee glinting in his eyes. "Oh, very. On a scale of one to ten? I'd say a million."

Vic is on my other side, and when I look up at him, he's not smiling, but he looks incredibly satisfied.

He should. After all, this was his idea. I didn't know quite what he was doing the night we cleaned up the construction site and dumped the bodies of my grandmother and her guards, but I should've known that nothing Vic does is ever an accident. Even then, his mind was racing ahead, setting up the pieces on the board for a checkmate that was still several moves away.

And today, we'll play that checkmate.

Our original plan was to just let my grandmother spend eternity buried in the foundation of the building, but instead, we've decided to use her death to our advantage. It was actually pretty fucking easy to lay a path of breadcrumbs connecting the Copelands to Olivia. They've done business together for years—some of it of the decidedly illegal variety—and it was easy to paint a sordid picture of two wealthy families having a falling out over tax fraud schemes and under-the-table deals gone wrong. Along with some evidence that Vic took from the construction site that's been planted at the Copeland's residence, we've created a slam dunk case for law enforcement.

If all goes well, Alexander and Stella will spend the rest of their lives in jail.

"I only wish I could be there to see them carted off in handcuffs," Malice mutters under his breath as we reach the car and pile inside.

I understand his sentiment, but honestly, I don't share it. I never want to see them again, not even for that.

Malice cranks the key in the ignition, and we pull away. Ransom reaches for my hand in the back seat, running his thumb idly over my knuckles as the men talk amongst themselves. Their voices fade into background noise for a bit as I get lost in my thoughts, chewing on my lip and gazing out the window.

Before we take the turn that will lead us back toward the safe house, I glance over at my men. "Can I show you something?"

"Sure, angel. Anything," Ransom says.

"Okay. We have to go somewhere to see it."

Malice's gaze snags mine in the rearview mirror. "What is it?"

"You'll see."

Leaning forward a little, I give Malice directions, guiding him to a spot in the city—a place where I found something the other day when I was searching online.

It's a warehouse, large and sprawling, recently built. And it's for sale.

We roll to a stop out front, and I open my door quickly, getting out. The men follow, glancing from the warehouse to me.

"What is this?" Victor asks.

"I want you to have a space to rebuild what you lost," I say quietly. "A place that can be a home for all of us. Where Ransom can work on his bikes, you can have an office for your computers, and Malice can have a room just for all of his tattoo stuff. We'll all live together, the way you guys used to live above your shop. You guys might not need to run a chop shop anymore, but I know you miss some parts of the old setup you used to have."

I can feel something building in all three of the men as I speak, and there's silence for a long moment after I stop.

Then Vic takes a step closer to me. "You want to buy this place," he confirms quietly. "And live here with us. Forever."

"Yes." I bite my lower lip, waiting to hear whether they like that idea or not.

I get my answer a moment later when all three of them scoop me up. I'm not sure how they manage it, but my feet literally don't even touch the ground as I'm encased between them.

"I hope you know what you're getting into, pretty girl," Ransom teases, pressing a kiss to my temple.

"Yeah," Malice growls. "Because we're never letting you go."

"Good." I grin, squirming as Vic nuzzles his face against my neck. "Because there's nowhere else I want to be."

41

VICTOR

Several weeks after Olivia's mysterious disappearance, things have settled as much as they can.

Willow and I are out shopping for things we need for the new place. It's become our thing, a task we always do together. Malice and Ransom don't really care about organization or decoration at all, but Willow and I do.

She's incredibly knowledgeable about home improvement stuff from the years she spent watching those shows, and we discuss the things we've learned and the things we want to change. It's funny to me that I didn't understand the shows at first, but now I feel as if I really do.

It's about building something from nothing.

Not just physically, but in a deeper sense as well.

This thing we're doing? It's not just building a house with Willow and my brothers. We're building a *home*. A future together. The choices we make aren't just about this paint color or that material for the furniture. It's about the fact that we're building the foundation of our life.

It's about thinking ahead to the future and imagining Willow lounging in the living room, or a baby in a crib in the corner.

"What do you think about this?" Willow asks, holding up a

paint sample as we make our way through the massive home goods store. "For the kitchen area."

"With the backsplash we've already picked out?" I purse my lips, cocking my head as I consider it. "Don't you think that will clash?"

"It shouldn't, because they're both cool tones. But we should get a few alternates just in case."

She scrunches up her nose as she considers her options, and I let her take her time, nodding whenever she picks up something I particularly like. The truth is, if Willow decided she wanted to paint our entire kitchen neon pink, I'd let her. So would my brothers, in a heartbeat. There's nothing she could choose that I wouldn't love, just for the simple fact that *she* chose it, but it's fun to do this with her, debating the merits of different colors and aesthetics.

It's time we get to spend together, and that's always my favorite thing.

The warehouse is a work in progress, still being turned into the living space for all of us, but it's coming along really well. Malice and Ransom have taken on more of the construction that needs to happen, doing their part while we do ours.

In the end, we leave with several cans of paint and place orders to have more things delivered soon. With that done, we head back to the car.

Willow insists on carrying some of the lighter purchases, even though she's visibly pregnant now.

She has a small baby bump, and every time I look at it, it does something to me. I didn't think I could feel anything stronger than what I feel for Willow, but there's a protectiveness that surges through my chest when I think of the little life growing inside her.

My brothers and I have essentially adopted this baby already. In our minds, it's all of ours. Troy's name is never even mentioned anymore, and our child will never hear it spoken.

As I load the stuff into the car, Willow leans over to help me. Her arm brushes against mine, and that little spark of contact is all it takes to make me reach for her. I pull her into my arms, pressing her against the car gently as I kiss her.

Just because I can.

Because it once felt nearly impossible to do this.

Willow kisses me back, her fingers sliding through the hair at the nape of my neck in a way that makes me instantly hard. She smiles against my lips when she feels it, and when we break apart, she rakes her nails gently down the back of my neck, making me shudder.

"What was that for?" she asks.

"Thank you for loving me," I reply softly. "Just as I am."

Her hand moves around to trace my cheek and the line of my jaw, her brown eyes warming. "I don't know any other way to love you, Vic. To me, you're perfect."

I kiss her again for that, and even though I could fuck her right here in this parking lot, I'd rather take her home. So I close the trunk of the car, and we head out.

When we get to the warehouse, Willow unpacks the stuff we got while I make lunch for her. I've done plenty of research on what she should be eating that will taste good but also be healthy for her and the baby. I've also been preparing myself to keep a straight face when she gets cravings and asks for strange things that should not go together in the future.

I'll make her whatever she wants. No matter how strange it is.

Even if it's crunchy peanut butter.

"You're gonna make a good dad, you know," Willow comments as she settles onto a stool at the high-topped table and watches me work.

"You think so?"

She grins, tipping her head to one side. "I know so. You'll make the best school lunches. And you'll cut the crusts off our kid's sandwiches so perfectly."

That makes me chuckle, and I gaze down at the chicken I'm preparing for a moment before I say in a quiet voice, "I wondered, a bit. After you first decided to keep the baby and raise it with us. If I would be any good at this. I know we all told you blood doesn't matter, and I believe that. But the only example I've had of a father figure was... awful."

"I know." Her voice softens. "I've thought the same thing about myself. But the thing is, your father and my grandmother *did* teach us something, just not the lessons they intended. They taught us what not to do. And I think—I hope—that we'll be better parents because of all the shit we went through."

I nod, because ultimately, I think she's right. It doesn't totally quell my nervousness about becoming a father, but it makes me happy to think that I can take the awfulness of my childhood and transform it into something better for our child.

We keep talking while I cook, discussing some ideas Willow had for the living room. A few minutes later, Malice and Ransom stride into the kitchen, deep in the middle of a debate about the floor plan for one of the upstairs rooms.

"If you put it by the window, it takes care of the whole problem, Mal," Ransom insists.

"And creates five new ones," Malice shoots back. "You're just still on about 'natural light' or whatever the fuck."

"Oh, excuse me, I forgot you prefer to brood in the darkness."

Willow laughs at their antics, and Ransom swoops in to kiss her before throwing me a look.

"Vic, please talk some sense into your twin," he says. "I can't deal with him."

"Don't drag me into this," I reply, checking the temperature of the chicken.

Malice kisses Willow in greeting as soon as Ransom steps away, grabbing the stool she's perched on and scooting it closer so that their lips meet. The chicken is done, so I turn off the burner and pause for a moment to watch as Malice murmurs something in Willow's ear that makes her flush and smile.

These sorts of moments, so full of domesticity and peace, are still unfamiliar in a way. But I like them. I like seeing my family this way.

There are some things, some remnants of my past, that I know I'll always live with. Some days I still get overwhelmed and have to rely on the tools I taught myself, counting until I can get my emotions back under control. I still like things to be organized, needing everything to be in its place.

In some ways, I haven't changed much at all.

But I know that in other ways, Willow has changed me so much. She crawled inside my soul and made a home there, and even though I was terrified of it, even though I felt like I might fracture into pieces... I didn't. My damaged heart reformed with her at the center, and that's where she'll always be.

"Right, Vic?" Willow says, glancing over at me.

That breaks me from my thoughts, and I shake myself. "Sorry, I zoned out when Malice and Ransom were arguing. It's just background noise to me now."

She laughs, shaking her head. "I was saying that you're not going to let me eat a chili cheeseburger right now. Ransom wants one for lunch."

"Absolutely not," I agree.

He makes a face. "Party pooper. Sorry, angel. I'll eat an extra one just for you."

"Thanks, Ransom." She blows him a kiss. "You're such a giver."

I plate up the lunch I made for her and bring it over to the table we're using for now, until we find one we like better. Malice and Ransom take their argument somewhere else, going back to work, and Willow leans up to kiss me.

"Thank you. This is way better than a chili cheeseburger. You take such good care of me," she murmurs.

The words she said to me in the parking lot filter through my mind, and I cup the back of her head, brushing my lips against hers once more.

"I don't know any other way."

42

RANSOM

My brothers and I all told ourselves that we didn't give a shit about having to leave our old warehouse behind when we fled Detroit with Willow. And it was true. Compared to losing the girl of our dreams to a monster, losing our home was nothing.

But damn, she really does know us well. Because this new warehouse, designed specifically for the four of us?

It's fucking perfect.

Vic and Willow have been picking out paint colors—although she isn't allowed to help with the actual painting—and switching out the temporary furniture with better stuff that we plan to keep for a while. It's starting to look less like a weird empty space that we live in and more like a home, which feels fucking amazing.

I've been working on the garage part of it, getting it set up just the way we want it. New tools gleam from the shelves and drawers along one wall, and new lifts and jacks and shit are installed and ready to go.

I've been working on a bike to replace my old one—and the one that got shot up by Ethan's old crew—fixing it up and overhauling it to run just the way I like. The chances of this one getting sprayed with bullets or burned are pretty low, so I feel like I can invest more energy into it.

I've got music playing, nodding along to the beat as I polish the sleek frame of my Ducati, in my happy place.

Well... it's *almost* my happy place. There's one thing that could make it better.

I wipe my hands off on the rag and then toss it into the dirty rag hamper before heading into the living area part of the warehouse.

Malice and Willow are on the new couch in the large, open space. My brother is holding a book open, and Willow has her head in his lap, both of them reading from the same page.

I smirk at the sight they make, shaking my head.

"I can't believe you're actually invested in these romance novels now," I tell Malice, waggling my brows. "You got them for Willow, but now they're kind of for you too, aren't they?"

Ever since we settled into our new place, it's become something the two of them share. They trade books back and forth or read the same one together, doing something called buddy reading that seems to be mostly Malice reading the dirty parts out loud to make Willow squirm.

Malice just gives me a deadpan look.

"What can I say?" he says in a flat voice. "I'm a romantic at heart."

I belt out a laugh, although the funny thing is, he's not lying. No one but me, Vic, and Willow will probably ever know that though. It's a secret he hides well from the rest of the world.

Shifting my attention from him to Willow, I jerk my thumb in the direction of the garage. "Hey, do you wanna go for a ride with me?"

She perks up at that prospect, sitting up on the couch. "Always."

"It's chilly out," Malice warns. "So you shouldn't go too long. And take a coat or something."

I roll my eyes. "You're starting to sound like Vic. Or Mom."

Willow crawls onto Malice's lap, grinning at him. "You're so protective," she teases, running her hands over his chest. "I bet you want to bundle me up yourself, don't you?"

He palms the back of her head and drags her in for a hard kiss before lifting her off his lap and depositing her on her feet.

"Get out of here," he says, smacking her ass as she walks away.

Her cheeks are a little flushed as she walks toward me, her skin practically glowing. I'm not sure if it's pregnancy hormones or just the lack of stress now that no one is trying to kill us, but she looks fucking luminous these days.

Draping an arm around her shoulders, I lead her into the garage. When she sees the bike, she perks up even more.

"Oh, wow. You've done so much on it. It looks great!" she exclaims, stepping forward. "I never totally understood why you'd want to get a used bike when you could have one new, but it makes sense now."

"Easier to customize," I tell her, watching as she trails her fingers over the chrome.

She looks good standing next to my new Ducati, like she belongs there, and I have a very vivid memory of fucking her on a different bike once.

Someday, I want to christen this one the same way.

That thought makes my heart race and my blood heat, and I have to take a breath and adjust my cock to get it to calm the hell down. The idea of bending her over the seat and sliding into her has a lot of appeal, but right now, I actually do want to go for a ride with her.

Willow catches me looking at her as she glances my way. My thoughts must be written clearly on my face, because she grins, walking back toward me.

"You know, I can tell what's on your mind right now," she murmurs. "You're thinking very dirty thoughts, Ransom Voronin."

"Of course I am." I smirk. "I'm thinking about you."

The gorgeous shade of pink in her cheeks deepens, and she tucks her bottom lip between her teeth. "I like that I make you dirty."

"And I fucking *love* making you dirty," I growl, pulling her into my arms. "You've got a wild streak, pretty girl, and I always knew it. From the moment we met."

She grins, shaking her head as her hands rest on my chest. "So where are we going?"

"You'll see."

I hand her a helmet and then pull one on myself. We get on the bike, Willow behind me with her arms around my waist. The engine roars to life, and I rev it a few times before peeling out of the open garage door and onto the street.

As soon as we hit the open road, I'm hit with an almost euphoric feeling.

Fuck, I missed this.

The sun is setting, giving the world around us a warm glow as the wind rushes past. Willow clings to me tightly, and it's as close to perfect as anything on this earth gets, if you ask me.

Willow laughs, giving a little whoop of joy as we take a turn, and that just makes my blood pump even hotter. I fucking love this side of her. The thrill seeker who loves this shit as much as I do.

As I take another turn, I feel her hand start to shift downward, heading for my crotch.

Truth be told, I'm already half hard from just having her on the bike with me, and having her stroke my cock through my pants makes my stomach clench.

The bike wobbles a bit, and my adrenaline spikes.

I can hear Willow's soft laugh even over the roar of the engine, and the feeling of her body pressed so close and her hand teasing me is enough to have all my blood rushing south. One of her arms stays locked around my waist as the other hand drags over my jeans-covered cock, and I try to stay focused on steering, but she's distracting as hell.

Her hips press forward, like she's grinding against the seat, and when I feel more than I hear her soft moan, that's all I can take.

I turn the bike into an alley without warning, pulling to stop before getting off. Then I pluck Willow off the seat and tug her helmet off, resting hers and mine on the bike.

"Bad girl," I chastise hoarsely.

Willow makes a face, her cheeks flushed as she bites her lip. "Sorry," she says, lowering her eyes. "I know I probably—"

Before she can finish that apology, I grab her and press her to the alley wall, kissing her hard. She sucks in a surprised breath, but then arches against me, giving back as good as she gets. A soft whimper spills from her lips, and I groan at the vibrations of it, kissing her harder.

Her hand slips down again between us, stroking me in earnest now.

I pull back enough to nip at her lip and arch an eyebrow. "Is that all you're gonna do? Tease me? You started this, pretty girl, but can you finish it?"

She smirks, her eyes flashing with desire and challenge. Her tongue flashes out of her mouth to lick her lips, and then, without warning, she drops to her knees in front of me.

"Fuck," I groan. "Jesus Christ, you're gonna kill me."

My hands go flat on the alley wall as she unzips my pants and then reaches in to draw my cock out. I'm rock solid now, and she strokes me a little, making precum drip from my tip.

"Do you wanna see how wild I can be?" she breathes, her voice husky.

"Goddamn. Yes."

Looking up at me through her lashes, she eases her mouth over my cock, enveloping it in that slick, wet heat.

We're in an alley, and not even a completely remote one, so I know we only have the illusion of privacy. There's a non-zero chance that someone could walk by and see us, but that thought only turns me on more. Willow is on her knees, sucking my cock in an alley, just because she wants to.

"You're so fucking amazing," I praise, the words spilling out of me. "So perfect like this. Harder. Get me off quick, angel, before we get caught."

Willow sucks me harder, hollowing her cheeks like a fucking Hoover, and my fingers curl against the rough brick of the wall.

Another moan comes from Willow, and the vibrations of it travel through my cock, making my arousal spark even higher. Gripping my ass with both hands, she starts taking me all the way down her throat, letting me feel and hear how turned on she is.

My eyelids droop, but I force them open, staring down at her in the dusky evening light. It's almost dark out by now, but I can see well enough to watch her head bob as she struggles to take me even deeper.

"Look at me," I urge. "Keep your eyes on me while you suck my dick with that gorgeous mouth."

She tilts her head a fraction, her brown eyes glinting as she meets my gaze. There's so much heat, so much need in her expression, that I curse under my breath as my balls start to tighten. But I don't want to come like this.

So I pull her off my cock and then lift her to her feet.

"Ransom," she gasps, looking like she's about to dive back down again. "Let me—"

"Shhh, pretty girl. I've got you. You've got me all fucking worked up, but I want to finish in your pussy. Want to make you come too."

I turn her around to face the wall, letting her brace herself against it. Impatient now, I shove her pants and underwear down, letting them stay bunched up around her thighs.

Her pussy is already slick and wet for me, and I curse as I tease her with the head of my cock, rubbing it through her arousal. Willow presses back against me, grinding as if she needs more, and I grab on to her hips to hold her still.

"Please, Ransom," she moans, her hair falling over one shoulder. "Fuck, please. I need it. I need you."

"I can tell," I whisper, pressing myself against her body. "You always beg so well for me. Because you always need it so bad, don't you? You can never get enough?"

"Never enough," she gasps. "Oh god, it's never enough, Ransom. Please, please, please."

I chuckle under my breath, and the sound is strained. I'm

405

teasing her, I'm also teasing myself, straining the bounds of my patience.

"Remember that time I told you I wouldn't fuck you because you didn't beg me quite enough?" I hum in approval. "Well, you've gotten better at it. How can I deny you anything when you put it like that?"

The answer is that I definitely can't, and I press into her body just a second later. She moans, and I echo the sound, caught up in how fucking incredible she feels.

"I need you to be a good girl and stay quiet for me, okay?" I rasp, clenching my jaw. "Otherwise people will hear you getting fucked in this alley. Can you do that?"

Willow nods, biting her lip to muffle her noises as I start moving inside her.

It's too much, too good for me to go slow, so I start fucking her harder and faster. Her pussy squeezes around me as she works herself back into my thrusts, meeting me in the middle.

Muffled moans and sobs of pleasure spill from her every once in a while, even though I know she's trying to stay silent, and it spurs me on. My fingers bite into her hips, and the pitch of her soft whines changes as she starts to come undone.

Something feral and possessive takes over me, and I drop my head, breathing into Willow's ear, "That's right, angel. You did so good. Now I need you to be a bad girl and scream my fucking name."

I pound into her, taking her with almost brutal thrusts, chasing the bliss that I can feel building in my balls.

Her mouth falls open as she cries out my name, arching her back.

"Shit," I curse, immediately following her over the edge.

I come hard, turning her head to kiss her, muffling the rest of her noises as we fall apart together.

It takes a few long minutes for us to come down, catching our breaths and standing on wobbly legs. I pull out and drag her pants back up, probably soaking her panties with my cum as it leaks from her. Then I fix my own clothes and turn Willow around to kiss her deeply, tasting myself and all the desire on her tongue as I do.

"Fuck, I love you," I murmur against her lips. "You have no idea."

"Well, I have *some* idea," she shoots back, grinning. Then her gaze slides to my motorcycle, mischief lighting in her eyes. "Does this count as christening the bike?"

I laugh, kissing her again. "It's a damned good start."

EPILOGUE

WILLOW

TODAY IS THE DAY.

Today, the last piece of Olivia Stanton's legacy will fall.

It's been three months since our final showdown with her, and I've finally stopped having nightmares about her and Troy—for the most part, at least. It's getting easier and easier to put that part of my life in the past, with so much good to focus on in the future.

It helps that Olivia is six feet under, and the Copelands are in jail for her murder. That makes it a lot easier for me to sleep at night.

The cops came poking around during their investigation of the Copelands, wanting to ask me questions as their daughter-in-law. We were prepared for that, and the guys coached me through what to say and what not to say, so by the time I had to answer their questions, I was ready.

It was actually pretty simple. I told a curated version of the truth, admitting that I had been married to Troy but also making it clear that my grandmother forced me into it. I told the cops that the Copelands and Olivia disliked each other and competed with each other, feeding into the narrative my men had already created of two nefarious families turning against each other.

My story contained just enough truth to make it believable and verifiable, and the evidence that Vic had planted factored heavily against the Copelands, implicating them strongly in Olivia's death.

And in her absence, her weakened estate finally collapsed.

Creditors came calling, and there was no one to negotiate with them or manipulate them into backing off. Her businesses were already struggling, and with her gone, they went under entirely. Especially because they were preyed on by Olivia's so called 'friends' who immediately gathered like vultures to pick apart her business interests once it became pretty clear she wasn't coming back.

Her mansion was repossessed to cover the estate's debts, and now it's being torn down.

My men and I all decided to come watch the destruction of the sprawling mansion, and there's something cathartic about seeing it happen. It feels like putting something to rest.

As I stand between the three of them at the edge of the property, I can't help but think of all the hopes and dreams I had in that house. How good it felt to finally have a connection to my 'real' family, and how I could see a good future ahead of me with Olivia's help. It felt like I had found my place after so long spent struggling on the outside.

Now I know it was never meant to be my place.

This was never where I belonged.

"Tear the motherfucker down!" Ransom whoops, startling me out of my thoughts. He's definitely enjoying himself, treating the destruction of the Stanton manor like some kind of spectator sport.

The wrecking ball swings, knocking out one side of the house, and he laughs. "Fuck, yes. Look at that! Clean shot."

I laugh at his antics, shaking my head at his enthusiasm. I'm glad he's here with me. Glad they *all* are. It's a reminder of the future that's waiting for me after I put this last ghost of my past to rest.

Another swing, and there's the sound of glass shattering as the bright sunroom is taken apart.

"Oh, to be a wrecking ball operator." Ransom sighs longingly.

"I think I missed my calling. I would've been great at that shit. And on a day like today, my job satisfaction would be off the fucking charts."

"Yeah, right." Malice snorts. "No one in their right mind would trust you with a wrecking ball."

"That's not true. People trust me with dangerous shit all the time."

"We let you handle dangerous shit," Vic comments dryly. "That doesn't mean we trust you with it."

The men keep bantering among themselves as more swings of the huge ball bring walls tumbling down. We stay until the mansion is nothing more than a pile of rubble on the ground in the middle of the lawn. Without Olivia around to pay them, the gardeners must have stopped coming, so the whole thing is over-grown and full of weeds, no trace of the immaculate landscaping left.

After a while, Victor checks the time and then puts a hand on the small of my back.

"We should get going, or we'll be late," he murmurs.

I nod, and we head back to the car, leaving the mess of what was once my grandmother's seat of power behind.

I think of Misty as we drive, and how her house wasn't where I belonged either. I think about the strip club I worked at, the school I fought so hard to get into. The whorehouse where I almost lost my virginity. There were so many wrong places that I ended up in over the course of my life, but they were all to get me to the right place. Here.

We pull up outside the doctor's office a few minutes later, and all of us troop in. We got a few odd looks the first time we came in for an appointment, but now people are mostly used to it. I know it's not uncommon for fathers to come with the mothers to ob-gyn appointments, but it's not usually so many of them at once.

After I get checked in, we're shown to the back. We settle into one of the exam rooms, and after I change into a gown, Doctor Simpson comes in.

"Ms. Hayes," she greets me. "And, uh, everyone."

I nod, grinning a little at the way she addresses my men. It's clear she's still not quite sure what to make of us, but I don't even give half a shit. I'm so completely over second-guessing myself or feeling ashamed of who I am. And at least this woman is professional enough to brush past it, focusing on the matter at hand.

"Alright, then. Let's get you up on the table, and we'll get started," she says.

She runs through a few standard questions, asking me if I've been eating well and about my morning sickness, which has improved a lot since the first couple weeks after I discovered I was pregnant. She also checks if I've had any pain or unexplained cramps or anything.

I answer all of her questions, then wince when she starts spreading the cold ultrasound gel on my stomach. She moves the wand around, and a sort of echoey sound fills the room.

It takes me a second to realize what it is.

"Is that—"

She smiles. "Yup. That's your baby's heartbeat."

A sort of wild awe fills me, a lump growing in my throat. Logically, I understood that I was growing a person inside me, but hearing the heartbeat really drives it home. After I first realized I was pregnant, I had such conflicted feelings about it. I wasn't sure I could raise Troy's baby without constantly being reminded of that hell. But it helped that my men made it clear from the very beginning that they would support me no matter what choice I made, and that they didn't consider sharing DNA with a Copeland to be a mark against the baby.

The guys look just as struck by the sound of the heartbeat as I do. Even Malice is standing with his jaw slack, a look almost like wonder on his face.

"And this..." Doctor Simpson taps a few keys on the keyboard attached to her equipment. "Is what the baby looks like right now."

She turns the screen so we can see it, pointing out the shape on the sonogram. My baby. *Our* baby.

Victor smiles, tilting his head a little as he studies the screen.

"Beautiful chaos," he murmurs. "Just like its mother."

Something squeezes in my chest, and tears prick at my eyes.

The exam finishes up, and Doctor Simpson assures me that everything is looking good and progressing normally. She leaves the ultrasound machine frozen on an image of the sonogram, and I keep glancing at it as she tells me I can get dressed.

"I'll see you in a month," she says, then leaves the room.

The space seems to shrink now that it's just me and my men. I can't quite seem to catch my breath. My heart is racing, emotions crowding in my chest, tumbling over each other. They rise up higher and higher, filling me up to the brim until finally, they explode out as words.

"Marry me," I blurt. "I mean... will you? Please?"

The men all react to that, surprise flickering across their expressions. They share a look, and then Ransom chuckles, glancing back at me. "Which one of us are you talking to, angel?"

"All of you," I reply, shifting my gaze to each one of them in turn. "Of course it's all of you. I know we can't do it that way officially, but I want to be married to all of you."

"Fuck," Ransom mutters. "I like the sound of that."

They all swoop in at the same time, taking turns kissing the breath out of me. Their hands and mouths are everywhere, and I figure I can take that as a yes.

"We need to get out of here," Malice growls, breathing harder. "Or I'm gonna fuck you right here in this room."

"Wait, wait, let me get dressed." I laugh, pushing him back. "We've already given Doctor Simpson enough to handle today."

I throw my clothes on in record time, hampered more than helped by the men, who keep trying to lend a hand. Clearly, they're better at undressing me than dressing me. It helps that I've started wearing pants with a stretchy waistband, so there are fewer buttons and zippers to deal with. Malice practically grabs the receptionists computer off her desk when she takes too long pulling up the software to schedule my next appointment, and finally, we hustle out of the building.

All of us crowd into the car, urgency building with every passing second. Malice shoves the key into the ignition and cranks it, making the engine roar to life.

Ransom, meanwhile, slides across the back seat toward me, cupping my face in his hands for a deep, hungry kiss. Our lips stay connected as his hands slowly start to wander, trailing over my extra sensitive breasts and the curve of my belly. One large hand works its way past the elastic of my pants, delving between my legs and making me whimper.

"Fuck you," Malice growls, glancing in the rearview mirror as he white knuckles the steering wheel. "I'm driving, you asshole."

Ransom just smirks. "More for me then. I thought you loved driving, Mal."

"Not right now, I don't," Malice mutters, sounding so put out that I have to laugh.

Vic, who doesn't have to keep his eyes on the road, turns around to watch from the passenger seat, and my blood heats as Ransom leans close to nip at my earlobe.

"Even though Vic likes to join in now, I bet he still gets off on watching too," he murmurs. "Should we give him what he wants?"

I nod, my breath catching.

Ransom tugs my pants all the way off and then helps me turn sideways in the seat so that my legs are spread. Then he wastes no time situating himself between my thighs, holding them open so he can bury his face in my pussy.

The first touch of his tongue to my clit makes me moan out loud, and Ransom devours me like he's starving. It feels so fucking good, the way he flicks his tongue, licking and lapping at me, and I give myself over to it entirely.

"Anyone driving by is gonna be able to see you," Malice comments from the front, his voice gruff with need.

The thought of what a filthy sight we must make sends a rush of arousal through me, and wetness gushes from me, soaking Ransom's chin.

"Yeah, I don't think she minds," he murmurs, grinning against my heated flesh.

He keeps lapping at me, running his tongue up and down my slit in long strokes before concentrating on my clit again, and even if I wanted to hold off my orgasm, there would be no way to stop it now.

"Ransom," I whimper, writhing beneath him. "Oh god..."

Malice steps on the gas, cutting around a corner so fast that I slide across the seat a little. Even though I just came, Ransom doesn't let up. He keeps going, fucking me with his tongue and teasing me with the piercing until I'm arching against him, tugging at his hair.

"You taste so fucking good," he mutters. "Could eat you forever."

I don't know how much time passes before the car screeches into the garage. Malice gets out, slamming his door and then yanking open mine so he can lift me out of the back seat.

"Wow, rude." Ransom licks his lips, complaining good naturedly as I'm taken away from him. "I was in the middle of something."

Malice doesn't even seem to hear him. He sets me down on the hood of the car and then shoves his pants down in one go. His tattooed cock springs out, rock hard and flushed, and I groan at the sight of it.

"Is it healed enough?" I ask, biting my lip as I stare down at his newest tattoo. My name, written right along the length of his dick alongside his other ink.

"Yeah, it's good." His voice is a harsh rasp.

He hasn't been able to fuck me while it's healing, and although that's been torture for both of us, he insists that it was worth it. And I have to admit, seeing my name emblazoned on his shaft is definitely a turn-on.

He's found other ways to get me off—watching his brothers

fuck me, fingering me, eating me out, and playing with toys—but god, I've missed this.

"Then fuck me," I beg. "Please."

My pussy is soaked between how turned on I am and the orgasm I just had, but even so, when Malice drives into me in one smooth motion, I can feel the burn of the stretch. He's clearly too pent up and desperate to wait, and I don't mind. I love when this man takes what he wants. When he fucks me hard and demanding, forcing me to keep up.

"So good," I gasp. "Don't stop."

I wrap my legs around his waist, pulling him in deeper, my moans echoing around us as he drives into me again and again.

"You're ours," he growls, the sound coming out harsh and guttural. "You're always gonna be ours. Our muse. Our beautiful whore. And someday soon, our *wife*."

His voice turns to pure gravel when he says that last part, and I nod frantically, panting for breath.

"Yours," I echo. "Yours, yours, yours. Always."

He groans, as if me saying that is making this even better for him, and I bite down on his shoulder as I come.

"Shit," Malice curses, his hands tightening on my waist he falls apart too, filling me up. "Take it all, Solnyshka. Fuck."

It seems to go on forever, his cock pulsing and pulsing as he fills me up, and even before we separate, cum is leaking down my thighs. After one more deep kiss, he pulls out and steps back, letting another gush of wetness spill from me. I look at his brothers, who are both out of the car now and watching us with ravenous gazes.

"I know Malice needed that," Ransom tells me, amusement in his voice. "But I need you too, pretty girl."

He steps up, cupping my face first so he can pull me into a kiss. It's searing hot but edged in gentleness, and I can taste myself on his lips.

That makes me moan into the kiss, and Ransom's eyes are dark as he pulls away. He slides me off the car's hood and turns me around, bending me over so that my hands are braced on the still-warm metal.

He grips a handful of my ass and spreads me open. "Look at you," he groans. "You're always so fucking hot when you're well fucked. I don't know how anyone could see your pretty pussy all wrecked and open like this and not wanna take you all over again."

"Ransom," I plead, pushing my hips back. "I need you."

"You've got me," he murmurs. "Always."

Then he presses into me.

His cock is different from Malice's, and the piercings rub against my sensitive flesh, working me up even more. He slaps my ass as he fucks me, the noise echoing and mixing with the sound of our sharp breaths and grunts.

"Beautiful," Vic murmurs. "So stunning."

I can feel his eyes on me, watching every movement. I'm pretty sure he remembers every time he's ever seen his brothers fuck me and could probably describe the specifics of each individual encounter. Heat curls through me at the realization that we're adding to that lengthy database in his mind right now.

"She truly is. That's our girl." Ransom's voice is strained as he fucks me, and I can tell he's close as well. His thrusts take on a frantic pace, and the pleasure starts to build in me, spiraling out and throwing me into another orgasm.

I scream this time, the sound bouncing around us, and I tremble against the hood of the car as sensation crashes around me. Ransom keeps fucking me through it, and then he finds his release as well, coming hard with a low groan.

After a few moments, he pulls out and helps me stand up straight on wobbly legs. He pulls me close, tucking hair behind my ear.

"You want your other future husband to fuck you too?" he asks, his blue-green eyes dancing. "I know Vic is starving for you, pretty girl. Do you still want more?"

I nod. "Yeah. So much."

"Not on the car," Vic says immediately, and I grin, because of

416

course he wants to fuck me someplace better designed for the activity.

Ransom shares a smile with me, then scoops me up and carries me into the main living area, bypassing the living room and heading straight for the big bed in the bedroom. He helps me take my shirt off while his brothers follow us in, then lays me out on the bed like a prize for Vic.

I swallow hard as Victor undresses and climbs up to kneel between my legs. He fists himself, gazing down at me with that intense look he always gets when he watches me.

"Was Ransom right?" I ask him. "Do you still like watching?"

"Yes," he answers, his voice tight. "But only because I know I can touch you afterward."

As if to prove it to himself, he touches me now. He gropes at my chest, squeezing my tits hard before pinching my nipples roughly. I arch, crying out for him as sparks of pain and pleasure shoot through me.

He drags his hands down my body, touching my scars on the way down before wrapping his fingers around my hips. I gasp as he hauls me closer, the head of his cock notching at my entrance before he presses in all the way.

He pauses when he's buried inside me, his eyes falling closed like he's experiencing a moment of bliss. Like he never wants to leave.

"Vic," I whine when he stays like that for too long, shifting underneath him to try to get some friction. "Please. *Please,* move. Oh my god."

Vic clenches his jaw and shakes his head. "Not yet. I want you to come on my cock first. Just like this. I want to feel you."

I groan, clenching around him. He's so hard and so big, filling me up so completely, and I grind down on him, rolling my hips to rub my clit against him. Using him to get off.

I'm so worked up and sensitive now that it doesn't take long at all. Something catches inside me, and that fire spreads, burning through me as I tip into pleasure again. I squirm on the bed, letting out a series of garbled pleas as I fall apart.

"Oh... oh, god. Feels so... fuck!"

His nostrils flare wide as he listens to me. Then, finally, he starts moving.

It's clear that holding out while I clenched around him like that used up all of his self-control, because his movements are wild and harsh as he fucks me in hard, fast strokes. He brings my knees up to my chest, exposing the mess of my cum-smeared pussy as he batters into me, and both of us stare down at the place where we're connected.

"Willow," he pants. "I love you. I love you. I—"

The words choke off, the muscles in his neck standing out as he throws his head back. Two more deep strokes, and he empties himself inside me.

His fingers slowly loosen their grip, and he releases his grip on my knees, allowing me to wrap my legs around his waist. It's as if I can see him putting himself back together in real time as he recovers from the intensity of it, and when our gazes lock, his eyes burn with contentment.

It looks damn good on him.

"I love you too," I whisper.

He smiles at me, and I smile back. Then he pulls out, leaving me a fucked out mess.

Vic slides a finger inside me, and I hiss at how sensitive my body is now. He gathers up a mixture of all the cum inside me and then holds it up to my mouth. I raise my head enough to lick that finger clean, savoring the taste of all of them like a perfect cocktail.

"Damn. You do shit like that, Solnyshka, and you make me want to fuck you all over again," Malice groans.

He and Ransom crawl up onto the bed to join us as Vic slips his finger from my mouth, the three of them surrounding me the way I like best.

"You should take a nap," Vic murmurs, brushing my hair back. "Sleep is important for you right now, and it's been a long day."

Ransom grins. "Plus, you'll need to be well-rested, because we have something very important to do tomorrow."

I turn my head to look at him, my brow furrowed. "What's that?"

"We have to go ring shopping."

I grin back, a happy warmth filling my chest.

On the night that I met these men, I was terrified of them. I watched them kill someone, and I was so sure they were going to kill me too. I had no idea that night that I'd met my soulmates.

But it's true. Soulmates exist, and these three men are mine.

And now, I'm going to marry them.

BOOKS BY EVA ASHWOOD

Clearwater University
(college-age enemies to lovers series)
Who Breaks First
Who Laughs Last
Who Falls Hardest

The Dark Elite
(dark mafia romance)
Vicious Kings
Ruthless Knights
Savage Queen

Slateview High
(dark high school bully romance)
Lost Boys
Wild Girl
Mad Love

Sinners of Hawthorne University
(dark new adult romance)

When Sinners Play
How Sinners Fight
What Sinners Love

Black Rose Kisses
(dark new adult romance)
Fight Dirty
Play Rough
Wreak Havoc
Love Hard

Dirty Broken Savages
(dark new adult/mafia romance)
Kings of Chaos
Queen of Anarchy
Reign of Wrath
Empire of Ruin

Filthy Wicked Psychos
(dark new adult romance)
Twisted Game
Beautiful Devils
Corrupt Vow
Savage Hearts

Magic Blessed Academy
(paranormal academy series)
Gift of the Gods
Secret of the Gods
Wrath of the Gods